Ship of Smoke and Steel

DJANGO WEXLER

Ship of Smoke and Steel

Book One: The Wells of Sorcery Trilogy

TOR
TEEN

A Tom Doherty Associates Book
New York

SHIP OF SMOKE AND STEEL

Copyright © 2019 by Django Wexler

Map by Jennifer Hanover

A Tor Teen Book
Published by Tom Doherty Associates
175 Fifth Avenue
New York, NY 10010

www.tor-forge.com

Tor® is a registered trademark of Macmillan Publishing Group, LLC.

Library of Congress Cataloging-in-Publication Data

Names: Wexler, Django, author.
Title: Ship of smoke and steel / Django Wexler.
Description: First edition. | New York : Tor Teen, 2019. | "A Tom Doherty
    Associates Book." | Summary: Isoka, an eighteen-year-old ward boss in the
    great port city, Kahnzoka, is sent on an impossible mission to steal Soliton,
    a legendary ghost ship, or her sister will be killed.
Identifiers: LCCN 2018044553| ISBN 9780765397249 (hardcover) |
    ISBN 9780765397263 (ebook)
Subjects: | CYAC: Fantasy. | Magic—Fiction. | Ships—Fiction. | Dead—
    Fiction.
Classification: LCC PZ7.W5358 Shi 2019 | DDC [Fic]—dc23
LC record available at https://lccn.loc.gov/2018044553

Our books may be purchased in bulk for promotional, educational, or
business use. Please contact your local bookseller or the Macmillan Corporate
and Premium Sales Department at 1-800-221-7945, extension 5442,
or by email at MacmillanSpecialMarkets@macmillan.com.

First Edition: January 2019

Printed in the United States of America

0 9 8 7 6 5 4 3 2 1

For Casey, who is the best

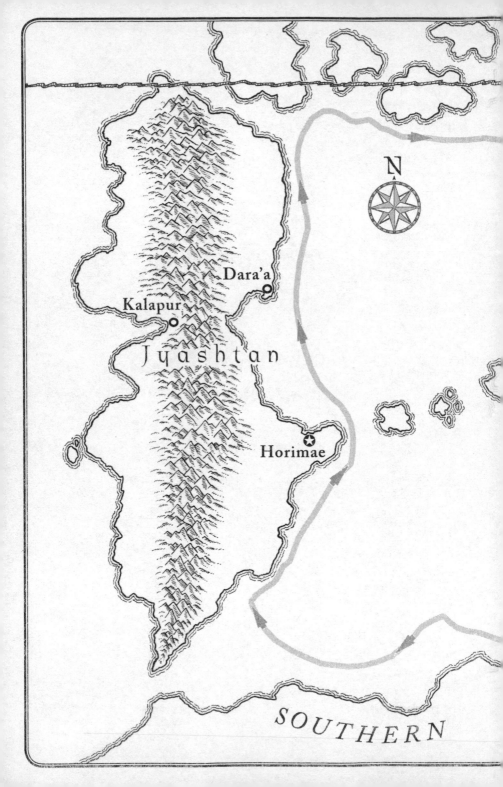

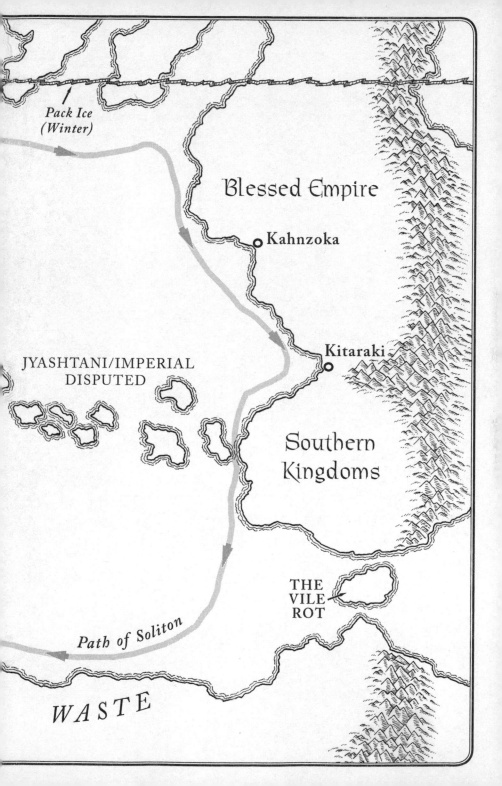

The Nine Wells of Sorcery

Myrkai, the Well of Fire

Tartak, the Well of Force

Melos, the Well of Combat

Sahzim, the Well of Perception

Rhema, the Well of Speed

Xenos, the Well of Shadows

Ghul, the Well of Life, the Forbidden Well

Kindre, the Well of Mind

Eddica, the Well of Spirits, the Lost Well

Ship of Smoke
and Steel

1

_____

It's time to get to work.

I move quickly, losing myself among the crumbling tenement blocks of the Sixteenth Ward. The streets smell of salt water and rotting fish, piss and misery. Huddled shapes crowd against the pitted brick, fearful faces staring. This is my Kahnzoka, my filthy, stinking city, and these are my people.

I walk a complex route, to make sure I'm not followed. When I'm convinced there's no one on my tail, I head to the building that houses my current bolt-hole and climb to the fourth floor. There's a strand of raw silk stuck between the door and the frame, looking like nothing more than a cobweb, but my eyes find it and I let out a breath. It reassures me nobody's been here since I left. I unlock the door, step inside, and shoot the heavy iron bolt.

The apartment is a tiny rattrap, not much more than a place to eat and lay out a bedroll. It only has one window, and I've shrouded it with thick curtains. There's no furniture other than a heavy wooden chest; this is just a hideout, not a place to live. It's not the only one I keep. There are always times when you need somewhere to go to ground.

I tug at the strip of fabric that belts my *kizen,* and when it gives way I struggle out of the tight formal wrap with a sigh of relief. I kick off the stupid little shoes that go with it, and reach up to free my hair. Unbound, it hangs ragged to the back of my neck. I breathe deep, enjoying the freedom to move.

One long scar traces a path from my collarbone, between my breasts, across my belly to my hip. Another crosses it, running horizontally over my ribs. There are more on my back, on my thighs. But they're all *old* scars, from *before*. History.

I kick open the chest with one bare foot and dress quickly. Leather trousers, a wrap for my chest, and a linen tunic, with a leather vest over that thick enough to turn a blade. It leaves my arms free, the way I like it. Heavy black boots, the bottoms still flecked with dried mud. The boots are a compromise. They slow my footwork, but anything lighter risks stepping on nails or something worse in the filth of the lower wards.

There are no weapons in the chest. I don't need any.

Hagan and Shiro are waiting at the agreed-upon spot, at the southwest corner of Rotdodger's Square. They've claimed a space among the beggars by virtue of the long knives sheathed at their belts. As usual, they're arguing about something.

"Oh yeah?" Hagan says. He's eighteen, my age, tall and wiry, with brown hair that hangs nearly to his eyes, and a neatly trimmed beard. "Like who?"

"You know Chiya's?" Shiro is sixteen, shorter and built like a beer barrel, with a wild puff of dark hair.

"Of course I rotting know Chiya's."

"You know Binsi, then? Tall girl, waist I could put my fingers around, tits out to—"

"I know that she costs more than you make in a year, you rotting liar."

"That doesn't matter, 'cause I never have to pay." Shiro grins in that way he has, which makes people want to punch him. The crooked angles of his nose show they haven't always restrained themselves.

"That is the most utter garbage I have ever heard," Hagan says. "I don't believe it for a minute."

"You can believe whatever you—"

He stops when Hagan punches him on the shoulder. Not a serious punch, just to get his attention. They turn to face me, and both give a little bow.

"Boss," Hagan says. "Was starting to think you weren't coming."

"I got a little held up." I survey the crowd. At this hour, they're mostly women, the able-bodied men off at their labor on the docks. They wear practical tunics, hair tied back under colorful cloths, off to work or to haggle for the daily meal. No *kizen* here.

"Nothing terrible, I hope?" Shiro says. He's new and a little too eager to please, like a puppy. Sometimes I wonder if he takes me seriously. If not, he and I are going to have a talk.

"Just business," I tell him. "Anything moving around here?"

"The usual," Hagan says. "Nothing to show they're worried."

"Let's go worry them, then." I slap him on the shoulder, and push off through the crowd. The two of them fall in behind me.

To an outsider, and maybe even to most of the people who live here, the lower wards look like chaos. A sea of humanity sandwiched between the harbor on one side and the upper wards on the other, living in ramshackle houses built to no particular plan, crooks and brothels and stores all mixed together.

If you were to see all this, and you were an enterprising sort, you might think it was the perfect place to set up shop. You might start, say, a gambling parlor in the gutted-and-rebuilt wreckage of an old countinghouse, fleecing the stupid, the gullible, and the drunk of coins they can't afford to lose. And you might think you owed your profits to no one but yourself, because the Emperor's tax collectors don't show their noses around here.

You'd be wrong. There are people who will get very upset with you. Not because you're taking money out of the pockets of the poor—since that's their business, too—but because you aren't paying the proper tithe. They'll start by sending you a message, nice and polite. If you're stupid enough to ignore that, then someone like me will kick down your door.

That's the other reason I like the boots. They're good for kicking down doors.

The broken-down countinghouse is two stories, made of crumbling red brick, but the roof and much of the second floor are gone. The largest surviving section is the old strongroom, a windowless block at the back of the building. Someone has added a new door, an ill-fitting thing nailed together from scavenged planks, with a slot to let someone look out.

I hope, as I pivot on one foot, that someone's at the slot and that they're not quick. My boot connects with a splintering *crunch* and there's a grunt that tells me my wish has been granted. The door opens a couple of inches, a broken bar visible in the gap. A second kick sends it slamming all the way ajar, catching a large man standing behind it in the shins. Already clutching a bloodied nose, he goes down in a heap, swearing.

There's not much to the place. A few tables, benches and chairs, big jugs of rice wine and small colored bottles of liquor stacked against one wall. It's too early for them to be open, so I assume the six people inside—seven, if you count the door guard with the broken nose—are employees. I size them up automatically. Two men are obvious toughs, broad-shouldered bruisers with short swords in their belts and scarred knuckles. One woman with a hook nose and a crossbow against the rear wall. Another woman in the corner also looks like muscle, dressed in battered leather, maybe a knife fighter or a grappler.

The last two, a man and a woman, are sitting. The woman's in a *kizen,* not a real silk one but a cheap linen imitation, bright with gaudy dye, her face heavily painted. The man beside her has a silk shirt and a fur-lined collar. He wears a sword but doesn't look like he knows how to use it. I read the pair as the brains of the outfit and his girl, probably not a threat. So figure four against three. Five if Broken-Nose stops blubbering.

"Watch the one behind us," I tell Shiro, under my breath. He still needs minding. Hagan, a veteran, has already done the same fast analysis of the room and catches my eye. I nod, minutely, to the woman with the crossbow, and he nods back.

"One of you," I say to the room at large, "is Ohgatani Firello." I fix the fur-collar man with my gaze. "I'm guessing it's you, but I've been wrong before. Anyone else volunteering?"

The woman in the *kizen* looks ready to dive underneath the table. Fur-Collar pushes her aside, angrily, and stands up.

"I'm Firello," he says. "Who in the Rot are you?"

"I think you can probably guess," I say. "But in case you're forgetful, there's money owing. You got a note saying there would be consequences if you didn't pay. I suppose you can call me consequences."

"Charming." He eyes the broken door. "And this is your idea of a polite visit?"

"Yup." I give him my best smile. I've been told it's unsettling.

"Who exactly are you claiming to represent?"

His eyes dart around the room, taking the temper of his guards. After the initial surprise, they've relaxed slightly, confident in their numbers. I can tell at that moment, from the set of their shoulders and the smiles on their faces, that I'm going to have to kill them all. But we'll play it out, for form's sake.

"Does it matter?" I tell Firello. "What's important is that I hold this turf in trust, which makes it my responsibility when someone moves in on it. If I let people get away with that, I might as well slit my own throat."

"Really." Firello's eyes narrow. "Rotscum. I think you've got no backer but the pair of limp-dicks behind you and you've been getting away with talking tough for years."

"From your point of view, does it make a difference?"

Firello smiles. "It means that if we slit your throats, nobody's going to care about three rotting kids going missing in the slums." One corner of his mouth rises. "Though I might save you to sell on to the brothels."

I'm trying to decide if it's worth wasting any more breath on this exchange when Shiro steps forward. His face has gone white with rage. I suppose he's not as used to the posturing and dick measuring that seem to be required on these occasions. His hand is on his knife.

"You have no idea who you're talking to," he says. "We—"

I'm already turning, because I know what happens next. Six people in front of us, one behind us. Shiro was supposed to be keeping his eyes on the one, and he's not. I don't need to see Broken-Nose start moving, because I can read it in the eyes of the other thugs. But I'm not *that* fast, not quite, and Shiro has stepped too far away from me. He cuts off in mid-sentence as Broken-Nose's knife slides into his kidney, point slicing clean through his leather vest. His eyes go wide, that moment of surprise before the pain hits.

Broken-Nose yanks his knife back, turning to face me. I can see he's surprised to find me already moving toward him, and he begins to backpedal. He's even *more* surprised when a blade of crackling, spitting green energy, emerging from my wrist, goes in through his eye and out the back of his head, his skull offering no more resistance than a rotten melon.

There are nine Wells of Sorcery, the pathways of magic the ancients burned into the fabric of the world. Most people can't touch any of them. Those who can reach at least one are called *mage-born*. Most of them can only draw a trickle of power, from one or two of the Wells; they are the *touched*. A few can manage more, enough to matter, enough to kill; they are the *talents*. And a handful, the *adepts*, have full access to the power of their Well.

That's me. My Well is Melos, the Well of Combat. War.

I should not exist. Adepts don't frequent the Sixteenth Ward. They certainly don't turn up at a rotscum gambling joint as gang enforcers.

So I can understand why Broken-Nose was (briefly) surprised.

Suddenly everyone is going for their weapons. Hagan's the fastest, snatching a triangular knife from his belt and whipping it in a perfect throw at the thug with the crossbow. She half-turns, taking it in the shoulder instead of the throat, but it startles her, and the bow clatters to the floor.

The two bruisers draw their swords. The woman in the corner has a knife in each hand, moving warily. Firello is fumbling for his sword, and I write him off as a non-threat. I step away from Broken-Nose's collapsing body and ignite my other blade. It snaps into existence with a distinctive *crackle-hiss*, about two feet of stuttering, shimmering energy, its brilliant bright green color characteristic of Melos power. The blades begin at the backs of my wrists and run parallel to my forearms, as though I'd strapped on a pair of glowing swords like bracers. They have no weight, but I can feel the heat of them, the power running across my skin in lines of crackling magic. Those lines get brighter and hotter the more energy I draw on. For an adept, it is entirely possible to burn oneself to death by drawing too much, as I can attest from painful experience.

Most people don't know how to fight a Melos adept. This clearly includes bruiser number one. He raises his sword in a useless overhand swing that does nothing but give me plenty of time to react. Accordingly, I'm not there when it comes down, stepping to one side, but my left-hand blade is in position. His own momentum does most of the work of severing his hand neatly at the wrist. Hand and sword hit the floor with a clatter, green lightning playing briefly over the severed stump as he stares in horror.

I've already moved on. His friend, bruiser number two, swings his sword in a flat arc, a slightly better move, especially when you're used to fighting people smaller and weaker than you. I'm *very* used to fighting people bigger and stronger than me, however, so I angle my parry, the steel edge scraping across the Melos blade with an earsplitting *scree* and a shower of sparks. He overcorrects, lurching backward, and it's no great trick to step forward and plant the end of my other blade in his throat. His stumble turns into a fall, his hands coming up to claw at the wound. Green lightning crackles across him for a moment, quickly swallowed in a spew of crimson foam.

Hagan, to my left, is facing off against the knife-wielding woman and not doing well. They've both got blades in hand, but he has a long, shallow cut down one arm, blood dripping from his elbow, and his face is locked in grim concentration. As I close, something *thrums* through the air, just behind me. Crossbow bolt. I step between Hagan and Knives, who gives ground at the sight of my blades.

"Take care of Crossbow!" I tell Hagan, and he nods and spins away. Knives takes a second step backward. There's uncertainty on her face—I figure her loyalty to Firello is a little shaky at the moment. I could probably talk the fight out of her, but we're past that now. If the Immortals get rumors there's a Melos adept on the loose, I won't last very long, so the only people who have seen my blades are either my trusted associates or dead. Knives is not my associate.

She has a wide stance, natural with a weapon in either hand. I bull right down the middle, straight at her, which she is not expecting. Her knives come in, reflexively, aiming for my sides. They get within an inch of my skin before Melos power erupts, a storm of wild green energy that stops the knives dead, as though they'd struck a steel breastplate. I feel the surge as a wash of heat across my skin, radiating outward from where the blows struck.

Meanwhile, my Melos blade has punched into her stomach, the tip emerging between her shoulders. She hangs there for a moment, suspended, and then vomits a gush of blood. I dismiss the blade, letting her crumple, then ignite it again with a *crack-hiss*.

On the other side of the room, the thug with the crossbow is on the floor, one of Hagan's knives in her back. She's crawling away, but he's already on top of her. Hagan has worked with me a long time, and he knows the rules. He lifts her head up by the hair and slashes her throat with a quick, efficient motion, and she shudders and goes still.

The bruiser with the missing hand is curled up around the wound. I silence him with a quick thrust as I walk past, and that leaves Firello and his girl. He's got his sword out, but his hands are shaking.

"Okay!" he shouts. "Okay! I get it. Blessed's Blood! We can make a deal—"

I don't feel like talking to him. What's the point? My left-hand blade strikes his sword, knocking it aside, and my right takes his head off. The spray of blood patters on the floor.

The girl collapses to her knees, her makeup streaked with tears.

"Please," she says, voice so quiet it's hard to hear over the crackle of my blades. "Please. I didn't do anything. I just serve drinks, I swear. You don't need to kill me. Please."

Hagan shoots me a questioning look. I glare at him. He should know better by now.

"Please," the girl says.

"Sorry."

The Melos blade punches into her side, under her left armpit. I slip it between the ribs to find the heart. The quickest death I know. It's all I can offer.

A lot of my colleagues, those who hold territories for the bosses, like to make up happy stories about their jobs. They're defending the people of their wards, they say, protecting them in exchange for a reasonable fee. I prefer not to dress it up. *This* is what I do. I hurt people for money. I hurt them until they pay, or I kill them if they won't, so that the next batch know better.

It's all right. The money goes to Tori, her perfect house, her obedient servants. Her gentle, sheltered life, miles from the stink of blood. She deserves it. She's smart, and kind, and loving, and she'll grow up among nobles and live a perfect life. She's not a monster, like I am. She can be generous and gentle. All I can do is hurt people.

Shiro is still moaning, but he's a dead man. I can see that at a glance. By the way Hagan kneels at his side, though, I can tell he's going to be difficult about it.

"We need a bandage for this," he says, staring at the wound. Blood has glued Shiro's shirt to his skin, and still flows in shallow spurts. "Can you tear up some cloth?"

"Why?" I say. "So he can bleed out tonight, or die a week from now when his bowels fester?"

"Isoka!"

"You know it's true. Look at him. Unless you have a tame Ghul adept you haven't told me about, he's done."

Hagan bites his lip. His hands are shaking. "You're saying we should just leave him here?"

"No, I'm saying we should slit his throat and be done with it. It's a mercy."

He winces as though I've hit him. "I . . . I can't—"

"You were quick enough to finish the woman with the crossbow." I frown. Hagan is usually more reliable.

"It's not the same! He was—*is* my friend. I can't just—"

"Then get out of the way."

Hagan looks at me for a moment, then stands. I kneel beside Shiro. His eyes are closed, and I don't think he's conscious. Thank the Blessed One for small favors, I suppose. My blade slides into his side, and he shudders and goes still. I stand up and let my power fade away, the Melos energy dispersing into shimmers of green lightning. It feels like stepping from a stifling room into a cool breeze, heat streaming off my skin.

"Let's go," I tell Hagan.

"There's probably money here," Hagan says, looking away from Shiro's corpse. "You don't want to look for it?"

"To the Rot with the money. We're here to send a message." I wave one blood-spattered hand at the bodies. "This is the message."

Hagan gives a jerky nod. I watch him surreptitiously as we leave through the busted door and slip back onto the Sixteenth Ward's busy streets. My other eye is on the crowd, but if anyone pays us special attention, they take care not to stray too close. In the upper wards, if a body was discovered, the Ward Guard would come out and pursue the murderer. Down here, the guards barely bestir themselves to clean up the corpses, and not until after they're picked clean.

Still, it's a good idea to get off the streets. There's another hide-out ready, halfway up a decaying block of shabby tenements. I'll lay low there until morning. Quite a few of the Sixteenth Ward's vagrant children are on my payroll, and they'll watch to see who finds the bodies and who those people tell about it. It's possible that the people in that room were the whole of Firello's organization, but it's equally possible he had another partner or two who might come over all revenge minded. If so, I'd like to know about it. I didn't go from street rat to ward boss by taking unnecessary chances, and even Melos armor is no protection from a knife in the throat while you're sleeping.

The bolt-hole is another empty, grubby room, with a rag-curtain window looking into a central courtyard the residents use as a garbage dump. There's a sack with fresh clothes, a clay jug of weak wine, another of water, and paper-wrapped parcels of food. Hagan stops in the doorway, one hand clutching the wound on his arm, breathing hard.

"Well." I look down at myself, the bloodstains already drying to dirty brown. "That could have gone better."

Hagan snorts and mutters something. I turn to look at him. "Are you okay?"

He looks up, face hardening. "Fine, boss."

"I'm sorry about Shiro." I'm not, but the lie won't hurt. "But he got emotional and paid the price. You know I warned him about that."

"So did I," Hagan said.

I frowned. "Was he your brother or something?" It's not like we hadn't lost men before. It happens. When you're in the business of hurting people, sometimes they hit back.

"I haven't got a brother," Hagan said. "He was just . . . a friend."

I shrugged. Who rotting knows what goes on in people's heads? Friendship wasn't a luxury I'd ever been able to afford. Life had taught me that lesson early on: there was Tori, there was me, and then there was everyone else.

"How's your arm?" I ask. "You look pretty bloody."

"Nothing serious." He pokes at the wound and winces. "I'll be all right."

"Go get cleaned up. I'll see you in the morning, once we know we're clear."

Hagan forces a smile. "Yes, boss."

I strip, wadding up my shirt and trousers, and do what I can to scrub the blood from my skin. It's something, but I won't feel really clean until I can get to a bathhouse for a proper soak. Once I'm in fresh clothes, I demolish the supper in the sack—rice balls, a roast chicken, sweet preserved cherries—and start in on the wine. It's all simple stuff, but with my body coming down from the combat high everything tastes good.

The dim light from the window turns redder as the sun slides down the sky. Jug in hand, I wander over and stare. From here I can see the harbor up close, pier after pier jammed with vessels, their bare masts like a strange, dead forest. I've heard that Kahnzoka is one of the greatest ports in the world, rivaled only by the Jyashtani capital of Horimae. Farther out are ships under sail, from single-masted junks to enormous square-rigged traders. The sleek triangular sails of an Imperial Navy galley, black trimmed with gold, cut through the riot of color like a shark through a school of fish.

I feel keyed up, jittery, unable to relax, like I've missed something and I can't quite put my finger on it. I'm like this, after a fight. It helps if I have someone to fall into bed with, a quick rut to burn off the extra energy. I thought about asking Hagan to stay—I've tumbled him a time or two—but he didn't seem like he was in the mood.

Wine's not as good, but I'll take what I can get. I bring the jug to my lips and swallow, as the last of the sun slips below the horizon and the light begins to fade from orange to black.

I dream of the people I've killed.

I don't know why. I don't feel bad about killing them. But their faces appear behind my eyelids when I sleep, standing around me. They're not threatening, not come to take vengeance from beyond the grave. Just . . . waiting, as though I should have something to tell them.

Firello is there, and his girl, and his guards. Shiro's there, too. He looks at me, silently, expectantly.

"Get lost," I tell them. "I don't know what you want from me, but you're not going to get it."

They just stare. No expressions, no sadness or pain. Just . . . expectation.

"This is a dream," I tell them. "You're all dead."

They don't react.

I struggle to wake up, to open my eyes. And it seems like it works, for a moment. Only it doesn't, because I'm still dreaming.

I'm lying on the thin, lumpy sleeping mat, empty wine jug near my hand. A slight breeze through the rag curtain raises goose bumps.

Above me there's a faint light. Tiny glowing pinpricks hover and dance, like dust caught in a sunbeam, leaving trails of luminous gray in their wake. They writhe like a bucket of eels. I raise my hand, and the gray trails shift, as though pulled toward my fingers.

Dreams. I close my eyes again, hoping for a more pleasant one.

2

Everyone has their addictions.

Mine isn't drink, or dice, or sex. That's not to say I never have a jug or three, or that I'm immune to the rush of clinking coin and clattering bone, or that I've never spent the evening in the company of a pretty boy from Keyfa's brothel. But these are things I could do without, if I had to.

My addiction is Tori. I can no more stay away from her than a plant can turn away from the sun.

Hagan picks me up after breakfast, at a suitably discreet spot far from our usual haunts. He's driving a battered old cab, with proper livery and permits. Nothing fake—I have an arrangement with the owner, and he keeps Hagan's name on the books as a licensed driver. Hagan dresses the part, too, in a cabdriver's shabby linen and slouching felt cap. The elderly mare in the traces gives a snort at the sight of me, and her ears flick while I climb aboard.

Then it's up to the Second Ward, up the great hill, climbing away from the sea and out of the miasma of smoke and poverty. It's like ascending the celestial mountain where the Blessed One dwells with the heavenly court. Except at the top of our mountain sit the nobles and the Emperor's favorites—more like rotspawn, in other words, than choirs of angels. We drive through the main gate under the suspicious eye of the Ward Guard, but our passes are in order, and a few coins encourage him not to ask unnecessary questions.

Hagan knows the routine, and he drives in silence. I'm back in my *kizen*, ridiculous, tight-bound thing, trying to look like the respectable lady I'm not. I don't know why I bother. It never works.

*   *   *

The house is beautiful, all wide porches, gently sloped roofs in elegant gray-green tile, manicured lawns, and a tiny, perfect pond. I stand outside, about as welcome as a dead dog floating in that pond. I can see it on the faces of the servants, when they think I'm not looking. The gardener in his broad straw hat stares at me and spits in the grass; the doorman's hand hovers near his sword as he lets me through the front door. A young woman brings me tea, moving with grace in spite of her restrictive *kizen*. She places the cup in my hand as courtesy demands but carefully avoids even the slightest brush against my skin. Then she hurries off, no doubt to wash thoroughly.

None of them know who I really am, of course. To them I'm just a strange visitor their mistress inexplicably tolerates, reeking of the dung of the lower wards. If they knew the truth, they'd be less polite.

The Rot can take all of them. They're not the ones I'm here to see.

After letting me cool my heels in the waiting room for a few minutes, another footman arrives to escort me to the inner garden. This is a private space at the very center of the house, stone walled and ringed by tall, drooping willow trees. Only a few trusted servants are allowed here. *They* know that my gold pays their wages and puts food on their tables—though even the most trusted don't know where that gold comes from, of course—and they've been warned, discreetly, of the consequences should any of this information be revealed.

They are considerably more respectful.

Ofalo greets me at the garden gate. He's an old man, balding and long bearded, like a statue of the Blessed One. He bows low, and I wave at him to get on with it.

Addiction. I've spent too much time here already. I shouldn't be here at all. Every minute is a risk. Every minute is weakness. Every time I leave I swear I won't come back, that next time I'll send some go-between who knows nothing and endangers nothing. Just knowing that this place is here should be enough, but it's not. I have to see her smile, or I start to feel hollowed out. I start to think dangerous thoughts.

"Welcome, Lady Isoka," Ofalo says. "Lady Tori will be here any moment."

"Good. Anything I need to know?"

If Ofalo objects to being snapped at by a girl of eighteen, he doesn't show it. That's one of the reasons I like him. He's been my factor here since the beginning, and he's never given me cause to regret it, never asked too many questions. Blessed knows I pay him enough.

"No, my lady. A few trivial disputes among the staff. Nothing that requires your attention."

"Anyone who troubles Tori is to be turned out immediately."

"Of course, my lady." Ofalo bows again. "Shall I send for refreshments?"

"No." I grit my teeth. "I'm not staying long."

"As you say."

He bows again and withdraws on noiseless feet. I go into the garden and sit at the little stone table, staring down at the tiny babbling brook. It's perfect, the epitome of everything a brook should be. Someone *made* it that way, placed every stone with careful consideration, taking into account the sound of the water and the way the light filters through the willows. The whole house is like that, smooth and deliberate, a work of art.

It's another reason I can't stay here too long. It makes me want to break something.

Tori moves so gracefully I don't even notice when she comes in. She's wearing a light blue *kizen*, fading to purple at the bottom, like a clear sky passing slowly from day to twilight. I can't stand the things. I hate the way they restrict me to tiny, mincing steps and pin my arms to my sides. But Tori wears hers effortlessly, as though she were born to it, as elegant at thirteen years old as any lady of the Imperial court.

We don't look much like sisters. We're both short, though she's still growing and she'll soon be taller than me. We have the same straight, dark hair, but mine is cut short and tied up, while hers falls like a black curtain to her waist, thick and glossy as a waterfall of ink. Her skin is smooth, her hands uncallused. She's so beautiful it makes me want to weep. And when she sees me, her face lights up, and I realize all over again why I can't stop coming here.

"Isoka!" She runs to me, as fast as the restrictive *kizen* will allow, all her decorum forgotten. I love her for that, too. She throws her arms around me and I hug her back. "It's been so *long*," she says. "I thought you'd forgotten about me."

"I know." Three months. Longer than ever before, weaning myself off her like an addict trying to get clean of dream-smoke. "I'm sorry. I've been busy."

"Are you going to be staying tonight?" Tori says. "I'll get Viala to make something special—"

"No!" I blurt out. "I'm sorry, Riri. I don't have long."

Her face falls, but there's still a hint of a smile at the pet name. She's too old for it. Another few years and she'll be something like a woman. I find it hard to imagine.

"Before I go," I say, "I need you to tell me everything that's been happening. I rely on you to keep an eye on things, you know."

That's all it takes to get her smiling again. She sits across from me and launches into a story about the cook's dog getting into trouble. I listen and make encouraging noises, and just *watch* her. *Remember this*, I tell myself, over and over. *Save this, for when you need it.*

"Isoka," she chides. "You're not listening."

"Sorry." I shake my head. "What happened to the dog?"

"Old Mirk only has three teeth left, poor thing. Last month Narzo said he wasn't good for anything and wanted to put him down, but I wouldn't let him. You can't get rid of someone just because they aren't useful anymore."

"That was very kind of you."

Her face clouded. "He died anyway, though. Last week. Tutor says that's the way of nature and I shouldn't be sad about it, but I cried anyway."

My sister, who cares for worn-out dogs and other broken things. I see Shiro's face, his last shudder, and my throat goes tight. Tori's a hundred times better than me, and if the only thing I do with my life is make sure she stays that way, it'll have been enough. Someday she'll be grown, and she'll have enough money that she'll never have to work, or to marry if she doesn't want to. She won't remember huddling under the bushes in the public gardens when it rained, or dodging the kidcatchers who snatch little girls for the dockside brothels.

". . . and when I told Garalo about it," she's saying, "*he* said that's the same way the nobility treat the common folk, working them to the bone and then throwing them away. I said they shouldn't be allowed to, and—"

"Wait." I fix her with a look. "Who's Garalo?"

"Just a boy I know." Tori's guilty look is blindingly obvious on her guileless face. "I talk to him in the market sometimes."

"How did you meet him?"

"Kuko wanted to listen to a speech, so she took me after shopping. Then I had questions, so we stayed and got to talking."

"Tori . . ." I take a breath.

"I know," she says. "I have to be careful. I'm not a *baby*, Isoka. Garalo talks to lots of people."

"It's still not safe to get involved in politics," I tell her. "You never know what kind of attention that's going to attract."

"But—"

"You have everything you need right here, don't you?" I venture a smile. "Don't go looking for trouble."

Tori looks away for a moment, and I think she's going to argue. Then the tension goes out of her, and she nods. I lean forward and wrap her in a hug, remembering the little girl who clung to my side when we huddled in the gutter.

I'm getting dirty, I want to tell her, *so you can stay clean.* But she can't know that.

Eventually, I have to leave, though not before cunning Ofalo, knowing my habits, comes back with roasted dumplings and plum juice. It's good to see him with Tori. I think he cares for her—I feel a stab at that dark jealousy, but I push it down. Who *wouldn't* fall in love with Tori? She's nothing but easy smiles and kindness and generosity. And if Ofalo's loyalty comes from more than gold, so much the better.

I know it's time to go when Tori starts asking me questions. "Is it true about *Soliton*? The ghost ship?"

"Ghost ship?" I glance meaningfully at Ofalo, who's clearing the plates, and he inclines his head in apology.

"She must have overheard some of the girls talking, my lady," he says. "Nothing but silliness."

"They said there was a ghost ship in the harbor. It comes to collect evil souls." Tori sounded excited. "Kuko said she saw Immortals watching for it!"

"There's no such thing as ghosts," I tell her. "And certainly no ghost *ships*." Though the Emperor's Immortals are real enough, unfortunately.

"That's right," Ofalo says. "I'll have a word with Kuko."

"And whatever happens," I add, "you've got the Ward Guard and all the servants here to keep you safe."

"I'm not scared!" she protests.

I say my good-byes, which means more hugs and a promise to visit again as soon as I can. Ofalo walks me out, back through the perfect house and its perfect gardens. With him at my side, the other servants know better than to sneer.

"There's a girl who takes her shopping," I tell quietly. "Kuko."

"Yes, my lady. She's a good girl, a hard worker."

"Did you know she's been taking Tori to listen to agitators?"

There's a long pause. "I had no idea, my lady. I'm terribly sorry."

"Just take care of it."

He inclines his head. "She'll be dismissed at once. I'll make certain whoever accompanies Lady Tori in the future is . . . reliable."

"Good." We pause at the front door. "I'll expect your next report in a month."

"Of course, my lady." He bows deep, wispy beard swaying. "We are honored by your trust."

His face is as calm as ever. I wonder what he thinks of me, if he thinks anything at all. Maybe he just sees me as a bottomless coin purse, a lifetime meal ticket.

If so, it's for the best. He wouldn't want to know the truth.

The cab is waiting in the street outside, Hagan lounging on his seat while the old mare munches from a feed bag. He straightens up as I emerge, his collar damp with sweat. From the halfsmile on his face, I can tell he likes the way I look in the *kizen,* all clean and feminine, like a noblewoman. I flash him an obscene gesture, and he laughs.

"Your command, my lady?" he asks.

"Take the highway to the Fifth Ward," I say. "We'll change and head to Breda's from there."

He nods, and I hop up to the carriage door before he can offer to help. Hagan clicks his tongue, and we move off at a slow walk. The Second Ward has wide, winding streets, lined with houses like Tori's, set well back among their gardens for privacy. Huge round stones sit on squat pillars, carved with the circular emblems of noble houses. Lesser houses, here. Anyone with real power would live in the First Ward, or better yet in the Royal Ward, in one of the palaces the Emperor bestows on his favored subjects. Still, seeing Tori in her comfortable place, among the residences of those who might once have sold her life for a few coppers, gives me a warm feeling. It's revenge on everyone who told us we weren't good for anything.

She's as good as any one of you rotting parasites. And all it takes is a bit of gold.

We pass back through the gate in the ward walls, waved through by bored guardsmen. Another difference between the Second Ward and the Sixteenth: here the fortifications only face outward, to defend the residents from the rest of the city. Back home, they face inward as well and we live under the crossbows and catapults of the Ward Guard.

It's an hour's ride to the Fifth Ward along the military highway that runs straight as an arrow from the docks to the citadel, cutting across Kahnzoka's ancient, tangled streets like a knife dragged through a plate of noodles. High ward walls line it on either side, with shacks and lean-tos at the bottom, growing up like mushrooms in spite of the guards' efforts to root out such unauthorized residents. A hundred hawkers have set up their wares along the road, wearing broad hats to keep off the brutal sun, shouting the virtues of fruit, sweets, cakes, pottery, silks, and a thousand other things. Small boys run alongside every carriage that passes, even my modest cab, announcing the services of their employers.

Far below, at the base of the hill, the Imperial Navy piers are visible, along with a slice of the bay beyond. The sleek, many-oared warships moored there show no signs of alarm. *Ghost ship.* A smile flits across my face. We'd both heard the stories of the dreaded *Soliton* as children, but I'd forgotten about them until now.

I'm more interested in the other carriages that pass us. I keep the heavy curtains mostly closed, peering out through a crack. The traffic is mostly transport wagons, hauling goods to the wealthy wards, with a few private vehicles mixed in. A squadron of Ward Guard cavalry rides past, hooves scattering mud. And, moving slowly, a matte black wagon pulled by gray horses, the driver anonymous under a hat fringed by a dark veil.

The Immortals *are* in town, and openly. I'd heard only rumors. Inside that wagon, behind mesh screens that hide them from view, the Emperor's elites watch the crowds.

For hundreds of years, ever since the Divine Emperor was chosen by the Blessed One himself, mage-born have been permitted only among the nobility. Commoners who are touched or talented are taken from their families; depending on their Well and abilities, they are either inducted into the Invincible Legions or parceled out to noble families as breeding stock to improve their bloodlines. But a few always slip through the net, and the Empire is not overconcerned. The fugitives find ways of employing their powers that keep them beneath the notice of the Imperial authorities. So touched and talented are not unknown in the lower wards.

Adepts are another story. We are too dangerous to be left alone. The primary responsibility of the Immortals is to make sure that every adept born within the Blessed Empire is placed at His Imperial Majesty's disposal. They are valuable assets for the Legions, securing the homeland against Jyashtani aggression or the machinations of lesser states. Their children—and they will be forced to have many—are adopted out into the noble families, who fight one another in the Imperial court for the privilege of taking them. The strongest make up new cadres for the Immortals, their loyalty the bedrock of the Emperor's power.

The Emperor's dark-armored personal guard have always been my private terror. Most of the young street children worried about being snatched by slavers, or being caught by the Ward Guard for real or fabricated crimes. And I'd fretted about those things, too, though more for Tori's sake than my own. But Ward Guards would usually let you off with a beating, and slavers could be bribed or escaped. If the Immortals caught *me*, though, there was no coming back.

I sit back and let the curtain fall. There's no reason to think I'm in danger of being found out. There are enough ghulwitches and deserters to keep the Immortals busy, not to mention Jyashtani spies. But my heart still beats a little bit faster as we drive on.

Breda's is the closest thing I have to a home in the Sixteenth Ward. I move around as much as I can, from flophouse to apartment, with a backup always ready in case I need to disappear. Being tied to routine makes you predictable, complacent. But there are times when I need to be seen, when I want people to find me, and that's when I set up shop in Breda's run-down winesink.

It's a big place, by Sixteenth Ward standards, on the ground floor of a half-ruined building right on the harbor. That's one reason I like it—there's always enough of a crowd to drown out a conversation, and plenty of eyes around to make sure no one tries anything stupid. The other reason is that Breda keeps things simple—no dream-smoke, no viper's milk, and definitely no credit. Just jug after jug of watery beer and sour wine, and a yard-long club under the bar that he can swing harder than a mule's kick.

I walk in, Hagan a respectful step behind me, and there's a satisfying pause in the buzz of conversation, three dozen people taking a quick glance before they go back to their drinks and dice. The air is thick with smoke and the smell of salt water, and the floor is gritty with sand and rotten straw. Apart from the bar in the back corner, which is made from timber as heavy as a ship's mast, the furniture is flimsy and cheap. Given how often things get smashed, I can't blame Breda for saving his coin.

Breda always holds a table for me by the fire. It's too hot in the summer, but I can sit with my back to the wall, and the crackle of the hearth adds another layer of protection against eavesdroppers. As soon as he catches sight of me, he scuttles out from behind the bar, all obsequious smiles. It's a strange look for Breda, who's near seven feet tall and thick as a side of beef, with a round, sagging gut and strings of greasy gray hair tugged over his bald pate. But he long ago decided it was better to be on my good side—or more accurately the good side of my employers.

It's too loud to hear much, but he just bows and gestures me to my table, then scurries off to fetch drinks. I take my time on the way across the room, looking over the regulars for anyone out of place. I get a few quiet nods, and offer a few in return. The majority of the crowd are honest folk, at least in theory. Sailors, dockworkers, fishermen. But here and there are thugs, prostitutes, thieves, and killers. My people.

When I sit, Hagan takes himself elsewhere. It's a small table, with just one other chair across from me. It's not long before someone takes a seat, a plump, well-dressed woman who's sweating freely through her too-thick makeup. She stares at me for a while, throat working nervously. I sigh.

"Spit it out," I tell her. "Or else go have some more drinks until you work up the nerve."

"Right," she says. "Sorry. It's just . . . sorry. I . . ." Then she pauses again, and I want to scream.

People. I don't rotting know how to talk to people.

But it's expected in my position. As long as the gold keeps trickling upward, I'm in the clear with my bosses, but there's a little more to it than breaking heads. As ward boss, people want to ask me for favors, or to adjudicate disputes, or beg me to cut them a break, just one more week, swear to the Blessed. I'd heard every story a hundred times over before I was fourteen, but I still make time to sit and listen. A little goodwill goes a long way. People are more likely to tell you things, or clam up when the Ward Guard pokes around.

That doesn't mean I don't sit and fantasize about doing horrible things to them while they blather on. I swear, if one more shopkeeper tries to tell me that he's behind on his payments because his grandmother is ill, I'm going to carve him *and* the old lady into chunks.

The well-dressed woman is here to ask me to find her daughter, who's working in one of the dockside brothels. Mom thinks she was captured by slavers, but my guess is the girl just ran off on her own. I promise her I'll look into it. I'm not in the business of returning runaways, but if she *is* being held against her will some brothel-keeper will need sorting out. Keeping slaves is illegal in Kahnzoka, and one of the few things likely to bring the Ward Guard down on all our heads.

I don't get any sick grandmothers, but there's a couple of bad backs and a fishing boat swamped in a storm. By the ragged state of the fisherman, his story is probably true, but I make a mental note to visit the others unexpectedly and make sure they know my patience isn't infinite. There's also a shopkeeper whose place was rolled by a gang from the Fifteenth Ward, which I'll complain about to the appropriate authorities, and a young prostitute who claims his client skipped out without paying.

"Who was he?" I ask the boy, a pretty little thing in soft silks.

"Some aristo." He snorts and tosses his long hair, a move I'm sure wins him many a customer. "Toyara something."

"A little detail would be useful," I tell him. "Find out his full name and send me a note. I'll have someone look into it." I will, too. It's bad enough when highborn parasites come down to the Sixteenth Ward to slum it, but if they start getting the idea they don't have to pay, it's going to cause problems for everyone.

After a few hours of this, I'm itchy and bored. The heat is stifling, and I've already loosened the collar of my *kizen* as far is it will go. Breda's beer is barely chilled when fresh, and not strong enough to even give me a fuzzy head. After another shopkeeper bows his way out, swearing that he'll pay any day, I decide I've had enough. Hagan rises from his own table and meets me on the way to the door.

"Getting on your nerves already?" he says, grinning.

"They were getting on my nerves an hour ago," I mutter. "I'm half a minute from kicking someone in the balls just to liven things up."

Still, once we step out the front door, I'm feeling good. The glow of Tori's company, of seeing the life I've built for her, step by painful step, is still with me. And now that I'm finished at Breda's I can get out of the damned *kizen*.

The sun is sliding down to meet the ocean, tinging the waterfront with orange. The docks are crowded, workers and sailors coming off shift and flowing up into the city, regular as the tides that float the ships. That flow, up to the wineshops, gambling dens, and brothels of the Sixteenth Ward, is what keeps us all alive. It pays for Tori's house and Ofalo's salary. The city breathes, in and out, and I feel it in my own chest. Kahnzoka may be halfway to the Rot, but it's my city.

"Where to?" Hagan says.

"Bleak Street." It's another of my hideouts, just a cheap room in a tumbledown building at the district's edge, but it has the virtue of spending the day in the shadow of the walls. "I need to get out of this rotting heat."

He nods and falls in. I stop at a street stall for dinner—fried gripper and chestnuts, wrapped in old rag paper. I eat as we walk the rest of the way, tearing apart the flaky fish with my fingers and blowing on it when it's too hot to touch. I'll take Sixteenth Ward street food over the "cultured" stuff they serve at Tori's every time. Except that plum juice. They get that right.

The apartment at Bleak Street is on the second floor, up a rickety exterior staircase. Hagan pauses at the bottom, and I wad up the paper from dinner and toss it in the gutter.

"I'll head back, then." He has his own place, down on Larker's Row. "Meet at the square in the morning?"

I cock my head. "Or you could come up."

"Or I could come up." He looks at me with a widening grin.

It's probably a bad idea, but I feel good enough that I don't care. I tug at the collar of my *kizen*. "If you're coming, hurry up. I need to get out of this thing."

He doesn't take much convincing. I turn on him as soon as he closes the door behind us, kissing him while I tug irritably at the knots that hold the *kizen* closed. Sometimes I'm tempted to take a Melos blade to the thing, I swear to the Blessed One. Hagan helps, with his strong, clever fingers, and I sigh with relief as the silk slides off and puddles on the floor. Then I sigh again, for other reasons.

"You really don't care, do you?" he says.

He's standing by the window, where the light is fading through the rag curtain, highlighting his smooth, lean muscle. I'm lying on the sleeping mat, sweat cooling pleasantly on my skin.

"Care about what?"

"About Shiro."

"Oh, blessed above." I sit up, cross-legged, and glare at him. "Do you want me to lie to you? Should I tell you I'm hurting deep inside?"

"I wouldn't believe you."

"Then why are you asking?"

"I'm just trying to understand you." He shakes his head. "We've worked together, what? Three years?"

"Four, by now."

"Four years. I knew Shiro for two months and I knew him better than I know you."

"Remember the first thing I said when I hired you," I tell him.

"Right. No personal questions." He turns away from the window and comes back to the mat. "I don't want to pry. I just wish I knew what you were thinking."

"What's to understand? I hurt the people I'm supposed to hurt and collect the money and pass it along."

"The perfect ward boss?" He gives a sour smile. "Like a little clockwork machine."

"That's right." Even Hagan doesn't know about Tori, of course. As far as he's concerned, the house in the Second Ward is just another part of my business. "Look. Shiro was just a kid I hired to back me up. If I'm going to feel bad about him, why not feel bad about those poor rotscum working for Firello?"

"They were trying to kill you."

"Because he paid them to back *him* up. Just because somebody took my money instead of someone else's I'm supposed to be broken up about him?"

"What if I'd gotten stabbed, instead of Shiro?" Hagan makes a face. "You know what, don't answer that."

There's a long silence, as the last of the light from the window dies. The room goes dim, only the aggregate glow of the never-sleeping city outside providing any illumination. I grab Hagan by the shoulders and drag him down, my lips finding his. He only resists for a moment.

It's easier than trying to figure out what to say to him. I don't rotting understand people.

It's probably a mistake, sleeping with Hagan. Not the sex, exactly. I'd never pretended to innocence, and when I was old enough to feel the urge I'd gone to a ghultouched—swallowing my disgust at dealing with such a creature—and for a ward against unintended consequences. And it's not really Hagan's fault, either. He's a good lieutenant, easy to get along with, a good rut. I like him. Which is the problem.

If it *had* been him instead of Shiro, would I have done what needed to be done? Or would I have gotten stupid? I don't want him to *understand* me. I want him to have my back.

It's a good image he used, and it stays in my mind as we clutch and kiss and gasp. A clockwork machine, like toys they make for little rich boys. A windup doll. It's all I want to be, all I *need* to be. No room for doubt or sadness. Just a machine.

When I open my eyes, it's to the sound of boots on the stairs outside. There's a pause, then the mutter of voices.

"Rot," I swear, coming fully awake. Hagan's eyes are open, but he looks confused. "Get up! I think—"

There's a splintering crash as the door bursts inward. Early-morning sunlight pours in, framing black-clad figures. A half dozen of them line up, three on either side of the doorway. I get to my feet as a seventh strolls in.

"Gelmei Isoka," he says.

He's wearing lacquered black armor from head to toe, with a subtle inlaid pattern that glitters in the sun, a pair of swords hanging at his side. His helmet includes a drape of blackened chain mail in front of his face. The others are the same. They might as well have come off a printing press.

"Who in the Rot are you?" I say, standing naked on the sleeping mat, Hagan still crouched at my feet. But even as I say it, I realize I already know. I've lived my entire life in fear of this moment.

The Immortals have found me.

3

Their leader doesn't respond to my question. Instead, he tilts his head slightly, chain mask jingling, and says, "You will come with us. Do not attempt to resist."

"What about the boy?" one of the others, a woman, says.

"Bring him in for questioning," the leader says.

Options, options. None of them good.

Nowhere to run. The back window is too small to fit through easily, and it only leads to the enclosed central yard. The walls are thin, but not thin enough that I can break them before the Immortals are on me.

Fight them? But these are *Immortals,* not street thugs. Every one of the seven could be an adept as powerful as I am. And if they're here, they know about my power, so I have no advantage of surprise. I could try anyway, and probably die. Not *necessarily* the worst option.

I'm not getting out of this room alive and free, then. What happens if I go along quietly? Unclear. Maybe rape, torture, breeding-stock for some noble family. Maybe execution. Maybe, maybe. Not enough information.

What happens to Tori? There's money stashed away, hidden against the event of my death. Secret letters with people I trust. Insurance. I'm not a fool. Can they find her? Only if someone talks.

Everyone talks, if you hurt them for long enough. But I'll always have the option of dying. If I ignite my blades and summon my armor, I can always make them kill me, and then the pain will stop. Tori will be safe.

Hagan. He doesn't know the whole truth. But he knows enough.

I've gotten sloppy. Has he put the pieces together? Would he, when they're pulling out his fingernails?

He meets my eye. It's the same look he gave me in the gambling parlor, a split-second silent conversation. *How are we going to play this?*

He's terrified. I can see it.

He'll talk. He doesn't owe me anything. He's just someone I pay to back me up. I've made that clear, haven't I?

My eyes say, *I'm sorry.*

I bring my left hand up, underneath Hagan's chin. I turn my gaze to the Immortal leader as I ignite my blade. There's a soft, wet sound, and a warm spray against my fingers.

Several of the Immortals take a threatening step forward. I dismiss the blade and raise my hands. Hagan's corpse collapses with a thud.

The Immortal leader crosses the room in a few strides and slams his gauntleted fist into my stomach. As I double over, my face meets his knee on the way down, and I feel my lip split. I hit the floor, and a moment later the first boot slams into my side. Bone *crunches.*

This time, I don't dream at all. Not even of Hagan.

When I wake up, I'm expecting pain. I've been beaten before, but never this badly. I think the Immortals had instructions to keep me alive, but I'd felt the sick-making crack of a snapped rib, and at least one of my fingers had broken where a stray boot had come down on it. So I open my eyes and keep absolutely still, waiting for the avalanche of agony.

It doesn't come. I have to breathe in, eventually, and my stomach and chest feel fine. Not numb, just normal. I raise my hand, to look at my mauled fingers, and find them straight and perfectly functional. There are long, pink marks, like freshly healed skin.

Either I've been asleep for weeks—which seems unlikely—or there's magic at work here. Ghul magic, the Well of Life, the Forbidden Well. I taste bile at the back of my throat.

The Emperor and his Immortals seek out all mage-born, for the good of the Blessed Empire, but none are so thoroughly policed as the unfortunates with access to Ghul. In the right hands, the Well of Life can do good. Ghultouched can calm a fever, ease a birth, or keep a cut from festering. Ghul talents can mend broken bones and close wounds. Ghul adepts, it's rumored, can do almost anything—regrow missing limbs, change a person's appearance, restore lost youth.

But they can be evil, or make mistakes, just like anyone else. And when you're toying with such primal forces, disaster follows easily. Far to the southeast, where the greatest city in the world once stood, lurks the Vile Rot, a festering, cancerous testament to the dangerous combination of arrogance and command over life itself. Since that time, Ghul mage-born have been feared, shunned, and executed almost everywhere in the world. The Empire is only slightly more lenient—a few ghultouched, after extensive training, are permitted to operate at the fringes of society, and Ghul talents are taken into the Legions. Ghul adepts are always killed, however, and ghulwitches—untrained, unauthorized Ghul mage-born— are hunted down by the Immortals.

The thought of some rotspawn mucking around with my insides makes my stomach contract, and I have to suppress the urge to vomit. My skin crawls. I breathe deep and swallow hard, trying to assess the situation logically. The Immortals were clearly supposed to take me intact, so in all probability they've simply healed me after their snatch squad got carried away. It's unlikely that they've seeded my body with fast-growing tumors, or given me a flesh-rotting plague, or—

Too much. I manage to roll over and push my hair back before I vomit, a thin, sour mix of wine and bile spattering the floor mat. Afterward, wiping my mouth on my sleeve, I feel a little better. Enough to take in my surroundings. I'm dressed in a light brown wrap, something a servant might wear. The room I'm in is small, just big enough for a sleeping pad, but the well-kept floor mats and plastered, painted walls tell me I'm not anywhere in the Sixteenth Ward. The door is open, leading out into a large sitting room, with cushions placed around a low table. The table is set for two, with decanters, glasses, and a bowl of oranges.

A door slides open on the other side of the sitting room, and a man enters. He's slim, balding, dressed in gray, with circular wire-frame eyeglasses. Seeing me through the doorway, he gives a thin, humorless smile, and beckons.

"Ms. Gelmei," he says. "Please. Come and sit."

I get to my feet, a little wobbly. He crosses the room and sits on one side of the table, gesturing for me to take the other. I do, cautiously, and watch as he pours clear water into two glasses. No point in being paranoid about poison—if they wanted me dead, I'd be dead. I drink deep, washing the taste of vomit out of my mouth.

"Welcome, Ms. Gelmei," he says. "I apologize for the way you were treated, but my operatives do not take kindly to a lack of respect. Your decision to silence your companion was . . . perhaps rash, although I must admire your cold-bloodedness."

"Your operatives," I mutter. My eyes go wide as I realize who I'm talking to. "You're Kuon Naga."

He inclines his head. "I am."

Kuon Naga. Childhood companion of the Emperor. Widely considered the second-most-powerful man in the Blessed Empire. Head of the Immortals. *Here,* talking to me.

I can't decide if this is good or very, very bad.

"What do you want with me?" I say.

He sighs. "I am a busy man, Ms. Gelmei. Please do us both the favor of not wasting my time. It would be best for you to assume that I know absolutely everything, and proceed on that basis."

"All right." I close my eyes, trying to decide how to play this. *Tori is all I can save.* "I'm a Melos adept. And ward boss for the Sixteenth, though I doubt you care I'm a criminal. You've got me. What happens now?"

"I'm sure you're aware that hiding the fact that you are mage-born is in direct contravention of His Imperial Majesty's wishes, and thus considered treason." Naga sipped from his cup. "Those taken as children are often spared, on the condition that they agree to use their talents to the benefit of His Imperial Majesty and the Blessed Empire. You are, unfortunately, too old for such clemency. Neither the Legions nor my Immortals would ever consider you reliable."

"That sounds bad for me." I give him a slight smile. "But you had one of your ghulwitches fix me up, so I'm guessing you're not going to have me executed."

"Insolence is the refuge of the weak." Naga picks up an orange, delicately. His long fingernails slice easily through the peel, which he pulls off in neat strips. "You think yourself desperate, that you have nothing left to lose. I have men in my employ who could show you how very wrong you are." He holds up the naked orange and pulls it in half. "There is always further to fall, Ms. Gelmei."

I keep smiling, because it seems to annoy him, and reach for one of the oranges myself.

"But I suspect we will come to an agreement," Naga goes on. "There is the matter of your sister."

I fumble the orange. It hits the table, bounces onto the floor mat, and rolls away. I feel like one of Naga's goons has punched me in the stomach all over again, but I try to keep my face still. *He can't know. He* can't *know.* "I don't have a sister."

Naga sighs. "What did I say about wasting my time?"

"I really don't—"

"Her name is Gelmei Tori, and she lives in the Second Ward, in a house you pay for. She enjoys paper folding and dancing. Once a week, she visits the Painted Market, and lately she's been meeting a boy to talk about how to address the problems of society. He's been giving her books—"

"Stop."

"Do I need to remind you how easy it would be for something to happen to her, Ms. Gelmei? She has no family, no protector, no one to petition the Ward Guard on her behalf. No one but you. If the alley she takes to the market happened to contain a gang looking for fresh meat for the brothels, who would know?" He separates a slice of orange, eats it with the delicacy of a bird. "There are clients who will pay well for highborn girls, or at least"—his mouth quirks upward—"convincing fakes. Have I made myself clear?"

I stare at the table as though the secret to saving Tori is hidden in the wood grain. So it had all been for nothing. All the work, all the blood, all the death. I'd climbed out of the dockside garbage heap one corpse at a time, lifting my sister over my head so she wouldn't be stained by the filth. And for all the rot-sucking good it had done, I might as well have slit my wrists and left Tori to fend for herself.

Hagan had died for this, because I'd thought he might talk. I suppressed a hysterical laugh. They might not even have interrogated him. Why should they? Naga already knows everything.

I feel like I'm in free fall, my fingers scrabbling at a crumbling rock face, searching for a handhold. *There has to be* something. I want to scream, to break the table in half, to break Naga's smug face. But I stop, because—

"You're about to tell me there's a way to save her."

He arches a delicate eyebrow. "And why would you think that?"

I hold up a hand, and one blade ignites with a *crack-hiss.* The green light shimmers and gleams off his glasses.

"Because if you know so much about me, you know there's nothing else I care about," I say. "And if you tell me there *isn't* a way I can save Tori, then there's nothing to stop me from carving you apart like a rotting turkey."

A pause. The crackling of Melos power fills the silence, green lightning arcing up and down the blade. The rush and heat of magic runs through me, giving me goose bumps. I'm so close to him. The slightest effort, and—

"You are quite clever, Ms. Gelmei," he says, finally. "But I suggest you conduct yourself with a little more respect."

"You want something from me. Given how careful you are with your time, I doubt you drop in on every prisoner to personally threaten to sell their family to a whorehouse." I let the blade die. "You know I can't refuse. So rotting well get on with it."

A very slight smile. "As you wish, Ms. Gelmei. What do you know about *Soliton?*"

For a moment, I'm speechless, back in the Second Ward house with Tori. I'm not sure what I was expecting, but it wasn't that.

"*Soliton,*" I manage after a while, "as in the ghost ship? The harborside spook story?"

"Yes," Naga says. "That *Soliton.*"

I shrug, wondering how I ended up talking to the second-most-powerful man in the Empire about *fairy tales*. "It's supposed to collect damned souls for oblivion. But it's a myth, right?"

"We in His Imperial Majesty's government have worked very hard to make that the general impression," Naga says. "But *Soliton* is quite real, I assure you."

"And it gathers damned souls?" I raise my eyebrows.

"In a sense. *Soliton* calls on the Empire roughly once a year. When it arrives, it collects a . . . tax. A cargo of young mage-born, including at least one adept."

"It . . . what, sails in and demands them?"

"It waits for us to hand them over."

"What if nobody does? Why would the Empire put up with this?"

"The port of Ghaerta, in Jyashtan, attempted to deny *Soliton* its due one hundred and twelve years ago. What happened is unclear, but the entire city burned to the ground in a single night, and the local garrison was slaughtered. Since then, to my knowledge, no one has run the risk."

I shake my head. "This is ridiculous. You can't expect me to believe that the Empire has been handing over its own mage-born children to a ghost ship for—how long has this been going on?"

"Since at least the time of the Blessed One. Five hundred years or more."

I stare at him, wondering if it's possible that he's mad. He wouldn't be the first Imperial councilor to go crazy.

"You don't believe me." He shrugs. "It doesn't matter. I just thought you might want to have all the information."

"You want to send me out as a sacrifice, don't you." It's not a question.

"Of course. We've had you under observation for some time."

"I'm assuming that the sacrifices don't make it back."

"No one has ever returned."

"Now who's wasting our time?" I shake my head. "You could have just tied me up and tossed me in a boat."

"Correct." The smug little half smile again. "We don't want you to become a sacrifice to *Soliton*. We want you to steal it."

4

"Steal it." My voice is deadpan.

"Yes."

"The five-hundred-year-old ghost ship that doesn't exist."

"It exists. And it is much larger and much faster than any vessel ever built by our own shipyards or those of Jyashtan." He waves a hand. "I will not trouble you with politics, but the Emperor expects war against the Jyashtani within five years. *Soliton* would have a drastic impact on the balance of power."

"Blessed above," I swear. "You're serious."

"I am."

"And how . . ." I pause, shake my head, and spread my hands. "I don't even know where to start."

"Don't bother. We have almost no information. There are people on *Soliton;* that is well established. We believe the sacrifices are not immediately killed, but as to what happens to them or who controls the vessel, nothing is known."

"So what makes you think this is *possible*?"

"It may not be. But we judged you to be suitable to make the attempt. You are young enough that the ship will accept you, personally powerful, and have spent your entire life working your way into a position of authority in a violent, degenerate society. And, of course, you can be properly motivated."

"Oh, rot." I stare into his cold eyes. "You mean if I agree to go, you'll leave Tori alone."

He blinks, and then actually laughs, a small, sharp bark of a sound.

"Oh no," he says. "As you said, if we simply wanted you to *go*, we could force you to do so. Your sister is necessary in order to make sure you *come back*." He leans forward. "Here is the deal, Ms. Gelmei, the only deal you will ever get from me. You will board *Soliton*. You have until it returns to the Empire—approximately one year—to assume control of it, by whatever method you can, and deliver it into our hands here in the harbor of Kahnzoka. For the next year, your sister will be unmolested. If you succeed, the two of you will be free. If a year passes, however, then rest assured Tori will suffer in some suitably horrific fashion. I hope that you don't doubt my imagination in such matters."

I'm having trouble breathing, and my heart is beating very fast. "That's not . . . you have no idea if I even have a *chance*. You can't hurt Tori—"

"I can," he interrupts. "I will. This is not a negotiation. I am telling you what the consequences of your actions will be. If you dislike one of the possible outcomes, I suggest that you apply your talents to avoid it."

There's another long silence. Slowly, I get my anger under control. Naga just stares, inscrutable behind his glasses. He peels off another slice of orange and pops it into his mouth.

"I will kill you for this," I tell him. "I don't know how. But I will. I swear to you."

He heaves a sigh. "Ms. Gelmei. Do you have any idea how many people like you have told me that? And yet." He spreads his arms. "You may have to wait in line."

Another pause.

"Nothing else? No further impotent threats to make? Very well." Naga brushes off the front of his coat and gets to his feet. "My men will be here to transport you to the docks at sundown. We wouldn't want you to be late."

For a girl who grew up on the docks, I haven't spent very much time in boats. My gaze was always landward, to the walled wards of Kahnzoka rising tier after tier on the hill. The sailors who flooded in and out of the harborside taverns and restaurants were a crude lot, and they'd only interested me when I could relieve them of their coin.

Now, as I leave Kahnzoka probably for good, I find myself regretting not spending more time out on the water. The city, my city, which had always reminded me of nothing so much as a bloated animal corpse teeming with ants, has a certain beauty to it from the harbor at night. Lights march up the slope of the great hill, marking the ward walls in a regular grid, while smaller lamps are scattered between them like earthbound stars. Along the docks, the lanterns twinkle as they're eclipsed by the forest of masts.

There are six Immortals in the boat with me, four rowing and two keeping watch. It's just possible I could escape. I can swim, and the harbor is calm. I could probably surprise the guards, kill one of them, jump overboard, and hope they can't find me in the dark. But then I'd be racing them to shore, betting that I can pull myself out of the harbor and get to the Second Ward to grab Tori before word gets back to Naga. No chance.

Naga's "take control of the ship" scheme is obviously crazy. But he's given me a year. All I need to do is find a way off *Soliton* before then and return to Kahnzoka without him finding out about it. Then I'll extract Tori and disappear. I have contacts, money salted away, favors owing. I can beat him.

Assuming I can get off the ship. Assuming I survive the first few *hours* on the ship, that it isn't some monster out of legend that devours its sacrifices whole.

Even in summer, it's cold out on the water. I shiver and wish this were over with.

The farther out we go, the more the fog closes in. The lights of the city are a vague blur behind us now, and the stars overhead are invisible. Even the steady splash of the oars is muffled, like we were wrapped in an enormous blanket. There's no longer any sense of movement, as though time has been suspended. I wonder if this is what oblivion is like, the non-life that waits for the wicked after they die. Just endless nothing, alone in the darkness forever.

I'm not alone, though. The head Immortal, a slim woman under the black armor and chain-link mask, sits ahead of me and concentrates. It would be hard to see in daylight, but there are lines of power around her head, faint streams of yellow energy circling her in constant, liquid motion. Yellow is Sahzim power, the Well of Perception. She mutters to the other guard, at the tiller, directing our course with her enhanced senses. I wonder what she sees.

It takes me a moment to realize we've reached our destination. There are no lights, no shouted greetings. Just a dark wall rising out of the water in front of us, as though we've come to the edge of the world. The oarsmen turn our little boat, bringing it side-on to the barrier, which extends upward and in both directions as far as the lantern's light reaches.

The head Immortal reaches out and slams her fist against the wall. It makes a hollow, metallic sound, like a gong. I wonder if Naga was lying to me all along, because this can't be a *ship*. It's too big, too dark, and it sounds like it's made out of metal. You can't make a ship out of metal; metal's *heavy*. It would sink, right?

The term "ghost ship," which I'd used so blithely a few hours ago, comes back to me. I shiver again.

For a while, there's silence. Then a demonic screech echoes down through the fog, like some enormous bird of prey. It's followed by a rattle of chains. I picture an army of the damned, bound and fettered with spectral steel, descending—

There are no ghosts, I tell myself. *Dead is dead.*

What finally lurches into view is a cage, lowered on a rusty iron chain. It comes down a bit astern of us, stopping a few feet above the water. The oarsmen push our little boat up beside it, and I can see that the door is open. It's big enough for three or four people to sit in, though not tall enough for them to stand. Thick, rusty iron bars are spaced only a few inches apart.

"Get in," the head Immortal says to me. Her voice is harsh, flat. It's the first she's spoken.

Last chance for a daring escape. But all six of them are looking at me now. I get to my feet, unsteady on the shifting deck, and take hold of the bars of the cage. It sways under my weight. I lift myself in, carefully, the cage rocking and squeaking on its chain. The head Immortal shuts the door and throws an iron bolt, then slams her hand against the vertical wall again with a *boom*. A moment later, the screech is repeated, and the cage begins to rise.

My heart starts to race, and I wonder if I've made a horrible mistake. Maybe I should have taken that last chance, however thin it might be.

I wait, sitting in the center of the cage, trying not to move, since every shift of my weight sets it swinging. The boat below me grows smaller, its lantern a single speck of light, and then it disappears into the fog. Total darkness envelops me, but I can hear the rattling of the chain, and feel the lurch in my stomach that means I'm still moving upward.

Finally, there's a hint of light. It's a gray, rotten light, not torch-light or a lantern. I can see a sharp edge, the top of the endless wall of darkness. Along the edge of the wall are figures, enormous things made of pale rock. The Jyashtani build statues to their heathen gods, humans with the heads of animals, but these are more like creatures out of some horrible nightmare. The closest one has a roughly equine body, with six legs all of different sizes and shapes. One wing emerges from its back, twisted and misshapen, and the head sitting on its thick neck looks almost human, but distended by an enormous bird's beak. The one beside it looks like a snake with human arms and legs emerging from its body at random.

And running over all of them is a gray light, a faint miasma that surrounds them completely. It shifts and swirls like part of the fog. It has to be magical energy, but it looks like nothing I've ever seen. The cage keeps rising, passing above the twisted creatures, and looking down I can see a line of them stretching off into the dark.

There's a sound, too. A susurrus of voices, down at the edge of hearing, mostly covered by the rattle and screech of the rusty chain. When it stops, though, just for a moment, I can hear them.

—"kill me kill her kill me kill her—"
—"around and around, push push push, one more time—"
—"make it stop; oh please make it stop—"
—"skin left on the bones—"
—"my baby you can't have her; she's mine to eat—"

"Blessed One." I haven't had much use for prayer in my life. But now I squeeze my eyes shut and *beg*. "Blessed One and all the heavenly hosts."

Another screech, thankfully banishing the voices. The cage swings sideways, and I open my eyes in time to see the edge pass underneath me. I'm over a flat surface, now, what I can only assume is the deck of the ship, though it looks like more metal. At the edge of my vision, the gray lights swirl, and something moves. Something big. My heart hammers.

Then there's darkness below me again. An opening in the deck, ragged edged, like a wound. The cage descends with another screech, the hideous statues passing out of sight. There are walls all around me, now, and I realize I'm being lowered into a pit.

The bottom of the pit is lit by actual lanterns, their wan glow welcome after the weird gray half-light. I can see dim shapes around the edges, crouching in the shadows. The cage comes to a halt about a foot above the deck, swinging slowly back and forth and spinning on its chain. I look around and guess there are a half-dozen people, but none of them seem to want to get close.

"Someone let the *lakath* out!" a voice shouts, from above me. It's a man's voice with a heavy accent I can't place. As the cage spins, I see one shape detach itself from the wall and come toward me. A young woman, about my age, with very dark skin and tightly braided hair. Her eyes are wide with fear, but she comes forward with slow, deliberate steps, and grabs the cage to stop its spinning. She struggles for a moment with the rusty bolt, then gets it free, and the cage door swings open with a squeal. The woman takes several quick steps back, with the air of someone who has just unleashed a wild beast.

I edge out of the cage and take a deep breath as soon as I'm standing on solid ground. My stomach lurches a little before settling down. It's hard to believe that I'm on a ship—the metal deck under my feet feels steady as bedrock. I wonder, again, if Naga has played some kind of trick on me.

Focus, Isoka. I draw a slow breath, let it out, pushing back against the fear. Whatever those things were up above, they're not down in the pit with me. I look around at my new companions. The girl who freed me wears a strange outfit, a long green dress in a style I've never seen, with asymmetric silver bands around her arms. She's not an Imperial—by her skin, I'd guess she was from the Southern Kingdoms, about which I know almost nothing. What she's doing in Kahnzoka harbor I have no idea.

Behind her, in the corner of the room, a large young man in rough leather stands in front of a girl in a *kizen*. The girl is younger than me. The boy has a fresh bruise on his forehead and a split lip. He looks like a low-ward brawler, a type with which I'm intimately familiar. He's sizing me up the same as I'm doing to him, and when our eyes meet, he bristles, like a dog's hackles rising.

Another young woman in the next corner, huddled in on herself. Her cheap, colorful wrap and gaudy makeup mark her as a streetwalker, one of the lowest rungs on the city's tawdry ladder of prostitution. Her garments are torn, and her makeup is smudged with blood where she's been beaten. Completing the group, in the last corner, is a scrawny boy with flyaway hair and threadbare clothes. He looks on the edge of panic.

Not a dangerous group, I assess. The southerner is an unknown, and the brawler could try something. The other three don't seem like a threat. Then I remember Naga telling me that they only send *mage-born* to the ship, and change my mind. If these are the latest sacrifices, which seems likely, then they can all touch the Wells. Which means I can't afford to ignore any of them.

I raise my hands, and attempt a smile. My heart is still beating hard against my ribs.

"Hello." Because, really, what in the Rot do you say at a time like this?

The brawler cuts me off, stepping forward and pointing with one hand, the girl clinging to the other.

"Are you the one who brought us here?" He has a thick low-ward accent. "Where in the stinking Rot are we? What do you want with us?"

"I didn't bring you here," I tell him. "I just—"

"Don't rotting lie to me!" he roars.

"She came down in the cage," the southerner says, her voice very soft but distinct. She speaks fluent Imperial with a lilting accent. "I think she was brought here like the rest of us."

"Then—" the young man begins. He's interrupted when the cage rises again, the screech and rattle of its mechanism drowning all speech. It passes upward, out of sight. A lantern appears, high overhead, and then several more. I can see the square room we're in has walls about fifteen feet high and above that is a metal catwalk with a railing. There are people up there, dozens of them, but the lanterns are aimed down at us, so they're nothing but faceless shadows. I hear laughter and shouting I can't understand.

The streetwalker starts to cry. I turn in a circle, shielding my eyes against the lights. There's something that looks like a ladder, hanging from the catwalk, but not quite low enough to grab with a running jump. I glance at the brawler, thinking that I might be able to make it if I stood on his shoulders, but that's as far as my plan gets.

Someone *jumps* from the catwalk. He falls fast, and then magic crackles and flares around him, the pale blue of Tartak, the Well of Force. It halts him in midair a few inches off the ground, and then he drops lightly onto his toes.

He has the copper skin and dark, curly hair of a Jyashtani, with high, sharp cheeks and shockingly blue eyes. I guess he's a few years older than me, perhaps twenty, with an athlete's build. His costume is outlandish, even by foreign standards. Jyashtani traders in the market usually wear loose white robes with tight black skullcaps, but this young man has cream-colored silk trousers embroidered with a blue-and-green design, a broad red sash at his waist, tied in an elaborate knot on his hip, and a dark shirt that doesn't fit, half-exposing one shoulder. There's a sword at his belt, a straight-bladed Jyashtani weapon. His hair hangs loose, longer than any Imperial man would wear it, brushing the nape of his neck.

"Greetings," he says. His Imperial is good, but not perfect, with the classic Jyashtani rasp. "Welcome to *Soliton*. My name is Zarun. I'm going to explain a few facts to you, so pay attention. You'll be here the rest of your lives."

5

Zarun looks at me first, then at each of the others in turn. I wonder if he's assessing them for danger like I did. Certainly he doesn't show any fear. His lips are slightly quirked, as though he finds us vaguely amusing.

"Where in the name of the Blessed is Soliton?" the brawler says.

"*Soliton* is a ship, not a place," Zarun says, turning to face him. "And you are all now part of its crew. The Captain is in command, and the officers, including me, carry out his orders. You, in turn, carry out ours." His smile broadens. "Is that understood?"

"To the Rot with that." The brawler steps forward, shaking off the grip of the girl behind him. "You're going to let us off right now."

"Oh, I don't advise trying that," Zarun says. "You saw the things at the rail when you were brought on board? We call them *angels,* and they serve the Captain. They take a dim view of crew trying to leave."

My skin goes cold. Were those twisted things *alive?* I remember the gray ripples of magic, the *voices,* and shiver involuntarily.

"I'm not asking again," the brawler says. "You don't know who you're dealing with, here."

He holds out a hand, and fire shoots up from his palm in a twisting column. Myrkai, the Well of Fire. I'd seen touched doing conjurors' tricks in the market, but nothing like this, and I have to work to keep my own power in check.

"Your Captain isn't here right now, is he?" the brawler says, the fire lighting his face. "So either you let us off, or I—"

Zarun moves *fast,* almost too fast to see. Bands of pale blue energy whip toward the brawler. The magic grabs both of the boy's hands, solidifying into glowing manacles of solid force that yank his arms up and apart. Power flares on Zarun's right arm, and I feel a sympathetic tug in my chest. Green Melos energy bursts out, forming a long blade like my own. In a single smooth motion, Zarun steps up to the brawler and slams the Melos blade into his chest, green lightning crackling from the impact.

For a moment, no one moves. The brawler's eyes have gone very wide, and the fire in his hand fades to embers and disappears. He tries to breathe, coughs, and spits blood. Zarun steps back and the Tartak fetters disappear. The brawler collapses like a broken puppet.

The girl behind him screams and runs to his side. I throw a quick glance around the room; the streetwalker is hiding her face, and the skinny boy is on his knees, his trousers damp with piss. The southern girl is staring at the spreading pool of blood as though it is the only thing in the world, her wide eyes very white in her dark face.

"Duro," the brawler's girl wails. *"Duro!"* I didn't get a good look at her earlier, but she can't be more than thirteen. Her *kizen* is soaking up blood.

"I'm sorry." Zarun looks down at her, still smiling. "There's always one who needs a demonstration."

"You . . ." The girl looks back at him, face twisted with rage and loss.

"He was your lover?" Zarun says, cocking his head.

"He's my *brother*," she spits at him. "I'm going to kill you, you rotscum, you filthy—"

"I see," Zarun says. "And is there anything I can do to change your mind on that subject?"

The girl's eyes are full of fury. She thinks she's being mocked. "I *will*; I swear it!"

"I believe you."

He spins, blade hand extended, then straightens up. There's a *thump* as the girl's severed head hits the wall. Her body collapses on top of her brother's, her blood pumping across him.

The southern girl gives a little shriek, and the others all look away from the carnage. I catch Zarun looking at me, and realize I was the only one who didn't flinch.

"This is a good lesson," Zarun says, in a thoughtful tone. "Here on *Soliton*, we mean what we say. If you tell someone you're going to kill them, be prepared for them to take it seriously." He lets the Melos blade fade away, and barks some foreign words into the darkness above us. Ropes fall, dark shapes swarming down them. "Bind them and take them to the Butcher!"

Our hands are tied behind our backs, and we're led out of the pit by a hidden door, escorted by at least a dozen armed people. The crew of *Soliton* are a mismatched bunch, drawn from every nation I've ever heard of and quite a few I haven't, men and women both, all young. Perhaps half are Imperials or Jyashtani, but there are a surprisingly large number of icelings, people from the Ice Kingdoms to the north of the Central Sea. They're all large and broad shouldered, with blond or brown hair and pale, almost colorless eyes. It's no wonder the first Imperial explorers thought they were ice spirits. Too uncivilized to trade in Kahnzoka, they survive on whaling and piracy.

There are four of us left: the streetwalker, the boy who stinks of piss, the southern girl, and me. My wrists chafe against the scratchy rope as we walk through an endless series of corridors, the way lit by lanterns carried by the crew. It feels more like an insect warren than a ship, every surface made of metal, streaked with rust. Here and there, something *grows* from the walls, irregular flat discs like shelf mushrooms, but the crew hurries us onward before I can take a closer look. They seem to know where they're going, but by the third or fourth junction I couldn't have found my way back to the pit for all the gold in Kahnzoka.

In spite of Zarun's brutality, I'm perversely feeling a little *better* than I was in the cage. Brutality I can handle. There's still a great deal I don't know about this ship—if it is a ship; I can't quite believe it—but there's *some* kind of society. We're not simply going to be devoured by monsters. I'm accustomed to dealing with people who use casual violence to make their points. Naga, the rotsucker, was probably right—working my way from gutter rat to ward boss prepared me for this.

Not that it's going to save him, when I get back to Kahnzoka. He's going to wish that he'd done what Zarun did, and taken me seriously.

Finally, we arrive at a door, jury-rigged out of wood scraps to fit into a metal hatchway. One of the crew knocks, and it opens from the inside. The space beyond has the feel of a barracks common room, with cushions, empty wine bottles, and dirty plates scattered everywhere. Weirdly, the cushions are made of fine fabric, battered with use but clearly very expensive. Some of the plates, chipped as they are, are gold-inlaid china, finer than anything in use at Tori's house in the Second Ward. I can see a statue of the Blessed One, his hand raised in the traditional benediction, made from silver with flashing blue stones for eyes; it would buy a tenement building in the Sixteenth Ward, and it's being used to weigh down scraps of paper.

The crew in the room, perhaps two dozen of them, pause what they're doing as we're led inside. Several games seem to be in progress, cards and dice and stranger things I can't identify. My attention, however, is drawn to the woman getting to her feet at the far end of the room.

It would be difficult for her *not* to draw attention. She's an iceling, and enormous even by iceling standards, a head and a half taller than me and at least twice as broad. The way she's dressed makes her look even bigger, swathed in rough leather and fur, with chunks of yellowing bone sewn in. The top half of a crab's claw, too big to have come from any crab I'd ever seen, adorns each of her shoulders. Her hair is twisted into thick, greasy dreadlocks, all tied back together, and the pale skin of her face is patchy with angry red blotches. She wears a thick, square sword at her side that looks more like an enormous meat cleaver.

This, I assume, is the Butcher.

"I thought I smelled fresh meat," she says. Her Imperial is atrociously accented, as though she were gargling rocks. She adds something in another language, and the lounging crew laugh. The sound reminds me of the baying of hounds. "Is this all they've brought?"

"Zarun had to put two down," one of the women who brought us says.

"And they call *me* a butcher," the Butcher says, to another laugh. "He ought to just hand them over; we'd whip them into shape."

"Zarun believes in the power of making an example," the woman says.

Something passes between her and the Butcher, some mutual animosity. I can feel the division between the crew who came with us and those in the room, like two gangs working on the same job while keeping a wary eye on each other.

"Well," the Butcher grunts. "It'll have to do."

She comes over to us, her footfalls loud on the metal deck. The boy must have pissed himself again, because a fresh wave of stench rolls over us, and the Butcher wrinkles her nose.

"Freeze and rot," she says, glaring at him. "Right. What's your Well?"

He blinks, eyes flicking back and forth.

"It's not a hard question," the Butcher growls. "What can you *do*?"

"M . . . Myrkai," the boy says, in a tiny voice. "It's Myrkai. But I'm not v . . . very strong. I swear."

Like me, he's probably spent his whole life hiding the fact that he's mage-born. Admitting it in front of strangers isn't easy.

The Butcher snorts. "Give him to Strom," she says over her shoulder. "She'll see if there's anything worthwhile buried in there."

One of the Butcher's crew grabs the boy's arm and drags him away, ignoring his yelps. The huge woman turns to the streetwalker, who stares up at her with red-rimmed eyes.

"And you?" the Butcher says.

"Tartak," she says. "But I'm only touched."

"Hmph." The Butcher looks the woman up and down. "Can you fight?"

"No." The streetwalker squares her shoulders. "I'm a prostitute."

"And not ashamed of it, I see," the Butcher says. "Officers' hall for this one, see if anyone wants her for their clade." Her face splits open, showing brown teeth. "I just might make an offer myself."

I can see the fear on the girl's face, but she keeps her back straight as she's led away. The Butcher stalks to the southerner, looming over her.

"Right," she rumbles. "Well?"

"I don't have one," the southern girl says. "I'm not mage-born—"

The Butcher's hand whips around hard, hitting the girl's cheek with a *crack*. She stumbles backward, hand rising to her face. It comes away covered in blood—the Butcher has something sharp on the back of her glove, a white wedge that might be a shark's tooth.

"I am . . ." The southerner straightens, and she looks up at the Butcher, ignoring the blood running down her cheek.

"I am Meroe hait Gevora Nimara, First Princess of Nimar." Her throat works as she swallows hard. "My presence here is some sort of mistake. My father, the King of Nimar, will—"

The Butcher's other hand cracks across her jaw, an open-handed slap that makes the girl reel backward. She steadies herself, looks up again.

"The King of Nimar," she repeats, staring right at the Butcher. "And he will reward you handsomely for my return. I will persuade him to forgive any offense you might have given me"—she touches her bloody cheek—"in return for your service."

Oh, Blessed. It's brave and honest and utterly, completely stupid. I tense for what I know is coming, but the girl, Meroe, doesn't move a muscle until the Butcher's fist slams into her gut with the force of a sledgehammer. She doubles over, folding up around the blow, and the Butcher grabs her hair to keep her from falling.

"First of all," the huge woman says, "you *never* lie to me. If you weren't mage-born, the angels would have torn you apart the moment you came on board. Second of all, no one *rotting* cares who your daddy is, and he sure as ice isn't going to protect you now. I'd give good odds he was the one who sent you here." She looks around at her crew. "We're all rejects on *Soliton*. The ones they wanted to get rid of." There's a chorus of assent, and some jeers. The Butcher turns back to Meroe. "If you're here, that means you're a reject, too.

The sooner you accept that, the longer you'll survive. Not that I'd give odds on you living very long in any case."

Meroe's lips work, but she can't draw a breath. The Butcher hauls her upright.

"Now tell me," she says, spittle flying into the southern girl's face. "What is your Well?"

"I don't . . ." Meroe's voice is a wheeze. "I don't have—"

The Butcher hits her again, and this time lets her collapse, following up with a kick to the midsection. Meroe has gone still, and the Butcher is winding up again.

"You'll kill her." I don't realize I've spoken until the words are out of my mouth.

The Butcher freezes, then turns slowly toward me.

"And what's it to you," she says, quietly, "if I do?"

Nothing. It's nothing to me. If I'm going to survive on *Soliton* long enough to escape, I need to start making allies. This is only going to antagonize this woman, questioning her in front of her underlings. It may *also* get me beaten to a bloody pulp.

But now it's too late. I've challenged her authority, and she can't let that stand.

"She may not know what her Well is, that's all," I say, trying for diffidence. "Some people don't find out until they're much older."

"So rotting what?" the Butcher says, stalking closer.

"So she's not lying to you, and there's no sense in beating her to death."

Her voice rises to a bellow. *"What makes you think you get a say?"*

"I just wanted—"

Her arm comes around. I know the backhand is coming, and it's hard work to keep my Melos armor suppressed, to let her hit me. My head rings with the impact, and the shark's tooth slashes my cheek open, letting a warm trickle of blood roll down to my chin.

I have to do that, have to let her get her own back, show me who's boss. She can't afford to look weak, not in front of everyone. I've seen this story a hundred times.

"And you?" the Butcher hisses. "What's *your* Well, rotscum?"

I step back and ignite my blades. The ropes around my wrists fall away as the energy sears through them, and I raise my hands, green power crackling. There's a hush among the gathered crew, broken only by the hiss of writhing magic.

"I see," the Butcher says. "Melos. I should have known. It rots the brain, makes you think you're invincible." Her lips curl into a snarl. "Are you going to fight us all?"

I shake my head and let the blades fade away. My cheek stings, but I don't touch it, just hold the Butcher's gaze. I may not understand people, but I understand *this,* the play of threat and counterthreat. She's a bully, which means she'll back away from strength and be merciless in the face of weakness. But she also has to keep up appearances with her people. I'm trying to show her I'm not a pushover without forcing her to prove herself by slapping me down.

I can see her going through this, too, the calculation in her eyes. She knows I took the blow when I didn't have to. Knows that if she pushes me too far, forces me into a fight, it's not going to be a bloodless beating. She's not stupid, in spite of her brutish appearance. Another thing I learned on the streets of the Sixteenth Ward—just because someone looks like an ogre doesn't mean you can assume they haven't got brains as well.

"I think I know just the place for you," she says, then looks at Meroe's still form. "For both of you, since you're such good friends. Pack Nine needs fresh blood, doesn't it, Haia?"

An iceling girl sitting in a nest of cushions, whippet thin and bald as an egg, gives a broad, nasty grin. "I'd say so. Yes, I certainly would."

Laughter spreads among the crew, the nasty chuckling of people who know you're not in on the joke. I try not to react. Blood drips off my chin.

"Very well. You two are assigned to Pack Nine." The Butcher gestures, and several of her crew move to lift Meroe and surround me, hands on their weapons. I note that they keep a respectful distance, now. "Show them the way."

6

Another trip through endless metal corridors. This time we're definitely moving downward, descending several flights of stairs. At first some of the hallways are lit by hanging lanterns, but they disappear as we descend, and the stains and rust become more prevalent. Sometimes parts of the wall or floor have fallen away entirely, leaving holes into dark rooms. There are more mushrooms, bigger than I've ever seen. Brackish water drips down the walls and stands in puddles.

There's a lantern sitting on a wooden table, an oasis of light in the darkness. Two crew sit beside it, guarding a heavy metal door with a thick wooden bar. They lift the bar as we approach, and our escorts carry Meroe inside, gesturing for me to follow.

It's a large room with a high ceiling, and a shaft, far overhead, lets in a small measure of daylight. Dawn must have come outside. The floor is half-covered in water, like a miniature lake, complete with a pair of small "islands" thrusting up out of the murk. On the dry side, there's a small collection of carpets and cushions pulled into a messy nest.

Waiting just inside the doorway is a tall, gawky young man with long copper-colored hair. I can't place his looks—his skin is light brown, darker than an Imperial's but paler than most Jyashtani, and while his features have an Imperial cast, they're thicker, with wide cheekbones. He has blue eyes, like the icelings, and wears weathered, practical clothes. He looks at me first, interested, and then his face falls when he sees Meroe.

"What's this?" he says.

Haia, the bald girl who led our escort, answers with a sneer, "Fresh meat."

"What's wrong with that one?" the young man says.

"Mouthed off to the Butcher," says one of the crew carrying her. He and his companion drop her awkwardly onto a carpet with a *thump*.

"Now you're back up to strength," Haia says. "After dinner, you're going out."

"You've got to be rotting kidding me," the young man says. "With *this* lot?"

"Don't work, don't eat," Haia says. "You know the Captain's law." She gestures to the rest of the crew. "Come on."

The young man stares after them in sullen silence as they troop out. Then he turns on me, looking furious. I'm still in the calm, disconnected world of violence and threat assessment.

"I suppose you only speak Imperial?" he says.

I nod, glancing back at the door. I heard the *thunk* of the bar, and there are no other exits. A prison cell, then. I've been in less commodious accommodations.

He takes a half step forward. "Rotting listen to me when I'm talking to you. That's your first lesson. My name is Ahdron, and I'm pack leader here. Don't forget that unless you want to end up like your friend."

Options. On the one hand, I could kill him. Not a guarantee, not on a ship where everyone is mage-born, but he's stepped inside my reach, and I'm fairly certain I could take him by surprise. He's locked in here with us, so he can't be too important. On the other hand, I have no idea what the consequences might be and I can't fight the Butcher and her whole crew. So probably best to be cautious, at least for now.

I square off with Ahdron and look him in the eye. He's a little taller than me and my guess is a few years older. Like the Butcher, he's a familiar type, the small-timer clinging to whatever scraps of power he has, blustering and cruel in his weakness.

"It would help if I knew what a pack leader was," I say. "Or a pack, for that matter."

"Fresh meat." He rolls his eyes. "A pack, like a hunting pack of wolves."

"Just you, me, and Meroe?"

Ahdron grits his teeth. "There's also the Moron and the Coward." He nods out toward one of the little islands, where a younger Jyashtani boy is sitting alone. "That's the Moron. The Coward is probably hiding somewhere." He cocks his head. "What about you? Can you do anything useful?"

"My Well is Melos. I can fight."

His expression shifts, just a little. Fear, greed, or a bit of both. "Can you, now?"

I nod again. He looks me up and down, appraisingly, then glances over at Meroe.

"What about her?"

I shrug. "She doesn't know her Well."

"Better and rotting better." He sighs. "At least she's toothsome."

"Don't touch her," I snap. Cautious is one thing, but some lines need to be made explicit immediately.

"Oh, fresh meat? You going to stand in for her?" He runs his eyes over me again. "I prefer my fresh meat with a little more *meat*, frankly."

I match his stare again for a long, quiet moment. Then his mouth twists, and he laughs.

"Relax, fresh meat. Captain's law. Any man takes a girl who doesn't want it, that man better look forward to having angels pull his arms and legs off. Or any girl who takes a boy, for that matter. Captain doesn't discriminate, and neither do the officers. This isn't like landside. *Soliton* is *civilized*." He cocks his head. "What's your name?"

"Isoka," I tell him. "And she's Meroe."

"Very well, Isoka. Since you're so worried about your friend, why don't you go make sure she's not going to bleed to death. I'll see if I can get someone to explain the facts of life to you."

I'm no doctor, but I've patched people up after enough street fights to know the basics. I roll Meroe onto her back and check for broken bones. It seems like she got lucky, or else the Butcher is fairly skilled at administering beatings; probably both. Either way, she hasn't broken any ribs. Aside from the cut on her cheek she'll probably get away with some bad bruises. I wrap her cut and mine with strips of linen slashed from an old pillowcase.

When I'm finished, I lean back against the pile of carpets, suddenly exhausted. The adrenaline that's flooded my veins drains away, leaving me shaky and weak. I haven't slept since Kuon Naga grabbed me, and that feels like a lifetime ago. I can feel my eyes drifting shut when there's a bit of movement across from me, and then I'm suddenly wide awake, heart slamming against my ribs, a half second from igniting my blades.

A slight figure shrinks back against the carpets. He holds a heavy canteen in front of him, like a peace offering.

"Sorry," he mumbles. "I just . . . Ahdron said I should bring this to you."

"It's all right." I rub my eyes and breathe. When he shuffles a little closer, I take the canteen and guzzle a long swig. "You just startled me."

"I'm sorry," he repeats. "You can keep that. Don't drink the water from the pool; it'll make you sick."

I sit up and look at him more closely. He's a couple of years younger than me, with a gauntness that speaks of hard, hungry days. He looks Imperial, though a darker tone to his skin might indicate some Jyashtani blood. His clothes are mostly layered rags.

"Thanks," I tell him, taking a slower drink. The water is tepid but tastes pure. "I'm Isoka."

"My name is Berun," he says. "Most people call me the Coward, though." He glances past me, at Meroe. "Is she going to be all right?"

"I think so."

"That's good."

He settles a little, coming out of his protective crouch. His eyes are still constantly moving, alert for danger. He reminds me of a rabbit, or a rat.

"Ahdron told me to come answer your questions," he says, after a moment's pause. "About *Soliton,* I mean. I'm sure you're confused."

"You've been here a long time?"

"Only a year," he says. "But it feels like longer."

I nod. All right. I don't know if I trust this strange boy, but information is information, and I need whatever I can get. I tighten the cap on the canteen and set it aside.

"First question," I say. "Is this really a ship?"

He nods. "I've been up to the deck, once. It's like being on top of a mountain. You can see *forever.*"

"Zarun said the angels would stop us if we try to leave. Is that true?"

"Yes." His voice is very quiet, as though he is worried they might hear. "They're *alive.* And they can find you anywhere. If you try to leave the ship, they come after you, and . . ." He swallows hard.

That might present a problem. I make a mental note that the angels need investigating.

"Who's in charge? Ahdron said something about a Captain."

"The Captain runs the ship," Berun says. "He decides where we go, and he controls the angels. But he only talks to the officers' council, and they make all the decisions for the rest of us."

A familiar pattern. Back in Kahnzoka, I'd never spoken to the shadowy bosses who were my ultimate employers.

"Is the Butcher an officer?" I ask.

Another nod. "She's in charge of the fresh meat. That's why they call her—"

"I gathered that," I deadpan.

"Sorry." He cringes a little.

"It's—never mind." I shake my head. "Why are we locked in here? Are they ever going to let us out?"

"The Butcher decides where newcomers should go. The officers each have a clade." He can see my frown at the unfamiliar word, and clarifies hastily. "That's like . . . their household. Servants. But not *just* servants. People who can do useful things and need protection. Then there's the packs. Most of the packs owe loyalty to one of the officers, too. They're the ones who go out into the ship and bring back food. There's hunting packs and scavenger packs. And then there's the wilders; they live out beyond the Captain's law and don't listen to anyone—"

"Slow down, please."

"Sorry," Berun says. His apologies seem to be reflexive. "It's complicated."

I don't need to know the details. The structure is familiar—bosses and gangs, just like in Kahnzoka, or for that matter just like a medieval lord and his knights. The strong rule, and the weak serve in exchange for protection. The oldest way of organizing a society.

I feel a little of my confidence returning. I can work with that.

"What about *us*? This is Pack Nine, they told me. Are all the packs locked up?"

"No." Berun speaks quietly again, and he glances nervously over his shoulder. "Pack Nine is on probation. Ahdron used to be one of the Butcher's lieutenants, but he made her angry somehow, so she stuck him here and sends him the dregs." He swallows. "There were six of us before the last time we went out."

Pieces fall into place, the cruel laughter of the Butcher's crew, her nasty smile. She's assigned me to a bunch of screwups, at the lowest rung of the social hierarchy, the equivalent of a trash-picker gang in Kahnzoka. A clever solution to the problem of what to do with me, once I'd challenged her authority.

I want to ask what he means by "went out" and what it is the packs actually *do* to find food, but Meroe shifts and groans. The movement startles Berun, who pulls back into a crouch, staring at her.

"I . . . I'll . . ." He swallows, looking between us, then gets to his feet. "I'll find some more water. For her. I'll be back."

Given the speed with which he darts off, I find that unlikely. I wonder what it is about Meroe that frightens him. She blinks muzzily, touching the bandage on her cheek, and tries to sit up. I put a hand on her shoulder to keep her in place for the moment.

"Easy. Give it a minute." I watch her eyes for a moment—they're red-brown, the color of freshly fired clay—and make sure they focus properly. "Do you want some water?"

Meroe nods fractionally, and I bring up the canteen. She gulps, swallows, and lets out a long breath.

"I guess I'm not dead," she says.

"How do you feel?"

"Like I was trampled by a . . . a . . ." She waves her hands vaguely. "A *zousan*. A big gray animal. There's no word for it in Imperial." She chuckles weakly, then winces, putting a hand to her stomach. "Okay. No laughing for the immediate future."

"I think you're going to be all right," I tell her. "No broken bones that I could find."

"That's a lot better than I expected," she says. "What happened?"

"You talked back to someone you shouldn't have."

"I remember *that*." Meroe pulls herself up slightly. "I mean what happened afterward?"

"I convinced the Butcher she was better off not killing you."

"You did?" Meroe raises one eyebrow, looking at the bandage on my cheek. "I'm sorry I missed that."

"It wasn't that impressive."

"Then you saved my life." A smile stretches her lips, thin and insubstantial. "Not that I'm not grateful and everything. But why?"

I feel myself flush a little. The truth is, I still don't know *why* I helped her. It's possible she could be an ally and having her in my debt might be useful, but that wasn't worth making the Butcher angry with me. Stepping in had been the wrong decision, unquestionably, but I couldn't help but feel like I'd do it again.

It was something about the way she'd talked to the Butcher. She'd been completely in the older woman's power, helpless, but there was no fear in Meroe's eyes. Just . . .

"Do I need a reason?" I say, irritably.

"I mean, people usually have reasons for doing things," Meroe says. "If you don't want to tell me, I suppose I can't complain. I just thought it might help me thank you properly."

"Don't worry about thanking me." I hand her the canteen again, and she takes another drink. "Is it true what you said? About being a princess?"

She nods. "First Princess of Nimar. But I'm not sure my father will really reward you if you bring me back. In all honesty I think the Butcher was right about him sending me here."

"Why would he do that?"

"Oh, I've lost track of the ways in which I've disappointed him. I suppose he finally got fed up with me."

"You seem . . . calm about it."

"I've been kidnapped before," she says brightly. "Twice by one of my uncles, and once by bandits. It's a hazard of my profession. This time they were nice enough to use some kind of drug, because the last thing I remember is strangers in masks getting aboard the royal coach. We're a long way from Nimar, aren't we?"

"I think so," I say, "but I have to admit that I don't exactly know where Nimar is."

She waves a hand, as if it's of small importance. "Is this really a ship?" She raps the floor with her knuckles. "I've never been on a proper ship before. Are they usually made of metal?"

"No." I'm having a little difficulty keeping up. Meroe seems to be speaking faster as her head clears, and the way she jumps from topic to topic is disconcerting. "This is *Soliton*. It's . . . unique. Have you heard the stories?"

She shakes her head, and listens raptly as I give her the abridged version, along with the information I've been able to glean from Berun.

"Nimar is well inland," she says when I'm finished. "So we don't get many ghost ships. My father must have *really* wanted to be rid of me if he sent me all the way to Kahnzoka. I'm surprised he didn't just slit my throat." She looks around. "So what now?"

I find myself staring at her. "You did hear what I said? That we're stuck here for good?"

She nods. "Sorry. I'm sure that must be very difficult for you."

"It's not for you?"

"Well, if it's true my father sent me here, that means there'd be no place for me at home anyway. So if I've got to leave, I suppose this is as good a place as any. And, well . . ." She pauses, looking at me expectantly.

"You're a very strange princess," I tell her.

"Yes! That." She smiles, broadly this time, cheeks dimpling. "I get that a lot. When's dinner?"

7

I sit against the stacked carpets for a while, eyes closed. Meroe has found Berun, and he's having trouble keeping up with her rapid-fire questions. Just listening to it is exhausting.

Focus. I think about Tori. About the house in the Second Ward, where she probably doesn't even know what's happened to me, has no idea that her beautiful, comfortable life is hanging by a thread. She won't learn that anything's wrong until I don't visit when I said I would. She'll be heartbroken and worried.

Rotting Naga and his rotting Immortals. He could at least let me send her a letter. I *will* settle things with him, one way or the other. Zarun and Ahdron were both certain there was no way off the ship—I think of the angels and their horrible voices, and shiver—but they can't be certain. There has to be *something.*

I'm coming back, Tori. I swear it.

Pleasant fantasies of what I'm going to do to Kuon Naga occupy me until dinner arrives, which fortunately doesn't take long. The door opens, and Haia and a couple of crew bring in a large steel bucket and a stack of chipped bowls. Whatever's in there, it smells wonderful.

Ahdron faces off against Haia, trying to puff himself up and act tough. Haia isn't buying it, though. She glances around at the rest of us with barely concealed contempt.

"You're going out in an hour," she says. "Be ready."

"I'm ready," Ahdron says, drawing himself up. "But I can't speak for these—"

"It's just the Silvercap Gardens," Haia interrupts. "Try not to muck it up."

"Or if you do," one of the crew behind her says, "don't bother coming back."

They set the bucket on the metal deck and leave, barring the door again.

"What's the Silvercap Gardens?" Meroe says, wandering over.

"I'll explain," Ahdron grates, "when it needs explaining." He goes to the bucket, looks in, and shudders. "Ugh. Crab juice again."

I can't resist the smell anymore, and I go to the bucket. It's full of a murky liquid, hot enough that it steams a little, with some greenish things and unidentifiable white bits floating in it. I've eaten crab, pulled from the ocean in wooden traps by fishermen from up the coast. It has to be rushed to the city on ice, so it's a delicacy, steamed, salted, and buttered. Not worth the coin, in my opinion, but edible enough. The smell of this concoction doesn't have much in common with what I remember, but I'm hungry enough that I don't care.

The boy from the island slips in front of me and grabs one of the bowls. He dips it in the bucket, pulls it out full and dripping, and retreats to sit on a folded carpet, drinking the liquid and scooping the soft pieces out with his fingers.

"This is the Moron," Ahdron says to me and Meroe. "Expect nothing from him and you won't be surprised. He only turns up for meals."

"It's nice to meet you," Meroe says politely.

"And he doesn't talk," Ahdron growls. "So don't bother."

I take a bowl and fill it, mimicking the boy. Whatever "crab juice" is, it's good. Shockingly good, even considering that I haven't eaten in more than a day. Spices I can't identify give it a tingling bite. The white lumps are meat—crab, I assume—and something spongy that I guess is mushroom. Either way, they're suffused with the delicious broth, and I gobble them down.

I glance at my empty bowl, then at Ahdron. He gestures wearily for me to go ahead—there's plenty in the bucket. I have a second helping, which is as good as the first, and a long drink of water.

"Melos, you said," he says as I'm finishing.

I nod.

"If we're lucky, we won't run into anything nasty," he says. "If we're unlucky, it's going to be on you and me to stop it. I'll stay back, and you get in close and pin it down. Just keep it away from me and I'll roast it." He opens his palm, letting Myrkai fire flare briefly. "Think you can manage that?"

As plans go, it's not much. But I nod again. No sense picking a fight here, not yet. I wish I had Hagan at my side, someone I could count on; then I remember what happened to Hagan, and my stomach knots.

Ahdron turns away, muttering. Meroe sits down next to me, a bowl of crab juice in her hands. She stares at it for a moment, as though unsure how to proceed.

"You use your fingers, apparently," I tell her. "Once you're done with the broth."

She nods and lifts the bowl to her lips with an air of determined curiosity, like a traveler trying the customs of a strange new land.

"You grew up in a palace, I suppose," I say, as she slurps her soup. "Silver spoons and crystal goblets, that sort of thing."

"Oh yes." She finishes the broth and attacks the rest with her fingers, shoveling mushroom and crab into her mouth. In between bites, she adds, "I had a tutor named Rimi just for table etiquette. How to tell a *demi-forchette* from a shell pick, and why you use one for nuts and the other for fruit, and so on."

I shake my head. "Important things."

"When my father dined with us, one of his courtiers would watch me for mistakes," she goes on, finishing the bowl. "If I made a mistake, I'd be punished."

"No dessert?"

"He had a black lacquer switch, about as wide as your little finger. There was a special box for it, in my anteroom."

"Your father beat you for using the wrong *fork*?"

"Oh no." She holds out her arms, showing smooth, unblemished skin. "I had to remain pristine against the day I married some prince. He beat *Rimi,* and made me watch. Every time I looked away, he'd add another stroke."

Aristos. Whatever country they're from, they live in a different world.

Meroe scrapes the bottom of her bowl with her fingers and sucks them clean. "That was good. Do you think I could have some more?"

A very, very strange princess. Wordlessly, I wave her on.

Haia and some other crew return after an hour, just long enough to let the crab juice settle. Ahdron calls us all together by the door, the two silent boys, me, and Meroe. The Moron looks at the two newcomers with interest, idly swiveling one finger back and forth in his ear. Berun is hunched in on himself, looking a little green. Ahdron looks from one of them to the other, sighs, and turns to me and Meroe.

"You. Southerner. Mero, is it?"

"Meroe," she says. "*Meh,* roh, ei."

"Whatever. Isoka explained how things stand?"

"She told me you're in charge. And we have to go somewhere and do something." She cocks her head. "I have questions, but—"

"She said you don't know your Well," he interrupts. "Are you good for anything?"

"I don't have a Well," Meroe says. "But I can dance, sing—maybe not *well*—speak seven languages, keep an account book up-to-date, follow trade law, and cook puff pastry."

"In other words," he growls, "you're useless."

"You haven't tried my puff pastry." Meroe grins at him fearlessly, and I suppress a laugh. Ahdron snorts. "If there's a fight, stay out of the way," he says, looking from her to Berun. To the Moron, he adds, "*You* can feel free to get yourself killed."

"The mighty pack leader," Haia drawls from the doorway. "Come on. You don't want to keep the crabs waiting."

We file out, and Haia leads us on another twisting journey through the ship. This time we don't have far to go, though the direction is even farther down, via a rusting staircase and a long ramp. We finally reach a place where the corridor dead-ends in a large metal door, secured in place with a double bar and guarded by a pair of crew. A stack of lanterns stands against one wall, beside a pile of crude spears.

"Here we are," Haia says. "Left at the second landing, then keep going until you get to the Silvercap Garden."

"I've done this before," Ahdron says, taking a lantern and ignoring the spears.

"Just thought you might have forgotten," Haia says, grinning. "It's been a while."

The Coward arms himself with a spear, but none of the rest of us do. We each take a lantern, and Ahdron lights them with a theatrical puff of Myrkai fire. The two guards undo the bars and open the door, which lets a cold wind and a strong smell of salt water into the corridor. The flames dance and flicker.

"Good luck," Haia says. I get the sense she doesn't mean it.

Ahdron strides forward, through the door and into the darkness, and the rest of us follow. It takes a moment for my eyes to adjust. By the sound, I can tell we're in a much larger space, almost as though I'm back under the open sky. I blink and make out a metal bridge, wide enough for two carts to pass each other, lined by a railing. It stretches on farther than I can see, and to either side is only darkness.

No. Not *quite* darkness. There are lights there, made tiny by distance, green and blue sparks like colorful stars. They hang in place or move slowly, as though swept by invisible tides.

"What *is* this place?" Meroe says. "This cannot be a ship."

"*Soliton* is the largest ship ever to float," Berun says, looking miserable. "It's bigger than some cities. That way"—he points to the door behind us—"is the Stern, where the crew lives. This"—he waves at the darkness—"is the Center. There are other bridges, ladders, stairways, hundreds of them. This is where we come to hunt." He huddles in on himself. "Where the crabs are."

Meroe steps to the railing and looks over the side. "What's down at the bottom?"

"The Deeps," Berun says. "No one goes down there and comes back alive."

"If there's a Stern, is there a Bow?" Meroe's face is animated in the lantern's half-light. "How does the Captain steer?"

"None of that rot makes any difference to *you*," Ahdron says. "Keep up."

"We should try to stay quiet," Berun says, as we start walking.

"Crabs can hear your footsteps half the ship away," Ahdron says contemptuously. "If they're around, whispering isn't going to hide you."

"Crabs aren't the only things out here," Berun says. But he doesn't argue further, only winces a little every time Ahdron's boots ring too loudly off the metal deck.

The bridge slopes down a little, and the surface is uneven, parts of it sagging or twisted. The railings are intermittent. In the darkness below us, colored lights move, fade out, and bloom again. We cross a circular landing, where several bridges meet and a spiral stairway descends dizzyingly out of sight. Most of the steps are broken in the middle, the rust-edged remnants clinging to the frame like a mouthful of shattered teeth. I think I can hear water rushing, far below us. Ahdron leads us across the landing and onto another bridge, where a crude arrow has been scraped into the rust.

I pause by a support pillar. There's a noise, down at the very edge of hearing, like someone talking in another room. And I swear I can see something *moving*, running along the metal surface in intricate, shifting patterns. Gray light. I blink, and look at Meroe, but she doesn't seem to notice. The others are already past, and I hurry to catch up, fighting a chill.

At the second landing, we turn left, as Haia instructed. Soon I can hear the patter of falling water, and we reach a spot where the bridge changes shape, splitting into four curving sections connected by long, arched buttresses. A little ways on, part of one section has broken free, leaning drunkenly against its neighbor. The paths divide and divide again, creating a labyrinth of interconnected bridges, like a hedge maze with bottomless pits instead of hedges.

Water falls from above us, not a steady rain but a constant spatter, drops splashing off the walkways or missing them and falling into oblivion. I hold out my hand for a few moments, and a heavy drop splashes into it, while another lands in my hair. I sniff my hand—freshwater.

"Don't try to drink it," Berun says. We all have canteens, though we didn't pack any food.

"Here," Ahdron says from up ahead. "This is what we came for."

He raises his lantern, and a hundred tiny gleams of light move with it. The curving paths are covered in weird fungal growths, huge shelf-like things veined with purple, sprigs of what looks like bright red grass, dangling tendrils that remind me of jellyfish tipped with electric blue. The dominant type seems to be a mushroom of a more normal toadstool shape, whose caps are plated unevenly with what looks like polished silver. They reflect the glow of the lanterns like stars.

"Silvercaps," Ahdron says. "They're good to eat. Here." He digs into a pouch and extracts several wadded bags. "Take the ones that are about as big as your hand. Just grab them right under the cap and snap them off the stalk. Try not to touch anything else. I don't know if anything *really* nasty grows here, but I wouldn't take chances."

The Coward takes a bag with bad grace, and the Moron accepts one with no sign of understanding. I exchange a glance with Meroe.

"That's it?" I say. "We're gathering mushrooms?"

Ahdron's face is thunderous. "We're doing the job we've been assigned to do, fresh meat. Be glad it's such an easy one."

Meroe and I take our bags and follow him inside the moist garden. The fungus is thickest on the edges of the path, so we walk in single file, staying clear of protruding growths. In places they tower overhead, tall spires of pale white flesh and sprays of leafy nodules.

"It's practically a forest," Meroe says.

"I've never been in a forest, so I wouldn't know."

"What?" Meroe turns to me. "You've never seen a *forest*?"

"We don't have them inside the walls of Kahnzoka. Until they brought me here, I'd never been outside the city."

"Oh." Meroe gives me an odd look, and goes quiet.

We stop to pick some of the silvercaps. They're a little rubbery to the touch, but their flesh parts easily under my fingernail. I drop several into the bag, and stop to look down at one particularly large specimen, nearly a foot across. Its silver coating reflects a distorted image of my face.

"It's pretty," I offer, feeling as though I ought to make conversation.

"It reminds me of descriptions of the Vile Rot," she says. "Mushrooms that grow to the size of houses, and plants that take root in living flesh."

I pause, halfway to picking another mushroom. "Charming."

"Sorry."

We work for another few moments in awkward silence.

"In Nimar," Meroe says, "there are women who pick mushrooms in the royal forest. They find them using pigs, trained pigs."

I'm not quite sure what to make of this. "That's interesting," I say, non-committally.

"The thing I could never understand," she goes on, "is how they keep the pigs from eating the mushrooms once they find them."

My only experience with pigs is when they're sliced up in bronze sauce, so I shrug. She's not looking at me, and I wonder if she's talking to herself.

"I always wanted to try it," she says. "My father wouldn't let me, of course. Not a proper activity, a princess grubbing around in the dirt with pigs." She pops a silvercap free. "I suppose I got the last laugh there."

"Meroe—"

She turns around, grinning. "Sorry. I'm rambling. I just—"

"Meroe, *move*!"

Something huge and blue comes up over the edge of the walkway.

It's a leg, as long as I am tall, protected by bright blue armor plating. It has four joints, and the end is tipped with a hairy, gooey ball that squishes against the deck. Another identical limb follows, rising over the edge and coming down gently amid the fungi.

"Ahdron!" I shout. I'm already backing away, letting the bag of silvercaps fall, looking around for the others. Berun is just ahead of us, and Ahdron is a little behind. The Moron is nowhere to be seen.

The body of the thing comes up over the rail. It's enormous, bigger than a horse, discshaped, with four limbs on each side. Six legs serve to stick it to the walkway, as easily as any housefly walking upside down on the ceiling. The two arms are much larger, thick as tree trunks, supporting a pair of grasping claws big enough to fit around my waist. Facing me is what I assume is the thing's mouth, a nightmare thicket of dozens of blade-tipped tendrils as long as my arm. Every bit of it is blue, the armor a bold sky color, the mouthparts closer to teal. There are no eyes, but the shell is covered in spiny growths.

I have fought men who were bigger and stronger than me, many times. When I was a little girl, I fought men who might as well have been ogres, compared to my slight frame. But at least they were human. I've heard stories of the monsters of the world—the tigers of Jyashtan, the great snakes of the Southern Kingdoms, the ancient nightwalkers of the iceling lands, and of course the horrible twisted things that set on anyone who gets close to the Vile Rot. But I'd never thought to see one with my own eyes.

So I freeze, for just a moment. Up ahead, Berun has frozen, too, clutching his sack of mushrooms as though they're the most precious things in the world. The crab glides toward him. It's so *quiet*, armor plates sliding smoothly across one another, and its padded, sticky feet make no sound at all. It steps forward almost daintily, entirely on the walkway now, one claw reaching toward Berun. The movement is oddly tentative, as though it doesn't quite know what to make of us.

"Hey!" Meroe shouts. A fist-sized bit of fungus flies through the air and shatters on the thing's carapace in a spray of spores. "Over here! Leave him alone!"

The crab's whole body shivers at the sound. It spins, and its claw swings toward Meroe, hard and fast. While its slow advance had me almost hypnotized, the quick motion activates instincts hard-won in a hundred street fights. I throw myself flat and pull Meroe down with me, and the claw goes over our heads.

"Run," I hiss at her.

I leave Meroe facedown in the padded fungus and spring up, igniting my blades. Melos power crackles from my wrists and runs over my body as the armor field stabilizes. As the crab brings its second claw down, I throw up an arm to push the strike aside, ready to move closer and jam an energy blade into its maw.

This turns out to be a very bad idea. I do it automatically—against a smaller, weaker opponent, many large men will go for a sweeping downward blow, even if they should know better. It's a great opportunity to end a fight before it really gets started. But I'm used to fighting humans, not crabs the size of carts. The claw meets my Melos blade and keeps coming, pushing my arm aside with no effort at all. It's like trying to deflect a lead weight dropped from the top of a building. I have to throw myself out of the way, wrenching the muscles in my side, to avoid getting crushed.

Even as I do, my second blade sweeps out, intercepting the crab's arm just behind the claw. Against a human, a Melos blade will take a hand clean off with a good hit. Now my blade scrapes over the crab's armor with a sound like a needle dragged over glass, leaving a dark, smoking scorch mark but no other damage. I feel heat wash across my arm as my power flares.

The claw hits the ground with a *crunch*. Fortunately, by luck or good reflexes of her own, Meroe rolled sideways out of the way. Unfortunately, that took her closer to the crab, just underneath the writhing, bladed tendrils around its mouth. Meroe sits up in time to see a half-dozen tentacles tipped with long, sword-like points reaching toward her, and starts scrambling backward.

Time to assess, now that I have a moment. The best option at this point would be to run away. Let the crab eat Meroe and probably Berun, too. Neither of them seems like they're going to be much help, and I think I can find my way back the way we came. Ahdron probably already took off. If Haia objects to my coming back alone, I can always kill her.

But I don't run. Meroe's not moving anymore—she grabbed the first two tentacles to reach her, and I can see her arms straining to keep them away. Blood leaks from her hands where they cut her, but she's not giving up, even as more tentacles stretch forward.

Rot. Oh, Blessed's rotting balls. What am I doing?

This is what I'm doing:

Running forward. Seeing the big claw coming, ducking underneath it, feeling the wind of its passage on my back. Swinging my Melos blade at the closest tentacle, which Meroe has pinned. Feeling the flesh part—no armor here—and seeing green energy crackle. Watching Meroe scramble free as I sever another tentacle, feeling a third slam against my belly and bounce off in a spray of Melos power, the lines of energy hot underneath my skin.

Seeing, too late, the second claw closing around my waist, catching me in its grip. I think Meroe screams my name.

The crab lifts me off the ground, my feet kicking, and it squeezes me like a nutcracker. My armor flares in response, two shimmering discs of Melos energy, keeping the two halves of the crab's claw from coming together and crushing my midsection. The lines of energy under my skin, where power from the Well runs, grow first warm, then hot, then unbearable, as though wire still glowing from the forge had been wrapped around me. I slam my blade against the claw, again and again, leaving a crisscross of smoking marks.

Something hits the crab from behind, bright and too fast to see. A bolt of flame, and then another, impacting against its shell with explosive force. I can see Ahdron, his hands ablaze with orange-red Myrkai power. A third firebolt catches the crab on one of its squishy feet, and it stumbles for a moment, off balance.

The pressure on my waist lessens, going from unimaginable pain to mere agony. The crab turns on its noiseless feet to go after Ahdron. It's shockingly fast, as fast as a galloping horse. Ahdron throws another bolt of fire at its maw, but his aim is off and the flames explode along its shell. They burn for a moment, then wink out, leaving scorches but no damage. Ahdron backpedals rapidly as the crab's other claw reaches out for him.

I've had a second to catch my breath and think. I've never had a proper instructor for magic, obviously. In the Legions, they have drills and techniques, perfected over hundreds of years. All I've ever had to work with are my instincts. The power has always just been there, like a trusty knife in a secret sheath, and it never seemed wise to question it too closely.

But now I need something different. Not a long blade for parrying, but something hard and sharp that will punch through this rotting armor. I exert my will, pushing the power down my arm, fumbling and uncertain. It feels like trying to *think* about something your body knows how to do automatically, like tying a knot, awkward at every step. But something shifts, and heat rises as green lightning crackles across my skin.

I let one blade vanish. The other *changes*, getting shorter and thicker. It looks less like a sword and more like a spike, and I can feel the potential inside it, like a coiled spring. I jam the energy blade as hard as I can into the crab's claw, aiming for the joint between armor plates.

There's a *crack*, like a lightning bolt, and a sharp metallic smell in the air. The blade goes in, armor plate snapping, the fracture spreading sideways. As it breaks through, I release the energy, and I feel power pulse through me and explode into the crab. There's a sudden stench, like charred fish, and the claw holding me spasms and lets go.

I hit the fungus-covered ground, feeling a wash of blessed chill as my armor vanishes. For a moment I lie still, breathing hard, but the crab is still moving. Another bolt from Ahdron hits it, and it charges toward him, legs churning as it passes *over* me. I roll onto my back after it goes past, in time to see him dodge another claw swipe. One of its tentacles licks out, slashing open his arm in a spray of blood. Ahdron desperately blasts the crab with a wave of fire, which forces it back a step.

I get to my feet and sprint after it. A running jump gets me high enough to grab the spiny protrusions on its back, prickles of heat flaring across my body as the armor keeps me from getting skewered. I pull myself up, hand over hand, until my dangling feet get purchase. I summon the spike again and bring it down as hard as I can. I can feel it break through, and the crab twitches as I release another wave of energy inside it. But it doesn't stop. Ahdron is down, on his back, a claw missing him by inches. I can't see Meroe. I'm hurting the crab, but it's like trying to kill an ox with a needle. I stab it again, pain flaring across my body with the ripple of heat. Rot rot *rot*!

"The brain!" It takes me a moment to recognize the source of the shout. It's Berun, on another walkway nearby, watching the fight across the gap. "Get the brain! Just above the mouth!"

Another wave of fire from Ahdron. The crab rears up, nearly tipping me off, then comes back down on top of him, sword-tentacles lashing. I pull myself forward, armor flaring, the spikes of the monster's back tearing my clothes. Now I'm almost upside-down, looking at where the eyes would be if the thing *had* eyes. I raise my energy blade, suck in a deep breath, and let the power build until I can't take the heat anymore.

Then I bring it down. The spike breaks through the armor with a *crunch* and a *crackle* of energy, and I hit the crab with everything I have, one rush of power that burns so hot it makes me scream. All eight of the crab's limbs flail as the Melos energy courses through it. It tips sideways, spilling me off to lie panting and helpless on the walkway while it twitches. And then, finally, mercifully, it dies.

8

I remember the return trip in bits and pieces. I think I walk part of the way, but at least once I wake up and find myself on Meroe's back, my arms dangling around her neck. Her hands are swathed in rough bandages, and she's breathing hard, struggling with my weight. I see Ahdron ahead of us, cradling his arm, his shirt awash in blood.

Before we reach the door to the Stern, I pass out for good, because the next thing I know I'm waking up in a bed, in a place I've never seen before. I lie still, and look around as best I can.

It's a strange bed, nearly as high off the ground as a table and much too soft. I sink into it with a feeling unpleasantly like drowning. I vaguely recognize this as the Jyashtani style, though why they can't have a proper sleeping mat on the floor like normal people I can't guess. There's a light sheet pulled over me—silk, I note absently—and beneath it my clothes are gone, replaced by a kind of half-length robe. More foreign clothing.

My body hurts, especially my right arm. I've pushed my power too far before, and I recognize the sensation, the aftermath we call powerburn. The initial agony has faded into an itchy numbness on my skin, with deep aches stabbing down to the bone. When I breathe, pain pulses through my abdomen, where the crab's claw almost crushed me.

The walls are metal, as is the floor underneath a threadbare carpet. I haven't been magically transported off *Soliton*, then, more's the pity. I take a deep breath and raise my head, stifling a groan. The room is small, not much more than the bed, with only a hanging curtain for a door.

"You're awake," Meroe says.

She's sitting in the corner of the room on a metal stool. The bandage I put on her face is gone, and the wound the Butcher's blow left there is covered by an ugly scab. There are circles under her eyes, almost black against her dark skin. She's replaced the clothes she came aboard in with an ill-fitting green dress, sleeves rolled up to keep from flapping over her hands. Her palms are wound round with linen bandages.

"I'd rather not be," I say honestly.

"I can understand that."

She gets up and offers me a canteen. I take it, nearly fumbling the thing as pain spikes from my right hand. That was where I'd concentrated my power to kill the crab, and every movement aches atrociously.

"How are you feeling?" Meroe says, watching with concern.

"Alive." I force myself to lift the canteen and drink. "Where are we?"

"A hospital run by someone named Sister Cadua. She has a lot of experience with powerburn, they say."

In the past, when I'd overused my power, I'd had to suffer through the aftermath alone. On a ship full of mage-born, I suppose the problem would be a bit more common. Though a horrible thought occurs to me—

"She's not a ghulwitch, is she?"

A shadow passes across Meroe's face, and she shakes her head. "Just handy with a mushroom poultice."

I let out a relieved breath. Having Kuon Naga's ghulwitch messing around with my insides is enough for me for one lifetime.

"The others are more or less all right," she goes on. "Ahdron needed some stitching up. The Butcher's people took them back down to the pack cell, but I convinced them someone ought to stay here with you."

"I'm surprised they care about me one way or the other."

"I think the Butcher would have been happy to leave you to rot," Meroe says. "But everyone's been talking about what you did, so she couldn't just ignore you."

"What do you mean, what I did?"

"The thing you killed was called a blueshell," Meroe says, grinning. "Apparently they're pretty rare, and not the sort of thing people fight all by themselves, even Melos adepts. The story's all over the place."

"Wonderful." I set the canteen aside, trying to figure this out. Having a reputation might help, but it's only going to make the Butcher angrier. "How long has it been?"

"A day and a half."

I groan, and pull myself to a sitting position. "You've been here the whole time?"

"More or less," she says. "We're still under guard, so I'm not allowed to wander around."

"You should have let them take you back to your cell."

"I didn't want you to be alone when you woke up," she says.

I give a sigh, which hurts. "You—"

"Besides, you've saved my life twice now," Meroe says.

"Maybe you should be a little more careful with it," I tell her. "What were you doing taunting that monster?"

"Getting it away from Berun, of course," she says. "He was scared out of his mind, and it was coming right at him."

"Berun is scared of everything." I wince at another ripple of pain. "He's useless."

"Which means I should let him get eaten by crabs?"

"If you have to." I shift awkwardly as she glares at me, and I try hard not to roll my eyes. Aristos. "Listen, *Princess*. You may have grown up in a happy fairy tale, but this is reality. You think Berun would jump in front of a crab to help *you*? He'd run for it, and more power to him."

"Don't talk about how I grew up like you know anything about me," Meroe snaps. "You came and rescued *me*, didn't you?"

"That's different."

"Why?"

"I have my reasons." Even if I'm not quite sure what they are at the moment. "Don't get the wrong idea about me."

"What idea would that be?"

I grit my teeth. "That I'm a good person."

She crosses her arms and sniffs. "Small chance of that."

"What's this?" a voice says from the doorway. "A lovers' tiff?"

I tense up, and Meroe turns. The rag curtain parts, and a slim figure enters. The newcomer has an Imperial complexion, with a long, wild half head of hair dyed bright purple and flopped over the other, shaven half. A boy, I assume at first, but I quickly correct myself; she's a woman, close to my own age, though with no chest and only the slightest of curves about the hips. She's dressed in the colorful silk that seems so common on *Soliton*, and her broad grin has a touch of madness about it.

"Hello, fresh meat," the newcomer says, without taking her eyes off me. "You're Isoka, is that right?"

"I am," I say, cautiously. "Who are you?"

"They call me Jack," she says, with a shallow bow. "Wide-eyed Jack, Quick-Fingered Jack. Mad Jack, if they don't fancy living much longer."

"Do you work for the Butcher?"

Jack giggles. "I wouldn't stoop to bowing to that oversized turd if I was reduced to begging in the street. No, I serve the most honorable Zarun, and gladly. He has heard of your exploits, you see, and wishes to buy you a drink." She brushes past Meroe, leaning forward on the bed, a little too close to me. "Are you game?"

"We can't leave," Meroe says. "One of the Butcher's people is keeping watch outside."

Jack turns to her as though seeing her for the first time. "*Was* keeping watch," she says. "Now I rather suspect he's scuttled off with the purse I gave him to enjoy his good fortune. But may I ask who you're supposed to be?"

"Meroe," I say. "One of my pack mates. She's new to the ship, too."

"More fresh meat," Jack says, licking her lips. "How delightful. She's welcome to join us, of course. But hurry, hurry. Zarun gets so sad when he's kept waiting."

"What about the Butcher?" I say.

"Leave the Butcher to me," Jack says. Her eyes are a bright sapphire blue, not a common color in the Empire. "What say you, Isoka, slayer of crabs? A drink?"

Options. As usual, not enough information. Zarun wants something, obviously. Going with her might anger the Butcher, but I think I've burned that bridge already. So what's left to lose?"

I glance at Meroe. "I could use a drink."

Jack bounces again and claps her hands, smile growing even wider. "Lovely. Let's, then."

I get dressed—my clothes have been cleaned but are still torn and ragged—and stretch, working out the residual ache of powerburn. Whoever Sister Cadua is, she does pretty good work, because I feel better than I'd expect to after that bad a fight. I join Meroe and Jack outside.

Jack leads the way, with an odd gait that's halfway between walking and skipping. There's another metal corridor with doorways on either side, and another curtain at one end. Jack hurries ahead, and I'm about to follow when Meroe grabs my elbow.

"Isoka, what are you doing?" she hisses.

"What does it look like?"

"She wants you to meet with *Zarun*," she says. "You remember what he did when we came aboard? That little girl?"

"I'm not likely to forget."

"Then maybe," Meroe says, "this isn't a person we should be getting friendly with."

I pull my arm away from her, irritated. This is what I was worried about—I saved her life on a whim, and now she thinks we're sworn companions.

"First of all," I tell her, "it's not *we*. *I* am going to meet with Zarun. You can do what you like."

Meroe stares, as though I'd slapped her. Her expression tears at something in my chest, but I push the feeling down ruthlessly.

"Second," I go on, "if you want to survive here, I promise you're going to have to do a lot nastier things than have a drink with someone who chops off little girls' heads. Zarun has *power* here. If I can use that to help myself, I will. I don't care if he slaughters his way through an orphanage."

For perhaps the first time in our acquaintance, Meroe seems at a loss for something to say. I give her my best nasty smile, and try to take some pleasure in the way she flinches.

"I'm just trying to stay alive, Princess," I say. "You might want to think about doing the same."

Jack clears her throat, an exaggerated *harrumph*. She's standing by the open door, one arm extended like a faithful servant welcoming the master home. I turn away from Meroe, certain she'll follow. Where else does she have to go? And, indeed, after a few moments I hear her footsteps on the deck.

I'm prepared for a lot of weirdness when I step outside—if *Soliton* has taught me a lesson so far, it's to be ready for strange things. What I'm not prepared for, apparently, is sun, and I take a half step back, eyes watering. As my vision clears, I discover we're standing in the center of a slanting shaft of sunlight, streaming down from an irregularly shaped hole in a metal roof several hundred feet overhead.

In front of me there's a—street, I guess you'd have to call it, if you can have such a thing aboard a ship. Sister Cadua's doorway is embedded in a wall that stretches off in either direction. Ahead is a much larger space, cluttered with small, ramshackle buildings that are definitely *not* part of *Soliton*'s original design. They're made of anything and everything—sheets of rusty metal, draped cloths, pieces of chitin, even slabs of what looks like dried mushroom. Some could be dignified with the title of "shack," while others are barely more than tents or lean-tos. The "street" is just a long, crooked area kept clear of obstruction, leading roughly from Sister Cadua's to a huge tower rising in the middle distance.

Overhead, a metal roof is supported by curved girders. Big chunks of it have rusted out, leaving ragged-edged holes that look up into a bright blue sky. That sight makes my throat thicken, just a little—it's surprising how quickly you get to miss the sky, when you're stuck in darkness. Patches of sunlight slide gently over the makeshift city, dappled by clouds.

"Where are we?" I ask, as Jack beams in the light and spreads her arms like an eager impresario.

"These are the Upper Stations," she says. "The highest deck. Home to the market, the officers, and the most successful packs."

"Where do the rest live?"

She glances at the floor. "Down below. There's the Middle Deck, and then the Drips."

The Drips sounds about right for where Pack Nine is locked up. I have a dozen other questions, but Jack is already moving again.

"Come, come!" she shouts. "We are expected, slayer of crabs. It wouldn't do to be late."

Jack caroms down the street like a puppy, rushing from one source of excitement to the next. In front of the shacks, people have set out sheets covered with small items, and I realize this is the market she mentioned. It's not much of a market, truth be told—the morning fish market in Kahnzoka would have swallowed it a hundred times over—but, again, not something I expected to find on a ship at all.

The items for sale are a curious lot. Some I understand—meat, mushrooms, plants that might be seaweed, armor plates and polished bones and a hundred other pieces of creatures worked into useful objects. But there are also things that could not possibly have been made aboard ship: china plates and crystal goblets, jade statues and silk dresses, fine things from all over the world. They're strewn around, casually, with no regard for their actual value. A delicate silver-inlaid egg with the gleam of real gold sits amid coils of seaweed rope and broken pieces of metal decking; a purple *kizen* fringed with pearls worth a king's ransom sits unfolded and unregarded beside a pile of carved bones.

"Where does it all *come* from?" I mutter.

Jack, to my surprise, answers. "Offerings," she says. "The Captain just wants mage-born children, but not every port knows he's so choosy. So they put their treasures in the boats with the sacrifices, and the angels leave them lying around topside. Our scavengers creep out and collect them in hopes of making a trade." She gestures at a young boy sitting by a collection of polished chimes. "The officers get their pick of the lot, of course. This is the dregs."

The dregs: gold and silver and silk. But, of course, it made sense. If you truly accepted that you were stuck aboard *Soliton* and were never going to leave, what good was a fortune in gems and precious metals? I wonder how much treasure there is aboard the ship, and whether Kuon Naga knows it's here. *All the more reason for him to send me to claim it all for the Empire.* Anger flares hot and bright in my chest, and I pause for a breath to get it under control.

More interesting than the trinkets for sale, now that I'm looking, are the people. There are quite a few around, sitting by the displays, visible in their small dwellings, or walking up and down the street. By Kahnzoka standards, it isn't a crowd—I could swing my arms without hitting anyone, which is unheard of on a busy street in the Sixteenth Ward. But the crew of *Soliton* make up for their lack of numbers with sheer variety. As I'd already observed, they come from every nation around the Central Sea—Imperials, Jyashtani, icelings, southerners, and still others I can't place at all. There seems to be no accepted standard of dress. Everyone simply wore what they pleased, either re-creating their native style from the strange blend of trash and treasure or making up something new with what they had at hand.

The one common element is that there are no *kizen,* nor the billowy robes wealthy Jyashtanis sometimes wear, or any other costume that might get in the way in a fight. Almost everyone carries at least a knife, which isn't so different from back in the Sixteenth Ward, but a good number have larger weapons, too. No one seems to throw a second glance at a sword, hatchet, or even battle-axe. And, I remind myself, there's every possibility that many of these people, like me, don't require a weapon to be dangerous.

Seeing them all sends my thoughts in an unpleasant direction. Small as the market is compared to bustling Kahnzoka, it's still more people than I'd imagined—hundreds, maybe thousands, living here long enough to build something like a city. The sheer number gives some credence to Zarun's claim that escape from *Soliton* is impossible. If there *was* a way, surely someone would have found it.

No. I grit my teeth. I'm not giving up yet. Tori is waiting for me.

And even if escape is impossible, I've already learned something critical. *Soliton* has a Captain. That means it can be controlled, which means it can be stolen.

If going through with Naga's mad plan is the only way to get back to Tori, then I'll do it. Crazy or not.

Then, once Tori is safe, I'll come back for him.

I brood for a few moments, then shake my head. Whatever the plan is, I need more information. As we walk in Jack's erratic wake, a few more common elements come to my attention. In spite of their differences in origin and dress, the people of the great ship are very similar in age. There's no one who looks much younger than twelve, and no one older than their mid-twenties. There also seem to be more women than men. While costumes might vary, groups who walk together often share a color or a look, which reminds me of Kahnzoka street gangs.

Packs. Or clades, I remember. The personal gangs of the officers. I make a mental note to learn the colors and symbols, so I can tell who's a friend and who's an enemy.

From time to time I look back over my shoulder and make sure Meroe's still with us. She's staring around as wide-eyed as I am, fascinated by the market and its people. When she catches my eye, though, her open face goes cold, and she looks away.

I ignore the little twist in my gut. She'll get over it.

"No lollygagging!" Jack says, waving to us with both hands. "Come, come. Time for shopping later. Now is the time for drinking!"

She spins on one heel and gestures ahead. A wider clear space on the deck is set up with dozens of tables and chairs, ranging from battered hardwood antiques to makeshift bits of decking and scrap metal. A small crowd of crew are eating and drinking from similarly mismatched plates and mugs, while a few younger children in gray tunics hurry back and forth fetching more. The rough street we'd been following intersects another here, and a large shack apparently serves as bar and kitchen.

"Welcome to the Crossroads," Jack says. "Best watering hole on *Soliton*. Only such, in truth, but 'best' has a better ring to it, I think. And now for the promised drink, and introductions."

Bemused, I follow Jack, feeling oddly at home here. It reminds me of Breda's, where everyone went armed, but there was a vague agreement that serious fighting should happen elsewhere. Meroe follows a few steps behind, torn between her anger at me and her desire to stay close. Before long, I'm attracting attention, crew whispering and pointing in my direction. Apparently my fame precedes me.

A bulky Jyashtani man at a table near my path gets up, glowering down at me. His lip twists into a dismissive sneer I find all too familiar.

"You're the fresh meat," he says. "Killed a blueshell all by yourself, did you?"

I pause, shrug.

"She killed it," Meroe says, to my surprise. "I was there."

"Sure." The man snorts. "I'll tell you what I think. I think you found a dead blueshell and you're looking to impress everyone your first day aboard. That it, eh?"

He matches my gaze, weaving slightly. Drunk. I wonder how much trouble I'd be in if I just killed him. Probably quite a bit, but I'm still tempted. A quick twist, inside his reach, a thrust to the throat, and that would be the end of it.

Meroe probably wouldn't like it. No sooner does the thought occur to me than I chase it away. What does it matter what Meroe would like?

I force myself to break eye contact, ceding the stupid pissing contest, and hope that's enough to placate him. Out of the corner of my eye, I see him take a step forward, and I get ready to kill him after all. Then Jack steps between us.

She's not intimidating, at least physically. She's shorter than me, and while my frame might charitably be described as "wiry," Jack looks like you could break her in half over your knee. But her wide, mad eyes meet the drunk's, and he recoils like he'd touched a hot coal. Whatever he saw there, it's gone by the time Jack turns around, grinning and leading me by the hand across the courtyard.

Another woman steps in front of us, and Jack breaks away to jump into her arms. She's one of the oldest I've seen on *Soliton*, maybe twenty-five, an iceling with broad shoulders and a solid, muscular build. Her long blond hair hangs in a spreading curtain past her shoulders, and her clothes are practical leather, layered with crab shell. There's a sword at her hip, a short, ugly thing whose grip is stained from long use.

Jack wraps her arms around her neck, and kisses her like none of the rest of us are watching. I blink, startled. Jack presses her thin, androgynous body against the iceling woman's ample curves, and I find myself looking away, feeling uncomfortable.

It's not as though I'm unaware of the fact that there are women who like women or men who prefer men. The Blessed One disapproved of such practices, but while that might hold some sway with the nobility in the upper wards, the people of the Sixteenth Ward are too busy trying not to starve to fret much about it. And, judging by the steady trickle of lonely aristos who work their way through our brothels, even high on the hill they don't pay much heed to the official morality.

Even in the Sixteenth Ward, though, it wasn't something you did in the *open*. Even if everyone knew—and everyone always knows, when you're packed into a tenement so close you can hear every board creak—you didn't . . .

Meroe has gone very still, like she's torn between staring and looking away in disgust. I wonder what they think of this sort of thing in Nimar.

Focus, I tell myself. There's more important matters to deal with.

Such as Zarun. He's sitting at the table beside the two women, grinning broadly. His clothes are different from the last time I saw him, but no less garish, maroon trousers and a dark vest sewn with interlocking circles of gold that hangs open across his muscular chest. He raises his eyebrows, then coughs gently.

The older woman pushes Jack away. "Sorry, love," she says, at the thin girl's pout. "But we've got company, remember?"

"Oh yes!" Jack spins around, beaming again. "This is Isoka, mighty slayer of crabs, and her pack mate Meroe. Isoka, this is Zarun, and his second, Thora."

"It's good to meet you," Thora says, with a half bow. "I've heard about what you did. Very impressive." She gestures to the seat across from Zarun.

"I didn't know killing the rotting thing would make me so notorious," I tell her, sitting down. Meroe stands next to me, hands clasped, eyes on the smiling killer on the other side of the table. "I was just trying to stay alive."

"It's not just killing the blueshell," Zarun says. "The Butcher thought she was throwing you to the crabs, putting you in Pack Nine. Now you've tweaked her nose quite nicely." His dazzling grin broadens. "I like that a lot. I have a feeling, dear Isoka, that we're going to get along."

He looks at Meroe, then up at Thora. "Perhaps you and Jack could show Meroe around Crossroads. And get us a drink while you're at it."

"I—" I begin, but Meroe interrupts.

"That would be fine," she says, all quiet dignity. "This is such an . . . interesting place."

Thora waves to one of the gray-clad children, who takes off for the bar at a run. As Thora and Jack escort Meroe away, the child comes back with a pair of small clay mugs, full of something frothy that smells alchemical. Zarun takes a swallow, and I follow suit, carefully. It tastes like rotten fruit, but there's a powerful kick that burns my mouth and leaves a trail of numbness all the way down my throat. I force myself not to cough and take another drink. He nods approvingly.

"So," he says. "Fresh meat, and for your first trick you mouth off to the Butcher. I have to say I'm surprised. Back in the pit I had you figured for the quiet type."

"Some people just rub me the wrong way."

"The Butcher rubs *everyone* the wrong way," Zarun says, leaning back in his seat. His eyes sparkle with mischief. "Most people are smart enough not to make an issue of it."

I shrug. He takes another drink and gestures with the glass.

"For some reason," he says, "she decides not to kill you, and instead sticks you in her punishment pack, under poor old Ahdron.

No doubt she hopes that you'll get yourself eaten, but instead you manage an impressive kill your first time out."

"Like I said, I didn't find out it was impressive until later," I say.

"It's a hell of a story," he says. "So where do you think it goes next?"

"Your guess is as good as mine." I match his gaze. "I'm thinking you might have an idea."

He laughs, and scratches his cheek. "That obvious, am I? I suppose it's never been my style to conceal my . . . interest."

"So, what? You want me to come work for you?"

"Something like that." For a moment, his eyes roam my body in frank appreciation. "I think we could do a lot for one another."

"Maybe." I sip from the drink—just the smell of it burns my nostrils—and stare right back. Zarun is certainly easy to look at, with his curls and his tight, muscular figure. "I don't pretend to know how things work here, but my understanding is that the Butcher gets a say in that."

"Unfortunately. The details may take a little time to arrange. It's just a matter of figuring out what she wants—"

"In that case," comes an unpleasantly familiar booming voice, "you're out of luck, Zarun."

The Butcher. I turn to see her pushing through the crowd, Haia and a half-dozen cronies behind her. Most of the other crew don't take much pushing, giving the huge woman a wide berth. Her attention is on me and Zarun.

"After all," the Butcher says as she stomps up to the table, "you were always worthless at figuring out how to please me."

"It's just that there's so *much* of you," Zarun says lazily. "I have to admit I kept getting lost."

"I can see why the skinny blackhair is to your taste, then," the Butcher says. "She's hardly a morsel." One of her hands rests on the hilt of her cleaver-like sword. "Unfortunately, this one is *mine*. You'll have to pass the night without another whore. No doubt the dozen you already keep will suffice."

"She's wasted in Pack Nine," he says, unruffled by the Butcher's crude barb. "Everyone knows you're just waiting for Ahdron to get himself killed."

"I don't see how that's any of your business," the Butcher booms.

"If she's got power enough to kill a blueshell by herself, then maybe it is Council business." Zarun looks down at his fingernails. "I wonder what Karakoa and Shiara would say about it? After all, you're supposed to be assigning the fresh meat for *everyone*'s benefit."

"You're welcome to bring it up at the next session," the Butcher sneers. "Though if you put your faith in those two, you're going to be disappointed. And *until* then, Isoka is part of my pack, and subject to my rules."

"As you say." Zarun catches my eye, and winks. "We'll see."

I'm reunited with Meroe on the way out of the market, but the Butcher's thugs still surround us. Getting back to Pack Nine's half-flooded cell involves descending a rickety spiral staircase down through the deck, passing another floor before reaching a rusty metal landing. The staircase continues on, but metal pieces have been layered into a barricade where it descends into the floor, blocking off the lower areas. We tromp through the same dimly lit corridors, splashing through puddles, walls flaky with rust.

"Since you're obviously fully recovered," the Butcher says, "you'll be eager for your next assignment. One of the scavenging packs brought back word of a hammerhead feeding in the Wrecks. All you've got to do is find it and kill it. We'll come for you in the morning."

I don't want to give her the pleasure of asking what that means, so I just nod. We reach the door to our cell, and the guard wrenches it open. Haia shoves me roughly inside, and another crew pushes Meroe after me.

"You're going out tomorrow morning," the Butcher says, loud enough that it echoes through the room. "Get a good night's sleep."

"What?" Ahdron surges to his feet. "Going where? I need—"

"Ask Isoka," the Butcher sneers. The door slams, and I hear the bar slide into place.

I'm left alone, again, with my pack mates. Ahdron strides over and slams a hand uselessly against the door. Then he turns to me, eyes alight with rage.

"What did she tell you?" he says. "Where are we going?"

"Somewhere called the Wrecks," I tell him. "She wants us to hunt a hammerhead."

I don't know what that means, but Ahdron's dusky skin pales, and he slams his hand against the door again and spits obscenities in a language I don't know.

"What's a hammerhead?" Meroe says. "Is it—"

"Shut your rotting mouth," he snarls, turning on her. "If I had a real pack instead of this rotting useless . . ."

Meroe tenses but doesn't step back. For a moment I think Ahdron is going to hit her, but he just turns away with a bitter laugh and walks off. Meroe looks at me, and I shrug.

"Do you have any idea what the Butcher was talking about?" she says.

"Only that it's probably bad news," I tell her. "Come on, let's see if they've left us anything to eat."

It turns out there's half a bucket of crab juice, still as delicious as ever in spite of being only lukewarm, and most of a loaf of stale bread, plus canteens of freshwater. We eat in silence. I spot the Moron, out on one of the little islands, sitting cross-legged with his eyes closed. Berun doesn't seem to be around. No doubt hiding somewhere.

Halfway through her second helping of crab juice, Meroe drops the bowl and swears. I look up to find her clutching her hands together, eyes squeezed tightly shut.

"Are you all right?" I say.

"It hurts, is all," Meroe says. "I'll live."

I look at her hands, and remember her grabbing the sword-tentacles of the blueshell, pushing them away as blood ran down her palms. The twisted place in my chest gives a twinge, like a cracked rib.

"It's probably time to change those bandages," I tell her. "Do you have any fresh ones?"

She nods, uncertainly. "Sister Cadua's people gave me a bag. Over here."

I pick up some canteens and follow her back among the nest of carpets. There's a hollow space where it looks like she's been sleeping, with the blood-spattered dress I'd first seen her in lying crumpled beside it. She produces a bag of reasonably clean linen strips, and I gesture for her to sit down. I kneel in front of her, and start untying the strips that bind her palms.

She winces as I work, looking over my head. After a while she says, "I thought you were angry at me."

"Why would you think that?"

"Because of what I said about Zarun."

"I'm not angry." The knot is tight, and I'm tempted to just slash it with a Melos blade. Instead, I tease it gently apart. "I just wanted you to understand. I'm not—"

"A good person," Meroe says wearily. "You mentioned."

"It's more than that. Where I come from, the streets of Kahnzoka, it's not so different from this." I get the knot untied, and unwind the tight linen strip. "I had to hurt people to survive there, and I'll have to hurt people to survive here."

"It doesn't bother you?"

"No. Grow up the way I did and it wouldn't bother you, either." The last of the bandage is stuck to her skin with dried blood, and I grab one of the canteens. "This is probably going to sting."

She hisses as I pour the water over her, still looking resolutely away. Once it's softened a little, I peel the bandage off, then clean the wound with more freshwater. It looks better than I was expecting, a nice clean cut, not too deep and no signs of festering. I wrap it in a fresh bandage and get to work on the other hand.

"So what about me?" Meroe says.

I pause for a moment, and look up to find her staring at me. "What *about* you?"

"What am I supposed to do?" she says. "To survive. I can't fight like you can, obviously."

I look down again. "Plenty of people can't. They manage somehow."

"Ahdron thinks I'm useless." Her tone is perfectly cheerful. "Should I ask him to kill me and be done with it? Or should I ask you?"

"I'm not going to kill you," I growl. She's making fun of me.

"Why not? I'd rather get it over with quickly than have some monster eat me."

"You're not useless." I peel the second bandage away and wash her slashed palm. "You just have to learn to be a little more pragmatic."

"Pragmatic. I like that." She laughs. "Not evil, just . . . pragmatic."

"Just stay close to me," I mutter, as I tie the bandage up again. "I'll keep you alive."

"How generous of you." She flexes her fingers with a grimace. "But if you're not a good person, you must want something from me. What is it, I wonder?"

"I told you I have my reasons."

Meroe stands up, abruptly. "There's one more."

"What?"

"Bandage." She pats her side. "I can't reach the knot. Can you help?"

"Oh. Sure." I step back. "Who did these in the first place?"

"Berun," she says. "I got him to talk to me, a little. He knows a lot about this place."

"He . . ."

I pause. Meroe has nimbly undone a set of buttons at the back of her dress, and now she shuffles her arms out of it. It's still belted, so the top flutters down to hang like an extra layer of skirt, leaving her naked from the waist up. Another bandage runs from under her left arm up around her neck.

She's not as shapeless as she seemed in that ill-fitting dress. And . . . toothsome, Ahdron had said. I glance over my shoulder to make sure he's not watching. When I turn back to her, she's looking at me with a curious smile on her face.

"What?"

"Nothing." She tugs at the bandage, arching her back. "Here."

I step close to her, untying the knot at her shoulder. Her breath tickles my cheek. When the linen comes free, I peel it off, stopping when it starts to stick to the wound, a long, curved gash under her arm and onto her back.

"Lean forward," I tell her.

She obeys, and I step behind her and pour more water from the canteen. It trickles across her deep brown skin, and I see muscles tense in her shoulders. When it soaks the injury, she hisses through her teeth.

Her skin is so beautiful, smooth and perfect. I think of the scars on my own body, a hundred little trophies from a hundred little battles. Faded, now. Since I learned to control my Melos armor, I haven't taken many scars, at least not where it shows. But my hands are still rough and callused, and my bloody history is written on my skin for anyone to see.

Meroe will have at least one scar to match mine, when this wound heals. The thought tugs at me in a way I don't like, as I rinse the injury and wind a fresh bandage.

"What did Zarun want?" she says, unexpectedly. "If you don't mind my asking."

"I don't mind." I shake my head to clear it. "I'm not entirely sure. I think he wants me to work for him—be part of his clade, I suppose it would be." I pause to tie off the bandage. "He may also want to rut me. I'm not sure how serious he was about that."

"To—" Meroe looks over her shoulder at me. "Really?"

"Like I said, I don't understand everything."

"And you're . . . considering his offer?"

"For the moment, I don't think it matters. The Butcher showed up and the two of them got into it." I shrug. "If Zarun can help, it won't be until after this assignment, at least."

"But if he *can* help, you'd take it?"

I feel myself flushing a little, and it makes me angry. "The Butcher seems to be *trying* to get us killed. I'd rather not spend more time under her thumb than I have to."

"Even if it means crawling into Zarun's bed?"

"I have rutted far worse men than Zarun," I tell her, "for far less."

"Oh." Her voice is small. "I . . . didn't know."

"Don't look so rotting shocked." I turn away from her. "And do your rotting dress up, unless you want the boys to come stare at you with your tits hanging out."

"Sorry." There's a hasty shuffling of cloth.

"Did you need anything else?"

"What?"

"With the bandages," I grind out. "Any more help."

"No." Meroe pauses. "If you go work for Zarun—"

It's obvious what she wants to ask. *What about me?* She's using me, for the protection I can provide, just like everyone else. It doesn't make me angry. Everyone uses the people around them, as best they can—the way I used Hagan and Shiro, the way my bosses used me, the way I'll use Zarun. That's just the way the world works.

"What?" I say, when she stays silent.

"Nothing," she says. "Never mind."

I snort. "Go get some sleep, Princess. You look like you need it."

I'm right about that, at least. Within minutes, Meroe is curled up in her nest, snoring in a genteel, aristo sort of way. I find myself too keyed up to rest just yet, although my muscles still ache from power-burn. I walk down to the shore, marked by a scummy, rusted line on the deck, and look across the half-flooded chamber. The Moron is still sitting on his little island, unmoving. I wonder if he's asleep.

"Isoka." Ahdron comes up behind me. "Can I have a word?"

"You're the pack leader," I say. "Do you need to ask?"

He snorts and steps up beside me, looking out at the little lake and the Moron.

"He just sits like that all day," Ahdron says. "Rot-for-brains."

"He managed to stay out of the blueshell's way," I say.

"He's got a talent for making himself scarce. Is there a Well for that?" Ahdron turns to me, running one hand through his hair. "Rot. Look. I feel like we didn't get the best start."

I shrug. "I can't say the last few days have been a great introduction to anybody."

"I know you're fresh meat and you don't know how things work here," he says. "But you understand the Butcher's got me in the dog-house, right?"

"I'd gathered that." I turn to look at him with affected casual-ness. "What did you do to make her so angry?"

"It's not important," Ahdron mutters, flushing slightly. "The point is that I'm not going to be down forever. Sometime—maybe soon—I'll get out from under her, and this is going to be a real pack in-stead of a trash heap."

"Glad to hear it," I drawl. "And?"

"Let's cut the rot," he says. "I saw what you did to the blueshell. We both know you and I are the only ones here who are worth a damn. I know you've got small reason to trust me, but if we can take down a hammerhead then even the Butcher is going to *have* to take notice. I need your help if we're going to have a chance."

"You don't have to ask for my help, do you? You just give the orders."

He swears unintelligibly. "I told you, cut the rot. You could have run for it and gotten away easily. I don't know why you didn't, but when it comes to the sharp end this time I'm asking you to stand by me again. It's not going to be easy, but if we pull this off, we can get out of this rotting hole." He gestures around. "We'll move up to Middle Deck, poach a few decent pack mates, and get comfort-able again. Pick our own battles. What do you think?"

He seems earnest. Excited, even. He wants to get back into the officers' good graces, and he thinks I'm his ticket. Whether he's right I don't know. I'm not sure he understands that the Butcher hates me more than ever.

"If you're asking whether I'll fight," I tell him, "then I'll fight. But it would help if someone told me what a hammerhead *was,* and how you kill one."

"I'll explain everything," he says eagerly.

"In the morning." I yawn, looking out across the water again. The Moron hasn't stirred. "I think I'd better get some rest, don't you?"

I feel him watching me as he walks away. He's no different from Zarun, or Meroe for that matter. Even on a ship full of mage-born, apparently my skill set is unusual enough that everyone wants to take advantage of it.

Which is fine. I can take advantage of them right back.

Everyone on *Soliton* seems convinced that there's no escaping the ship. If I assume for the moment that I believe them, that leaves one option to save Tori's life—figure out how to deliver *Soliton* to Kuon Naga. The only lead I have is the Captain. I'm going to have to get close to him to find out more, and for that I'm going to need allies. Some of those allies will probably end up with a dagger in the back, of course. That's the way these things work. I just need to make sure they don't do the same to me.

I dream about angels, the twisted, alien shapes that haunt the ship's rail. In the dream they're clustered around me, like eager dogs gathering for a treat, except I feel like they're trying to *talk* to me. Voices babble at the back of my mind, endlessly, unintelligibly. Someone is shouting in the distance, trying to cut through the chatter, but too far away to hear. The angels bleed gray light, which swirls around me, tiny specks of glowing dust trying to burrow through my skin.

I also dream about Zarun, which is more explicable and considerably more pleasant. I kiss the taut muscle of his stomach while his hands run up and down my back. Zarun, I suspect, would not mind my scars. Unfortunately, this pleasant scenario means I wake up with an itchy, unfulfilled feeling that leaves me badly wanting to rut, or at least find a comfortable spot with some privacy and take care of things for myself. I don't seem likely to get either, since Ahdron is already shouting for everyone to gather.

We do, though in the case of the Moron it's clearly more because Ahdron is holding our breakfast bucket than for any respect for the pack leader's orders. Ahdron sets the bucket and a couple of loaves of bread in front of us, and starts to talk while we dip our bowls. Meroe sits beside me, and I catch her looking at me uncertainly. She doesn't say much, for once. Berun sits as far as possible from Ahdron, shoveling bits of crab into his mouth between nervous looks up at the pack leader. The Moron eats in beatific silence, apparently ignorant of everything spoken.

"The Butcher wants us to hunt a hammerhead," Ahdron says. "Obviously that isn't easy. She knows where one's been feeding, which takes care of the first problem, but that leaves the issue of killing the rotting thing." He shakes his head. "Normally you need a whole set of beaters, a Tartak adept to hold the monster down, and someone to carve a way through its thick skull. We've got . . . us. But we haven't got a rotting choice if we want to eat, so we're doing it."

Berun has frozen. "We can't kill a hammerhead. Is she *crazy*?"

"I think she knows exactly what she's doing," I say.

Meroe shoots me a look. Berun tosses his bowl aside and starts to get up, and Ahdron's voice cracks like a whip.

"Coward! Sit down and shut up. You're part of this, and if you try to run off gods help me I'll burn you alive. Understand?"

Berun sits, white-faced. The Moron, having finished his breakfast, sets his bowl down and wanders back to the shore. He plunges easily into the water, swimming out to his island in a few quick strokes.

"Obviously he's not worth anything," Ahdron says. "But Coward, you're Tartak. So we need you on this one."

"I'm n . . . not strong enough," Berun says, looking at the floor. "I'm only a talent. I c . . . can't hold a *hammerhead*."

"You can rotting well try," Ahdron says.

"Meroe saved you from the blueshell," I tell him. "Now's your chance to return the favor."

"I didn't . . ." Berun looks at Meroe, then back at the floor. "I'm sorry. I don't mean to be . . . I'm just not strong enough, that's all."

"We're not going to be able to do it the usual way," Ahdron says. "We're going to have to get it to come to us, instead of flushing it out with beaters. Meroe, that's your job."

"How?" Meroe says.

"By being bait," Ahdron says. "When we start seeing signs the hammerhead is close, you'll cut yourself and make some noise. That'll bring it out, sure as winter."

"I don't—" I start, but Meroe interrupts.

"All right," she says. "Then what?"

"Then Coward here holds it. It doesn't have to be for long; a few seconds will do." He leans down and sketches an elliptical shape on the deck, then puts a couple of dots in the middle. "The only way to kill a hammerhead is to hit the heart or the brain. But they're both too far inside to get to easily. So Isoka, I want you to go for the legs instead. Damage enough of them and we'll slow it right down. Then I can take my time and blast it apart. May not make the best steaks for the officers, but they can go rot."

"It won't work," Berun moans. "I *told* you, I can't hold it."

"Would you shut it?" Ahdron closes his fist, which ignites with a *whoomph.* "I swear, I'm going to—"

"Let me talk to him," Meroe says. "Please."

Ahdron glares at Berun, but he nods. Meroe takes the boy's trembling hand and leads him away, speaking to him in a low voice. Ahdron rolls his eyes and starts on his own breakfast, ripping one of the tough loaves of bread in half.

"So, the hammerhead," I ask him, "does it have claws like the blueshell, or tentacles, or what?"

Ahdron shakes his head. "Just a mouth. A big, wide mouth, full of tiny, sharp teeth." He rips a hunk off the bread and chews with some difficulty. "Rotting gods. Would it kill them to bring it to us fresh?"

"What do they make bread out of, anyway?" I tear a chunk from the loaf. "It can't be flour."

"Mushrooms," he says. "There's a kind you can grind up like grain."

"Amazing," I mutter. Crabs and mushrooms seem to be the two things *Soliton* has in abundance.

Meroe comes back, with Berun in tow. To my surprise, the boy is looking more determined, his clenched fists still shaking slightly.

"Well?" Ahdron says.

"I'll . . . try," Berun says. "I don't think . . . I mean . . ."

Meroe touches his arm, lightly, and he looks up at her. I almost laugh out loud at the puppy-dog devotion in his eyes. He's fallen for her, hard.

"I'll do it," he says. "I don't know how well it will work, but I'll do it."

"That's the spirit, Coward," Ahdron says.

I drift over to Meroe and lower my voice. "What'd you tell him?"

"Just that I needed his help," she says. "I *talked* to him instead of threatening him. It wasn't difficult."

"And you think he'll hold up?"

"He gave me his word."

"Sure, because he wants you to rut him."

"He doesn't. . . ." She hesitates, though if she's blushing her dark skin makes it invisible. "All right, maybe he does. But still I think he'll try to help."

"Boys have done stupider things for a pretty girl."

Meroe snorts. "You were the one saying you'd be happy to sleep with Zarun if it got you what you wanted."

"If it got me what I wanted. He's not just a boy with a pretty face."

"Not *just* a boy with a pretty face. But he does have a pretty face."

I glance at her, and there's a faint, mischievous smile on her lips. I smile a little, too. Trading barbs, in a strange way, makes me feel closer to her than anything else. It reminds me of Hagan and Shiro, standing on the street corner and swapping insults and improbable exploits.

"What about the other boy?" she says. "The Moron."

"Not to my taste."

She rolls her eyes. "No, I mean, can he help?"

"According to Ahdron, he never talks and doesn't seem to understand anything anyone says to him."

"Maybe he doesn't speak Imperial or Jyashtani."

"He *looks* Jyashtani."

"There are a lot of languages in Jyashtan," Meroe says. "Especially in the south."

"You'd think he'd have said *something*, then, even if no one could understand him."

"I wonder if anyone's tried."

Her thoughts on the matter are interrupted by the clang of the cell door opening. Haia is waiting for us on the other side with a mocking grin.

"All right, Pack Nine," she says. "Time to go down into the dark again."

9

When Ahdron warns me about rattlers, I picture some kind of snake. This turns out to be almost completely wrong, and I find myself wishing he'd been a little more descriptive.

These rattlers are spherical creatures a bit larger than my head, looking like nothing so much as a ball of rust-red needles. They move by rolling across the metal deck, their spines making a distinctive rattle-click sound. Two fleshy pink "feet" like stubby tentacles emerge from either end to give them periodic kicks, enabling them to move at high speed.

And, I discover, to jump several feet off the ground with unexpected force. Three of the creatures had careened into the circle of light shed by our torches, then come at us all together. I step toward them, putting myself in front of the others as I ignite my blades. A blast of flame whips past my shoulder, blowing one of the rattlers into a spray of smoking fragments, but the other two keep coming. I get ready to slash the leading one in half, winding up and ready to swing, when the damn thing springs into the air with a quick thump of its foot against the deck. I try to get my other blade around in time but don't make it, and it slams into my chest. Melos armor crackles, keeping the needles from my skin, and a wave of brutal heat rolls across me. The impact sends me reeling backward, and the rattler bounces away. It does a quick roll on the deck and starts coming back at us, ready for more.

There's a scream from behind me. It's Berun, who's down on his knees, clutching at his arm. The rattler that hit him skids to a halt farther on, and another bolt from Ahdron intercepts it and blows it to bits. I return my attention to the creature that bounced off me, which has gotten back up to speed for another try. Now that I'm expecting the jump, I'm ready for it, and my blade is in just the right place to slash the thing clean in half. The two pieces thump to the deck, oozing watery fluid and crackling briefly with green lightning.

Meroe is kneeling beside Berun. The Moron, as usual, is nowhere to be seen now that the action has started.

"Is he okay?" I ask.

Before Meroe can answer, though, Ahdron points. "The rest of the pack is coming!" he says.

I hear more rattle-clicks. A lot more, like a barrel full of knitting needles rolling down a hill.

At this point, we're deep into the Center. Haia gave us a map, a crude, sketchy thing on a bit of torn cloth, and slammed the door behind us.

Wherever they found the hammerhead, it's much farther away than the Silvercap Garden, and much farther down. We descend several spiral staircases, walking along bridge after bridge until I'm thoroughly lost. The whole Center seems to be a mess of bridges, pillars, and stairs, some sturdy-looking with solid railings, others rickety and rusted, or infested by fungus. Far below us, strange colored lights shift in the dark, moving slowly into new constellations. Now and then, I catch a whiff of something that smells like the sea over the tang of rusty metal.

A few small crabs, about the size of dogs, scurry away from our approach. The people of *Soliton* use "crab" to mean any of the monsters of the Center, but these look like the crabs I'm familiar with. Berun says they're called scuttlers and they don't attack humans unless they seem weak. I guess we look strong enough, because the scuttlers leave us alone, and we don't run into any serious problems until we reach a wide bridge four levels down and the rattle-clicking begins.

Rattlers, apparently, hunt in packs. I rotting well wish people would take the time to explain things.

Apparently they hunt in *big* packs, too. At least two dozen of the red creatures roll out of the darkness, already moving fast, feet kicking out every few yards to push them ever faster. If I wait for them to come to us, they'll knock me down and Meroe and the others will be easy prey. So I run toward them, angling diagonally across the bridge, slamming my boots hard against the metal deck to make it ring like a gong. Crabs are supposed to be attracted to sound, and the rattlers are no exception. They start to turn in my direction, the whole pack slewing around to come after me. The closest one jumps, and I slash it in two. Another Myrkai bolt sends a rattler careening off the bridge wreathed in flame.

Then the rest of them have made the turn, and they're jumping at me, too. I duck and roll out of the way as a half dozen fly through the space where I was standing, bouncing off the deck and spinning to come back at me. I cut another down as it gets too close, and feel a pulse of heat as one of them caroms off the backs of my legs. Three more jump, and I intercept one and duck another. The third catches me on the shoulder, hard enough that I stumble backward and land on my ass.

"Ahdron!" I shout. "Now!"

He says something in response, but I'm not listening. I curl up, putting my head down, and let my blades fade away as I put all the energy I can muster into my armor. It thickens, power crackling over me as the rattlers slam against me again and again. Their spines scrape against the solidified magic with a sound like blades on glass, green lightning arcing all around me.

All at once, everything goes white, and my armor flares hot enough that I want to scream. There's a rush of sound, like the *whoomph* of igniting oil, and then sudden quiet. A single rattle-click rapidly fades into the distance.

I open my eyes and push myself to my feet.

I'm standing in the middle of a huge patch of blackened deck. All around me are the rattlers, cooked to a crisp by the enormous fireball I was just at the center of. Ahdron is standing some distance off, arms folded, looking smug.

I take a step toward him, stumble a little, and concentrate on breathing for a moment. Stray sparks of green light still shimmer over my clothes, earthing themselves on the deck and the dead rattlers.

I don't know if the things are good to eat, but they smell *delicious*.

"If you could do that," Meroe says, "why didn't you just do it in the first place?"

"For starters, it wears me out," Ahdron says, grinning. "And it's not very accurate. I needed them all together and well away from us, unless you fancy getting cooked, too."

Meroe takes my arm, carefully, and puts it across her shoulders.

"Here, lean on me," she says. We start walking back toward the others. "Are you all right?"

"Medium-rare, at worst," I tell her, sucking in a breath. In truth, my limbs feel a little wobbly from the rush of power, but it's passing. Momentary impacts and flames are easier on my armor than the sustained pressure the blueshell put me through. "What about you?"

"I'm fine. I think something got stuck in Berun's hand, though."

"That'll be the needles," Ahdron says. "The tips are barbed, and they break off. Let me see."

Berun whimpers and opens his hand. There are three long spines embedded in his palm.

"Those aren't in that deep," Ahdron says. "There's a trick to getting them out. It doesn't hurt, if you do it right."

Berun stares up at him. "Do you know how?"

He nods. "You have to hold very still, though. Take a deep breath. I'll unhook them on three."

Berun grits his teeth, white-faced. Ahdron crouches and grabs the spines.

"One," he says, and then immediately yanks hard. The spikes come out, blood running freely from the cuts they leave behind. Berun screams and clutches his hand to his chest, smearing his shirt with crimson. Meroe jolts.

"*What* are you doing?" she says.

"He'll be fine," Ahdron says. "If that's the worst injury we get today, we'll count ourselves lucky."

"That's still no reason to be—"

"Realistic?" Ahdron smiles. "Come on. If these two can stumble a little further, there's a pillar up ahead. It'll be safer to rest there."

Meroe mutters something in another language. I gather it's uncomplimentary. I wait, getting my breath back, as she wraps Berun's hand in a bandage. She's brought the sack of linen with her, along with a makeshift knapsack full of extra canteens and leftover mushroom bread from breakfast.

"Are you planning on staying down here longer than the rest of us?" I ask, as she knots the bundle back up.

"You never know," she says. "It might help, and at least I can carry some extra weight." She catches my eye and adds in a quiet voice, "I don't like being useless."

"You're doing better than Berun."

"Don't you start on him," Meroe says. "Did you ever think that if Ahdron was encouraging him instead of threatening him he might not be so afraid of everything?"

I doubt that, but Meroe's expression tells me it wouldn't be productive to say so, so I only shrug. I have a hard time understanding why she's coddling this boy, who seems to deserve his nickname. Any gang in Kahnzoka would have kicked him to the gutter long ago as not even worth killing. Meroe may not have a Well, but she's got an inner strength that I wouldn't trade for a hundred craven fools like Berun. Or a dozen insecure bosses like Ahdron, for that matter.

And the way Berun looks at Meroe makes me want to slap him, halfway between a boy at his first peep show and a supplicant looking on the image of his goddess. She doesn't seem to notice, or pretends not to. The Moron has reappeared, standing at the pack leader's side as calmly as if nothing had happened. Ahdron regards him sourly for a moment, then turns and leads us onward.

We reach the pillar, a massive metal spire at the intersection of four bridges, with a circular platform ringed by a rusted-out railing. Shelf mushrooms grow on its side, and tiny beetles with iridescent red carapaces scuttle among them. I hold back for a moment, waiting for Ahdron to tell us they're flesh-eating monsters, but he doesn't give them a second glance, so I relax. The pack leader sits in a soft pile of fungus with his back to the pillar, taking a long swig from his canteen.

"Take a break," he says. "It's another hour's walk to the edge of the Wrecks, and I don't want us exhausted when we get there."

I sit down against the pillar a little ways away from them and take a long drink. Another hour, Ahdron says, and we'll reach the hammerhead's hunting ground. If we find it, and if this rotting plan to kill it actually works, then I'll need to figure out what to do about Ahdron's offer, and Zarun's. And—

There's something moving, under the surface of the pillar. It's hard for my eyes to focus on. At first I think it's a horde of ants, but the moving specks are smaller, and glow with a faint gray light that feels unpleasantly familiar. They're all flowing in the same direction, up from the deck toward the ceiling lost in darkness above us. As they move, they weave around one another, a delicate dance of near collisions like they really *were* ants. I put my hand against the pillar, tentatively, and watch the flows shift around it, like a stream twisting around a rock.

And there are voices, down at the edge of hearing. Most of the words are unintelligible, but a few break through the babble. "Hurts. Please." Someone—*something*—is begging. And then another, "Kill, kill, killkillkill—"

I snatch my hand away and scramble back a pace, heart pounding. Meroe looks up at me, questioningly. I blink, and wave her away. She's touching the pillar. So whatever it is, she can't see it, or hear the voices.

"Isoka." It's Ahdron, climbing to his feet. "You ready?"

I nod, my throat suddenly dry. "I'm ready."

It's not hard to guess why they called this place the Wrecks.

We reach it after descending another staircase. In the midst of the labyrinth of bridges, a wide, flat expanse of decking stretches out ahead of us, beyond the range of our lanterns. It's supported at regular intervals by more pillars, and I give these a wide berth. In between the pillars there are holes in the deck, too clean and rectangular to be rusted-out patches, each the size of a building. On the sides of the holes are huge stanchions, as tall as I am, from which dangle lengths of arm-thick chain.

The first few holes we find are empty, just drops into the unknowable depths of *Soliton*. Eventually, though, we come across one that's still occupied. It takes me a moment to understand that the ugly, rusted thing hanging in the gap is a ship, albeit one of a design I've never seen before. It has two parallel hulls, long and narrow, with a gracefully curved deck bridging the gap between them. The chains are attached to it, suspending the small vessel in midair at roughly the level of the deck.

So this is a dock, of a sort. I wonder if the small vessel was some kind of ship's boat—it's the size of a war galley, but given the enormity of *Soliton* it doesn't seem unreasonable. Why a dock would be hanging in midair with no water in sight is beyond me, but once again, it's a weird ship.

It isn't just rust that has damaged the small vessel. Parts of its hull are shattered into jagged, twisted shards, or torn open by parallel rents I can't help but interpret as the marks of enormous claws.

"Wow," Meroe says, eyes wide. She looks from the vessel to the empty holes, then out into the distance. "How many are there?"

"Dozens," Ahdron says indifferently.

"Do any of them still work?" Meroe says, taking a step forward. "Is there a way to get them into the water? You could—"

"Don't," he says. "People have tried going out to them. Even if you don't slip and fall all the way to the Deeps, there's nothing to find."

"And they're cursed," Berun says.

"They're not cursed," Ahdron says.

"People who climb out there die," the boy insists.

"It doesn't *matter*," Ahdron says, "because we're not going near them. Meroe, time to play hammerhead bait."

"Right," she says. "My crucial role in this adventure. You're ready, Berun?"

"I . . . think so." Berun shifts awkwardly. "If it comes, I'll try to hold it."

"Here." Ahdron tosses Meroe a small object, which makes a *clonk-clonk* noise. It turns out to be a bell, bent out of shape. "Just cut yourself a little, and make a racket."

Meroe nods, and takes a deep breath. She pulls a knife out of her pocket and offers it to me, hilt first.

"Would you mind?" she says.

I take her hand, palm up. It's shaking a little. "Close your eyes," I tell her.

She does. I make a quick gash across the meat at the bottom of her thumb, just below the bandage. Blood wells quickly, drops running down her arm.

She holds her hand out to Ahdron. "This enough?"

"Should be," he says. "You and Isoka go out ahead. Berun and I will keep our distance."

Convenient for him. Meroe waves her hand around, letting blood drip on the deck, and rings the bell with a *clack-clonk*. It echoes weirdly off the metal.

"I guess we just . . . walk," she says. "Come on. I want to see if there are more of the little ships."

"Does it matter?" I say, falling into step beside her.

"You're not *curious*?" she says.

"About what?"

"About *this*!" She waves a hand. "Who *built* this thing? *How*? What was it for?"

I think of the voices in the pillar, and the angels. "I'm not sure I want to know."

"Really? *I* certainly do." She rings the bell again. "I mean, have you even heard of anything like it?"

I shake my head. "Whoever built it, though, I think they're long gone." I gesture at the small ship as we walk past it. "Otherwise they'd have kept things in better shape."

"Does the Captain know, do you think?"

There's a thought I hadn't considered. I've been assuming the Captain can steer *Soliton*—that's what it means to be a Captain, isn't it? But I wonder if he understands any more about how the ship works than the rest of us.

"I'd love to talk to him," Meroe says.

"You like figuring things out, don't you."

She nods. "My father always told me I shouldn't be so interested in everything. It wasn't . . . seemly, for a princess. But I suppose I can't help it." She rings the bell, and waves her wounded hand back and forth. "There was a eunuch at our court who studied the stars. I used to sneak in and play with his telescope."

"What's a telescope?" The word is Imperial, but I've never heard it before.

"It's . . . you know what a spyglass is? For looking at ships?"

I nod cautiously. I've seen those on the docks.

"A telescope is like that, but stronger. You use it to look at the stars, or the moon."

"Why?"

She shrugs. "Curiosity?"

Which is, of course, a very aristo way of looking at things. Why *not* stare at the sky when you don't have to work for your dinner?

The next bay over is empty, so we change directions, and come alongside another wrecked vessel. This one is dangling nose down, with only the chains at its aft end still holding it in place. It shifts back and forth, very gently, producing faint metal-on-metal creaks.

Meroe rings her bell. "I feel like I'm calling the castle to dinner," she says.

"You're calling *someone* to dinner." I look over my shoulder and make sure Ahdron and Berun are not too far behind us. They're hanging back, but still in sight. "Hopefully it'll hear us soon."

The hanging ship creaks again. Then I become aware of another sound, a rapid drumming. It comes up through my feet as a vibration in the deck, making my teeth buzz. Meroe tenses.

"I think you can get rid of the bell." I look around again, but I can't see any sort of monster. The sound comes from every direction at once. "Where in the Rot is it?"

"I think . . ." Meroe hesitates, closing her eyes, then takes a step away from the closest gap. "Underneath!"

The hammerhead crawls up over the side of the gap. Chunks of rusty decking break and fall away under its weight, but it keeps coming. It's big, as tall as the blueshell but considerably more compact, with a long, oval body split into many narrow segments of gray chitin. Each side of it is lined with legs, hundreds of stubby little things that keep it only a few inches off the ground. They move with eerie, mechanical coordination, ripples of motion running down each flank. At the front of the creature, its body flattens out into a broad head, protruding out to either side and shaped vaguely like a hammer. A huge mouth splits the head almost in two, and as it yawns wide I can see row after row of needle-like teeth, short but viciously sharp.

The legs, Ahdron had said. Meroe is already backing away from it, and I fade to one side, ready to attack its flank if it stays focused on her. All of a sudden, though, I don't like this plan. Meroe is all alone, and if something goes wrong—

"Berun!" Meroe shouts. "Now!"

Berun, at Ahdron's side, swallows hard and concentrates. For a moment, pale blue light flickers around the hammerhead, which is still moving toward Meroe at a leisurely pace. The Tartak force makes it pause for a moment, but no more than that.

"I can't," Berun says. "I can't hold it!"

"Try again." Meroe's voice is remarkably steady. "I trust you."

Oh, rot. Rot rot rot.

Pale blue light gathers one more time, but Berun doesn't seem to know *how* to apply his force to the enormous creature. Bands of light press against the massive head, trying to hold the thing in place, but he's just not strong enough. Given the size of the thing, it's like trying to stop a runaway cart full of rocks. It pushes through with ease, moving faster now, right at Meroe.

I should have rotting known this wasn't going to work.

I run at the hammerhead, igniting my blades and shouting at the top of my lungs. The noise at least distracts it, and it slows, wide snout turning in my direction. It doesn't change course fast enough, though, and I still catch it in the side, one blade held out in front of me like a lance. The green energy sinks into the hammerhead's flesh, actinic crackles of magic spidering out along its hide, until my knuckles brush against its skin. Clear, sticky blood wells, coating my fingers.

I'm just about at the middle of the creature, and down around my knees its hundreds of legs are pumping away like pistons. I pull my blade free with another spurt of watery fluid and slash low, hoping to salvage Ahdron's plan. But the legs are chitinous and hard, much tougher than the rubbery skin of the creature, and my Melos blade scrapes and sparks across them without inflicting much damage.

The hammerhead lurches sideways, and I have to jump backward to avoid being slammed aside. I definitely have its attention now, and its segmented body curves in my direction, blunt head straining blindly toward me. The mouth gapes wide enough for me to see two black tongues twisting around each other like wrestling snakes.

Rotting wonderful.

Fire blooms in the darkness, a bolt that whips across the deck and slams into the hammerhead's side. It barely seems to notice. Another blast impacts near its head, shattering into globs of liquid flame that burn briefly on its thick hide before guttering out. It's coming faster now, legs churning, and I back away.

"Isoka!" Meroe shouts.

"Keep it moving!" says Ahdron, hurling another gout of flame.

You're not rotting helping, I want to say, but I can't spare the breath. Picking away at something this size is like trying to kill an ox with a slingshot. The heart or the brain, Ahdron had said. I try to picture the location of both, based on his crude drawings. The heart, back in the center of the body, is buried too deep in the rubbery flesh to get at without carving the thing apart. The brain should be just behind the bulbous hammer-shaped head. So maybe . . .

Oh, Blessed's rotting balls. This is going to hurt.

I spare a glance over my shoulder, making sure the ground behind me is clear, and settle into a defensive crouch. The thing is coming at me like a loaded wagon barreling downhill, and a traitorous part of my brain insists that it's not too late to run away. But I need this— if I'm going to climb *Soliton*'s hierarchy, get out from under the

Butcher and into a position where I might be able to get something done, I need to take risks.

This is definitely a risk.

A moment before it reaches me, I jump, hoping to get clear of its jaws. At the same time, I stab down with both my blades, aiming at the back of the snout, trying to punch through enough rubbery flesh to reach the brain.

It nearly works. I get my blade in, sizzling Melos power slashing through flesh, but the brain must be farther back than I thought. The creature never slows. And my standing jump isn't quite high enough, because one long black tongue licks out and wraps around my ankle, yanking me down. My blades come free in a spray of clear blood, and for a moment I'm falling. I jam one blade in, right above the creature's jaws, and twist it so it holds me in place. That keeps the tongue from pulling me in entirely, so its bite closes on my calf, rather than my waist.

Melos armor flares wildly around my leg, green energy forming a nearly solid shell that crackles and spits as it tries to keep the monster's teeth from my flesh. But this isn't like deflecting a sword cut or a brief blast of fire. It's more like trying to hold up a building, and I give a full-throated scream as the magical energy flowing under my skin builds to an unbearable heat. Wisps of smoke rise from my leg where arcs of green lightning strobe across it.

I let the armor fail. I'm not sure it's even a conscious decision, but I have no choice. In another few seconds, Melos power would sear my leg into ash and blackened bone. The hammerhead's straining jaws close, and a new, exquisite agony blooms as needle teeth tear into my flesh. There's a nauseating *crack* as the bone breaks, and blood bubbles through the monster's clenched teeth.

Definitely not the best plan I've ever been a part of.

The hammerhead is still moving fast, turning back toward the others. I'm hanging on the front of its head, supported by my mangled leg and the blade driven into its nose. If I let go, then I'll fall down and be crushed under the thing's onrushing bulk. If I hang on, I'll pass out from loss of blood. My vision is already going gray at the edges. *So what now, Isoka?*

Die, most likely.

I'm not eager to die. And more than that. If I die, I *fail*. If I die, Kuon Naga will do whatever he wants to Tori and everything I've worked for will be for nothing. If I die now, I never meant anything to anyone.

The rot with that. I'm not going to let that rotsucker win. Not like this.

I twist my head and spot Meroe and Berun. My voice is a strangled yell, twisted by pain.

"Get its mouth open!" I wave my free hand, blade humming as it parts the air. "You rotting little *coward*, just get this thing to open up!"

I'm not sure Berun understands, but Meroe does. She grabs him by the shoulders and shakes him, hard. His eyes are wide as saucers, but he brings his hands up, focusing his Tartak power. I see the wisps of pale blue energy hover around the hammerhead's mouth, tentatively at first, then pushing harder as Meroe shakes Berun again.

The creature's jaw levers open. I'm sure Berun wouldn't be strong enough if it were bearing down, but he's caught it by surprise, and in a few moments the thing is yawning wide. I purposely don't look at my leg, catching only a sidelong glimpse of a mess of torn fabric and skin, painted liberally in crimson. Instead, I grab a tooth in my free hand and swing myself forward, *into* the hammerhead's mouth.

This is, to put it mildly, completely insane.

The two black tongues writhe around me but don't grab hold yet, the creature unsure what to make of this development. Pulling my leg free from where it's still impaled on the hammerhead's teeth hurts so much I nearly black out, but I cling to consciousness like grim death, crawling toward the back of the thing's gullet. I plant my boot on the base of its tongue, and push upward, slamming both of my blades into the roof of its mouth. They cut through its palate and slice deep enough, I hope, to reach the brain.

This time, I managed to hit *something*. The hammerhead wobbles, slewing like a cart with a snapped axle. I stab again and again, ignoring the lash of its tongue against my waist. I feel it when the creature starts to roll, legs losing their coordination and going out from under it. It falls heavily and flips over, sending me crashing against the roof of its mouth, then flips again, ending up on its side. I lie curled inside the monster's cheek, its tongues twitching and shaking against me, as it slides to a halt.

There follows one of those timeless moments that could be an instant or a thousand years. It's dark, and warm, and smells of spoiled meat. My leg no longer hurts, but I can't feel anything below my knee, which I suspect is a bad sign. In spite of the heat of the hammerhead's bulk all around me, I feel cold, which probably has to do with the rate at which blood is leaving my body.

Now what, Isoka? Going to die now?

This admonition manages to get me wriggling forward. But the hammerhead's mouth is almost fully closed, and the most I can do is put my hands on its teeth. Prying its jaws apart is beyond my strength, and I can't even think of trying to resummon my blades.

Rot.

A shudder runs through the hammerhead. For a moment I think it's going to get back up, and then its jaw levers open. Meroe is standing in the gap, breathing hard, arms trembling.

"Isoka!"

She reaches past the rows of needle teeth and grabs me under the arms. I scrabble weakly, trying to help her, but only push her off balance. She stumbles back, and I end up in her lap as she sits down heavily. I'm soaked with a mix of hammerhead blood and my own, my skin caked and sticky with the stuff, and Meroe frantically brushes it off my face.

"Isoka!" she says. "Hang on. I'm going to find a bandage."

I almost laugh, because I need a hell of a lot more than a bandage. It comes out as a cough. Some ways off, I hear Berun shout, and Ahdron swearing in his own language.

"I have never seen something so crazy," he says. "Is she all right?"

"Of course she's not rotting all right!" Meroe shouts. "Get over here and help!"

"I—" Ahdron says.

Berun cuts him off. *"It's moving!"*

There's a crunch of twisting metal. I manage to raise my head.

The hammerhead's dying tumble took it close to the edge of one of the holes in the deck, and Meroe and I are still lying beside it. We're several yards away from the hole, but the deck beneath us is flaked and pitted with rust. The hammerhead, which had been lying still, begins to thrash, clear fluid spraying wildly from its mouth, legs twitching in uncoordinated spasms.

"Run," I gasp at Meroe. She won't let me go.

One of the monster's mindless tremors lifts it off the deck as its back arches. It slams down with a tremendous crash, hundreds of pounds of flesh hitting the rusty, rotten deck. There's a scream like a dying giant as a whole section of metal warps under the impact, supports giving way with a rapid *pop pop pop*. Plates of rust at the edge of the gap flake away, and then the deck beneath me tilts as one end dips toward the abyss.

The hammerhead begins to slide as it thrashes, and its weight pulls the deck down farther. I feel Meroe lose her balance and fall, then start to skid toward the edge. I grab her wrist, but I have no strength, and nothing to hang on to. Metal rasps at my clothes as the deck dips again, becoming a ramp leading into darkness.

Someone is screaming. Possibly me. The hammerhead goes over the edge, flailing aimlessly. I reach out with my free hand, trying to get a grip, but the ragged, rusty deck only shreds the skin on my fingertips. When we reach the gap, I try again, bloody palm grabbing for the edge of the deck. It crumbles in my grip, and we're falling.

I pull Meroe close, wrapping myself around her, putting every scrap of my energy and will into summoning my Melos armor. Then I close my eyes, knowing it won't be enough.

10

The same dream. The angels cluster around me, a mass of twisted, monstrous shapes, their voices overlapping, indistinct, but full of madness and terror. It's like they want something I don't know how to give them, pressing against me in their need until I want to scream.

". . . Isoka?"

A human voice, barely audible above the babble. There's a figure behind the angels, visible in glimpses, outlined in soft gray light. Wavering, indistinct, but still familiar.

". . . oka . . . listen . . . something . . ."

Hagan?

I always dream of the people I've killed. Even when I'm dead, apparently.

Am I dead?

I don't feel dead. But that may not mean much.

I open my eyes, and see the stars.

In Kahnzoka, between the city lights and the ever-present haze, we don't often see the stars. But while I'm not an expert, I'm pretty sure they're not supposed to be moving, and that none of them should be green, red, or blue.

"I don't think I'm dead." I say the words aloud, as an experiment. They come out as a raspy whisper, but I can hear them.

If I'm not dead, where am I?

That's enough to bring it all back, and I close my eyes, throat working.

Rot. Rot, rot, rot, Blessed's rotten balls in a rotting teacup.

Okay. That's enough of that. Focus.

I open my eyes again and try sitting up. Somewhat to my surprise, I manage it easily, though my head spins for a moment. I'm in no immediate pain. The light of the stars isn't much to see by, so I run my hands along my leg, searching for the wounds left by the hammerhead. While my trousers are torn and squishy with blood, my skin is smooth and unbroken underneath. The bone that I *felt* shatter is in one piece.

This whole scenario is unpleasantly like waking up in Kuon Naga's custody. But then I'd only been beaten, not half bled out and dropped off a cliff.

I ignite one of my Melos blades. Energy sizzles out of my wrist, a solid wedge of white-green power. It doesn't cast *much* light, but it's better than nothing, illuminating my immediate surroundings in a ghostly, flickering green. By Melos light, I can see that I'm sitting on fine white sand, which stretches away in all directions, its small hills and undulations casting long shadows. A few steps off, a dark shape is huddled in on itself.

Meroe. I roll over and stumble in her direction, Melos blade held aloft like a torch.

She's lying on her side, breathing softly, her features slack. The sand around her is disturbed, and I guess that she crawled a short distance. I kneel beside her, searching her for injuries. Her left leg is obviously broken, crooked underneath her at a bad angle, and there are strange dark lines running across her. Charred marks, marring her clothes and skin.

Powerburn. I was holding her when we hit the ground. My armor must have flared, trying to protect both of us. But if the backlash was strong enough to burn *her*, it should have cooked me into roast beef.

Her skin is hot to the touch. She needs water. So do I, for that matter. Meroe's pack is nowhere to be found, but my canteen is still on my belt. I pull the stopper and tip the water gently into her mouth, but it's barely more than a couple of swallows. I swear quietly and get back to my feet, raising my blade higher.

There. The green light gleams off a rippling surface. I shuffle in that direction, sand sliding away from my feet. It turns out to be a fairly large pool, flat and black in the darkness, reflecting my glowing blade and the stars overhead. I kneel at the edge, put my hand in, and take a cautious sip.

It's freshwater, thank the Blessed, sweet and cold. Ahdron said that drinking the standing water would make me sick, but I'm going to have to risk that, because I don't see another alternative. I hold the canteen underwater until bubbles stop rising, then gulp greedily, letting more of the water run down my neck into my sweat-and-blood-soaked shirt. When the canteen's empty, I fill it again, and stand up to take it back to Meroe.

And then stop. My reflection stares back at me, dimly, from the surface of the pool, and there's something . . . wrong. I bend closer, dropping the canteen, and wait for the water's surface to settle.

My breath catches in my throat. There's something wrong with my *face*. Markings, like graceful, curving strokes of a pen, cross it in a pattern from below my right ear up diagonally to my hairline. They look like a series of curves written in deep indigo, each intersecting the tail of the next, sometimes branching and recombining. It runs down onto my neck, and from there onto my torso. I pull my shirt up, frantically, and spot more of the strange marks, swirling crosshatches running over my breasts and down across my stomach. Now that I'm looking, I can see more on my legs, through the gaps in my trousers left by the hammerhead's teeth. The marks seem particularly dense where it bit me, the flesh turned almost solid blue.

What in the *Rot*?

I stand still for a moment, trying to breathe, mind racing. There are gangs in Kahnzoka that tattoo their members, but it doesn't look anything like this. The only thing I can remember bearing anything similar is a mark like a green and red stain that marred the right shoulder, under the skin, of an old man in the Sixteenth Ward. He was an auxiliary for the Legions, as he tells the story, and took an iceling spear to the shoulder. The wound festered, and he would have died if one of the legionary healers hadn't tended it. But the healing—*Ghul* healing—hadn't been perfect, leaving the strange colors.

And then everything falls into place. The marks, and why I'm alive.

Meroe is a ghulwitch.

A moment later, I'm standing over her, Melos blade still burning, breathing hard.

She's a *ghulwitch*. No wonder she didn't want to tell the Butcher what her Well was. I put my life on the line to help her, and she was lying the whole time.

No wonder the King of Nimar was so eager to discard his princess. He must have found out that she's an abomination.

My blade hovers over Meroe's still face, the point an inch or two from her cheek. She reached into my body with her magic, *changed* me. Blessed only knows what she did aside from leaving marks on my skin. There could be tumors growing in my brain, or insects nesting in my intestines, ready to chew their way out. She could have turned my fingers to claws, my eyes to fungal growths.

Melos energy spiders out, lightning crackling from the tip of the blade and dancing across her features before earthing itself. Killing her would take less than a heartbeat. *Monster. Abomination.* Her kind created the Vile Rot, and came close to destroying the entire world.

She must be strong. Certainly no mere touched, to heal me as she did. A well-trained talent might have managed it, but who could possibly have trained Meroe? She must be an *adept*, a full-fledged Ghul adept, the one thing every nation around the Central Sea agrees must be destroyed at birth. If I put my blade through her skull, I'd be doing the world a service.

I close my eyes for a moment, and see Hagan's face. I've killed better people than this *creature*, for far worse reasons. For practically no reason at all. The girl in the gambling den begged for her life, my blade at her throat. I stabbed her through the ribs, right to the heart. A quick death.

Shaking, I put my foot on Meroe's shoulder, roll her onto her back, and put the tip of my blade below her breast. Another fork of green lightning arcs, raising a thin string of smoke where it burns her shirt.

So she saved my life. So what? I didn't ask her to. She didn't ask if I'd rather die than have her muck around inside me with her tainted hands.

Rot rot *rot*.

I see her standing up to the Butcher. Her face, blood running down her cheek, as she continued her calm appeal after the first blow. She must have known it wasn't going to get her anywhere, but she had to try, and she wasn't going to beg. When I saw that, I thought . . .

Rot. I can't do it, can I?

I let my blade fade away and clench my fists, staring down at this beautiful girl, this abomination who'd kept me alive and done who-knew-what else. I feel a scream bubbling up inside me, rage and fear mixed in an acid brew, and I turn away from her before it can work its way out. I start walking, feet shuffling the sand, no idea where I'm going except *away*.

The white sand seems to go on forever. After a while, my eyes adapt to the faint light—the "stars," far above, are the same colored lights I saw from above in the Center. We really are in the Deeps, the part of the ship Ahdron said nobody ever comes back from. Which is just rotting wonderful.

Though I can see a little, I still hear the crab before I catch sight of it. Sand crunches as its feet come down in a complex eight-legged rhythm, moving steadily closer. I turn to face it, and make out a sil-houette. It's smaller than the blueshell, but still taller than I am, an ovoid central body hanging from eight multi-jointed limbs. No claws on this one, and its hide is bright orange, speckled with silver.

I could run, as I could have run before. But I don't. I turn to it and ignite my blades, green light washing over the sand. The scream

I pushed away refuses to be contained any longer. It tears at my throat as I charge.

Long after the creature has collapsed, I continue my work, severing each leg in turn until the body lies on its back, stumps flailing.

"I," I tell it, "have had. Rotting. *Enough.*" Power crackles across my armor as I plant my foot on it. "You hear me?"

It answers me with a hiss, not that I was expecting anything else. I let one blade fade away and summon the armor-piercing spike I used against the blueshell. It takes form, slowly, my right hand hot and sparking with green energy. I punch down, driving the spike into the crab's carapace, and let all the power go. It floods into the creature's body, sizzling through it with a sound like meat hitting the frying pan. All its stumps twitch at once, strobing with actinic lightning, and then it goes still and dark.

"Enough," I whisper, breathing hard.

I don't have time to waste here. I have an appointment with the Captain, and it's time to get to work.

It's not hard to follow my tracks back to Meroe. It's a little harder to make the walk with all eight of the crab's severed limbs tucked under my arms, but the smell wafting up from where my power cooked it is appetizing, and I have a feeling we're going to need all the food we can get.

11

By the time Meroe wakes up, I've made some progress.

First I splint her leg. It doesn't seem like a bad break, in the sense that the bone isn't actually sticking out anywhere. More than that is beyond me, but I know enough to straighten it and strap it to something firm. A length of crab-shell works quite well. For straps, I've sacrificed most of my trousers, hacking the tattered cloth off above my knees.

She gasps and shudders as I pull her leg straight, then relaxes when I tie the straps tight. I trickle water into her mouth for a while, then get to work on the crab meat. Cooking with my Melos blades is not an ideal process. I manage to sear the meat by holding it close to the crackling green energy. The middle of each strip still feels raw, but it's the best I can do, and I devour a few. In spite of the preparation, it's palatable. As to whether it will make me sick—as with the water, no other options seem to be available, so we'll find out.

I cut some thinner strips and sear them a little more thoroughly, hoping that will help them keep longer. I've got most of one leg carved when Meroe groans, and her eyelids flutter. I let my blades disappear and station myself at her side.

Her eyes open, and find mine immediately. We stare at each other for a long moment.

"I'm not dead?" Meroe says.

"You know, that was my first question as well," I tell her.

"And?"

"You're not dead. We're in the Deeps."

"My leg hurts." She shifts, and beads of sweat pop out on her forehead. "Really hurts."

"It's broken. I've got it set as best I can."

"Oh." She swallows. "I thought it might be."

"Do you think you can drink some water?"

She nods weakly, and I hand over the canteen. She finishes it, then looks up sheepishly.

"Sorry. I probably should have saved that."

"There's more," I tell her. I set the canteen aside and pick up a strip of meat. "Food?"

Another nod. She pops the crab meat into her mouth and chews thoughtfully, watching me out of the corner of her eye. Tension is thick in the air, and for a moment I feel sorry for her. After all, how *do* you ask someone if they've figured out you're a ghulwitch?

"Isoka—" she starts, after the second strip of meat.

"I know," I tell her, tapping the line of blue marks across my face.

"Oh." Her eyes fill with tears. "I'm so sorry. I didn't mean to. I could feel you dying and I'd never done anything like it before, but I wanted to save you, and I just . . ." She shakes her head, not looking at me. "I didn't know it would leave marks. I don't really understand anything."

"I was dying?"

She nods. "We hit hard. Your armor protected us some, but not enough. And the powerburn was . . . bad. You'd lost so much blood already. . . ." She swallows again. "I was just lying there and I could *feel* you slipping away. And I didn't . . ." Meroe looks up at me, brown eyes shining. "I didn't want to be alone. That's what I was thinking. I'm an awful person, Isoka. You were dying and all I could think was, oh, gods, I don't want to be alone down here."

There's a long pause. Meroe presses the heels of her bandaged palms into her eyes, scrubbing away the tears.

"So you're a ghulwitch." I hesitate. "A Ghul . . . adept."

"I . . . think so," she says. "I've never tested my power."

"Why not heal yourself?"

She shakes her head. "It doesn't work. Believe me, I've tried. I can't affect my own body."

I'd heard that was true for ghulwitches, but I'd never met one to ask before. Looking down at Meroe, battered and crying, I found it hard to square her with the monstrous stories everyone tells.

"Does anyone else know?" I ask her.

"Not anymore." She takes a deep breath. "When I was little my keeper was a servant named Gigi. She was the one who noticed my power. I had been playing in the garden, and the plants were . . . strange."

I nod silently. Most mage-born, especially adepts, are noticed at a young age, when they do something clearly unnatural. The power comes to us when we're too young to know any better, or to control what feels like a perfectly normal part of ourselves. I'd been lucky enough that I could lose myself in the slum, staying away from anyone who'd seen my occasional outbursts until I eventually learned enough control to keep myself hidden.

"She saved my life," Meroe went on. "Gigi told everyone I was ill. Do you have the crowfoot pox in the Empire?" When I shrug, she says, "It's an uncommon disease in Nimar, but not unknown. It's dangerous for children, but almost always deadly for adults who catch it. Gigi told everyone I had the pox, and isolated herself with me in one of the monastery towers. We lived there for nearly a year, servants leaving our food outside the door. All that time, Gigi tried to make me understand what my power was, and what it would mean if anyone found out."

"They would have killed you, I assume."

Meroe nods. "Mage-bloods are venerated in Nimar, and given honorable placements. Every Well except Ghul. A few weak touched and talents are apprenticed into a monastic order, but adepts . . ."

"It's the same in the Empire," I say. "Ghul adepts are too dangerous to let live."

"I know." Meroe shakes her head. "Believe me, I know. Do you have any idea how often I've thought of just . . . doing what Gigi should have done? I had a spot picked out, a tower in the palace with a hundred-foot drop onto hard flagstones. I even went up there a few times, but I never . . . I was never strong enough."

"It's no shame to want to live."

She laughs bitterly. "Tell that to my father."

"He found out?"

"I don't know for certain. But"—she waves a hand—"it would explain how I ended up here, wouldn't it?"

I nod, and we lapse into silence again. Meroe stares at me, studying my face, and ventures a weak smile.

"It doesn't look . . . bad," she says. "Almost pretty. South of Nimar, there's a tribe who practice ritual scarification, and I always thought—"

"I don't care how it looks."

She cuts off, swallowing. After another moment, she says in a small voice, "What are you going to do now?"

The meaning is obvious enough. Meroe can't walk, nor can she defend herself against the crabs. If I abandon her, it's the same as if I slit her throat, and we both know it.

I'm not prepared to do that. I may still not fully understand why, but it's time I accepted it. "*We* are getting out of here. Ahdron said nobody comes back from the Deeps, but there's got to be a way back up. We'll stay away from the crabs as much as we can, and I'll kill them if I have to."

"What about the wilders?" she says. I frown. I recall Berun mentioning the term, but not the details. Meroe goes on, "People who ran away from *Soliton*'s 'civilization.' They're supposed to live out here. Maybe they can help us."

"Didn't Berun say they hate the people from the Stern?"

Meroe shrugs. "I doubt Berun ever met one himself."

"If we meet any wilders, we'll ask for help," I say. "And if they get in our way, I'll kill them, too."

She gives me an odd look. "You've done that before, haven't you?"

"What?"

"Killed people."

It hadn't even occurred to me that this might be new ground for her. I nod, a little uncomfortable. *Rotting aristos.*

"Okay," Meroe says, after a moment's pause. "Can I make the obvious point that I can't walk?"

"I'll make you a sledge, at least until we have to start climbing."

I glance around at the rolling, empty sand. "That's the hard part. I'm going to have to go and find some supplies, and you'll need to wait here for me."

Meroe blinks. I can see the fear in her eyes, just for a moment—fear of being alone here, hurt and helpless, easy prey for anything that happens along. Then, as always, she steadies, and gives a decisive nod.

"All right," she says, no hint of worry in her voice. "Can you help me to the water before you leave?"

Blessed above. Sometimes I think this princess is twice as tough as I am.

I walk. And walk. And walk.

Soliton is a ship. A big ship, but still. There has to be an end to it, doesn't there? An outer hull. But if there is, it's invisible to me, far beyond the tiny circle of light thrown by my Melos blade. After a while I dismiss the magic and let my eyes adapt, walking by the light of the moving stars.

I keep my course as straight as I can. I *should* be able to follow my footprints in the sand to return to Meroe, but I'm still wary. There are two red stars, neither moving much, that hang directly behind me. Hopefully, when I turn around, I can just walk toward them.

Eventually, something huge looms out of the shadow, blotting out the stars as I come near. I approach slowly, wary for crabs, but nothing moves. It's a metal tower, a dozen yards across at the base. I imagine it stretching upward to the Center, narrowing as it rises, supporting decks and platforms and bridges. A few shelf mushrooms grow around it, but there's no sign of a ladder or stairs. It's just possible I could climb it, but not for long enough to make a difference, and I'd never get Meroe up.

At the base, there are large chunks of fallen mushroom lying on the sand, dried and desiccated. I pick one up, curiously. It weighs almost nothing, but it's far too crumbly and brittle to be of use building a sledge. The tower itself looks too solid to carve a piece off of.

Something moves, inside the pillar. The specks of gray light flow steadily upward, denser here. They seem to well up from under the sand, as though the pillar were a giant siphon drawing them skyward. When I touch it, I feel . . . something, a faint tug and a whisper that quickly fades away.

Looking over my shoulder, I see one of my two guide stars has started to move sideways, crawling slowly across the darkness. I pick up a couple of the larger chunks of shelf mushroom and head back along my footprints.

I relax a little when my pool comes into view, with Meroe a darker lump beside it. She sits up as I return, and I drop the bits of mushroom on the sand.

"Welcome back." She's huddled tightly in on herself. "Did you find anything?"

"Not much." I indicate the mushroom. "I'll try a different direction tomorrow."

"Tomorrow?" Meroe says, with a slight smile. "How will we know when that is?"

"After I get some sleep, then," I tell her. "How are you feeling?"

"My leg hurts," she says. "No worse than it did, though." She hugs herself a little tighter. "I'm cold."

"I thought of that." It's chilly down here in the dark, a wet, stygian cold that starts to creep in as soon as I stop moving. "Give me a minute."

I snap one of the pieces of mushroom into a few smaller bits, and arrange them in a rough pile. Half an hour later, I'm still trying to get my makeshift campfire going, holding my Melos blade near enough to it that green lightning arcs and pops. Wisps of smoke rise, now and then, but it won't catch, and eventually I slump back in defeat.

Meroe, sitting next to me, gives me a sad smile. "It was a good idea."

She's shivering. I take one of her hands, and she looks at me questioningly. Her fingers are like ice.

"Lie down," I tell her.

She does. I prod her onto her side, and lie down next to her, pressing myself up against her back. I feel her stiffen slightly, then relax.

"Better?" I ask, after a while.

"Yeah." She gives a little giggle. "Your breath is tickling my neck."

"Sorry."

Another silence. I think she's fallen asleep, but then she says, "Will you tell me something about yourself, Isoka?"

I feel myself tense up. "What do you want to know?"

"Anything." She yawns. "I talk about myself a lot. I just thought . . ."

Another pause.

"If you don't want to . . . ," she says, worried.

"I have a sister." I don't realize I'm speaking aloud until the moment after I've done it. Pressed together, it feels like the two of us are alone in the universe, a tiny bubble of warmth and life in the middle of cold, unfeeling darkness. "Her name is Tori. She's four years younger than me." I pause for a moment. "We used to sleep like this, when it got cold and we were on the street, or squatting in some rattrap. Whenever it snowed, street kids would freeze to death. We'd find them in the mornings, just like they were asleep, only turned blue. They were always smiling, and I thought it wouldn't be a bad way to die. But when I slept with Tori, I was always warm. I used to joke that she had a belly full of hot coals."

I keep talking a while longer, and I feel Meroe's breathing go slow and deep, her body relaxing. After a while I close my eyes, press a little tighter against her, and let myself drift away.

12

When I wake up, Meroe's face is inches from mine. Her eyes are closed, her features calm, and in the strange moments after waking I feel an odd urge to *kiss* her. That's enough to make me blink and come fully awake, and I prop myself up on one arm and brush sand out of my hair.

She opens her eyes as I sit up, and groans.

"And here I was hoping this had all been a dream," she says. "Why is it only a dream when you really *want* it to be real?"

"I've wondered that myself."

First we drink water, filling and refilling the canteen until we've both had enough, and then we eat a few more strips of badly cooked crab meat. I push Meroe's dress up to examine her leg, and she does her best not to wince as I prod it gently. I have no idea if it's set properly, but it doesn't seem to be festering or swelling too badly.

"Right," I say. "Last time I went that way." I gesture to where a few of my footprints are still visible, then turn ninety degrees. "This time I'll go this way. Maybe I can find the edge of the ship."

"Would that be helpful?"

I shrug. "It'd be something."

She nods, then looks away nervously. "Before you leave, can you help me with something?"

"What do you need?"

Her eyes stay fixed firmly on the ground. It takes me a second, but I get it, and I find myself grinning. "Oh."

She rolls her eyes at me. "Please hurry."

Through a combination of carefully averted gazes and loud humming, we manage to give Meroe a chance to piss without either of us dying of embarrassment. I get her settled back near the pool, and wave with as much cheer as I can muster.

"Be careful," she says.

"You too."

"Don't worry about me." Sleeping seems to have restored her spirits, and she grins broadly. "If the crabs come for me, I shall disarm them with my rapier wit."

I smile back, with an effort, and start walking.

Once again, I find two "stars" that haven't moved in a while and use them as guideposts, in case something happens to my footprints. This time I find one of the massive pillars much sooner, with several dog-sized green crabs gathered around its base. I veer well clear, and though they freeze at the sound of my shuffling feet, they don't follow me.

Walking through an endless expanse of white sand gives you too much time to think. I think about Tori, in her Second Ward house, and wonder if she's realized I'm gone yet. Maybe she's worrying about me. Maybe Naga has already killed her, just out of spite, and all this is pointless. But no—if I *do* somehow take command of *Soliton*, he'll need her to make sure I hand the ship over to the proper authorities. So she's safe. Until he decides I've failed.

I turn my mind in other directions. I think about Meroe, back at the pool, but then I worry about whether she's all right. And I think about how we spent the night, and what *she* thinks about it, which is, frankly, confusing. I try to think about Zarun instead, but that's just frustrating, and in spite of my best efforts Meroe keeps intruding. So in the end I try to think about nothing at all, just my boots brushing slowly through the sand, which works about as well as you might imagine.

It's with some relief, therefore, that I discover that there's an end to the sand after all. I've passed several more pillars, but now the faint light ends at a wall of utter darkness, stretching up far higher than I can see and running perfectly straight in both directions. This can only be the hull of the ship. It's so large and so featureless that it's hard to gauge how far away it is. After another hour of trudging, the thing seems no closer, until I spy small discolorations at the base.

As I approach, I can see that they're buildings, of a sort. A collection of small huts and shacks, leaning against the massive wall of the ship for support. All of them have at least partially collapsed, and some are little more than piles of rubble. Not a promising site, but more than I've found anywhere else, so I turn my steps in that direction.

Something catches my eye when I get close, faint movement in the sand. I freeze, watching carefully, and catch tiny gray particles whipping across the dunes. They look like the flows I can see inside *Soliton*'s pillars, and they're converging on the village, drawn inward like they're caught in a whirlpool.

That gives me pause. I ignite my blades, the green light harsh after the near darkness, banishing the faint wisps of gray. Shadows dance as I move closer to the wrecked village. Down at the very edge of my hearing, the whispering voices are back, speaking words I can't quite understand.

The village is full of corpses.

The people who lived here have clearly been dead for a very long time. For the most part, the bodies are practically mummified, reduced to skeletons wrapped in dried-out skin and dressed in shredded rags. None of them are intact, not because of the passage of time but from the manner of their deaths, which is gruesomely clear. Several large shells, bleached white, lie among the villagers. One crab's corpse is half-covered by the ruin of a demolished shack, as though it were killed while wrecking the building.

There are people who live in the Deeps, then. The ones the crew called wilders. Or were, at least, until the crabs came for them. I walk gingerly into the village, blades ready. Nothing moves. There's no sign of living people, or living crabs for that matter. The shacks themselves seem to be made of long, spongy poles, which I guess are dried mushrooms of a more useful species, along with a few little bits of fabric. Not sturdy, but how sturdy do they need to be, here inside *Soliton*?

The skeletons, up close, are . . . strange. The bones seem *twisted* in places, not broken but grown into strange new shapes. One body has what looks like a third arm, fixed bizarrely between its shoulder blades. Another skull has bone spikes growing from it. A foot seems to have . . . blossomed, each toe stretching into a twisted corkscrew shape that looks like it was trying to become another limb.

Closer to the great wall of the ship, there's a faint flicker of movement, gone before I can focus on it. My lip twists, but I extinguish my blades, counting quietly as I give my eyes time to adapt to the dark. The gray light emerges, gradually, flowing stronger here, mounding up into silent, shifting waves like a torrent of water spilling through a river gate, converging on one of the shacks. Once I'm sure there's nothing moving beyond the strange lights, I approach, my power tightly coiled.

Two human skeletons lie under the dead crab, bones scattered. People fought and died, down in here in the dark, and no one ever knew. I step over them carefully, edging around the big shell and smaller, scattered pieces, following the intangible flood of gray.

The shack backs against the wall of the ship itself, the huge metal barrier that stretches off into the dark. But here, at the back of the shack, there's a *hole*, a square about as tall as I am. A smaller dead crab lies there, a spearpoint emerging from a hole in its shell. The gray specks rush over it, cresting like a wave over a rock.

I'm not sure exactly what I'm looking for. There are useful materials in the village, but . . .

I step through the hole. The white sand of the Deeps gives way to metal floor, without the patina of rust and decay that covers the rest of the ship. There's a chamber here, inside the wall, a large cube-shaped room lit only by the flickering gray of that intangible light. Apart from a scattering of sand, it's empty.

No. Not quite empty. My eye follows the gray motes, which converge on the far side. There a semi-circular pillar runs from floor to ceiling, like half a pipe stuck to the wall. The flow of gray stuff rushes into it, pulled upward and out of sight, like what I saw in the pillars outside but much brighter and more powerful.

Beside the pillar are two more corpses. They sit side by side, one grinning skull on the other's shoulder, their hands entwined between them. This place's last defenders, perhaps, who retreated here when the crabs came. They don't look like they died fighting, and I take a few steps forward to get a closer look.

". . . soka . . ." The voice rises from the faint babble, stronger than the others. For a moment I think I've imagined it. ". . . Isoka . . ."

Rot. I turn in a slow circle, just to confirm I'm alone.

". . . hear . . . it's . . ."

"H . . . hello?" My own voice isn't as strong as I intended it to be. But rot, there's *no one here.* I grit my teeth and take another step forward, bringing me within arm's length of the pillar. "Is someone there?"

No answer. The gray motes swirl around me, my legs making eddies in the flow as they rush onward. I reach down to touch them, and they swirl around my fingers like smoke.

"Isoka." The voice is definitely stronger.

"Who's there?" Then, without really knowing why, I ask, "Hagan?"

The voice could be his. And—rot, that was a *dream.* I *killed* Hagan, and dead is dead.

I raise my hand, and brush my finger against the pillar.

Something moves.

Perhaps not my most brilliant idea, all told.

The gray motes curl around me, thickening into spinning bands of light that spin like a berserk gyroscope. The distant voices get louder, the susuruss of quiet whispers rising into a high-pitched mosquito *whine* that seems to bore right into my skull. And then . . .

I can *feel* it, something vast and alien, turning its attention in my direction. The gray light mounds up in front of me, and before I can do more than blink it rushes inward like a striking cobra, streaming in through my eyes and mouth and ears. It's spreading through me, *investigating* me, cataloguing me with the dispassionate attention of a naturalist dissecting a specimen. It's gone in an instant, before I even have time to scream.

It doesn't speak. The communication is more basic than that, a feeling blasted directly into my mind, so strong it drives me to my knees:

UNAUTHORIZED/REJECTED

". . . Isoka! . . . coming . . ."

Blessed's *rotting* balls in a vise. I surge back to my feet, igniting my blades. The green Melos light pushes back the darkness, fading the gray to wraith-like wisps. My heart pounds, but the familiar feeling of my power crackling through my arms helps me stay calm. I back away from the pillar, turning in a slow circle.

Something has changed. Silently, one of the walls of the room had opened, revealing a long passageway stretching off into darkness. In the depth of that shadow, something glows blue.

The glowing figure takes a step forward, and the ground shakes, sand jumping across the metal deck. It's too big to make out, by the light of my blades, and I can only see fragments of it, sliding through the shifting radiance. Smooth, gray skin, like rock, big, bulky segmented legs surrounded by rings of waving, clutching human arms. Along its flank, a row of smooth, gray faces, living death masks with eyes that follow me and mouths open in an endless scream. High above, a faceted crystal that shines from within with pale blue light, a gemstone bigger than my fist embedded in the thing's skin.

It's not a crab. I saw something like this when I was brought aboard, lining the edges of *Soliton*'s deck.

An angel.

UNAUTHORIZED/REJECTED

It takes a step forward, shifting between me and the door, limbs stretching toward me like something out of a nightmare. I back away, closer to the pillar.

Oh, rot.

The gray light flickers. Something is moving, *writhing*, in the shifting mix of gray and blue and green. The motes fall inward until they're nearly solid, shaping themselves into a man-sized figure. It grows more distinct as the angel advances, arms and legs and a head, clothes of a familiar cut, a face—

It holds out a hand. Wisps of gray light lash out, wrapping themselves around the angel, and the huge thing freezes in place. The figure turns to face me.

Hagan. It's Hagan, though he's warped and distorted, as though I'm seeing his reflection in a shifting pool of mercury. His eyes meet mine, though. When he speaks, there's a crackling buzz like a swarm of wasps that nearly drowns out his words. Nearly, but not quite.

"Isoka."

No. Not possible. Hagan is dead, dead, dead; I rotting killed him myself.

I'm going mad.

"Way." He grimaces, as though each word costs him an enormous effort. "Way. Out."

Blessed's *balls*.

"The way out?" I shake my head. I can't believe I'm *doing* this. "You know the way out?"

He nods, with difficulty, and raises one hand. Gray light floods my senses again. For a moment there's *something* at the back of my mind, a vast, complicated web of tunnels and decks, a map that's far, far more intricate than I can comprehend. Then it's gone, draining away. Hagan looks frustrated. He grits his teeth, and light shifts in front of him, forming a ball of gray. With a gesture, he sends it floating toward me.

My hand comes up to catch it, automatically, but it passes through my fingers like they're not even there. It hits me in the chest and sinks into my skin, without even a flicker from my Melos armor. It feels strange, as though someone had latched a thread around my breastbone and given it a gentle tug. When I look down, a gray thread emerges from my chest, leading off into the darkness.

"Follow," Hagan says.

"I . . ." I shake my head. "This is impossible. Hagan—"

The angel shifts, its twisted limbs grinding toward me. Hagan turns to it, and it freezes again, but the strain on his face is obvious.

"Go," he says.

I don't need to be told twice. I edge around the angel, which remains motionless as a statue. When I reach the door, I pause and look back. Hagan is still there, outlined in glowing gray, watching me.

I have to say something. I can't just . . .

"Hagan. Are you—"

"Isoka." His voice is harder to make out, the distortion louder. "Listen. Anomaly . . . coming. Danger. Garden." He grows louder for just a moment. "*Find Garden*. Or die."

The angel shifts again, trying to turn around.

"Go!"

I back through the doorway. An instant later, the metal slides shut in front of my nose, leaving an unbroken expanse of wall. It's just me and the dead village, alone in the dark.

For a while I just sit, among the ancient corpses, and stare at the wall.

What in the Rot was that?

Hagan—except it's not Hagan, because Hagan is dead—stopped an angel from tearing me apart.

But the last time we met—I can't believe I'm even *thinking* this—I put my blade through his skull. So I can't imagine he'd be well-disposed to me, if he were still hanging around. Which he's not.

And then there's this . . . thing in my chest. The gray thread stretches out of me and curves off into the dark, shifting slightly as though with an intangible breeze but always pointing in the same direction. I'm supposed to follow it, which makes even less sense than anything else. If Hagan *is* here, how in the Rot does he know the way back to the Stern?

I never even *asked*. That thing, that *presence*, rooted around in my mind, and apparently didn't like what it found.

But—

I put my head between my hands and groan, fingers digging into my hair. No matter how many times I go over it, it doesn't make any rotting sense.

Maybe I *am* going mad.

Eventually, I have to get up. Meroe is waiting, unprotected. That

thought gets me worried enough that I hurry through my prepara-
tions, grabbing what I need from the wreckage of the village before heading back the way I came.

When I finally get there, Meroe is asleep beside the pool. I kneel
to check on her, worried, but she just seems cold and exhausted. I'm
tired, too, but after what happened inside the wall I don't even think
of sleep. I'm not sure I could pass another quiet night in this place.

Instead, I get to work on my supplies. I brought one of the larger
crab shells from the ruined village, a few of the long, flexible dried
mushroom poles from the buildings, and as many intact scraps of
fabric as I could manage. Being a Melos adept, fortunately, means
never being without a handy cutting tool. I start slashing and tying,
and by the time Meroe wakes up I'm nearly finished.

"Good morning," I tell her. "Or whatever it is."

"Morning." Meroe yawns, sits up, winces, and puts her hands on
her leg.

"How do you feel?"

"About the same." She takes a deep breath. "Better, now that
you're back."

"We're getting out of here."

"You found something?" Meroe looks at my project and frowns.
"What happened?"

"It's a long story." And how in the Rot am I supposed to explain
that a boy I murdered turned up to give me a helping hand? "I found
a ruined wilder village, and I think I might know how to get out of
here. This"—I gesture—"is to help me bring you along."

Meroe looks at the crude construction, tilts her head, then laughs.
"I get it. It's like a sled."

"More or less."

I've lashed two long poles to the dish-shaped crab shell, which is
large enough for Meroe to sit in. When I take the poles in hand, I
can more or less drag the whole contraption across the sand. It's not
elegant, but it's easier than carrying her.

I hand her a couple of other poles that I've cut to roughly the
height of her armpits. "You might be able to use these for crutches,
too. I don't know how far we'll have to go."

"Very thoughtful," Meroe says. "You're practically an expert at this."

I bark a laugh. "Believe me, I'm making it up as I go along."

We have only the one canteen between us, and I don't know when we'll find more freshwater, so we both drink from the pool until we're squelching. Meroe puts the rest of the half-cooked crab meat in the shell, then climbs in herself, and I pick up the poles.

"What can I do to help?" Meroe says.

"Just don't move too much." I shift my grip until I find something comfortable. "Here goes nothing."

After a few false starts, my rigged-up travois actually works fairly well. The most difficult part is coming down the shallow slope on the face of each dune, where the thing has a tendency to slide and tug me sideways, but I learn to walk a little faster to get ahead of it. I don't ignite my blades, the better to see the tiny thread of gray light. For Meroe, it must feel like we're hiking through the darkness with no guide at all, but she doesn't question me.

Not on that subject, at least. After a while, she says, "You were telling me about yourself, the other night, before I fell asleep."

I grunt, hoping responding in monosyllables will keep her from getting too interested. But she persists, and I have to admit that talking is easier than trying not to think at all. So I end up going over my life story, one little piece at a time. I leave out some of the details, and my capture by the Immortals and the aftermath, but that still leaves Meroe with a thousand questions.

What's hardest for her to understand is how mage-born are treated in the Empire. Things in Nimar are very different, apparently.

"Why would you have to *hide* being a Melos adept?" she says. "With that kind of power, couldn't you find a job better than a ward boss?"

I shrug, as best I can while holding the poles. "Mage-born owe their lives to the Emperor's service. According to the Emperor, anyway, and since he's got the army his is the vote that counts. Mage-born from the noble families get trained and serve in different ways, according to their talents. For them it's supposed to be a great honor. If you're a commoner and they catch you young, then you might get adopted by a noble family or sent to the Legions. But if they think you're too old to be trained properly, then their only real use for you is as breeding stock."

"You're not serious," Meroe says.

"Of course I'm serious." I can't keep a bit of venom out of my voice. "You think the rotting aristos care what happens to a commoner? They stick you in a room, rape you until you get pregnant, and then take the kids away to be raised as their own. It 'improves the noble bloodlines.'"

"Gods," Meroe says. "No wonder you hate them."

I shrug again, uncomfortably. It's not that I *don't* hate the aristos. It's just that it never occurred to me that there was any other way to feel. How else is an alley rat fighting over scraps of rotten fish supposed to feel toward people who live in manicured gardens and eat hummingbird tongues? A specific reason seemed somehow superfluous.

"In Nimar," Meroe says, "any position is open to anyone who passes the examinations for it. It doesn't matter who your parents are."

I snort. "I'm sure a lot of nobles' daughters end up as fishwives."

"It's not perfect," Meroe concedes. "But we can't afford to waste mage-born as 'breeding stock.'" She shudders. "You'd have taken the examination and been given a high position."

"What if I didn't like what I was given?"

It's Meroe's turn to shrug. "If one of your fishermen decides he doesn't want to be a fisherman, what does he do?"

"Sell his boat and try his hand at something else, I suppose."

"What if he's no good at it?"

"Then he starves, or goes begging."

She shakes her head. "That doesn't sound very efficient. Wouldn't it be easier to figure out in advance what he's best off doing?"

"So does that mean you had to take an exam to be princess?"

"No." She goes quiet. "It's different for royalty."

I don't get the chance to enquire about this, because the gray thread I've been following suddenly twitches, the far end rising so it slants upward. It gets more vertical as we keep moving, and ahead I can see one of the big pillars. It looks like every other one that I've seen, flecked with rust and crusted with shelf mushrooms, but with one important difference: a broad, flat stairway spirals around it, vanishing upward into darkness after a couple of turns.

If Hagan's gift is to be believed, it must connect to the network of stairs and bridges in the Center, which leads ultimately back to the Stern. A way out. I let out a long breath, not sure if this makes the "Isoka is going insane" theory more or less likely.

One immediate problem presents itself, though. The stairs don't come all the way down to the level of the sand. The bottom step is about eight feet up, just high enough that I can't touch it with my arms outstretched.

The sight of the stairs makes Meroe suck in her breath. "You knew this was here?"

"Sort of," I mutter, staring at the inconvenient gap.

"So how do we make the stairs come down?" Meroe says eagerly. "Is there a secret switch or something?"

I give her a withering look, and her enthusiasm fades.

"Oh," she says. "Well. We could . . ." She trails off.

"I'm thinking," I growl, letting the travois fall and going over to the pillar.

The shelf mushrooms, much as they *look* like a stairway, aren't strong enough to support my weight even briefly. I tear a couple away from the metal, then fling them aside. If I put my arms up and jump, I can *almost* reach the step, but not quite. And that doesn't help Meroe.

I turn back to the pillar. Its face is smooth, apart from patches of rust, and I can't get much of a hold on it. But . . .

"Meroe," I say. "I'm open to ideas."

"If you could stand on my shoulders, then you could probably pull yourself up," she says. "But if I could stand up properly, you wouldn't have had to drag me all this way."

"I think I can get myself up there," I say. "But then what?"

She looks at the poles I've been using to pull the travois, and her brow furrows.

"It might work," she mutters to herself. "And what have I got to lose, other than falling onto my broken leg?"

I give her a dubious look.

Step one: get Isoka up onto the bottom stair.

I summon my Melos blade, lighting up the sand with shimmering green, and apply it to the metal, pouring in as much energy as I can muster. It takes about ten minutes of steady pressure, but when I'm finished there are two notches carved into the metal. I wedge my boot into the foothold, then reach up for the handhold, hauling myself up. From here, the first step isn't so far away, but reaching it requires a back-wrenching maneuver, pushing away from the pillar and grabbing the edge in one motion.

Now I'm hanging from my palms, my feet dangling, and all I have to do is pull myself straight up with the rusty edge of the step cutting into my fingers. *No* problem.

By the time I crawl onto the step, I'm sweating freely and my biceps are trembling. I lie on my back for a moment, focused on breathing.

The canteen nearly hits me in the face, and I grab it out of the air. Meroe throws up the rest of the supplies and I set them all aside. She's sitting just under the step, with one of the poles I used from the travois in her hands.

"Ready?" I ask her.

"Probably not," she says.

"If you can't hold it, just fall," I tell her. "You can try again."

"And again, and again. Until we starve to death." Meroe grins and lifts the pole. "Just don't drop me."

The pole is long enough that when she raises her arms I can grab the end. I haul it upward, hand over hand, and Meroe uses it to pull herself to a standing position, her good leg underneath her.

Step two: get Meroe up to the bottom stair.

Step two is going to hurt.

Meroe grips the pole, squares her shoulders, and then reaches upward and starts to climb. As soon as she puts her weight on it, I know this was a bad idea. I struggle to maintain my grip, the edge of the stair digging into my arms, and try hard not to scream.

Meroe climbs, hand over hand. One of her legs kicks free, the other secured by the splint. It's only a couple of feet between us, but it feels like the gulf between worlds. A few seconds stretch into an eternity of pain.

Her fingers brush the back of my hand. I don't dare let go of the pole, not yet.

"Grab my wrist." The breath required for speech is almost too much. Meroe nods, pulls herself up one more hand's width, and her fingers close around my wrist.

I let go of the pole, which falls to the sand below, and grab her hands. Now she's dangling from my grip, with nothing to brace her legs against, and my arms are already screaming in agony. All I've got to do is unwedge my feet, sit up, and lift her up over the edge. *No* problem.

When I finally pull her up, I collapse backward, and she falls on top of me, dead weight. We lie there for what seems like hours, damp with sweat, gasping for breath. My arms are trembling, with all the strength of wet noodles.

Meroe's head is on my shoulder. I can feel her body pressed against me, the swell of her breasts, the triple-time slam of her heart. Beads of sweat roll from her hairline down the dark skin of her cheek.

"You're pretty strong," I murmur. "For a princess."

"Told you . . . I wasn't . . . useless." She rolls off of me, flopping on the step with her arms spread. "I also bake a mean quiche."

"What in the Rot is a quiche?"

"You Imperials are barbarians." She sucks in a breath. "Have I said thank you yet? For, you know, not leaving me to die when you probably should have."

"You haven't." I sit up. "And don't. We're not finished yet."

To climb the stairs, I lift Meroe onto my back, her arms around my neck, splinted leg sticking out awkwardly in front of me. Fortunately, the steps aren't very steep, winding around and around the pillar in a lazy spiral. The gray thread points straight up, as though it were a fishing line descending to snare me through the sternum.

We climb, and climb, and eventually we reach one of the circular platforms, with bridges extending out into the darkness in several directions. The gray thread points to one, taut and certain, but I set Meroe down and collapse against the pillar.

"Rest," she says, looking at me worriedly.

I take a long drink from the canteen, then heft it thoughtfully.

"I know," Meroe says. "We're going to have to make it last."

I offer it to her, and she takes a single sparing swallow. I'm too tired to argue. I lean against the pillar, head resting on Meroe's shoulder. The strange voices are there, almost comfortingly familiar in their unintelligible babble.

When I wake up, I've slumped over farther, so my head is in Meroe's lap. She's asleep, too, mouth wide open and drooling a little. Not very princess-like at all. I sit up, my abdominal muscles aching, a dull pounding in my skull. The gray thread is still there, still pointing in the same direction. I poke Meroe.

"We need to go." I still feel exhausted, but I'm not sure I'm going to get any stronger sitting here. Not once we run out of water.

"Mmm." Meroe blinks and sits up. "You're sure you're ready for this?" She yawns. "You don't want to sleep for another, you know, six days?"

I find myself grinning. "I don't want to hear any complaining. *You* can sleep on the way."

"I offer moral support," Meroe says. "Moral support can be surprisingly tiring."

In truth, she doesn't look great. There are bags under her eyes, and the flesh around her broken bone is distinctly puffy. She wraps her arms around my neck, chin on my shoulder, breathing hard.

In fairly short order my thighs are a mass of pain, my shoulders ache abominably, and each step drives knives into my lower back. We stop when I can't take it anymore, resting against a railing and chewing the strips of crab. I take another careful swallow from the canteen, and pass it to Meroe.

I can't see more than the next few steps. The Center is an enormous, three-dimensional maze, hanging in open space, but I can make out none of it. All I have to go on is the gray thread, unreeling steadily in front of me. I can feel Meroe's curiosity when we come to an intersection, but she never asks how I know which way to go.

She's gotten very quiet, in fact. When we stop, I deposit her against the rusted railing and kneel in front of her. Sweat beads on her forehead, and her hair is soaked. I press my hand to her skin, and it's hot to the touch. I ruck up her skirt to get a look at the wound, and the flesh of her thigh is dark and swollen.

"Cheeky," she says weakly, as I slide my hand up her leg. "Take me dancing first."

I roll my eyes, and pull out the canteen. It's heavier than I expected, nearly half-full, and it takes me a second to understand. "You haven't been drinking, have you?"

"Wasn't thirsty," Meroe says. Her lips are cracked, and her tongue rasps over them. Her voice has gone dreamy. "'Sides. Logical. If you collapse, we both die. If I pass out, you're already carrying me." She closes her eyes. "Or just leave me. 'S all right. Doesn't hurt. I'll just sleep awhile, and come after you when I'm feeling better."

"Meroe." When she looks up, I force the canteen into her mouth. She gags for a moment, then swallows. When I take it away, she coughs, and looks up at me resentfully.

"What are you so eager to get back for, anyway?" The water seems to have revived her a little. "You want to get back to working for the Butcher? Fighting crabs?"

"Better than dying here." I strap the canteen to my belt, significantly lighter now.

"Is it?" She looks at me, and I can see tears in her brown eyes. "Nobody leaves the ship. Is that really a life worth fighting for?"

"You fought for *your* life, even after you found out . . . what you are." I grit my teeth. "Are you giving up now?"

"Maybe my father was right."

I want to slap her. I want to take her in my arms until she stops crying. For a fleeting, weird moment I want to kiss her. Meroe's not the only one feeling a little loopy, clearly. But I push all that away and grab her by the shoulders, hoisting her up once again on my back.

"Isoka . . . ," she says.

"Listen." I take a deep breath. "I am *not* going to die on this ship, do you understand? My sister is waiting for me. She needs me. That means I'm getting out of here, no matter what."

"It must be nice to have someone waiting for you," Meroe says, talking into my shoulder.

"And I'm not leaving you behind," I go on. "Not after I've hauled you this far. You can come with me to Kahnzoka and do . . . whatever you want to do. I don't care. But you're not going to stay here, and you're not going to die."

There's a long pause.

"Always wanted to see the Empire," Meroe says in a small voice.

"You will. We'll . . ." I pause, at a loss for what Meroe might actually like about my filthy, smoky Kahnzoka. "We'll climb up the hill and visit the Emperor." And maybe pay a visit to Kuon Naga while we're at it.

"Sounds nice."

"And get the best noodles in the city. I know a place. And plum juice."

"Mmm."

I start walking. Meroe is hot against my back, like I'm carrying an oven. She's fallen asleep again, her wheezing breath whistling in my ear.

My arms have gone past pain and into tingling numbness. I don't dare stop, not now. I'd never start moving again. I follow the gray thread up stairs and around corners, across bridges and through intersections. If a crab finds us now, we're finished, because I don't have the strength left to fight a butterfly. Fortunately, all we see are more strange mushrooms and the tiny gray lights that live inside the pillars.

When change comes, I'm almost too far gone to notice it. There are lights ahead, not the distant, colorful stars but ordinary torchlight, its flickering glow supremely alien here in the darkness. Specks of it swim in front of my vision, like fireflies. I run my sticky, dry tongue over my lips.

I'm supposed to do something. What is it?

Oh yes.

"Here!" The reedy screech is the best shout I can manage. "Over here! We need help."

The torchlight pauses, then shifts. Someone has heard me.

So that's all right, then. I lay Meroe down, as gently as I can, and fall over. I'm unconscious before I hit the ground.

13

This business of waking up in strange rooms with no memory of how I got there is getting *really* old.

The unfamiliar ceiling this time is metal, the rust-flaked fabric of *Soliton*. I'm lying on a proper sleeping mat, with a heavy, tasseled blanket pulled up to my neck. The room is small, lit by oil lamps, with the usual eclectic decor. It's certainly a step up from the half-flooded cell Pack Nine called home, or even Sister Cadua's.

There's a table and two chairs on the other side of the room. Zarun is sitting there, a book open in front of him. He looks at me as I move my head, and smiles.

I sit up abruptly. The blanket falls to my waist, and I realize belatedly that I'm naked underneath. One of Zarun's eyebrow quirks, very slightly, but I refuse to frantically cover myself for his benefit. If he wants to stare at my chest so badly, let him. Blessed knows there's little enough to stare at.

"Isoka," he says. "How do you feel?"

"Better than last time," I mutter. My limbs ache, but with the deep pangs of exhaustion, not the stabbing pain of injury. "Where am I?"

"Back in the Upper Stations, in the guest quarters of my clade. It was some of my people who found you."

"Where's Meroe? Is she all right?"

"At Sister Cadua's." Zarun cocked his head. "I'm told that she had quite a severe fever, but Sister Cadua expects her to recover with treatment. She hasn't woken up yet."

A little tension goes out of my shoulders. I have no idea what position I'm in here— as usual—but at least the nightmare march wasn't all for nothing. I hike the blanket up enough to cover myself and let out a long breath.

"You're the talk of the ship," Zarun says. "Again. This is becoming a habit."

"It's not something I'm aiming for," I say. "I'm just trying not to die."

"I imagine." He smiles. "Like it or not, I'm afraid, this time your fame will be considerable. Other people have fought blueshells and won. *No one* has ever fallen into the Deeps and survived."

"Lucky me."

"They're calling you 'Deepwalker.' It has a certain ring to it."

I roll my eyes. "What are you doing here, Zarun? Just waiting for me to wake up in hopes of getting an eyeful?"

His smile widens. "I'm afraid that's only a side benefit. I wanted to speak to you before anyone else had the chance."

"Speak, then. Because I have to piss something fierce." Not a lie. Someone must have given me water while I was sleeping.

"As you wish. I would very much like to hear the story of your survival, but that can wait." He sits up a little, and his smile disappears. "The Butcher, predictably, is pressing for me to return you to her . . . care. As we discussed before your little adventure, I would not be averse to having you in my service. So, if you're willing, I am prepared to exert my influence on your behalf. It helps that you are already here, in my custody. In spite of her protestations, I can find something that will persuade the Butcher to drop her demands." He spreads his hands. "Just say the word."

"And what exactly would I do, in your service?"

"Given your talents, I imagine I'd put you in a hunting pack. Considering how well you've handled yourself so far, I'm excited to see what you could accomplish with a proper team. And, of course, you'd have better accommodations and freedom of the market, like any of my other crew."

I wouldn't be a prisoner, in other words. Definitely a step up. Which is the goal—keep moving upward until I get to the top— but there are a few complications.

"Can I think about it?"

He shrugs. "If you wish, but not forever. I can only stall negotiations for so long."

"Just give me a few minutes." I glance at the door, which here is a real door instead of a curtain. "Alone, if you don't mind."

"Of course." He picks up his book and gets to his feet.

"And I'd like my clothes."

He wrinkles his nose. "I'm afraid what you were wearing was . . . not in a fit state. I've taken the liberty of having new clothes made ready." He waves to a silver-inlaid wooden trunk in the corner of the room. "If there's anything you need, please ask."

"Fine." I don't like taking gifts from Zarun, but it can't be helped. Between my blood and the crabs', my old outfit had gotten a bit foul.

"And . . ." He hesitates, still looking at me. "I'm not sure if you had the chance to look in a mirror, on your adventure, but . . ."

This confuses me for a moment, until I remember the marks. I touch my face, where I know the blue lines criss-cross my skin, though it feels no different under my finger.

"I'm aware," I tell him.

"They suit you, I think." He grins. "I look forward to hearing the story of exactly how you acquired them."

I stare at him pointedly until he leaves. Once the door is closed, I kick off the blanket and get to my feet, stretching and wincing as my muscles pop. My skin is clean, which brings up the unpleasant image of someone washing me while I was unconscious. I thrust that thought aside and kick open the chest to find a set of trousers, a tooled leather vest, and underclothes, along with my old boots, now washed and brushed. The vest has a low scooped neckline and is a little more *decorative* than I like, but it's a hell of a lot better than nothing.

There's a silver ewer of water on the table, and a chamber pot underneath it. After making use of first the one and then the other, I'm feeling considerably more comfortable, and ready to think a little harder about Zarun's offer. I knock at the door, and it's opened by a young Imperial boy in a similar outfit. He bows and directs me through a larger room, where several mismatched chairs are set in a half circle. Zarun sits in one, and Thora and Jack share another, the slight Jack sitting half on Thora's lap. Two more chairs are occupied by people I don't know. Flunkies of Zarun's, I assume.

"Welcome," he says, waving a hand but making no offer to find me a place to sit. "You look much improved, I must say. Your resilience is remarkable."

"I've often been compared to a cockroach," I deadpan.

"A very pretty cockroach," Jack says dreamily. "I like the blue. It's a good look for you, Deepwalker. Ow," she adds, as Thora knuckles her on the head in warning. "Just stating a fact."

"Have you considered my offer?" Zarun says.

"What about the rest of Pack Nine?" I don't want to give away that it's mostly Meroe I'm concerned about, though I suspect Zarun can guess.

"Ahdron is Pack Nine's leader, and he's still pledged to the Butcher," Zarun says. "So they stay with her."

Is it my imagination, or is there a hint of expectation there? "What if he wasn't leader?"

Zarun shrugs, his expression all false innocence. "If Pack Nine were to get a new leader, through a formal challenge, then in theory that leader would be free to choose an allegiance or stay independent. In practice, independence is . . . difficult."

"Why's that?"

"'Cause if you don't have anyone backing you up," Jack says, "there's nothing to stop the Butcher from sending a pack round to break your legs if you don't swear service."

"Fine." I lock eyes with Zarun. "And if I were to swear allegiance to you?"

"Then I suppose I would be obligated to exert my influence on behalf of my new pack," Zarun says. His eyes twinkle.

I grit my teeth for a moment. I would rather *not* be in debt to Zarun, but it looks like on *Soliton*, like on the streets of Kahnzoka, trying to live without a patron is futile. Zarun is currently the best candidate in a field of one. At least pack leaders have some status, so I'll be better off than if I simply joined his clade. And Meroe and the others will be safe.

I can always betray him later.

Pack Nine, they tell me, has been moved to quarters on the Middle Deck. Thora escorts me outside to provide directions. Zarun's clade lives in one of the nine square towers that define the limits of the Upper Stations, according to Thora generally considered the most desirable real estate on the ship.

Once we go outside, smaller buildings are packed in tight, edged by the same street market I saw the last time I was here. The ceiling is high above, and I can see a cloudy night sky through the rusted-out gaps.

"So why is *this* the place to live?" I ask her, as she leads me through the crowd. "This ship is so big every person here could build a palace with room to spare."

Thora smiles at me. She has a kind face, for an iceling, ringed by stray blond curls. Like many of the northerners, she's enormous, a full head taller than me and broader in the shoulders than most Imperial men. Among the icelings, the Butcher must count as merely oversized instead of gigantic.

"You've seen the rest of the ship by now. More of it than anyone else, actually, if the stories are true. The problem isn't lack of space; it's keeping the crabs out." She points into the middle distance, beyond the nearest row of shacks. "See the wall?"

It takes me a moment. It's a ramshackle thing, uniform only in its ten-foot height, made out of metal plates, pieces of crab shell, broken planks, and whatever else came to hand. At first I'd taken it for the back of another line of houses.

"*That* keeps the crabs out?" I ask.

"The smaller ones. The hunting packs intercept anything bigger." She gestures at the huge square towers, arranged in a regular grid. "Originally we only defended the space between four of those, in the corner of this deck. Five years ago, the Council decided to expand the wall to nine. Someday we'll have enough manpower to push it out again."

"What about the Middle Deck and the Drips?"

"They're all just corridors, so they're easy to block off with doors and barricades. But the rooms are smaller and the ceilings are lower, so everyone would rather live up here if they can afford it."

I smile, just a little, because it reminds me of home. The Sixteenth Ward, crammed in along the shoreline and breathing the stink of rotting fish, with the rest of the wards stacked up above it one after another, all the way up to the Imperial Ward on the breezy summit of the hill. If the Emperor could have devised a way to build the higher wards directly on top of the lower ones, no doubt it would have made things easier.

"Here we are," Thora says. Where two streets cross, there's a hole in the deck, and a stairway leading down. "Your pack's quarters should be right down there; take the first left and look for a door. If you get lost, just ask around."

"Thanks."

She looks down at me, considering. "Zarun's not as bad as he seems, you know."

"Five minutes after I arrived, I watched him cut a little girl's head off."

Thora winces. "He can be . . . harsh. But he rewards loyalty with loyalty. If you prove you're trustworthy, he'll always back you up."

"I'll keep that in mind," I say.

"I still want to hear what happened in the Deeps," she says. "Come find me, and I'll buy you a drink. I suspect a lot of other people will, too."

"I'll take you up on that," I say. "The story's not as exciting as you're probably hoping, though." Because I'm certainly not telling them about Hagan.

"Add a few flourishes, then." Thora smiles again. "Good luck, Deepwalker."

The name makes my skin prickle, but I just nod cordially. Thora turns away, back toward Zarun's quarters.

It occurs to me that, for the first time, I'm free in the "civilized" part of *Soliton*. No one is escorting me or dragging me anywhere or locking me in, and part of my mind urges me to run for it. Find somewhere to hide, disappear, gather information until I'm ready to make a move.

These are well-honed instincts from years on the streets, but they're almost certainly wrong. *Soliton* just isn't big enough for these kinds of tactics to be effective. The ship itself is huge, of course, but the crew here in the Stern can't be more than a few thousand people. You can't *hide* in a place like that, where everyone knows everyone else at least by reputation. It makes me feel horribly exposed, deprived of the anonymizing crowds of the city streets that I could wrap around myself like a comforting blanket.

Besides, I don't have time to take things cautiously. And when Meroe wakes up—

As though in answer to my thoughts, a few people on the street are staring openly at me. One says something to another in a language I don't speak, but I catch the word "Deepwalker."

Spectacular.

I trot down the stairs, two at a time. The Middle Deck is where I was first brought to see the Butcher, I realize, a maze of metal corridors opening on to rooms of various sizes. I turn left, as instructed, and walk quickly down an empty hallway to a curtained doorway. I hesitate at the threshold; am I supposed to knock?

From inside, someone short-cuts my dilemma. "Isoka? Is that you?"

I push the curtain aside. The room is smaller than the cell we were in previously, but in much better shape, with no standing water or rotting carpets. Sleeping mats are set against one wall, a low table with cushions in the center, and a few heavy clay jars stand by the door. Other than that, it's empty, bare metal floor and walls. I suppose Ahdron hasn't had the time to decorate.

In the back, a doorway leads off to a smaller room, blocked by another curtain. The pack leader is nowhere in sight, but Berun is at the table and the Moron is sitting cross-legged in one corner, in much the same position he used to sit in on the little island.

"Isoka!" Berun gets up. "I heard they found you, but . . ."

"Yes," I confirm wearily. "I'm still alive."

"They told us Meroe is at Sister Cadua's," Berun says, anxiously. "Do you know—"

"I haven't seen her, but I heard she'll be all right."

"Thank the Blessed." He swallows. "What . . . what happened to your face?"

The blue marks. Rot. Time to lie.

"It's fine," I tell him. "I hurt myself in the fall. We found a mushroom that helped a bit, but it left these marks behind." I offer my arm, where another line of curlicues wraps around my biceps.

"It's . . . interesting," he says. "I'm glad you're all right."

"Thanks." My patience for Berun isn't particularly strong at the moment. "Where's Ahdron?"

"In the back. He's taken it for his bedroom."

I stride past Berun, and he turns to follow me, almost skipping to keep up.

"Um," he says. "Do you know what's going to happen to us?"

"Not yet," I growl, and push aside the curtain.

Ahdron's "bedroom" is just another metal space with a blanket and cushions on the floor. I suppose the sacrifices to *Soliton* don't include a lot of furniture. He's sitting with his back to the wall, a clay jug in one hand, and he grins at me as I come in.

"Isoka," he says. "Gods be damned. Or should I call you Deepwalker now?"

"'Isoka' is fine," I tell him. He looks much as he did before we left to fight the hammerhead, though his hands are wrapped in bandages. Powerburn, I assume. He really was trying to kill the thing.

"I didn't think . . ." He shakes his head. "You can't blame me for not expecting you to come back from that."

"I wasn't so optimistic myself, to be honest."

I watch his eyes search my face, hesitate for a moment on the new marks, then move on. "You're all right?"

"More or less."

"And you want to know where we stand," Ahdron says. He takes a pull from the clay jug. "As you can see, Pack Nine's circumstances have improved."

"No doubt the Butcher was grateful to you for coming home without me."

"She would have been happy if we'd all died down there," he says. "But since we didn't, and since you killed the hammerhead, she's happy to take advantage of our success. I'm not sure if she and I are *entirely* square"—he takes another drink, and I get a whiff of alcohol—"but we're not on probation anymore."

"What did you do that made her so angry, anyway?"

He shrugs. "Rutted the wrong girl. How was I supposed to know she had her eye on her?"

I had figured it was something like that. Men like Ahdron are always letting their pricks get them into trouble.

Quit stalling, Isoka.

The problem is that I can't hate Ahdron. He acts like a bully because a bigger bully is sitting on his back, a situation with which I'm intimately familiar. He was probably earnest about helping me, even if it mostly meant helping himself. At the very least, he's not actively trying to get me killed.

And I'm about to cut his legs out from under him. Or kill him, if it comes to that.

Oh, well.

"—I think we can keep working our way up," he's saying. "Now that we're off probation, we can choose our own targets, and between you and me we should be able to make a lot of scrip quickly. That might let us bring in another—"

"Shut up and listen for a minute," I tell him.

He pauses, eyes narrowing. "Someone wants you to leave?"

I shrug.

"The Butcher won't stand for it." He cocks his head. "Are you going to do it?"

"No."

"Good choice. They may say they can protect you, but—"

"I'm not leaving. I'm taking the pack." I fix him with a stare. "Consider this my formal challenge."

There's a long silence.

"You're not serious," Ahdron says, lifting the bottle to his lips.

"Of course I'm rotting serious."

"Do you have any idea what the Butcher will do to you?"

"Let me worry about the Butcher," I tell him.

"You *are* serious." He sets the bottle aside and clambers to his feet. "You haven't been here a rotting week, *Deepwalker*. You think you know how things work on *Soliton*?"

He steps closer, squeezing my space, and I don't give ground. "It's not a matter of what I know," I say. "It's a matter of whether you think you can take me on."

"You rotting Melos types are always so rotting confident," he sneers. "You think I've never killed one of you before?"

"You've never fought *me*." I force a smile. "Concede the point and you can stay in the pack. You'd make a good subordinate."

"Freeze and rot," he says. "We had a *deal*."

"Circumstances have changed."

"Get out."

"I want an answer."

"As the challenged party, I have a day and a night to respond." His lip curls. "Not that you would know the first rotting thing about it."

"Tomorrow, then."

"I was wrong about you," he says. "I thought you were smart, Isoka."

"If it's any consolation," I tell him from the doorway, "I was right about you."

Ahdron is correct on one point—I don't really know what I'm doing. I don't know my way around *Soliton* yet, much less the rules of power struggles. I don't even know how to buy food, or a place to sleep.

But all that can wait. If this works, I'll have time to get my legs under me. And if it doesn't work, I'll be dead, which means Tori goes to the whorehouse and Blessed knows what happens to Meroe. So it has to work.

When you're on the bottom, you have to take risks. It's the only way up.

I find my way to Sister Cadua's in a series of false starts and bad directions. A tall Imperial woman meets me at the familiar curtained doorway, and now that I'm looking for it I can see her eyes flick to the marks on my face before she looks away.

"Yes," I say, before she can speak. "It's me. From all the rumors."

"You want to see your friend?" she says.

"Please."

She nods and leads me inside. We pass a number of doorways before she gestures me into a small room, where Meroe is laid out. I'm relieved to see that she already looks better than I remember, scrapes and bruises fading, breathing easily. My makeshift splint is gone, replaced with a sturdier version.

There's a chair beside the bed, and I sit down, suddenly feeling a weight of exhaustion. For a while I just watch Meroe breath, staring at the rich brown of her skin, the delicate little upturn of her nose.

I remember the first night in the Deeps, pressed together for warmth. It's warm enough, here, but I imagine climbing into bed beside her, huddling close. Just to be there when she wakes up. Just to feel . . .

Blessed's rotting balls. I don't understand myself anymore.

"Miss Isoka?"

I startle. I must have fallen into a doze without realizing it. Now another woman is in the room with me. She looks Jyashtani, though her skin is almost as dark as Meroe's. Shorter than me, broad and heavyset, she has an air of unmistakable authority.

"Sister Cadua?" I guess.

She nods. "It's good to meet you." Her Imperial is accented, but fluent, like that of most of the people I've met here. She nods to Meroe. "She's doing well. Were you the one who set her leg?"

"I hope I didn't screw it up too badly."

Sister Cadua gives a small smile. "Not *too* badly. It should heal clean, though it will take some time."

"Good." I look back at Meroe. "Do you know when she'll wake up?"

"Soon, I imagine. By tomorrow, unless there's something wrong I don't know about."

I nod. Sister Cadua leans close to me, examining my face with a professional eye.

"You look exhausted."

"It's been a busy day," I admit.

"You can go home," she says. "I'll send someone when she comes to."

"Home is . . . a bit tricky at the moment."

"Ah." She pauses. "There's an empty bed in the next room. And we could spare you a bowl of crab juice, I daresay."

"Very kind," I say. "And the catch?"

"I'd like to examine you."

I turn that over in my head for a while, but it seems only fair. Sister Cadua is all brisk efficiency. She hustles me into the next room, and I strip off my new clothes and stand patiently while she walks around me. She touches the marks, carefully.

"They don't hurt?"

I shake my head. "Feels perfectly ordinary."

"And you say these came from some kind of mushroom?"

"Yes," I say, belatedly realizing this might not have been such a good idea. Sister Cadua seems sharp enough to poke holes in my hasty cover story. "It wasn't like anything I've seen up here," I improvise. "Probably only lives in the Deeps."

"Hmm." She frowns. "Could you sketch it?"

"Meroe would do a better job, once she wakes up."

She nods. "It sounds like a useful thing to add to our repertoire. I may suggest an expedition to retrieve some."

"I don't know if I could find my way back to the exact spot," I say.

Sister Cadua waves a hand. "It will be difficult, of course. But without a Ghul talent in the crew, we need all the help we can get."

I yawn. "You must get some ghulwitches as sacrifices."

"Less frequently than you might think," she says. "The only one

I know of served in Shiara's clade, but he was killed more than a year ago."

There's more to that story, but her expression warns me not to dig into it. I'm certainly not about to tell anyone Meroe's secret, even if it still gives me the creeps when I think about it too hard. Sister Cadua indicates that I should get dressed, and leans out into the hall to summon a bowl of crab juice.

"It'll be just the one night, you understand," she says. "We need the space for the injured, most of the time."

"Don't worry," I tell her. "After tomorrow, I'll have somewhere to go."

14

I spend another uncomfortable night in the stupid Jyashtani-style bed, suspended several feet above the floor for no readily apparent reason. At least the crab juice, the soup of miscellaneous crab parts and mushrooms ubiquitous on *Soliton*, is hot and delicious.

In the morning, I go back to Meroe's room. She's still asleep, and a young man in dark robes is carefully giving her water. He pauses as she moans, and shifts uneasily.

"Her fever has come down nicely," Sister Cadua says, when she bustles in. "She's going to be fine, though of course the leg will take some time to heal."

I remember the feeling of the hammerhead's jaws closing on my own leg, the snap of breaking bones and the hot gush of blood from shredded flesh. Now the only evidence is a ring of curling blue marks around my calf, thanks to Meroe. My stomach still lurches when I think about her power, but not as badly as it once might have.

Sister Cadua and her assistant leave me alone with Meroe. Her features are smooth now, calm. Her eyes quiver, shifting restlessly under closed lids. I wish she'd wake up.

There's a knock on the wall beside the curtain doorway, and a hesitant voice. "Isoka?"

It's Berun, looking even more nervous than usual. I force a smile, trying to put him at his ease, but it doesn't seem to have the intended effect. I don't have a lot of practice *not* frightening people. Better to get to the point.

"What's going on?" I ask him.

He's looking past me, to Meroe. His eyes are wide. "Is she really going to be all right?"

"Sister Cadua says she'll be fine," I say, irritably. The way he looks at her bothers me. "What are you doing here?"

He looks back at me and swallows hard. "Ahdron sent me."

"Is he ready to talk?"

Berun shakes his head, miserably. "He says . . . he accepts your challenge. He'll be waiting in the Ring at midday."

I look at him blankly. "The Ring?"

"It's where formal challenges are fought," Berun says. "So there can be witnesses."

Rot. I'd hoped Ahdron would come to his senses. "Did he tell you anything else?"

Berun shakes his head again. "But . . ."

"But what?"

"I shouldn't tell you this." He glances at Meroe. "The Butcher came to our quarters last night. She and Ahdron talked for a long time."

Which explains a lot. No doubt the Butcher promised him her favor if he kills me. So much for Ahdron coming to his senses.

Rot them both, then. We'll do this the hard way.

"Okay," I tell Berun. "I'm going to go and get this over with."

"But . . ." He looks like he's about to cry. "Ahdron is . . . strong. You should apologize. He might—"

"Stay here with Meroe," I say, ignoring him. "If she wakes up, tell her I'll be back soon. Can you do that?"

"I'll tell her. But what if—"

"Tell her," I grate, "I'll be back."

Berun blinks, and nods.

It can't be long until midday, so I don't have time to waste. Fortunately, the Ring isn't hard to find. All I have to do is follow the crowd. Apparently the news that the infamous Deepwalker will be fighting has spread rapidly, and a steady stream of crew drifts down the ragged street. Word of what I look like has spread, too, and I can hear the whispers around me, see the glances at the marks on my face. I keep my eyes fixed ahead, ignoring them.

The Ring isn't as elaborate as I imagined. It's just a large, clear area of deck, roughly circular, surrounded by a chest-high barrier improvised from scrap metal. A single gate leads inside, and rising platforms around the perimeter provide somewhere for crowds to stand and watch. Opposite the gate, there's a dais, like one of the fancy boxes at the theater, with a half-dozen chairs.

Much of the arena is already ringed with crew. The sound of conversation dies as I walk through the gate, leaving a moment of silence. Then it returns, much louder. I look around, but I don't see Ahdron. I must be early.

The platform is occupied, though. I assume it's for the officers, because I recognize Zarun's lean, handsome face, and the massive, armored figure of the Butcher. I don't know the others. An Imperial girl, younger than me, in a silk *kizen* with a wide-brimmed hat and wispy veil, sits in an elegant, correct posture. Beside her is a tall, broad-shouldered young man, with the same light brown skin and broad features as Ahdron, wearing martial leathers and an inscrutable expression.

The final chair is occupied by a boy close to my own age, with classically Jyashtani features and wearing the loose black-and-white clothes I've seen on their traders in Kahnzoka. He has round spectacles that catch the light, reminding me for a moment of Kuon Naga, and holds a tall wooden cane in one hand, tapping it idly against the platform. While all eyes are on me, he seems to be watching with particular interest. I return his stare for a moment, then glance at Zarun, who raises his eyebrows knowingly. The Butcher is glaring, but I avoid her eyes. Then the tenor of the crowd noise changes, and I turn around.

Ahdron comes in through the gate. He's dressed in thick, dark leather, closer to armor than what he wore on our hunts, and he has a round shield strapped to his left arm and a sword at his belt. I watch him carefully as he crosses the floor of the Ring. Fighting crabs, Ahdron didn't seem particularly well trained, but there's a confidence in his stance now. He stops a few feet away from me, scowling.

"Forgive me if I don't know the procedure," I tell him. "Are we supposed to bow?"

"Go and rot," he says, jaw clenched.

"You don't have to do this," I say. "This is your chance to get out from under the Butcher's thumb for good. What did she offer you to kill me?"

He glances up at the officers. "We had an agreement," he says. "And you stabbed me in the back."

"Forgive me if I'd rather not spend my life working for someone who wants me dead." I yawn, stretching my arms over my head. "And I haven't stabbed you anywhere. Yet."

"So rotting cocky." His right hand clenches tight, and wisps of smoke rise from between his fingers. "Is that how you got chosen as a sacrifice? Mouthed off to the wrong person?"

"More or less."

"Ahdron, leader of Pack Nine." One of the officers stands up, the big warrior, his voice booming across the ring. "Isoka Deepwalker. Are you ready?"

Ahdron nods, tightly. I give a nonchalant wave.

"The challenge is recognized by the Captain and the Council," he says. "The victor will be the new pack leader. The winner will accept the loser's surrender, and show mercy." He raises a hand, then lets it fall. "Begin."

I'm not expecting any mercy from Ahdron. Killing me would please the Butcher, and I'm certain he's eager to curry favor. And, all bluster aside, I'm having doubts.

I've spent my life fighting. Half the time, that alone is enough of an advantage. Most people, even criminals and thugs, avoid violence if they can help it, unless it's against people who can't fight back. When you go up against a gang of street toughs, you can see in their eyes who the real hard men are, and who's spent their time kicking people while they're down.

Ahdron has the look. He's done this before. And, in a crucial way, he's more experienced than I am. On *Soliton,* everyone's a mage-blood, and if he's not bluffing, Ahdron's even faced Melos users before. I've never fought anyone with their own Well before, much less an adept.

Some things are obvious, though. I have to stay close to him. If he opens the range, he can throw fire at me until my armor overheats and I have to choose between being cooked by powerburn or Myrkai flames. In close, if he has to face me with an ordinary sword and shield, my blades and armor should give me an advantage. I hope.

I ignite my blades with a *crack-hiss,* and Melos green shimmers across my body, earthing itself in crackling lightning on the deck. To my surprise, Ahdron doesn't back away to gain distance, or even go for his sword. Instead, he flexes the fingers on his right hand and drops into a crouch. A ball of flame appears in his palm, the air around it shimmering with heat haze.

First move to me, then. I come in fast on his unshielded right side. He releases the fireball as soon as I move, and it impacts on my arms as I bring them up to block. A wash of heat ripples across my armor, but it's nothing serious. More dangerous is the fact that for a moment he's hidden from view by the flash and smoke, and when I come out the other side he's shifted stance, leading with his shield.

I swing my left-hand blade at his head, a wide, slow stroke he can see coming a mile away, then shift my balance at the last minute and punch out with the other blade, going for his belly. If he'd bought the feint, it would have run him through, but he's too good for that. He ducks, letting one blade slash over his head, and takes the second blow on his shield. Energy screeches against steel as my blade slides off in a shower of sparks and crackling green lightning. I spin past and away, but not before he reaches for me with his empty right hand. I get a brief glimpse of white-hot fire—

There's a moment of blinding heat and exquisite pain. I'm not certain if I scream.

Blessed's rotting *balls,* that hurts.

Between blinks, I'm on the deck, curled up on my side, wild

discharges of green Melos power arcing and sputtering all around me. Ahdron is standing over me, his hand still glowing, gouts of smoke rising from it. The air smells like scorched metal.

"I *told* you I'd fought your kind before," Ahdron says. "You didn't believe me. I knew you wouldn't. Too cocky by half, all of you Melos types." He closes his fist in a puff of smoke. "Your armor may stop a bolt of fire, but up close, I can make things a lot hotter."

No rotting kidding. But I'm not as badly wounded as he seems to think. My armor *did* stop the blow, even if the powerburn hurt like the Blessed's own cattle brand. Ahdron hasn't fought a Melos adept as strong as I am. I lie still a moment longer, blades sputtering and arcing to the deck. He takes a step closer.

"I'm not going to ask you to surrender," he says, too quietly for anyone but us to hear. "But lie still and I can make this quick."

Unfortunately, he's not stupid. Before he bends down to jam that white-hot fist into my face, he puts his boot on my arm, and he keeps his shield in front of him. That reduces my options, but he's still clearly not expecting me to be able to move. I swing my free arm low, under the rim of his shield, and the blade chops into the meat of his leg with a *crackle* and a smell of burning flesh. He shouts and stumbles back, and the injured leg gives way underneath him, sending him to one knee. I roll away, gaining distance.

Pulling myself to my feet brings a fresh wave of pain from my side, and I blink away tears. He gets up at the same time, teeth gritted, clearly hurt but still able to stand. I raise my blades, staring at him through a field of crackling green.

"Surrender?" I force a smile.

"Rotting . . . *bitch*," he hisses, through clenched teeth.

I take this as a no. He raises his free hand and unleashes a gout of flame, Myrkai power washing over me. My armor flares, but it's mild compared to the concentrated heat he can deliver up close, a distraction rather than an attack. I charge, swinging left to get out of the blast, and he turns to meet me shield first. I lash out with one blade, then the other, Melos power leaving blackened streaks on the metal and notches in the rim. When he tries to counter, open hand darting forward full of white-hot flame, I step back and slash down, and he has to retreat to avoid losing his fingers.

For long seconds, we dance like this, my blades hacking at his interposed shield, him trying to get a hand on me without getting it chopped off. His power may be vicious, but it means he lacks reach, and we're briefly at a stalemate. I become aware, for the first time, of the sound of the crowd, a vast, ocean-like roar of cheers, screams, and curses. As we circle, the officers come into view, the Butcher watching with a sneer, Zarun regarding us calmly over folded hands.

Ahdron backpedals, pelting me with small bursts of fire, hoping to wear me down. I bull through them, trusting my armor. Between the washes of fire and smoke, I watch him. I watch his feet, the way he drags his leg, and when the time is right I lunge.

He takes one strike on his battered shield, but I aim the other low, and he has to give ground. But he's off balance, and when he puts his weight on his bad leg it folds. He goes down hard, shield ringing against the metal of the deck, and he's wide open.

Step forward, reach down, thrust, and twist. The easiest thing in the world. I've already begun the motion when something catches my eye, movement in the stands, a familiar face forcing her way to the edge of the ring. Meroe.

Berun is beside her, but in that instant all I can see are Meroe's eyes, wide as a cat's at night. I hear her voice in my head.

"You've done that before, haven't you?"

"What?"

"Killed people."

I see Shiro's face. The girl who'd been unlucky enough to be in Firello's when I came calling, begging through her tears. Hagan's last look at me, his trust.

I see myself through Meroe's eyes. *Monster.*

I don't pause for long, but it's long enough. Ahdron fights through and lets loose with another blast of flame, blinding heat raging all around me. I have to back away, gasping for breath, the pain from my armor rising to bone-deep agony. I can't keep this up much longer.

"Surrender," I manage. Now I'm the one gritting my teeth.

Ahdron, somehow, is getting back to his feet. Blood drenches his calf, and he's limping, but he's still up. He can see me weakening.

"Go rot," he says.

The crowd is screaming, and my armor crackles and sparks. Through it all, I hear her calling my name.

"Isoka!" Meroe's voice is hoarse. *"Isoka!"*

I lock eyes with Ahdron.

So I'm a rotting monster. It's not like I didn't know that already.

I come at him again, as his hand blazes white fire. A descending slash with my right-hand blade and he raises his shield to meet it. I bring the other blade around, and he twists to intercept that, too—

—and I let the blade vanish. I grab the jagged rim of his shield, green lightning shimmering and crawling as my armor touches the metal. I pull, hard, and he takes a stumbling half step forward, hopping on his good leg. Too close. I shift left, inside his guard, and as he tries to lean back and get his shield between us I bring the other blade up, an underhand blow that punches the spike of Melos power into his ribs. Then I spin away, fast and smooth, because he's still flailing with his white-hot palm.

Ahdron stays on his feet for a couple of breaths, weaving like a drunk. His eyes find mine again, and there's nothing in them but bewildered pain, as though he doesn't understand how this happened. Then he coughs, and blood coats his teeth and dribbles down his chin. He falls, first to his knees and then facedown on the deck, and goes still.

I take another step back, letting my armor fade, the air wonderfully cool on my superheated skin. My breath is ragged, and my side feels like it's been shredded, but I manage to turn to face the officers' box. I can't find Meroe in the crowd anymore.

The rage on the Butcher's face is easy to see. The Imperial girl smiles and licks her lips, as though she's seen something appetizing. The big warrior, who'd spoken to start the duel, gets to his feet.

"Isoka Deepwalker. Your challenge has been witnessed." He nods, gravely. "Pack Nine is yours."

*   *   *

For once, I manage to stay on my feet after a fight, though it's a near-run thing.

Whatever custom kept the crowd out of the Ring while the fight was in progress apparently doesn't apply once it's over, because the spectators vault the wall and crowd around. The air is full of excited shouting in a dozen languages, young crew in the outfits of the officers' clades mixing with scavengers and civilians. Objects were changing hands—bits of dyed crab shell, collected on long strings. Money, I realize, or what passes for it here. Of course they were betting on my life or death.

A group of younger girls pushes their way through the crowd to Ahdron's body. Once they lift it, people make way for them. His blood patters to the deck as they bear him away, and one arm dangles limply. I wonder what they'll do with him.

"Isoka!"

I have only a moment to brace before Meroe is on top of me, wrapping her arms around me and pulling me close. I feel hypersensitive, as though every nerve in my body had been scraped raw. There's pain from my burns, the dull ache of exhaustion in my muscles, the twinges from old bruises. The slam of my heart against my ribs, slowing down from its galloping pace, and the rasp of breath in my lungs. Meroe, pressed tight to me, the frizz of her hair on my chin, the shape of her body against my own. The smell of blood, sweat, and burnt flesh.

She must have said something, because the next thing I know she's peering at my face in concern.

"Isoka, can you hear me? Do you need to go to Sister Cadua?"

"I'm all right." I can barely hear myself over the noise of the crowd. They're all around me but hesitate to come too close, leaving me and Meroe in the middle of a small, empty space. "Are you . . ."

She nods. I notice for the first time that she's leaning on me to stay up, her broken leg still splinted. Berun is standing at the edge of the circle, holding a leather-topped crutch.

"I think we need somewhere to sit down," I tell her.

But where do we go now? I crane my head, looking for the

officers' platform and trying to find Zarun. The chairs are empty, except for the Jyashtani boy with the glasses, who's watching the crowd with an amused expression. I spot the big warrior talking to some crew, but the others are lost in the mob. There's no sign of the Butcher.

"Fresh meat no longer!" Someone steps into the circle. It's Jack, tall and slim, wearing a fey grin. "Isoka Pack-Leader, now. Isoka Deepwalker. And beautiful Meroe, of course." She bows. "Zarun has sent me to fetch you from this mess, if you require fetching." She cocks her head. "Do you? Or would you rather bask in your glory a little longer?"

"I've basked plenty," I tell her, and Meroe nods agreement. She reaches out to Berun, who hands over the crutch. I stay close behind her, ready to grab her if she falls, but she's surprisingly adept.

Jack moves her hands like she's parting a curtain, and the crowd opens up in front of her, the crew once again giving her a wide berth. She laughs delightedly and leads us down the narrow corridor.

"Make way!" she says. "Make way for the fearsome Deepwalker and Clever Jack!"

Outside the Ring, we reach clear streets and Jack directs us to the tower where I'd first awoken. I'm expecting to return to the chambers where I met Zarun, but we go in a different door, and then through a curtained doorway off a long corridor. It leads to a large, nearly empty room, with three more doorways at the back. A rickety wooden table and a pair of elaborately carved chairs are the only furnishings.

"Where are we?" I ask Jack, when she turns and spreads her arms in a grand gesture.

"Why, the quarters of the illustrious Pack Nine!" she says. "Only the best for the latest and most deadly of Zarun's hunters."

"Quarters *here*?" Berun says, from behind us. "In the Upper Stations?"

"As I said," Jack said. "Zarun is a generous master."

"I thought . . . ," Meroe says, looking at me.

"I'll explain in a minute." I look at Jack. "It's done, then? Between Zarun and the Butcher?"

She nods. "Yes, I believe it is. My master can tell you more. I'll go and find him, if you don't mind. He asked to be summoned when you were comfortably ensconced." She turns to Berun, then back to me. "I understand there is one more member of your merry company?"

"The Moron," I say.

"Don't call him that," Meroe says.

I shrug, uncomfortably. "I don't know his real name."

"I'll go get him," Berun says. "There's some things I want to pick up."

"Well and good!" Jack practically skips to the door, taking Berun by the arm. "We shall all reunite anon."

There's a moment of silence after the two of them slip out.

"'Anon'?" I shake my head. "Who *talks* like that?"

"She's certainly . . . colorful." Meroe carefully lowers herself into one of the chairs, leaning her crutch against the table. I take the other chair, gratefully. My side twinges, and I wince. She frowns. "Are you sure you're all right?"

"It hurts," I say, with a shrug. "I'll live. But what about you? I left you with Sister Cadua—"

"I think I woke up about a minute after you left," Meroe says. "Sister Cadua wanted to keep me in bed, but Berun let slip that you were fighting someone, and I couldn't just . . ." She shakes her head and takes a deep breath. "I had to see."

"I'm sorry I wasn't there."

"Isoka, please. When I woke up I was honestly shocked I wasn't dead." Her voice goes quiet. "You dragged us out of the Deeps."

"Where I would have died, if not for you."

"I—" She grins. "All right. Let's just agree that we made a good team."

"Fair enough." I find myself fighting a grin of my own. I can still see Ahdron's puzzled face, feel his shudder as I ran him through. I'm still a monster, and my side rotting *hurts*. But Meroe is smiling at me.

"So what happened with the Butcher and Zarun?" she says. "Why were you fighting Ahdron?"

My grin vanishes. I take a deep breath and explain, as best I can—Zarun's rescue, and the deal he offered. My counteroffer, and his terms.

"Why?" Meroe says. "What's so important about being leader of Pack Nine?"

My hands tighten, gripping my trousers. "I wasn't going to leave you for the Butcher."

"Oh." Meroe looks down at the table.

"I didn't—" I swallow. I keep seeing myself through her eyes, bloodstained and brutal. "I didn't *want* it to work out this way. I hoped Ahdron would give in without a fight. I thought—" I shake my head. "Sorry. No excuses."

"I . . ." Meroe hesitates. "I can't say that I *liked* Ahdron. But I didn't ask you to kill him for me."

"I know." My stomach roils, like I'm about to vomit. "I told you I'm not a good person, Meroe. This is what I do. I hurt people."

There's a long pause.

"I don't blame you," Meroe says. "I . . . don't want people to get hurt. But sometimes there's no other way. My father told me that, once." She's smiling again, a sad smile full of old pain.

"I'm still going to get us both out of here," I tell her. "Trust me."

She meets my eye. "I do."

There's the sound of footsteps in the corridor outside, and a moment later Zarun enters, with Thora and Jack behind him. He gives a little half bow, blue eyes sparkling.

"Forgive me if I don't get up," I tell him.

"Of course," Zarun says. "You're the champion of the hour. And it was well fought, I must say. I knew you were tough, but I had no idea you were such an artist."

I shrug, uncomfortably. "You've got what you wanted."

"I have indeed. The Butcher was kind enough to wager the fate of Pack Nine on the contest, so she has grudgingly agreed to accept my terms. As of now, you are under my protection." He repeats the bow in Meroe's direction. "Welcome, Princess."

"Just 'Meroe,'" she says, voice guarded. She still doesn't trust Zarun.

"Of course," he murmurs, turning back to me. "As pack leader, you'll be responsible for choosing your own hunts."

"With your . . . advice, I imagine."

"I strive to be helpful, with you being so new." Zarun smiles. "To that end, Thora and Jack will be joining you."

Jack is grinning like a lunatic, which seems appropriate for her. "Pledges of eternal loyalty, pack leader!"

"We'll try to earn our keep," Thora says, more subdued.

I don't think any of us doubt for a moment what's really going on here. Zarun used my challenge to steal Pack Nine from the Butcher, and he needs to protect his investment. Thus he assigns me "subordinates" to serve as minders.

I don't object. He's right that I'll need the help, and if the time comes when we need to move against Zarun I'm sure we can evade them. Or kill them.

"Thank you," I tell the three of them. "I appreciate the assistance."

Zarun waves a hand at our surroundings. "The quarters are yours for as long as you want them. And if there's anything else you need . . ."

I bow my head respectfully. "Again, thank you."

"One more thing. Next week, the Council of Officers will meet in public session. My colleagues have asked me to say that they would be very pleased if you were to present yourself."

I'm sure the Butcher will be *thrilled*. But there's no use trying to duck her. If I'm going to use my new position to get to the Captain, getting close to the officers is the next step. I give a quick nod.

Zarun steps forward, unexpectedly, and takes my hand. I have to work not to snatch it away. "The public sessions are . . . somewhat formal occasions. You'll need an appropriate costume." He grins again, mischievously. "I would be honored if you'd let me assist you in finding something suitable."

I manage another nod. He stays close a bit too long, watches me a little too close for comfort. Then he pulls away, bows again, and turns to leave.

"We'll be back in a few hours," Thora says, and she and Jack move to follow him. "Just need to collect some stuff."

"Various and sundry treasures," Jack says, "looted by Clever Jack. Also more underwear."

I wait a few moments after the curtain closes behind them, until the footsteps fade into the distance. Then I look at Meroe.

"Why am I feeling like I've stepped in something vile?" I ask her.

"Zarun wants something from you," she says.

"I think he's made *that* clear."

"Something other than just wanting to rut you, I mean," she says, without a hint of embarrassment. "It must be something to do with the Council."

"I know." I lean back in the chair with a sigh. "I need *time*. How am I supposed to play the game without even knowing what the sides are?" Back in Kahnzoka, I'd had years to learn the lay of the land, which boss controlled which streets, who was safe to cross and who to avoid at all costs. I'd been aboard *Soliton* most of a week, at best, and all I knew was that one officer wanted to kill me and another wanted me in bed.

"Leave it to me," Meroe says.

I look up at her. "What do you mean?"

"I mean, you focus on keeping us alive and I'll make sure you know where to stand when it comes to the Council." Her smile is broad and genuine. "I'm not going to just let you carry me everywhere."

"But . . ." I wave a hand weakly. "You don't know anything more about it than I do."

"No. But I will." Some of my skepticism must have showed, because she rolls her eyes. "Isoka, you grew up on the street, and you know about gangs and brawls. I grew up in a palace, and I know about people smiling and being courteous while trying to stick a knife in your back. I had my own food taster since I was six years old."

"Oh." She hadn't talked much about herself, down in the Deeps. "I had no idea."

"Trust me. However nasty things are on *Soliton*, they're not worse than the Royal Palace in Nimar." She cocks her head. "Fewer pastries, though."

I laugh, and she smiles wider.

"You don't have to get me out of here," Meroe says. "*We* will get *us* out of here. I don't know what your plan is, but just tell me what you need."

"It's not much of a plan," I admit. "Not yet. But first of all, I need to get close to the Captain."

Meroe nods. "Then that's where we start."

15

I feel a chill, and threads of black magic shiver across my vision. Then Jack is standing beside me, arms crossed.

"Our prey is there," she says, "all unsuspecting."

"Good," I say. "You're sure you can keep its attention long enough for Thora and Berun to hold it?"

"Of course. But also unsuspected. There are two of them." She flutters her eyebrows. "Lovebirds, perhaps? But what shall we do, fearless leader?"

Two shaggies, where we'd expected to find only one. That's certainly a complication.

"Any chance we can pull one of them away?"

She shakes her head. "Doubtful. Close as two crows in a cage, those two. I suspect they will have to be taken together or not at all."

"Can Thora hold a shaggy, with Berun helping her?"

"Perhaps," Jack says. "She's a mighty one, our Thora. But surely not for long."

"It just has to be long enough for you and me to take down the other one." I raise one eyebrow. "I trust that won't be long."

"Oh, delicious confidence," Clever Jack says, "of course not." But Clever Jack is never less than supremely overconfident in her own abilities.

"Thanks for the assessment," I deadpan. "Go back to Thora and tell her to grab whichever one looks smaller. When she does, you and I will take the other one, like we planned."

"Orders heard and understood," Jack says. "Through this next hole, to the left. I will give you a few heartbeats to get into position."

The Center isn't the only place the crew goes to hunt crabs. The Stern is enormous, extending down many levels from the paltry three the Council can claim some authority over, and even on those three large sections are barricaded and abandoned to the scuttling, squirming creatures of the dark. That's where we are now. Instead of trekking across endless bridges and platforms, we're stalking through broken-down corridors, floors and walls flaking with rust, with jagged-edged holes in addition to the usual doorways. Given what happened last time I went to the Center, it's a relief that here there isn't too far to fall.

Meroe, much to her irritation, stayed behind, unable to keep up on her broken leg. I left the Moron with her. Now that we're trying to work together as a pack, he'd only get in the way. That leaves me, Berun, Thora, and Jack. I've worked with worse gangs, in spite of a few . . . eccentricities.

I duck through a rusted-out hole in the wall and turn left, moving just slow enough that my footsteps won't echo. When I reach the next doorway, I pause. Unlike the Deeps, here it isn't *truly* dark during the day. Enough sunlight seeps in through the holes in the deck to take the edge off the gloom.

Up ahead is a dark silhouette, a long, low thing bigger than a horse. I stare a little longer, convincing myself that I can make out features that match the description of a shaggy—six fat legs, a long neck, hung all over with curtains of dripping moss and fungus. It's hard to tell, but Jack seemed certain, and she knows what she's doing. Probably.

Thora and Berun are still getting into position. I grip the metal at the edge of the hole—When they're ready, I—

"Isoka . . ."

I practically jump out of my skin, clenching my jaw tight to avoid a yell. My blades come alive with a *snap-hiss* and I spin, but there's nothing but darkness behind me.

For a long moment, there's no sound but the crackle of Melos power.

"Hagan?" I say, very softly.

No answer. I turn back to the hole, and faint movement catches my eye. Gray motes, flowing in a stream through part of the wall, skirting the edge of the broken section. Hesitantly, I reach out my hand, laying one finger on the metal. The gray energy swirls around it.

"Isoka." It *is* Hagan's voice, a little stronger now.

Blessed's balls. I'd just about convinced myself I was crazy.

"Hagan, can you hear me?"

There's another pause, the faint crackling buzz that accompanies his voice rising and falling.

". . . not strong enough . . . ," he says. ". . . somewhere . . . power . . ."

"I'm not strong enough?" I blink. "I don't understand."

"Garden . . . anomaly coming . . . *Garden* . . ."

His voice fades again. Before I can speak, I hear a bellow and there's a flash of blue. Jack has made her move. With a shout of frustration I turn around and throw myself through the doorway.

The room is a large one, with holes in the ceiling letting a few rays of sunlight dapple the chamber. As my blades add their light to the tableau, I see the shaggy is aptly named. It looks a bit like an ox, if an ox had six legs and were taller than I am at the shoulder. Where the head of an ox would be, there's a long, flexible neck, ending in a small sphere equipped with a wide, toothy jaw. Along its flanks and neck, curtains of dark green moss hang like matted hair, swaying with every movement.

Jack is standing in front of it, arms crossed, grinning like a fool. The shaggy gives another hooting bellow, swinging its head toward her. Jack bows, her shadow stretching behind her and up the wall. The shaggy bellows again, and lunges, its neck moving with the speed of a striking snake. Before it can hit home, Jack vanishes with a flicker of dark magic.

Her shadow remains, skipping neatly away from the confused shaggy. Jack's well is Xenos, the Well of Shadows. It's supposed to be one of the rarest wells, to the point that there isn't a full-fledged Xenos adept in the whole of the Empire. I don't know if Jack's an adept, but the little I've seen her do is impressive. With another dark flash, she reappears atop her own shadow, in time to attract the shaggy's attention again.

I have to admit it's a thrill, fighting alongside other mage-born. I've spent my life in the certain knowledge that, no matter how much I trust them, none of my allies can truly match me. Now I have my pack. I wonder for a moment if this is how the Invincible Legions feel, going into battle, or the Immortals.

Bands of blue light have materialized around the creature, spreading across its legs and along the curve of its neck. Thora and Berun, on the other side of the chamber, are both concentrating hard, wrapping the shaggy in bonds of Tartak force. Intent on Jack, it doesn't notice until it's too late. The thing tugs against the binding, and I see Berun flinch, but it's stuck fast.

Which is my cue. I come out from the doorway, running alongside the beast until I can get at the base of its long, curving neck. I duck forward, blades slashing, sending strands of thick green flying. Liquid spatters across me, beading on my armor, and starts to sizzle. I feel pinpricks of heat as the stuff tries to eat its way to my flesh. Charming. I grit my teeth and push forward, surrounded by crackling green lightning and acrid smoke. One of my blades makes contact with something solid, and I swing in that direction, barely able to see. I can feel the cut, though, and the gush of fluid. I hack at the long neck again, like a lumberjack trying to fell a tree.

There's another bellow from the shaggy, and I turn to get a glimpse of its mouth coming at me, the neck doubling back on itself. I duck, reflexively, but before it reaches me Jack is there, her shadow rising from the deck in front of her like a paper cutout. The shaggy's head collides with the flat black shape and recoils as if it had struck a wall.

"Finish it!" Jack says. She's grinning, as always, in spite of the fact that threads of smoke are rising from her clothes where flecks of acid have landed.

I leave her to watch my back, and turn to my task. It doesn't feel like a fight. More like a chore, a butcher hacking apart a carcass with measured strokes, only with a lot more blood. Eventually, I hit something vital, and black blood spews forth in a torrent. The shaggy gives a despairing gurgling bellow. I skip sideways and it staggers forward and collapses to the floor.

It's getting hot inside my armor, coated as I am in acid, but I don't dare drop it for fear of letting that stuff onto my skin. I glance at Jack, who is still smoking slightly. Berun is on his knees, gasping for breath. Thora kneels beside him, patting his shoulder.

"There," she says. "You did well, lad. Better than I would have given you credit for."

"What about me?" Jack pops up beside Thora, emerging from a shadow like a fish jumping from a lake. "Any praise for Clever Jack?"

"You were brilliant," Thora says, patting Berun's shoulder again and getting to her feet. "As always."

"And my reward?"

Thora gathers the slender girl close with a hand at the small of her back and kisses her thoroughly. My ground-in instinct to look away from such a display wars with an undeniable interest, and under other circumstances I might have left them to it. As it is, though, I give a loud cough.

"A little help?" I spread my arms, which are still steaming with acid. The heat inside my armor is getting seriously uncomfortable.

Thora pushes Jack away, ignoring the disappointed noise she makes. "Sorry, pack leader," she says. She uncorks a waterskin and lets the stream play over my armor, the water making strange patterns as it runs along the flickering surface of the energy field. It takes two skins before I feel like I can risk letting my power drop, sucking with relief at the cool air.

"Did you know that stuff burns?" I ask Thora.

She shakes her head. "I hadn't heard of anything like that. Maybe this one has something different growing on it than most shaggies."

"Maybe it'll flavor the meat," Jack says, looking the dead beast over. "Good eating on these."

I nod, then glance back at the doorway I'd come from. "Good work, all of you. Just . . . give me a minute, would you?"

"I sometimes get like that after a fight," Thora says to Jack behind me. "You get carried away and don't realize how much you've been holding it in."

"The general Hespodar's two greatest military maxims," Jack says, in all seriousness, "were 'never let the phalanx press into broken ground' and 'always piss before the battle.'"

"You made that up," Thora says.

"Possibly."

Around the corner, I press my hand back against the edge of the torn metal. But the flow of gray light has faded, and Hagan's voice is gone.

Rot. Because what I need is more mysteries.

The aftermath of a hunt, I've learned, is as well planned as the system of tithes and protection payments that keeps the Sixteenth Ward running.

When a hunting pack brings down large prey, we report where we left the bodies to one of the clades, who send out a scavenger pack to drag them back to safety. In return, the clade leader gives the pack etched bits of crab shell called scrip, which work more or less like ordinary money. Money without gold or silver in it still seems strange to me, but no stranger than everything else on *Soliton*.

Pack leaders are free to choose their own targets, based on reports from scavengers and other hunting packs. When two groups want to hunt the same prey, the Council decides, either awarding it to one or ordering them to work together. The Council seems to decide everything, in fact. Berun told me the Captain doesn't stick his nose in everyday life much, but as far as I can tell he doesn't intervene at all, except for occasionally sending the angels on mysterious tasks of his own.

There's not much everyone agrees on about the Captain—that he's a man, that he lives in a tower that sticks up from the deck near the stern of the ship, and that he controls the angels through some means no one understands. He seems to have been here longer than anyone else; at least, no one I've talked to came aboard before him. Other than that, though, there's almost nothing.

It's frustrating, because aside from my investigation of the Captain and how he controls the ship, things have been going well for a change. For all that Zarun sent them to spy on me, Thora and Jack can handle themselves, and between us we've been able to bring down enough prey that we have plenty of scrip for food and enough left over for furnishings. Our rooms, which I've learned are in a place called Tower Five, have grown steadily more comfortable. Mostly this is Meroe's doing, since her leg keeps her out of the daily hunts.

When we return home, she's sitting on the floor in the common room, which is now equipped with several more chairs and a thick carpet. The Moron is sitting opposite her, cross-legged, and there's a book open on the floor between them. I blink at the sight of the Moron—who, as far as I know, has never responded to any attempt at communication—pointing eagerly at the book, while Meroe stares intently.

"What's this?" Jack says. "Has the Princess managed to tame the savage beast?"

"He's not a beast," Meroe snaps. "*Or* a moron." She catches sight of me and grins. "Isoka! Come and see!"

I drop my pack in the corner and flop down beside Meroe, and Berun quietly follows suit. Thora and Jack retreat to their room. Probably to rut; I swear, I've known dogs in heat that are more restrained than those two.

"Welcome back," Meroe says, a little belatedly. "Is everyone okay?"

"No problems." Aside from my encounter with Hagan. Thinking about it makes my palms itch. I'll tell Meroe about it, but later, once I've figured out how to explain. Which may be a while.

"Good," Meroe says, and turns back to the Moron. "I've figured it out. *Finally.*"

The boy is staring down at the book in deep concentration, dark brown skin furrowed. He taps it again, looking at Meroe, and she holds up a hand for him to wait.

"He can read?" I say.

"I tried writing messages to him," Berun says. "He never seemed to understand anything."

"Because you didn't use the right language," Meroe says.

"He's Jyashtani, isn't he?" Berun says.

"He's a little dark for a Jyashtani," I say. "I thought he was from the Southern Kingdoms."

"He's technically Jyashtani," Meroe says. "But Jyashtan is a big place. The people we *usually* think of as Jyashtani are from the north, where the capital is. Their empire rules the south, too, but there are a lot of peoples there who speak their own languages." She grins. "And, in this case, use their own system for writing. Look."

I examine the book. The letters are, indeed, unrecognizable, strange square glyphs instead of the thin-lined characters of Imperial. Jyashtani use the same script we do, I think. I hadn't known there *were* others.

"This is a book from . . . well, I don't know exactly where," Meroe goes on. "The point is he can read it. And so can I, a little." She shakes her head. "He's deaf and dumb, I think. Can you imagine being dumped in here and not being able to hear or make anyone understand you?"

I look at the boy, who meets my eyes with a calm, curious gaze. "I'm amazed he's still alive," I say.

Meroe nods. "His name is Aifin. I may be pronouncing that wrong. I'm not *exactly* sure what language he speaks, only that it uses these Fertani characters. I'm going to have to see if there are any more books in the market."

There are a surprising number of books on *Soliton*. The various ports think they make good sacrifices, I guess. For the most part, the crew don't have much use for them.

"Well. It's good to meet you, Aifin," I say, and then feel stupid because of course he just keeps staring. "Meroe, could I speak to you alone for a moment?"

"Of course."

"I'll get dinner started," Berun says. There's a small hearth in one corner, below a convenient rust hole in the ceiling. I'm almost used to the smell of the dried mushroom they use in place of firewood.

I help Meroe to her feet, and she slips the crutch under her arm. Berun and the Moron—Aifin—have been sharing one of the three bedrooms, and Thora and Jack claimed another. That leaves the last for me and Meroe. We found sleeping mats in the market—they sleep properly in Nimar, apparently—and she's added other odds and ends. A few books stand in a pile beside her bed, next to a bowl of beaten gold and a small collection of charms made from parts of crabs.

"How's the leg?" I ask, as the curtain closes behind us.

"Itchy," Meroe says. "But it shouldn't be long before I can walk at least a little. Sister Cadua's remedies really do work wonders."

Meroe herself, of course, can literally work miracles, but I let the irony of that pass. She doesn't like to be reminded of what she is, and if we're being completely honest neither do I.

"Any luck today?" I ask.

She crutches to her sleeping mat and lowers herself onto it. "No. Nobody knows anything."

"That they're willing to say."

"In that case, they're very good liars." Meroe sighs. "I don't understand."

In the couple of weeks since we moved into Tower Five, Meroe has been helping me dig up information on the Captain. More accurately, she's been doing the digging, while I chop unfortunate crabs into pieces. She's become well versed in the ins and outs of *Soliton* society remarkably quickly, but the Captain himself remains elusive.

"It doesn't make sense," I say. "Someone has to bring him food, clean his rooms, warm his bed. There has to be *something*."

"I know," Meroe says patiently. "The officers take care of it is all anyone will tell me."

"Personally?" I can't imagine the Butcher fetching the Captain's towel or cooking his crab juice.

"I don't know." Meroe sighs. "But I think Zarun is still our best chance."

Our clade leader has been a frequent guest, eager to check up on his latest acquisitions. His interest in me, specifically, is obvious, both because the crew is still abuzz with talk of the Deepwalker and for . . . other reasons. Lately, he's renewed his invitation to find me something to wear for the Council meeting.

"I don't like relying on him so much," I mutter.

"We're not relying on him," Meroe says. "We're *using* him."

I can't help but smile. "I'm rubbing off on you."

"Please." She grins back. "Princesses can be as ruthless as gang bosses, believe me."

"I believe you." I rub my eyes, trying to get my heart to slow down before a flush shows in my face. That smile. Rot.

"He said he'd come by tonight," Meroe says. "Go out with him. See what you can find out."

"If you say so." I sigh. "Let me change clothes, then."

Meroe nods. "I'm going to keep working with Aifin."

She gets her crutch under her and makes her laborious way out of the room. As the curtain falls behind her, something slams against the metal wall beside me and I hear a moan, followed by a string of unfamiliar profanity and heavy breathing.

The thing is . . . I mean . . .

Rot it. The thing is, under other circumstances, I would have happily returned Zarun's unsubtle interest. He's handsome, with a touch of the exotic by Kahnzoka standards, and the suggestion of corded muscle under the loose shirts he wears makes me want to investigate more thoroughly. He's dangerous, of course, and a murderer, but I can hardly complain about that. But.

But . . .

But it has become clear to me, through a couple of sleepless nights and several extremely explicit dreams, that it isn't Zarun I want to rut. It's Meroe hait Gevora Nimara, with her bright grin, her quick laugh, her thick, heavy braid. Her smooth, dark skin, the curve of her hip, the quick smile on her soft lips.

I've never wanted someone so badly. I want to kiss her; I want to feel her hands on me; I want to nip at her throat and hear her gasp like—

Well, like Jack is gasping in the next room, as Thora does whatever Jack keeps asking her not to stop doing.

It doesn't help that I've been lacking good opportunities to relieve my frustration, either alone or in company. I sleep six inches from Meroe, and while I've never been shy of myself, it feels . . . awkward. I don't know what she'd think. Certainly I've never heard *her* indulge.

I could, of course, go to the brothel. There's one aboard ship, run by the Imperial girl I'd seen on the officers' dais, whose name is Shiara. A few shells of scrip would get me a couple of hours with a pretty boy—or, rot it, a girl, if that's what I need. But . . .

But it's not what I want. I don't want *anyone*. I want her.

The trouble is, I don't know what *she* wants. Whether she'd laugh at me or hate me forever. And it's become increasingly obvious that I need her to help me make sense of the tangled mess of *Soliton's* politics. I can't risk my relationship with my most valuable ally over a couple of wet dreams.

Blessed's rotting balls. Is it something about this rotting ship, or is there something wrong with me?

I emerge from our room in the loose trousers and green silk tunic I've been using for everyday wear. *Soliton's* market has plenty of clothing, but the selection is eclectic. Meroe, fortunately, learned to wield a needle and thread in her early years, and she's managed to alter a few things to a reasonable fit.

She's sitting with Aifin, while Berun watches and pokes at something on the hearth. Aifin is trying to get some point across, poking the book and then rapidly sketching a character in the air with his finger. Meroe frowns, clearly not getting it but determined to keep trying.

I shake my head. Anyone else would have written the Moron off after a few tries. Leave it to Meroe to keep pushing until she gets through. She shifts a braid away from the long, delicate curve of her neck as she bends over the book, and my heart double-thumps.

Rot, rot, rot. *There's a job to do here, Isoka. Remember Tori and Kuon*

Naga. The clock is ticking, and it's not going to stop just because my body has gotten confused.

There's a knock, a gong-like sound on the metal wall. The front curtain pulls open, and Zarun is standing in the doorway, smiling his shark's smile. He's dressed as flamboyantly as ever, in a style I don't recognize—a swathe of deep blue cloth pinned at one shoulder and hanging to his waist, with the other arm and shoulder exposed. It leaves a lot of nice-looking skin on display, just in case I wasn't distracted *enough.*

"Good evening, Isoka," he says, with a brief nod at the others. "Congratulations on your hunt today."

Word spreads fast in the small community of *Soliton*'s crew. I shrug.

"Do you still have time this evening?" he says. "The Council meeting is the day after tomorrow. If you're going to be presented to the officers, you'll want to make a good impression."

People telling me I have to look nice instantly sets my teeth on edge. Unfortunately, he's right. The Council is the only way to get closer to the Captain.

"They saw me in the Ring, didn't they?" I say. "It's hardly being presented."

He shrugs. "This is more . . . official."

"All right." I stretch, with a show of reluctance, and reach for the string that gathers our stack of scrip.

Zarun waves a hand.

"Please," he says. "I'll take care of everything."

I slip the scrip into a pocket anyway. Zarun's grin widens a notch, and he gestures to the door. I follow him out through the corridor and into the crowded chaos of the Upper Stations. He leads the way through the streets, toward a section of the market I haven't visited before.

"So," he says, falling into step beside me. "Are you getting accustomed to how things work here?"

"More or less," I tell him. "It's not that different from back home. I get paid to kill things. Here they just tend to have more legs."

Zarun chuckles. "That's what I like about you, Isoka. You're so refreshingly direct."

By the way he looks at me, it's clear that's not *all* he likes about me. Fair enough. I've snuck a few admiring glances, too.

"These Council meetings," I ask him, "does the Captain ever attend?"

He shakes his head. "Not since I joined. When we want to see the Captain, we visit him in his tower."

"When *did* you join? How long have you been on the ship?"

I've picked up enough of *Soliton*'s etiquette to know this is something of a daring question. Everyone on board, no matter how comfortable they seem in their current circumstances, came from *somewhere*, and not by choice. We're all prisoners here, and not everyone is happy to be reminded about it. Fortunately, Zarun only smiles slightly.

"It will be . . . eight years, now?" He looks up at the ceiling, where the sun slants in through rusted holes. "I think. It can be hard to keep track, in here." He glances back at me. "Did they tell you I'm a Jyashtani prince?"

"I may have heard that somewhere, but I didn't believe it."

"You're wiser than most, then," he says. "My *father* was a prince of Harzashti. And my mother was a weed picker's daughter. When I became an embarrassment, *Soliton* provided a convenient solution."

If I'm right about his age, he wouldn't have been more than twelve at the time. Hell of a place for a child to get dumped. "And the Council?"

"That came later. I built a successful hunting pack, won the respect of my fellow crew, and eventually . . . ." He spread his arms. "You're full of questions today, Deepwalker."

"It's sinking in that I'm really going to be staying here," I ad-lib. "Seemed like I should learn the ropes."

"You've made a good start, at least. I hope Thora and Jack have been helpful."

"They have." It was true, though I'm sure they also provided Zarun with regular reports. "Thora has been training Berun, too."

"Thora is extremely reliable," Zarun says. "And your princess? Is she recovering?"

"She is." I don't particularly want to discuss Meroe. "Where exactly are we going?"

"In here."

He gestures down an alley, which leads to a side door into a nearby tower. There's no sign, and I look around curiously as he walks up and knocks.

"This is a shop?" I say.

"Of a sort. The best of the scavenger's finds aren't laid out in the street." Zarun gives me the shark's smile again. "And you deserve the best, Deepwalker."

"Who's there?" says a voice from inside. It sounds like a little girl.

"Zarun, and a guest."

There's the sound of muttering, and the door creaks open. A girl of thirteen or so, slim and dark-skinned, stands in the doorway in a baggy, oversized dress. She yawns ostentatiously.

"Another girl, Zarun?" she says. "You were just in last week. What happened to Ralya?"

"Ralya is well," Zarun says. "Though we have, regrettably, parted ways. But this is Isoka Deepwalker."

"Deepwalker." The girl leans forward, rising onto her toes to study the blue lines across my face. "Hmm. Is it true?"

"What, that I survived the Deeps?" I give another shrug. "It's true. Though I'm not the only one. Meroe was with me."

"Ah, but one of you walked out carrying the other," Zarun says. "Isoka, this is Feoptera, queen of scavengers."

"I told you not to call me that," Feoptera snaps. "It makes me sounds like a vulture or a hyena. And I'm not anybody's queen."

"Forgive me," Zarun says, giving me an amused glance. "Just a young lady with exquisite taste."

"Your price is getting higher by the minute," Feoptera says. "Come inside before you talk it up beyond your means."

She stalks away, and we follow. The metal corridor is lined with junk, so tight we sometimes have to squeeze past sideways. There are metal sheets, rusted at the edges, piles of dried mushrooms, and large fragments of crab shell. In and among these products of *Soliton* are bits of salvage: cups and plates, furniture, crates and boxes, wine bottles. Open doorways lead into rooms crammed with even more stuff.

"So what is it this time?" Feoptera says over her shoulder. "Jewels? Perfume?"

"Something for Isoka to wear to the Council meeting."

"Ah, yes."

The girl stomps into a room on her left. Several tables take up most of the space, and makeshift shelves line the walls. Every inch of horizontal surface is covered with fabric, a galaxy of brilliant colors and glittering adornments. There's silk, and Jyashtani lace, and a hundred other materials I couldn't hope to identify. A lamp in the corner gleams off cloth of gold and sparkles from precious stones.

I can't help but let out a low whistle. On *Soliton*, I know, bits of pretty cloth aren't as valuable as a nice set of tools or a fine blade, but back in Kahnzoka the contents of this room would buy Tori's estate several times over. Old instincts make my palms itch.

"Take your pick," Feoptera says. "Try not to damage anything."

She stalks out, with one last glare at Zarun.

"She doesn't seem to like you very much." I say, in low tones.

He chuckles. "Feoptera is very fond of me. You should see the way she treats people she really doesn't like."

"And . . ." I gesture around at the mounds of finery, feeling a little helpless. "What do people wear to these Council meetings?"

"It's less that there's a specific standard," he says, running his fingers over a long black silk dress. "It's more that we like there to be a sense of occasion. Here, hold this."

I take the wisp of fabric he hands me. He looks at us together for a moment, shakes his head, then takes it back and sets it aside.

It turns out this is only the beginning. Zarun digs through the heaps, pulling out garment after garment. Some of them are familiar to me—Imperial *kizen* and Jyashtani robes—while others are more exotic. Dresses with wire stays, to spread one's skirts across half a room, and slim, slitted sheets that would barely qualify as underwear back in Kahnzoka. Elaborate lace confections, dripping with gleaming gems, and loose-woven fabric in an overlapping pattern of colorful threads.

Soliton had visited every city with a harbor and fine clothing was apparently a popular sacrifice. The collection stretched back in *time,* too—I could see double-fastened *kizen* of the kind that only grandmothers now wore. It was a remarkable collection of frippery, and I couldn't help but marvel at the *waste* of it all. Every one of these dresses represented days, probably weeks, of labor, all to give some fine lady a way to impress her friends for an evening.

Rotting aristos.

Zarun sorts through the piles, holding garments up to me like I was a paper doll, then rooting around for new ones. I fidget uncomfortably while he works.

Eventually, out of awkwardness more than anything else, I say, "Can I ask you something?"

"Of course," he says, glancing between a frothy blue lace confection and something black that shimmers like ravens' wings.

"Why are you helping me? Why all of this?"

He looks up at me with a slight smile that doesn't touch his pale blue eyes. "Oh. A *real* question."

"I'm just struggling to understand what you get out of it."

"Having the Deepwalker associated with my clade helps my prestige," he says, looking back to the piles.

"But you came to meet me before that," I say. "Try again."

"Even at that point, it was obvious you were a superb fighter," he says. "Any of the officers would be happy to have you."

"You've got plenty of fighters. You haven't given Thora or Jack their own pack to lead."

"Thora prefers a more personal role," he says. "And Jack . . . is Jack."

It *was* hard to imagine the mercurial girl getting anyone to follow her. But I shook my head. "Still. You don't need me."

He pauses for a moment, then holds up another dress. Or part of a dress—it's hard to tell. It's slashed open in so many places it looks like it was attacked by wolves. Being naked would be more modest.

"Fine," he says. "Ever since I saw you in the pit, I wanted you in my bed. When I heard you could fight as well, I was sure of it."

I smile, crookedly, and take a step closer to him. "Please. I'm honest enough with myself that I know I'm not the sort of beauty that turns men's heads."

"Maybe not most men." Zarun's smile widens. "I have particular tastes."

I break eye contact for a moment to look down at myself. "You like skinny, gristly girls?"

He puts one finger on my chin and lifts my head up to face him again. "I like girls," he says, "who can hold their own."

We're close enough that I can feel his breath on my face. My heart beats faster, and my chest feels hot and tight. For all that a certain princess has infested my dreams, there's no denying that Zarun is *toothsome*, to use the late Ahdron's word, lithe and lean, dark curls just the right length for me to twist in my fingers, sparkling eyes. And there's a flush in his cheeks that says his interest is genuine.

But he's also lying.

I turn away, grabbing a dress at random from the piles. "What about this one?"

I hear him let out a breath, not quite a sigh.

Zarun ends up handing a half-dozen dresses to Feoptera, who looks me over with a practiced eye and says that she'll see what she can do. We leave the shop before I fully realize that we're done, back out into the muted sunshine of the Upper Stations, which feels bright after the gloomy interior of the tower. Around us, the market is in full swing, hawkers shouting the virtues of their scavenged morsels to the passing crew.

"So what happens at this Council meeting?" I ask Zarun, as we walk side by side. "Aside from you introducing me to the other officers."

"The Council will meet in closed session beforehand," he says, sounding bored at the prospect. "At the reception we'll talk to the pack leaders and other notables."

"And what happens in the closed session?"

"We take any decisions that need to be made. Unless there's instructions from the Captain, of course."

"Can you bring issues to him, if you need to?"

Zarun shrugs. "I suppose we could, but it almost never happens. The Captain is . . . not like the rest of us. He controls *all* of *Soliton*, not just the Stern, and he's mostly concerned with where we'll head and whether the sacrifices are adequate. Dealing with the crew he leaves to us."

"He could help, though. What if he sent the angels to fight the crabs? Or—"

"He has his reasons," Zarun says, cutting me off. He gives me an irritated glance. "You won't get very far asking questions about the Captain."

"He doesn't like being questioned?"

"He doesn't care a bit, as long as he's obeyed. But there's no point in asking about things nobody understands."

"I don't know about that," another voice says, with a thick Jyashtani accent. "In my experience, those are the only really important questions."

I look up to find another group approaching us. At the head is the Jyashtani I saw on the officers' podium, with the round glasses that reminded me of Naga. He has the light brown skin of northern Jyashtan, dark, curly hair long enough to be a bit shaggy, and he wears a modest robe. He has a silver-headed walking stick in one hand, and as he comes closer I notice his right leg drags behind his left, foot sticking out at an odd angle.

Beside him, enormous even without her crab-shell armor, is the Butcher. She's wearing civilian clothes, a leather vest and trousers stitched together from a patchwork of oddly colored pieces. Without a helmet on, her surprisingly curly blond hair hangs in a loose tail at the back of her neck. She glowers at everyone, but her face darkens considerably on her sighting Zarun, and then goes positively stormy when she sees me with him. Behind her are a half-dozen crew, including the bald-headed Haia.

"My esteemed colleagues," Zarun says, making a little bow.

"The fop," the Butcher rumbles. "And the famous *Deepwalker* everyone finds so precious. What a lovely pair." Her lips twist. "Has he bent you over a bench yet, or are you still just sucking his dick?"

"Now, now," Zarun says. "Just because *you* no longer have access to my bed—"

"Not that he can manage much else," the Butcher says, looking down at me. "If he finds the right place to stick it, you can count yourself lucky."

I admit I have a hard time imagining the Butcher rutting with Zarun. She's a head taller than him and easily twice his weight, her limbs wrapped with slab-like muscle, with a neck like an ox and breasts like overgrown summer melons. She seems like she would crush anyone not built to her own heroic scale.

"I believe you know the Butcher," Zarun says, ignoring her. "And this young man we call the Scholar." Zarun puts a hand on my shoulder, with a possessive air. "I'm bringing Isoka to the Council meeting for formal introductions."

"Lovely," the Butcher snaps. "I'm sure we'll all enjoy making conversation with your whore."

Zarun's hand tightens on my shoulder, as if in warning. It's unnecessary—it's clear that making trouble here would be counterproductive, and in any event I'm used to people insulting my virtue, even if they're usually men I'm about to kill. It's amazing how many people, in the face of a cold-blooded killer, think the worst thing they can say about her is that she spreads her legs. So I keep up a smile, because I know it will annoy the Butcher. She stomps past us, brushing deliberately too close, and her crew follows suit.

"I look forward to getting a chance to speak with you, Deepwalker," the Scholar says, inclining his head. "I've been hoping to interview you about what you saw in the Deeps."

"The Scholar is the one who likes to ask questions about *Soliton*,"

Zarun says. "The rest of us put up with him because he occasionally comes back with something useful."

"I putter," the Scholar says modestly. "There's so much that's beyond our understanding. I've always thought—"

"Scholar!" the Butcher roars over her shoulder. "Hurry up, if you want your rotting piece of junk."

"Another time," the Scholar says, with a smile. He nods again and hobbles off after the Butcher and her crew.

"Is it true?" I say quietly. "You and her?"

"Hard to picture?" Zarun grins at me. "The truth is that I used her, to get where I am today. She didn't take it well."

"Apparently."

"You wanted to know why I'm helping you?" He nods in the Butcher's direction. "It's because *she* hates you. You made her look weak and foolish when you came aboard, and every inch you rise is a twist of the knife in her back. She never could get over a grudge."

"So you're helping me out of spite?"

He laughs. "Don't be silly. *I* don't hold grudges." He turns back to me and flashes his dazzling smile again. "Hate makes people stupid. If this keeps up, sooner or later she'll make a mistake. And then . . ."

He gives an eloquent shrug, and turns away.

The package from Feoptera arrives that evening, couriered by a breathless young man whose eyes go wide at the sight of the Deepwalker. I wave him away with a sigh and retreat to my room, where I'd been recounting my conversation with Zarun and the Butcher to Meroe.

"The last thing he said, about the Butcher," she asks as I re-enter. "Do you believe it?"

"I'm not sure. It sounded more plausible than the rest." I toss the package down beside her and sit on my sleeping mat. "They obviously have a history."

"Does he hate her as much as she hates him?"

I shrug. "If he does, he hides it well."

"Then what's the endgame? Why does he need to damage her?"

"From our point of view, does it matter?"

Meroe nods. "It does. We still don't know what Zarun is *after*. He and the other officers are already on the top of the heap here. Is he just defending himself against the Butcher? Or is there another step?"

"The Captain." I grimace. "If he's ambitious, that's the only place left for him to go."

"We don't know how the Captain was chosen. What happens if he dies or steps down." Meroe spreads her hands. "It's possible is all I'm saying."

"There's too much nobody wants to talk about." I frown. "The Scholar seemed friendly. Maybe we can pin him down. And the Butcher . . ." I sigh. "We may have to kill her, whatever Zarun is planning. He's right about how she feels about me. Every time she tries to hurt me and fails, it makes her look worse. She can't back out now, not without making herself a laughingstock to her own people."

Meroe looks pained at the thought, which sends a needle of guilt through my chest. She may have been raised under a threat of murder, but she's not as comfortable with violence as she pretends. My princess.

"There might be another way out, but right now I can't see it," I say. "Keep your eyes open."

"If Zarun's driving you two at one another, it doesn't seem likely." Meroe shakes her head, and looks down at the package. "Let's see what he got you."

I'm honestly a little afraid to look, but I untie the string and unfold the linen wrapping. Inside is . . . a dress, I suppose. It's a dark blue-green, with overlapping folds and fringes of fine lace. Small silver charms click against one another as I lift it up. Underneath, Feoptera has thoughtfully included a hand mirror, an elaborately gold-inlaid thing that would be worth a small fortune on its own.

"It's . . . elaborate," Meroe says.

"I'd say 'ridiculous,'" I mutter, looking at it. A *kizen* is one thing, but this?

"Try it on," Meroe says.

I pick the dress up, struggling to figure out how the separate parts go together. I can't even tell which is supposed to be the inside and which the outside, much less how they're connected. I look up at the sound of a sputter, and find Meroe hiding her smile with both hands.

"Sorry," she says. "Just the look on your face."

I roll my eyes. "I suppose you know all about it."

"I think I can manage," she says. "The style isn't *that* far from what we wear in Nimar." She gets up, leaning on her cane, and takes the dress out of my hands. "Come on, strip off, and I'll see what I can do."

There was not a lot of room for modesty in my upbringing. Tori and I cleaned ourselves in public fountains, changed clothes in back alleys, and splashed naked in the cisterns in the summer heat with the other street children until the guards ran us off. While the servants I hired have struggled to mold her into a proper young woman, there was no one minding *me*. In theory, therefore, taking off my clothes and letting Meroe dress me should be no great affair.

In practice, I feel her eyes on me like a shaft of sunlight, warming my skin wherever it touches. I shuck out of my trousers and pull my tunic over my head. Then, with a glance at the straps and stays of the dress, I undo my chest wrap as well. I keep my eyes resolutely on Meroe's sleeping mat.

Is she staring at me? What if she is? What if she isn't? I feel my face flushing.

The featherlight touch of her hand on my back makes me jump, heart pounding. She flinches away.

"Sorry," she says. "Are my fingers cold?"

I give a lying nod. When she touches me again, I only shiver a little. Her fingers are wonderfully warm, in fact. She pushes my hair aside and traces the line of blue marks around my back and onto my flank.

"I forgot how far these went," she says, softly.

I don't know what to say. I want to tell her it's all right, that she saved my life. I want her to keep touching me, so badly that my skin practically tingles at the prospect.

Instead, she returns to the business at hand, and with some reluctance I pose as she instructs. Raise my arms, lower my arms, step
into one skirt, and buckle another around my waist. Breathe in as she
cinches up some ties, stand tremblingly still as she fusses with small
knots at my collar, her breath hot on my neck. Finally, she steps
back, looks me over, and raises an eyebrow.

"Well?" I say.

She picks up the mirror.

Feoptera, to her credit, has done her best. The dress flares out
from the waist down, but above that it shoves and prods my
stubbornly uncurved body into something like a proper woman's
shape, with a high bodice that gathers every available ounce of flesh
to create the illusion I have breasts. The lace spills from the cuffs
and the neckline, the silver charms gleam, and the layers of skirts
swish against one another as I turn. It's a beautiful dress, and yet . . .

"I look ridiculous," I say flatly.

"You look ridiculous," Meroe says. "Because it's not *you*. It's like
someone tried to put a fancy ball gown on a . . . a tiger."

I raise my eyebrows, then spread my fingers into claws and mouth
a roar. Meroe laughs out loud, and after a moment I join her.

"This is what Zarun thinks the Council wants to see," I say,
testing my range of motion.

"Rot that," Meroe says. "We can do better."

I look up at her. "You think?"

"Trust me." She grins. "It's a princess thing."

16

"Almost ready," Meroe says. "Stop squirming."

I do my best, sitting in our room on a borrowed chair, while her strong, clever fingers work on my hair. She slides in the steel pins, long, dangerous-looking things like miniature stilettos, fixing the carefully crafted braid in place like a butterfly in a collection box.

"There," she says. "That's not going anywhere."

It's odd, having my hair up. I haven't worn it like that in years. The back of my neck feels cool and vulnerable.

"I still don't know where you found all of this," I say.

"I've been out in the markets while you've been fighting crabs," she says. "I've gotten to know a few people."

Meroe's ability to insinuate herself into *Soliton*'s society has been, frankly, astonishing. When we went to the market together, she seemed to be on a first-name basis with half the hawkers, and every one of them was happy to see her. I don't think I knew my ward in Kahnzoka half as well as she's come to know the Upper Stations in just a few weeks.

She holds up the mirror. "Want to see?"

"I'm not sure I do."

"Have a little faith," Meroe says.

I'm not sure why this bothers me so much. Back in Kahnzoka, clothes were never more than a means to an end. Maybe it's the fact that Zarun and Meroe both seem to think they're important that puts my teeth on edge. Regardless, I'm being stupid; I steel myself and look into the mirror.

"That's . . ." I blink. "Not bad."

It's a long way from skirts and lace; that's for certain. The trousers are worked leather, accented with carved crab shell, tight and dark. More crab shell on the top covers the shoulders, decorative but nonetheless suggesting armor plate. Deep red slashes are worked into the leather, visible only briefly as I move. It doesn't flaunt my chest, but it doesn't hide it, either. And it leaves my midriff bare where the line of twisting blue marks winds across it.

When I turn my head, the steel points of the hairpins wink at me. Meroe is watching, and I suddenly realize she's nervous.

"It's good." I look down at my hands, which are wrapped in leather cords. "Very good. Definitely more . . . me."

"I don't know what Zarun and the others will think," Meroe says, setting the mirror aside. "But *I* think it makes you look beautiful and dangerous." She puts a hand on her stomach, where the marks are on mine. "You're the Deepwalker. You should look the part."

Beautiful and dangerous. Not a description I've heard very often. I clear my throat to cover a moment's hesitation. "It's unfair, isn't it? You came back from the Deeps as much as I did."

"Technically, I didn't do much walking," Meroe says. She leans on her cane to add the last part of her own costume, a thin silk shawl around her neck. Then she spreads her arms. "What do you think?"

I hadn't been so wrapped up in my own problems that I'd neglected to watch Meroe changing. Her dress was modest, with a high neckline and long sleeves, but it clung to her figure in appetizing folds. It was cream and light blue, contrasting with her skin, and blue gemstones sparkled at her ears and in her hair.

"Beautiful," I say. "And dangerous."

Meroe smirks. "Good."

Berun gapes visibly as we leave, and even Aifin sits up to watch. Jack is waiting, her hair slicked back, crisp in a white shirt and black tailcoat. She gives Meroe a smile, then raises an eyebrow at me.

"Thora is with Zarun," she says. "Shall we proceed, brave companions?"

"Lead the way," I tell her, looking back at Meroe. "Slowly, if you please."

Jack is surprisingly solicitous of Meroe's limited pace, given the way she usually skips across the deck. We leave the tower and wend our way through the Upper Stations. It's well after dark, which only means the markets are a little more subdued. By the light of torches and mushroom-fed braziers, we make our way to a corner of the deck I haven't visited before, up where the rear wall rises like a mammoth curtain of darkness.

Up against that wall is a steel cage, unpleasantly similar to the one that brought me aboard ship. For all I know, it might be the same one. Two armed crew stand in front of it, and they nod to Jack as we approach.

"There's a stairway," Jack says, "but for our princess I thought this might be more comfortable. It's a long way up."

"Thank you," Meroe says, though I can tell the cage brings up the same associations for her. She steps into it unhesitatingly nevertheless, sitting down near the center. I follow, sitting opposite for balance's sake.

"More than two would be a strain," Jack says, "so your valiant hero will take the stairs, for the good of all. See you at the top, pretties."

She bounds off, and the crew close the door. A few moments later, at an unseen signal, the cage starts to rise. Points of light from torches and lanterns outline the Upper Stations as clearly as a map, a two-by-two square defined by the nine towers that stretch up to meet the distant ceiling. Behind me is the rear wall of the ship, and to the right another slab-like section of hull rises up. To the left and in front of me, only the man-height wall of scrap metal separates the civilized part of *Soliton* from the crab-infested wilds.

It brings home how *small* it is, everything the officers and crew have built, compared to the vastness of the great ship. The darkness of *Soliton* swallows them like the ocean swallows a flung stone, stretching out into the unknowable distance. . . .

Not my concern, I admonish myself, and lift my head to look *up*. That's what I need to worry about. I can see starlight through a square hole in the deck, with the chain a black slash through the center.

"Are you nervous?" Meroe says.

"A bit." I look across at her. "I have to keep reminding myself nobody's going to be trying to kill me."

"Hopefully."

I smile. "Hopefully." Then my expression turns sour. "I wish we had a better idea what we were looking for."

"Play it by ear. Ask about the Captain, but don't push too hard." She takes my hand in hers. "If all else fails, try to have a good time. It can't hurt."

"Stick close, would you?" I give her hand a squeeze. "This sort of event . . . isn't my strong suit."

The cage rises through the hole in the deck, and suddenly the sky is alive with stars. It takes my breath away for a moment, a river of light stretching from horizon to horizon, diamond dust gleaming on the deepest black velvet. In Kahnzoka, the stars are a few flickering points, visible on a clear night through the haze and the ever-present lights of the city. Here, though, there's no urban glow to drown them out, and they shine down in their uncounted millions.

It's only been a few weeks, but I've almost forgotten what it's *like* to see the sky. I take a deep breath, my chest expanding like a weight has come off. I'm so busy staring upward that I barely notice as more crew grab the cage and bring it to a halt over the deck. Meroe touches my hand again, gently, and I look down to see that the door is open.

We step out, carefully. A few lanterns provide enough light to see the deck, but no more than that. Beyond them, there's nothing but darkness. *Soliton* is visible only in silhouette, its shape outlined against the spectacular starscape. I can see the vast bulk of it, stretching off into forever. Distance is impossible to judge.

Behind me, a single spear of darkness rises far overhead. It's a spire, tall and slender. From the descriptions I've heard, this can only be the Captain's tower, set on the very stern of the ship. At the top, a pale light glows, hard to distinguish from the stars around it. I wonder if the Captain is looking down at us.

Beyond the sides of the ship, there's only darkness. The ocean must be out there, but I can't see it, only the curtain of stars descending to the horizon on all sides. There's no sense of motion, though I know the ship is under way. It's much too big to sway with the waves, so the only hint that we're moving is a steady breeze.

"Deepwalker," says one of the crew, a tall, dark-skinned young man with a grave manner. "This way, please."

We follow him, toward the ring of lanterns. They're set in a rough circle on the deck, revealing the rusted metal underfoot. And more that that; at the far side, two huge figures stand, barely outlined in the light. They're twisted amalgamations of human and animal forms, one a coiled serpent with a woman's multi-armed torso and the head of an ant, the other a bull with a bird's beak, a human face screaming from inside its open mouth. Angels. I remember the one I saw in the Deeps, its smooth, uncanny motion, and I'm very grateful these two are inanimate.

"Isoka Deepwalker," a woman says. There's a small crowd of people inside the ring of lanterns, and while I was staring they noticed our arrival. The woman facing me is an Imperial in a kind of *kizen*, except it's been slashed indecently short, well above her knees. A pair of gold snakes twine through her hair. I blink at her, trying to get my bearings, and send up a silent thanks when Meroe steps between us.

"This is Gaetica," she says. "The head of Pack Two, in Karakoa's clade."

I bow slightly. "An honor to meet you."

"And you." She's staring at the blue marks on my face. "I've been hearing nothing but stories of your exploits of late."

I give an uncertain shrug. "I'm just trying to stay alive."

Gaetica watches me with an unreadable expression, leaving me feeling like I've failed some sort of test. By this time, though, more of the crowd has gathered, eager to make my acquaintance. I feel like I'm back at Breda's in Kahnzoka, except none of the gathered pack leaders have petitions for me. Mostly, it seems, they just want to gawk at the Deepwalker.

Meroe squires me from one to the next, her memory for names

and positions apparently infallible. Few of the guests pay her much attention, which makes me feel obscurely offended on her behalf. Instead, they bow to me, or shake hands, or salute. I get more invitations to drinks or dinner than I can count, a half-dozen proposals for friendly sparring matches, and three explicit offers to rut. The last of these comes from a young woman, who looks between me and Meroe with a knowing smile. I'm glad it's shadowy enough that Meroe can't see me flush.

"Do you really know *everyone* here?" I ask her, when we finally find ourselves in a quiet corner for a moment.

"Most of the important ones," she says.

"How in the Rot can you keep them all straight? And don't tell me any princess ought to be able to do it."

She giggles. "My sister Vera used to forget the names of the High Council. It made Father so mad I think she was doing it on purpose." She shakes her head. "I suppose I've always had a knack for it."

"I feel like a monster in a menagerie," I say. "They all just want to stare at me."

"Let them." She puts her hand on my shoulder. "You're doing fine, Isoka."

"I'm not getting us any closer to what we need."

"This is just the beginning. The officers will be here soon, I think."

Just the beginning. Rotting wonderful.

There's food laid out on a great wooden table, and rows of crystal glasses that belonged in a palace somewhere. I fight my way to the center of the scrum and help clear a path for Meroe. Once she arrives, tapping her cane on the deck, I hand her a plate of unidentifiable fried bits and a goblet of something amber. For myself, I take only a goblet.

Whatever the stuff is, it's surprisingly good, a bit like wine but considerably stronger. I can feel the liquor at the back of my throat as the initial sweetness fades. Meroe sips, and raises an eyebrow.

"Well," she says. "I could get used to that."

"Good, isn't it?" Zarun steps up behind us. For a wonder, he's dressed less garishly than usual, in a sleek dark green robe that's almost subdued, matched with a floppy silk hat that hangs rakishly over one ear. "Lots of cities include liquor as part of their tribute, so the scavengers are always bringing back crates of the stuff, but the quality can be a bit hit-or-miss."

"When did you arrive?" I ask.

"Just now." He waves a hand. "It wouldn't do for the Council to be the first ones here."

Meroe nods. "The most important person always arrives late."

"Let me make the introductions," Zarun says. He slips his arm into mine, so smoothly it almost feels natural. "If you don't mind, Meroe?"

"Go ahead." I catch Meroe's gaze, and she mouths, *Eyes open.* I nod.

I can see the massive form of the Butcher, towering over the crowd. Somewhat to my relief, Zarun leads me in the opposite direction. Another large figure stands at the edge of the ring of light, surrounded by a smaller group of hangers-on. It's the tall warrior I saw the day I fought Ahdron. He shares the light brown skin and broad features of my former pack leader. I've learned that these are characteristic of the people who inhabit what the Empire calls the Southern Wastes, who as far as I know have never been encountered by His Imperial Majesty's explorers. The far south is notoriously treacherous sailing, with little but sand and snow to make up for the risk of foundering in a sudden blizzard. But *Soliton*, of course, knows no such hazards, and has scooped up its share of the people who call themselves Akemi.

The circle of courtiers opens up as we approach. The southerner pauses to exchange a lingering kiss with his closest companion, a slight, younger man with a Jyashtani look, before he looks up to greet me. He has handsome, chiseled features, and dark hair braided close to his scalp. He's dressed in tooled leather, not dissimilar from mine, but accented with small bits of twisted steel threaded onto silk cords.

"Isoka," Zarun says, "this is Karakoa. He's the longest serving of our little Council."

"Deepwalker," Karakoa says. His voice is a low rumble. "You were impressive in the Ring."

"Thank you," I say. There's a confidence about the man that's a little intimidating, even for me. I've met many braggarts on the streets, but Karakoa has an altogether different air.

"It has been a long time since *Soliton* had another Melos adept," he says. When he smiles, his teeth are huge and white. "Your technique is primitive, but you show promise. I look forward to watching your development." Then, as an afterthought, "If you survive."

"Thank you," I say again, and mentally add, *I think.* "You've been on the Council—"

"Almost from the beginning," he says. "Fifteen years."

He can't be more than thirty. I frown as he goes on.

"When I came aboard, Jarli ruled the ship in the Captain's name. I was the one who convinced her to share power." He shakes his head. "Now *there* was an adept. Melos and Rhema both. Deadly as a scorpion and fast as sin."

"What happened to her?"

Karakoa falls silent, and it's Zarun who answers. "She died, trying to get beyond the Center."

"She said there had to be something there, at the other end of the ship," Karakoa says. "Something more than mushrooms and crabs. Foolishness."

"Did Jarli introduce you to the Captain?" This feels about as subtle as a brick to the face, but this sort of thing isn't my strength. "Or did that happen after she . . . was gone?"

"She introduced me," Karakoa says, glancing at Zarun.

"Can you tell me what he's like?"

The big warrior purses his lips for a moment. "Not what I expected."

Someone else is trying to get Karakoa's attention, so Zarun steers me away. "He's a good sort, in the end," he says in a low voice. "A bit . . . unsubtle, perhaps. But a hell of a fighter."

"I can imagine," I murmur. There's something bothering me, looking out at the crowd, but I can't put my finger on it.

"Now," Zarun says. "Where—" His face falls, and he heaves a sigh.

"What's the problem?"

"The Scholar." Zarun's lip twists. "I was hoping he'd stay with his precious books tonight. He usually does."

"You didn't seem worried about him the other day."

"I'm not *worried*," Zarun says. "He's just tedious." His eyes flick to me. "Incidentally. You didn't care for the dress?"

I look down at myself with a slight grin. "I thought this was more . . . *me*."

"Do you know, I think I agree with you?" His gaze lingers deliberately. "It's . . ."

"Dangerous?"

"Exactly." He reaches for my midriff and strokes it gently with the backs of his knuckles. "I hadn't realized these marks went all over. I'd be . . . interested to examine the rest."

"Of course you would," a woman says. "Honestly, Zarun, you call Karakoa unsubtle, but you're about as delicate as a bull in heat."

"Shiara." Zarun turns around, and I turn with him. "How lovely to see you."

It's the other person I saw on the platform, the Imperial woman. She's my age, or maybe even younger, and a spectacular beauty in the classical style: long, slim legs and a narrow waist, delicate features, and night-black hair falling in a torrent nearly to the deck. She's wearing a dress, not a *kizen*, and it leaves little to the imagination, baring her shoulders and a deep neckline. Her skin is almost as pale as an iceling's, and her lips are painted a deep, bloody red.

I may not have Meroe's facility for learning the lay of the political land, but I've heard a bit about Shiara. The other officers won their positions through skill and strength, but she'd taken hers by cunning, beginning as nothing more than a desperate hawker in the market. Careful trading had seen her rise to leader of a scavenger pack, and then beyond. Now her clade included the most successful traders on the ship, not to mention running the only brothel.

Beside her is the Scholar, in his round spectacles. Unlike everyone else, he's made no effort to dress up for the occasion, and still wears the slightly shabby robe in which I'd last seen him. He nods to me, as though we were old friends, the flickers of the lanterns reflected in his lenses.

"You are a pretty man, Zarun, but somewhat empty-headed," Shiara says. There's a playfulness in her tone, unlike the Butcher's mockery. "Go on. Make your introduction, since it pleases you so."

"Isoka, this is Shiara," Zarun says. "She has a wasp's stinger for a tongue, but she's not as bad as she seems."

"Oh, is that how we're playing?" Shiara steps forward, red lips crooked. "I could tell you stories about *him,* my dear. But tell me. You were taken from the Empire?"

"Kahnzoka," I say, cautiously.

"It's been nearly a year since we left Imperial waters," she says. "I'm dangerously behind on the latest gossip. Did Princess Ariane ever figure out who the father of her baby was? Is old Barei still alive?"

I can't tell if she's putting me on. That sort of story, treating the affairs of the royal family like the twists and turns of street theater, was everywhere in Kahnzoka's taverns and winesinks, lowborn getting a bit of their own back by gawping at the antics of their betters. I'd never paid much attention, since the tales changed with the teller and had little bearing on anything that mattered.

Zarun, apparently, agreed with me. "Why not just make up your own story, Shiara?" he says. "It'll have just as much relevance."

"Knowing it's real always adds a certain something," she says. "Come on, Deepwalker. What's the latest?"

"You're asking the wrong person," I say. "I never kept track of all that who's-sleeping-with-whom stuff."

Shira makes a disappointed pout. "Well. At least you've stirred things up a little around *here.* I've been so bored lately."

Zarun gives her a look I can't interpret, and Shiara sighs. She's turning to leave when something catches my eye. She's wearing a necklace, a long silver chain with a chunk of metal on it. It's dull and a little rusted, unlike the rest of her jewelry, and it seems to be a piece of something larger. Both ends are a filigree of tiny hairs, hanging loose, like an old, frayed rope.

That's not what captures my attention, though. Something is *moving* inside the metal, tiny points of soft gray light slowly churning in an endless spiral. They're barely visible in the glow of the lanterns, but I'm certain it's the same light I've seen in *Soliton*'s support pillars, the light that seemed to gather around the angel and shape itself into Hagan.

Is she *wearing* a piece of the ship? But there's scrap metal everywhere and I've never seen anything similar.

"Isoka, dear. You're welcome to keep staring, but after a certain point I usually charge a fee."

"Sorry." I blink and look away, and find myself locking eyes with the Scholar, who is watching me intently. Shiara smiles, this time with a nasty edge, and slips off into the crowd.

Zarun touches my arm. "Did I miss something?"

"Just . . . the wine. Or whatever it is. It's been a while since I had any."

"I think that means you need a bit more," he says.

"Not just yet." I look around for Meroe, surreptitiously pulling myself free of Zarun's grip. "Do you—"

"Do you think I could have a moment?" It's the Scholar, stepping forward, his cane rapping sharply on the deck.

"I suppose," Zarun mutters. "*I* will have another glass of wine, at least."

He turns back toward the table, leaving me at the fringe of the crowd with the Scholar. We look at each other in silence for a few moments, until I start to feel awkward.

"You wanted to talk to me," I prompt.

"I did," he says.

"If you want the story of what happened in the Deeps, this probably isn't the best time."

"It's not," he agrees. "I'll have it later." He pauses again, holding up a hand just as I open my mouth to speak. "I'm considering," he says, "the best approach."

"The best approach to *what*?" He's starting to remind me of Jack, although a bit less excitable.

"You talked to Karakoa."

"I did."

"And you asked him about when he joined the Council." Apparently he'd been listening. "What did he say?"

"That he helped found it, fifteen years ago." I frown at him. "You must know this, right?"

"Did he tell you," the Scholar goes on, ignoring me, "what *Soliton* was like fifteen years ago?"

"No. Other than that someone named Jarli was in charge." I was starting to see Zarun's point.

"One woman, ruling in the name of the Captain. Ruling over a single clade of perhaps . . . a hundred people?" He shrugs. "I arrived not long after, you see. Though it was years before I was admitted to the Council."

"All right. So what?"

"At the time we had barely begun to secure a single tower in the Upper Stations. Now we have nine, and they're nearly full."

I recall the ride up in the cage, the endless darkness. "There's plenty of room."

"Not the point," he snaps.

"Please *get* to the point."

"One hundred people then," he says. "How many now, do you know?"

"I don't—"

"One thousand three hundred twenty-one," he cuts in. "Not counting any deaths that haven't been reported yet. I keep track."

"Good," I manage, "for you."

"Which means a little more than eighty people added as sacrifices per year. Net of deaths, of course."

The tickle in my mind from earlier is back. "And not counting any children."

"No children on *Soliton*."

"What?"

"Women can't conceive on the ship." He gives a tight smile. "It just . . . doesn't happen."

At some level, it made sense. I hadn't seen any babies or expecting mothers, and as far as I could tell there were no ghulwitches to provide family planning. But . . .

"Why not?"

"Good question." He looks over my shoulder, at the rest of the crowd, and sneers. "They're not fond of asking questions. But think a little harder. Eighty people added per year. Which means?"

I speak slowly. "What were things like a few years before Karakoa came aboard?"

"Death rate is high. Few survivors. Hard to say. But another good question."

"Hang on," I say. "*Soliton* has been going around for *centuries*. And there were people here a lot longer than twenty years ago. I saw a village in the Deeps. . . ." I trail off, as he stares at me with interest. "It was a ruin. But it had been there a long time."

"Indeed." He cocks his head. "I like you, Isoka Deepwalker. You have the air of someone who asks questions."

There's a long drumroll, drowning out conversation for a moment. The Scholar bangs his cane on the deck and bows.

"That," he says, "is my cue. You must come and visit me, I think. We can . . . ask questions. In the meantime, I'll leave you with one." He waves his cane at the crowd. "Apart from the children, what's missing?"

He stalks away before I can answer, twisted foot dragging. I watch him go, hardly sure what to think. He seems half-crazy. But . . .

I think back to Kahnzoka, to crowds like this one. Men and women, children and adults, rich and poor. The fish market, where they all came together. Old men sitting in doorways, telling tales to a crowd of street kids. Old women, bent double under the weight of a load of fish, still capable of a shocking turn of speed.

Karakoa *might* be thirty. A few others I'd seen look a touch older, but not much. No one past that.

People come on board as teenagers. The Captain and the angels wouldn't accept anyone younger or older, or so I'd been told. So if someone had been brought on board fifteen years ago and they'd been nineteen, that would make them thirty-four today. The math works out.

No one in this crowd, no one I'd met on *Soliton*, can date from

much before Karakoa arrived. Some people die, of course, but . . .
everyone?

What in the Rot is happening on this ship?

I manage to find Meroe, still waiting by the table of food, working
her way through a plate of fried . . . things with evident relish.

"Do you have any idea what those are?" I ask her.

She shrugs, mouth full. "'ey're goo'." I roll my eyes, and she swallows. "Did you find anything?"

"Maybe." I'm still not sure what to make of the Scholar. "I'll tell
you later."

The drumroll sounds again, and the crowd goes quiet. A couple
more lanterns come alight, revealing the officers standing in a line
between the pair of massive, motionless angels. The Butcher waits
with her arms crossed, looking uncomfortable and even larger than
usual next to the petite Shiara. Karakoa and Zarun seem more relaxed. Off to one side is the Scholar, leaning on his cane.

"Is he an officer or not?" I ask Meroe.

"He's on the Council," she says, "but he doesn't have his own
clade or any hunting packs. The others keep him around because
he's useful."

"Fellow sacrifices," Karakoa booms, and there's a ripple of
laugher. "Thank you for joining us. As always, we are honored by
your trust, and the Captain's." He glances in either direction at his
fellow officers. "We will come to the point. There have been . . .
irregularities, as I'm sure you've all noticed. Scholar, would you
summarize?"

The Scholar steps forward with a click of his cane. "Our last stop
was in Kahnzoka. We haven't gotten any fresh meat since then, and
Soliton has been staying mostly out of sight of land. Our speed has
increased, too." He gestures to his left. "Somewhere off that way is
Cape Wall."

I hear Meroe's breath catch, and I lean close to her. "What does
that mean?"

"Cape Wall is halfway down the Southern Kingdoms," she says.

"Well south of Nimar. We're more than a thousand miles from Kahnzoka."

A thousand miles. I can't even visualize that distance. The Sixteenth Ward is a bit more than a mile from end to end, long and skinny as it crams against the waterfront. I try to picture a *thousand* of them, laid one after the other. It's easy to forget that *Soliton* moves at all when I'm belowdecks; now I feel the wind on the back of my neck, and shiver.

A stray thought, infuriating but true: no wonder Kuon Naga wants this ship. Big enough to carry an army, faster than anything with sails, impervious to the unreliable wind and the waves. No arrow or siege engine could do more than scratch its metal hull. Forget some border squabble with Jyashtan. Control *Soliton* and you could rule the world.

People in the crowd have started shouting back, a confusing jumble of accents and languages. The gist is clear enough, though.

"What's going on?"

"Why has the Captain changed course?"

"Where is he taking us?"

The Butcher steps forward, her voice a roar. "Shut up and listen!"

The crowd quiets again. Karakoa says, "Believe me, we heard your concerns, and we share them. Naturally, we petitioned the Captain."

Now the hush is so quiet I can hear the whistle of the breeze, like when the priests intone the sacred names of the Blessed One.

"Of course," Karakoa says, into the silence, "the Captain's reasons are his own, and we do not question them. But he assures us that the disruption will be short-lived. Our regular stops will resume soon."

"In other words," the Butcher says, "try not to panic like a flock of rotting chickens! There'll be more fresh meat and more sacrifices to scavenge soon enough. Just keep your heads down and keep hunting."

Mutters from the pack leaders. They don't sound happy.

"Speaking of hunting," Zarun says, ignoring the glance of pure loathing the Butcher directs at him. "I imagine you've heard that

Pack Twelve lost two men looking for blueshells six levels down from the Drips. One of my packs went looking for the bodies, and found what was left of them." He pauses. "It wasn't a blueshell that got them. It was a dredwurm."

The name means nothing to me, and Meroe looks confused, too. But there's a sigh from the crowd, a sort of collective intake of breath that indicates it's very significant indeed.

"It cannot be allowed to run loose, and that means a Grand Hunt," Zarun says. "The Council hereby makes this offer: whatever pack brings us the eye of the dredwurm can claim any boon within our power to grant, in addition to the usual bounty of scrip." He beams at us. "I expect quick results, my friends."

With that announcement, the party seemed to be over. There was a brief crush as the assembled pack leaders looted what was left of the food and drink, and then a general movement in the direction of the stairs. I stick by Meroe's side and wait as they disperse. Eventually, Jack appears, looking a bit sweatier and more disheveled than before, and gives us a grave bow.

"I trust that you enjoyed yourselves?" she says. "These audiences are the closest thing *Soliton* has to a social scene, not counting Shiara's occasional debauches."

"It was . . . interesting." I glance at Meroe, who nods agreement. "Jack, what's a dredwurm?"

"Ah, yes." Jack's eyes light up. "A truly legendary beastie, the king of crabs, risen from the Deeps. Or so we're told." She shrugs. "Each one looks different, but they're all strong enough to break through the decking and tunnel wherever they like. They're impossible to keep out with walls and guards, so the only option is to destroy them whenever they show their fangs."

"And the eye?" Meroe says.

"That's what makes it a dredwurm. Every one of the monsters has a single crystal eye, and the Council is bound to collect them for the Captain. Hence the bounty. Whoever takes the beast can name her price." She grins. "Zarun will try for it, you can be certain. If you ask nicely, he'll let you take part and we'll all split the reward."

Meroe and I exchange looks, and I can tell our thoughts are running on similar lines. If the Captain himself wants these eyes—

"But that's for later," Jack says. "Back to the cage, friends! Time to leave the angels to their silence and descend back to the world of mortals." She winks at me, looking a little tipsy, even for Jack. "Thora will be waiting."

17

I sit opposite Aifin, with a writing slate and some crumbly, chalk-like stuff on the table between us. He watches me with bright, intelligent eyes. I've never looked at him up close before; while his skin is as dark as a southerner's, his features are more Jyashtani.

"His progress has been amazing," Meroe says. She's standing at my shoulder, holding her cane but not putting any weight on it. She's still cautious of her leg, though Sister Cadua says it should nearly be back to full strength. "I've tutored him a little bit, but once he got the basics he started going through every book he could get his hands on. Go ahead, ask him something."

It's hard to imagine this is the boy we used to call the Moron, when he's so obviously keenly alert. I clear my throat, then feel stupid for doing so and pick up the chalk instead. Carefully, I write out: "My name is Isoka," in simple block letters.

He nods, takes the slate, and scribbles in a rough but readable hand: "M. tells me about you. Says you are leader of . . ."

He taps the chalk against the slate, thinking. I take it back and write: "Pack. Like wolves."

"Pack," he writes. "Yes. To fight monsters."

I wipe the slate clean with my sleeve and start again. "Yes. We fight monsters, to get food to eat."

"I will fight," he writes, smudging the letters with his eagerness.

"Before, when Ahdron was leader, you didn't fight."

He taps the word "Ahdron" and shakes his head. I gesture, indicating a tall young man, and eventually he gets the idea. He writes:

"Did not understand. So long without understanding. No one reads my words here. Could not read yours."

"You could have made us understand, couldn't you?" I gesture at my tongue and my ears, to demonstrate.

He gives an uncomfortable shrug. "Tried. Others didn't listen. Hurt me. Stopped trying." He hesitates, then adds: "Thought I had died, and in hell."

"May I?" Meroe says. When I hand her the chalk, she writes: "Who taught you to read your language? How did you get here?"

Aifin wipes the slate again. "Father taught me. Loved me, even though broken." He taps his throat. "But Father died. Uncle wants rid of useless mouth. Sell to slaver for monster ship."

So many on *Soliton* have some variant of the same story. For all her cruelty, what the Butcher told Meroe wasn't wrong.

"We'll practice sometime soon," I write. "So you can show me what you can do."

Aifin nods enthusiastically. He holds up one hand, and for a moment it's outlined in golden light, his fingers moving so fast they're a blur.

"Rhema," I say aloud, surprised. The Well of Speed is relatively rare. Picking up the slate again, I write: "That will be useful."

Aifin nods again. A curtain shuffles in the back, and Jack emerges with a flourish. "Dinnertime! Are you lot coming to the Crossroads?"

"Isoka and I will," Meroe says, before I can say anything. She takes the chalk and puts the question to Aifin, who shakes his head. "And Berun is still shopping."

"Thora is still *snoring,* so the three of us will have to make do." Jack strikes a heroic pose, like an explorer pointing the way. "Onward!"

I don't grumble. But Meroe has become adept at reading my expressions, and she rolls her eyes at me as we follow Jack down the corridor.

"Eating dinner in public is hardly torture," she says. "It's good to get to know people."

"Getting to know people is your department. I handle cutting them into pieces, remember?"

"You're the pack leader. And the Deepwalker. Like it or not, that means you've got a role to play."

I make a face, but the truth is this argument is mostly for show. Meroe makes much of the small talk anyway, so all I have to do is nod along. And the food is usually better, though you never quite know what you're going to get.

I have to admit, as we emerge from the tower and start threading our way through the market, that living on *Soliton* is starting to feel almost normal. The mix of people from every country on the planet no longer seems odd; when I get back to Kahnzoka, it will be strange to be surrounded by so many Imperials. I've gotten used to the haphazard clothes, the weird mix of primitive makeshift tools and luxury goods from the scavengers. I'm even coming to appreciate the differences between breeds of mushrooms, and know where the best meat comes off a crab.

I'm losing my edge, in short. Getting comfortable. At night I close my eyes, listening to Meroe's soft breathing, and try to think about Tori. I try to picture what Naga will do to her if I don't return.

It should be *all* I think about. But I keep getting distracted. Just now, I'm watching the way Meroe's hair bounces as she walks, the sway of her hips.

Rot, rot, *rot. Stay focused, Isoka.*

When I first visited the Crossroads, it seemed like chaos. Now that I know what to look for, it's still chaos, but *organized* chaos, if that makes any sense. The tables are roughly divided into clades, with pack leaders and important clade members drifting toward the center, and the rest surrounding them. There are no emblems for the clades, no explicit symbols, but it's not hard to tell who's who after a while. The Butcher's people, for example, wear more trophies than anyone else, forever covering even their everyday clothes with bits of crab shell. Karakoa's fighters wear plain, unadorned clothing, following the example set by their leader, whereas both men and women in Shiara's clade seem to have some kind of competition to see who can wear the most jewelry.

Not everyone in Zarun's clade dresses as gaudily as Zarun, but enough try to emulate him that a gathering of his servants is easy to pick out. My status as pack leader and Deepwalker gets us a place at the inner table, and a few others even push out of the way to make room. Jack seats herself at my left hand, Meroe at my right. One of the Crossroads' young servers quickly comes over to offer us drinks, and I raise a mug in greeting, receiving nods from around the table.

At Meroe's prodding, I've come to recognize a few of them. Pack Seventeen's Attoka, an Imperial girl with a shock of bleached-white hair, chats with the somber Marcius, the southerner head of Pack Eleven. Sketor, a tall but skeletally thin iceling boy who trades in weapons, flirts with a trio of young men from one of the hunting packs. There's a general buzz of conversation, and I'm pleased to see that the others are getting used to *me,* too. The first few times we joined the group, I spent the whole time fielding questions about the Deeps, none of which I particularly wanted to answer.

The conversation, of course, is about the dredwurm. The hunt for the creature has stretched on longer than I expected, but Jack says this is normal—just *finding* a dredwurm is hard enough, let alone killing one. Hunting packs are flooding the lower sections of the Stern, looking for the telltale holes torn in the deck plates, and along the way cleaning out the crabs that cross their path. There's talk of expanding the Middle Deck and the Drips, pushing the barricades outward to incorporate freshly cleared areas into the "civilized" part of the ship.

The gossip is all about who's found fresh signs, who's been hurt, who brought home a good kill. I listen with only half an ear as Meroe and I tuck into mushroom-and-crab pies, seasoned with some spice brought back by a scavenger. It's hot enough to make my eyes water, and tasty enough that I send off for a second helping.

"Aifin," I ask Meroe, as she guzzles water, "you really think we should bring him out on a hunt with us?"

"He volunteered," she said. "After he quizzed me about *Soliton*. I think he's desperate to fit in." She shakes her head. "Imagine how lonely he must have been."

He thought he was in hell. If that's what hell is like, count me glad we Imperials don't have such a thing.

"Well," I say. "We'll have to see how strong he is. I've never worked with someone who used Rhema before."

Meroe nods. "He and I should both be able to come along soon."

"You're sure?" I glance at her cane.

"I think so. It feels much stronger." She stomps her foot and grins. "Practically good as new."

Frankly, I'd rather Meroe stay behind. It would be one less thing to worry about, but she'd never permit it. Princess or no princess, she doesn't want to be coddled.

"And Berun's been making good progress with Thora," Meroe says.

"Speaking of progress." I lower my voice. "Any luck?"

"Not much." She looks irritated. "People don't *write* anything here. All the books are from sacrifices. There's no records that I've been able to find."

"I don't think the scavengers have brought back a printing press yet."

Meroe snorts. "Most of the people I've talked to don't understand why I would care what happened twenty years ago, much less further back than that."

"But you *haven't* found anyone old enough to remember?"

She shakes her head. "No. The Scholar was right—there's no one who's been on board longer than Karakoa."

"There *were* people here, though. Scavengers find old gear all the time. So what happened to them?"

"Maybe they just died out?" Meroe says. "It takes a lot of effort to keep the crabs out of the Stern. Maybe they broke through, and everyone died."

"Maybe." But I find it unlikely. A settlement of ordinary people might be wiped out by crabs, but a town full of mage-bloods?

"Isoka . . ." Meroe hesitates. "It's definitely strange, but are you sure this is the right thing to be asking questions about? I thought we were trying to find the Captain."

"The two fit together," I say. "If the people on the ship were wiped out somehow, what happened to the Captain? Did he die, too? If he did—"

"Then someone on board eventually became the new Captain." Meroe nods. "*That* makes sense."

"The succession is the important part," I say. "If we can figure that out . . ."

I trail off. We've always left the most important part of the plan unstated, as though speaking it aloud would make it clear how silly it is. But it's there: one of us has to *become* Captain, if such a thing is possible.

I've told Meroe that this is my plan for getting us off the ship. If it's the angels that stop people from leaving and the Captain controls the angels, then the Captain and anyone close to him must be able to leave.

I'd be the first to admit that it's not a *great* plan. But it's what I've got, until we get more information. The problem is, the only people who know anything about the Captain aren't talking.

We get our second helpings, and I happily dig in. Jack is talking to Attoka about how the romantic adventures of a mutual friend are going—not well, apparently—and I find my attention drawn to a conversation at the next table, where some of the less senior pack members have gathered.

"And you believe it?" one boy says, with a thick Jyashtani accent. "Nobody can remember this happening before, but we asked the Captain and 'everything's fine; everyone just carry on.'" He snorts.

"You think the Captain doesn't know what's happening?" a girl beside him says.

"Don't be stupid. But if the Captain told the officers, 'Sorry about this, but I'm dropping you all in deep rot,' do you think they'd tell *us*?"

"Don't know about that," another young man says. "But I do know that some of the officers are worried. Word is Shiara's been buying up food and storing it away. She's got some kind of private fortress in the Drips."

"She's always been a paranoid bitch," the girl says. "Might not mean anything."

Someone behind me coughs politely for attention. I half-turn and find myself facing a tall, blond iceling girl, a few years younger than me, with a white robe and complicated braid that give her a priestly look.

"Deepwalker?" she says.

I raise an eyebrow. Given the evidence literally written on my face, the whole ship should be able to pick me out by now. "Yes?"

"I serve the Scholar," she says. "My apologies for the interruption, but he would like to ask if you could attend him this evening."

I look at Meroe to make sure she's listening, then ask, "What does he want?"

The girl bows her head. "He's told me only that he has some information you might find to be of interest."

"That's not very specific." Meroe gives a little nod, though, and I sigh. "All right, why not? Where does he want to meet?"

"He asked me to bring you to his observatory," the girl says. "If you are not finished with your dinner, I will wait."

"Oh." I look down at what's left of my meal and find my appetite suddenly lacking. "Now's as good a time as any, I suppose."

The girl leads me out of the market, and somewhat to my surprise makes for the long staircase that leads from the Upper Stations to the open deck. We start to ascend, walking in a tight spiral, and it's not many turns before I'm wishing we'd taken the cage up instead.

"What's your name?" I ask.

"Erin," she says. I wait a moment to see if she'll offer anything else, but that seems to be all.

"I thought the Scholar didn't have a clade of his own," I prompt.

"He does not," Erin says. "But he helped me and my sister Arin, and in gratitude we tend to his needs. He is a kind master."

There's something off here—for one thing, this kind of quiet obedience seems antithetical to the other icelings I've met, women like Thora and the Butcher. Maybe there are different nations and cultures among the northerners.

"And he lives up on the deck?"

She nods. "He must be able to view the sky to do his work. You will see."

After more turns than I'm really prepared for, we reach the top, both of us panting slightly. The staircase rises through a circular hatch, letting out on to the rust-mottled outer skin of the great ship. It's evening, and the sun is nearly to the horizon, lighting up a band of clouds in pinks and oranges. The eastern sky is already darkening from purple to black, and a few bright stars have appeared.

In the darkness of the Council meeting, I didn't appreciate how many structures there were on the ship's deck. The Captain's tower is the largest, rising like a great black spike at the Stern, but there are dozens of oddly shaped protrusions, cubes, half spheres, and stranger objects. Some have collapsed, undermined by rust, and others spill thick rivers of vegetation and fungus from the holes in their roofs. It reminds me that we're beyond the defensive perimeter of the Upper Stations, here. This is the domain of the crabs, and I itch to summon my blades.

"You're perfectly safe," Erin says. "The master understands the crabs better than anyone else on *Soliton,* and he keeps careful track of any dangerous ones whose territories might encroach."

"Good to know." I keep looking around, just in case.

She leads me to a large cylindrical structure, like half a barrel embedded into the deck. It's several stories high, and the rusted holes in the sides have been patched with scrap metal and fabric. A small door at the bottom stands open, and Erin reaches it, then steps aside, gesturing for me to enter first. Beyond is warm, musty darkness, and I blink as my eyes adjust.

The interior of the cylinder is a single large space, full of a bewildering array of chests, cabinets, desks, and dressers. It looks as though the Scholar has grabbed any furniture that might be useful to keep things in, in some cases stacking them on top of one another in unwieldy arrangements. The desks are covered in . . .

junk, pieces of broken tools, metal fragments, sections of mushroom, and organic debris that must have come from dead crabs.
There are bones, as well, human skeletons both fresh and yel-
lowed with age.

One set makes me pause for a moment. They're dry and brittle
looking, but still recognizably *wrong,* twisted and deformed. Limbs
bifurcate where they should run straight, or twist into spirals. A
skull bulges like it struggled to contain something growing within.
Another, so small it might have belonged to an infant, has two extra eye sockets. These bones look older, but . . .

"You've seen something like this before, haven't you?"

The Scholar is coming down another spiral staircase, this one
wrapped along the outside wall of the building, leading up to a second level that's half rusted away. His cane raps on each step as he
descends.

"In the Deeps," I say, cautiously. "There was a village, all ruined.
The bodies there looked like this."

"I'm not surprised," he says. "I wish you could have brought some
back for study. You can never have enough bones, I say." He reaches
the bottom of the staircase and gestures at his bizarre collection with
his cane. "Thank you for accepting my invitation."

"You said you had something interesting to tell me."

"I do." He smiles, and pushes his glasses up his nose. "And I have
reason to think you might be willing to listen, which is more than
I can say for the others."

"What others?"

"Our oh-so-wise *officers.*" He snorts. "Zarun and the Butcher
can't decide if they're going to rut or kill each other, Karakoa can't
see past the next hunt, and Shiara cares only about herself. Whereas
you, you have been asking questions." He cocks his head. "At least,
your princess has."

"I don't—" I begin.

"Don't play stupid. These things get back to me, you know. And
there's nothing wrong with asking questions, at least as far as *I'm*
concerned. Some of the others might not take such a benign view
if they knew what you were really after."

"We're just . . . curious." I shrug. "We live on this ship, but we don't understand it at all. And mostly no one seems to *want* to."

"Curiosity is difficult," the Scholar says, tapping his way closer. "Better to fight out your little feuds, hunt the crabs, and try to forget about it, especially when the answers aren't easily forthcoming." He stops across from me, beside the desk full of bones. "You've been thinking about what I said at the audience."

"A bit," I admit. "We know there were people on *Soliton* generations ago."

He taps the desk. "These bones are two hundred years old, give or take."

"But there was almost no one here fifteen years ago. Sometime before that, there must have actually *been* no one, except maybe the Captain."

"Very good."

"So something wiped everyone out."

"Exactly." He gestures at the bones and other artifacts with his cane. "And I can tell you this. It wasn't the first time. I've found fragments from a half-dozen generations. Never much, but enough to tell me people were here, and then that they weren't. Over and over."

"And? What happened to them?"

"I can only guess." The Scholar sighs. "So few things get written down."

I chuckle. "Meroe was complaining about the same thing."

"And has she found any answers?"

"Not really." I shake my head. "Why are you telling me this? Just because I like to ask questions?"

"Oh no." He beckons. "Come upstairs. There's more to the show."

Another set of stairs, my legs groaning in protest, keeping pace with the Scholar's slow ascent. The second level of the tower is set well above the first, and covers only half the circular space, with a ragged-edged drop looking over the floor below. The stair reaches a landing and then continues upward, through a hole in another, more intact floor, the opening currently blocked off with a cloth.

This level, apparently, is where the Scholar actually lives, inasmuch as there's a large bed shoved against one wall like an afterthought. A table beside it is piled high with dirty dishes, which look as much like archeological specimens as some of the debris below. The rest of the space is devoted to more tables, all covered in carefully arranged trash.

"Arin, dear," the Scholar says. "Go and help your sister fetch water."

There's a yawn from the bed, and a girl in a long white robe sits up, kicking back the sheets. She's identical to Erin, except that her hair is loose instead of braided. When she sees me, she looks interested, but not alarmed. The Scholar says nothing while she puts on shoes and troops down the stairs. Only when she's out the door does he turn back to me.

"You don't trust your . . . servants?"

"Erin and Arin are very dear to me, and I would never question their loyalty," he says. "But I wouldn't want to upset them unnecessarily."

"What exactly are you planning to show me?"

"Just this." He walks to one of the tables and raps on the wood. "What do you see, Deepwalker?"

I look. The thing on the table is like a rope, if a rope could be woven of steel strands. It's coiled around several times, and roughly severed at both ends. The individual fibers untwist at the cuts, opening out like a flower into smaller and smaller filaments, until they reach the limit of vision and become a vague fuzz.

"Metal rope?" I ask.

"Look closer." He sounds oddly eager. It makes me want to leave this place and not come back, but I bend down instead, squinting.

Movement, inside the thing. Tiny sparks of gray light, streaming in both directions, a twisting flow that follows the spiral of the fibers. And I realize what the rope reminds me of—Shiara's necklace, the night of the Council meeting, only much larger.

My face must have given something away, because the Scholar is smiling in quiet satisfaction. He touches his glasses again, and his hand is shaking very slightly.

"You can see it, can't you?"

"See—" I look from the rope to him and back. "What *is* this thing?"

"It's a piece of the ship, from one of the support pylons." He takes a step forward, cane tapping. "You *can* see it. I could tell the night of the Council meeting. I suggested Shiara wear that necklace; it's another fragment, a weak one, but—" He shakes his head in wonder. "And if you could see *that* then you're stronger than I am, much stronger. Finally. *Finally.*"

"Slow down." I take a half step back, and make a conscious effort not to summon my armor. "*You* can see those lights, then?"

"You were a gang enforcer, back in Kahnzoka. They're already telling stories about you. And you're a Melos adept. You killed people, didn't you?"

"I—" My head is spinning, trying to follow him. "So what if I did? Here on *Soliton* you—"

"I don't care about the *morality*. Leave that to the gods." The Scholar's glasses reflect the lanterns burning around the room, tiny bits of light shining in his eyes. "Afterward, you dreamed about them, didn't you?"

My throat seizes up for a moment. My mind goes to Hagan, and I swallow hard. "How could you know that?"

"I dreamed of the first person I killed," he says. "She was nothing to me, a street rat who tried to knife me in an alley. I didn't mean to hurt her, but she came at me, and . . ." He waves his hand, as though to dispel the memory. "I thought she was haunting me."

"No such thing as haunting," I say, automatically. "Dead is dead."

"Not entirely." He takes a deep breath, calms a little. "You—we—can touch a Well no one else can. The Lost Well, the Well of Spirits. Eddica."

18

Eddica. The first Well, the Well of Spirits. Lost, according to some; a myth, according to the Blessed One.

A month ago I would have said the priests had the right of it. Now . . .

"No one can access Eddica," I say. "There hasn't been even an Eddica-touched in the history of the Empire."

"I suspect your illustrious rulers are lying to you about that, as about so many things." The Scholar shrugs. "Eddica is real enough. But rare, now, and so subtle that even those who have it usually don't know it's there. Only on *Soliton* does it become obvious."

"Why here?"

"Because *that* is Eddica energy!" He raps the table again. "The whole ship runs on it. You've seen it, in the pylons, the towers." He lowers his voice. "You've felt it from the angels."

"I've seen *something*." I'm sure as rot not going to tell *him* about Hagan. "This is a strange rotting place, but that doesn't make it *spirit energy*."

"Did you dream of Ahdron, after you killed him?"

I shake my head, frowning.

"If you die here, you go into the ship. Children can't be born here, because the spirits can't reach them. The whole ship is like a giant cage for souls."

"That's . . ." I take another step away from him. "No wonder the others won't listen to you. You're off your head."

There's a pause. He takes a moment and visibly restrains himself, straightening up. His cane taps the deck, twice.

Because that's what anyone would say, isn't it? Anyone who hadn't been guided out of the Deeps by what looked very much like the ghost of her best friend.

Could he be *right*? Rot, rot, rot. I need time to think.

"You don't have to believe me," he says. "I didn't expect you to, to be honest. It took me years to work it out." He paces a few steps, tap-tapping, then turns. "But you must admit that you and I share a power that no one else on the ship has. That we can see this . . . energy. And if we can see it, perhaps we can manipulate it."

I remember how Hagan had thrown lines of the strange gray energy at the angel to halt it in its tracks, and used it to show me the way home. Whatever it is, the Scholar is right that it flows throughout *Soliton*. Is that the Captain's secret? If this power can control an angel, can it control the ship itself?

The Scholar misinterprets the look on my face. "You see the possibilities, don't you?"

I shrug. "So why aren't you running the ship?"

"I'm not strong enough. Only Eddica-touched, not even a talent. I can see the flows, if I concentrate hard, but they remain beyond my reach. But *you* saw the power in Shiara's necklace, without even trying. You must be a talent, or even an adept. You might be what I need."

"What *you* need?" I narrow my eyes. "What do you want from me?"

"Only what's best for everyone, of course." He grins. "Come. One more flight of stairs, and I'll show you the third act."

I'm about ready to walk out the door, or possibly cut this madman in half. But I don't. Because he may be crazy, but I'm not sure that I'm not crazy, too, and he's the best lead I have. And crazy or not, he's on the Council, and he can get to the Captain. If he needs my help so badly, I can get what I need from him.

And if he's right about this power, then . . . maybe . . .

We climb, again. When we reach the top of the spiral stair, he pushes the leather cover aside with his cane. I'm a little surprised to see sky above us, the light now almost totally gone, the river of stars broken by wispy clouds. No lanterns glow up here. We're still inside the cylindrical structure, but the roof and most of the walls above this floor are gone, leaving a flat expanse of deck bordered by a jagged, rusty edge. The floor is stained by rain and salt spray.

A single table stands in the center, surrounded by three bronze instruments on tall stands. Two look like spyglasses, while the third is a complicated arrangement of interlocking circles whose purpose I can't divine.

"This is why they let me on the Council, you see," the Scholar says, having regained his calm. "I figure things out. From here I can see the stars, when it's clear, and that tells us our position."

I nod, cautiously, as he walks to the table. I know that sailors at sea use the stars to figure out where they are, though I have no idea how one might actually go about doing it.

The table holds a couple of thick books, with leather covers to keep the rain away from them, holding down the edges of a big leather-backed map. It's a fine one, painted in a delicate hand, with tiny mountains and decorative sea serpents now cracked with age, and it shows all the lands around the Central Sea, the entire known world. Jyashtan in the west, the Blessed Empire in the east, with the divided bulge of the Southern Kingdoms beneath it. The islands of the icelings in the north, with glaciers carefully picked out in white and blue, and the gray expanse of the Southern Wastes, which the mapmaker has filled with fanciful imaginary beasts. Various islands stand out in the great ocean, including the string that stretch like stepping-stones from east to west, where the war fleets go to fight and die.

The Scholar puts his finger on the map, just below where the island chain comes closest to the Southern Kingdoms. I lean forward and read the label for Cape Wall, painted in tiny, tiny brushstrokes. Automatically, my eyes track north, and find Kahnzoka, tucked into its broad bay.

A thousand miles away. Full of things I never thought about, any more than I thought about the air I breathe. Now I find myself missing . . . everything. The food at Breda's, the way people in the Sixteenth Ward nodded to me as I passed, the feeling of walking streets I'd walked so many times the map was ground into my bones. And

Tori, beautiful, brilliant, *clean* Tori, untainted by the blood that stains my hands.

I take a deep breath, feeling it catch in my throat. At that moment, I would give anything to be able to visit her. To sit in her garden and listen to her earnest insistence that everyone could help one another if they would only *try*.

I would introduce her to Meroe. I think they would get along.

Tears prick the corners of my eyes. I blink them away, furious, and look up at the Scholar. He's staring at me, his expression unreadable.

"Well?" I ask him. "You've already tried to convince me that this ship runs on the spirits of the dead. You're going to have to work hard to get crazier than that."

"This, I'm afraid, is a bit more . . . mundane." He taps the map. "As you heard at the Council meeting, this is roughly where we are now." Tracing a line due south, his finger crosses the deep ocean between the Southern Kingdoms and the wastes, then turns west. "For fourteen years, *Soliton* has followed this path. Never precisely the same, but never varying much. We stop in different cities each year, for example."

The line continues across the wastes, then north along the coast of Jyashtan, all the way to the ice. Then east again, skirting the icelings' islands, until it returns to the Empire and turns south once more. A great circle, clockwise around the Central Sea.

"And now it's going faster than normal," I say. "You told us already."

"We passed Cape Wall several days ago," he says. "And we're still in sight of land. We're going *the wrong way*. East, not south."

My lips twist. "Maybe the Captain realized he forgot a city, and wanted to make a special trip."

"Perhaps. Perhaps we'll turn south, any day. But if we don't . . ."

I examine the map under his finger. The Southern Kingdoms and the wastes form a narrow strait, leading right off the eastern end of the map. Just at the edge, an island sits in the strait like a cork in a bottle, painted in blotches of green and red.

The Vile Rot.

"Don't be stupid." I straighten up. "No ship goes near the Rot." I'm from fifteen hundred miles away, and *I* know that.

"*Soliton* is hardly an ordinary ship." The Scholar shrugs. "Suppose that, every twenty years or so, it breaks from its usual pattern and takes this route. Through the Green Strait, to the Rot."

"That's . . ." I shake my head. "That's impossible. *Nothing* survives the Rot, not even *Soliton*. If the Captain took the ship in there, he wouldn't be around to take it out again."

"I wouldn't be surprised if everyone aboard died. But the ship?" He taps the deck with his cane. "Steel doesn't rot."

"What would be the point?"

"To clean us out, maybe? Like washing out a teapot in hot water. Clean the ship in the Rot and start over."

"Then why gather us in the first place? That makes no sense."

"Unless our deaths *are* the point." He leans closer. "If our souls *power* the ship. It picks up fuel, and then it *burns* it like firewood." He straightens up. "Or maybe the Captain has his own reasons."

"Why don't you ask him?"

"He's not inclined to share his thoughts with us," the Scholar says, with a slight smile.

I look down at the map again, and fight down a chill. *"Anomaly . . . coming . . . ,"* Hagan had said. *"Find Garden. Or die."*

Is this what he meant?

"I've heard enough," I say out loud. "They warned me you were a little mad, but I have to say this is worse than I expected."

There's a long pause.

"I didn't think you'd believe me," he says, surprisingly calm.

"I don't. And I'm leaving."

"You haven't heard my offer."

I snort. "I'm not interested in more crazy theories."

"Nothing so complicated. I know what you want, and I can get it for you."

"Oh, really?" I glare at him. "What do I want?"

"I can get you into the Captain's tower."

I stare for a moment. "Why should I believe you?"

"The crew guards the main entrance, but I can show you another route."

"It can't be that simple."

"It's not." He grins. "There's an angel on the bottom floor. But the Council has a key that will get us past it. I'll lend you mine."

"And then . . . what?"

"That's up to you." He spreads his arms. "You and your princess have been asking about getting to the Captain for weeks. I assume you have some plan for what you want to say to him."

I wish I did. But . . .

"And what's in this for you? I assume that if the rest of the Council found out, they wouldn't be pleased."

"You assume correctly." The Scholar raises his eyebrows. "I want you to bring me the dredwurm's eye."

That's not what I expected to hear. "I thought the Council already had a bounty on that."

"They do. Let's say that we disagree on what should be done with it."

"Why?"

"It doesn't matter." He grins again. "More of my 'craziness.' But that's my price."

"Even if I thought I could kill the dredwurm," I say carefully, "nobody knows where it is. Half the crew is out looking for it. If I ever see the thing, it'll be as part of some big team Zarun puts together, and I won't be able to get the eye for myself."

"As it happens, Zarun has just received a report from one of his scouting packs," the Scholar says. "He's putting together his team now, but it will take him a few days. If you hurry, you can beat him to the punch."

"Assuming he tells me what he knows. Unless you have the location already?"

"Unfortunately, my informant didn't quite get that far." He taps his cane against the deck. "But you're the Deepwalker. I have every confidence in you."

"If I do this . . ." I shake my head. "If anyone found out, Zarun or the other officers, they'd kill me."

"As they'd kill me, if they knew I let you into the Captain's tower. I think it's a fair trade."

"I'm not sure I do."

"It's my price," he snaps. "If you don't like it, you're welcome to try to find another way to get to the Captain." He glances at the map, then back at me. "If you think you have time."

I sit in my room, back against the wall, one foot tapping out a fast rhythm on the floor.

The Scholar may be crazy, but he's right about one thing. This is a hell of a bet. *He* thinks it's worth it, because he believes we're all headed to the Rot.

If he's right, we're all going to die. And if I die here, that means Tori—

Rot, rot, Blessed's rotten balls in a vise.

The curtain rustles, and Meroe comes in, looking worried.

"Are you all right?" she says. "Berun said you were looking for me."

I beckon her over, and she sits beside me, favoring her bad leg only a little. She's still carrying the cane, but she doesn't use it much.

"Isoka?"

I hold up a finger, close my eyes, and listen. The walls here aren't thick, Blessed knows Thora and Jack have proved that often enough. I don't hear anything now, but best to be careful. "Try to stay quiet."

Meroe obliges by whispering. "Isoka, what's going on?"

"I met with the Scholar."

"And?"

"He's mad."

She eyes me. "Is it contagious?"

"He made me . . . an offer. If we bring him the dredwurm's eye, he can get me in to see the Captain."

Meroe frowns. "I thought nobody knew where the dredwurm was."

"Zarun does. If I can get the information from him, we can beat him to the prize."

I see her eyes widen in understanding. "By 'we' you mean—"

"You and me. Berun. Aifin, if he's willing."

"Not Thora and Jack."

I shake my head. "I like them, but they were Zarun's people long before they were part of this pack."

She nods, slowly. There's a long silence.

"Do you really think we can kill the dredwurm? The four of us?"

"We killed a blueshell and a hammerhead."

"*You* killed them, you mean."

I shrug, uncomfortably. "Honestly? I don't know. But this could be the best chance we get."

It sounds like a weak argument, even to me. Why not wait, and look for a better opportunity? Get closer to the Council. If not for the Scholar and his rotting map, I would have agreed. But as it is . . . if there's a chance . . .

"If you think we can do it," Meroe says, "then I'll help."

I want to hug her and swear at her at the same time. Tell her she shouldn't put so much trust in me. What in the Rot do I know?

She shifts uncomfortably, working her fingers idly through her braids. "What about Zarun?"

"I'll figure that part out."

"We'll be betraying him."

"Does that bother you?" I cock my head. "You didn't want to accept his help in the first place."

"I . . ." She bites her lip. "I can't forget what he did the day we got here. That poor girl. But . . . he's done everything he promised since then. I don't *like* him, but I feel like I can trust him, if that makes any sense."

"He's using us, just like we're using him. We don't owe him anything."

"But if he finds out—"

"He'll kill us." I feel my fist clench. "Or I'll have to kill him. But he doesn't have to find out. I have a plan."

"Okay," Meroe says, and the trust in her voice tears at my heart. "When?"

"I'll get the information from Zarun tonight. We'll go looking

tomorrow morning. We can't risk someone else getting there first."
I hesitate. "Can you talk to the other two?"

She nods. "They'll help, I'm certain."

Of course they'll help. Berun is half in love with Meroe, and she's
the only friend Aifin has ever had. They'll do it for her, and she's
doing it for me. Which means it's all my responsibility.

Rot, rot, rot.

"Okay." My chest feels tight. "Then we're on."

"Okay." Meroe waits for a moment, looking at me. "Isoka? Are
you all right?"

I'm not all right. I'm trying hard not to stare at her, my hands
laced together in my lap. I know what I want to say, but it feels like
my throat has swollen shut.

"It's . . . ," I manage. But that's all.

Meroe scoots closer, until she's sitting directly opposite me, our
knees touching. She takes my hands in hers and holds them gently.

"I know what this means to you," she says, still whispering. "Getting off this ship and back to your sister. You're doing what you
have to do, Isoka."

"I know." She doesn't know the half of it. Doesn't know about
Kuon Naga, or the threat hanging over Tori's head. But I'm suddenly certain that even if she did, she'd understand. "Meroe . . ."

She's *right there*, face inches from mine, her lips slightly parted.
All I would have to do is lean forward, put my arms around her.

What I want to say is:

*I didn't think it was possible for someone to be as kind, as smart, as
brave, as you are.*

*I didn't think I could care about anyone but Tori. I thought I'd burned
that out of myself. Blessed knows I tried.*

*I have never wanted a girl before. I have never wanted someone so
badly in my life. I want to kiss you, touch you, drag you down, and rut
until we're both too tired and shaky to stand. To fall asleep with you in
my arms, listening to you breathe.*

But my arms hang dead, and my lips won't move. Because I have
no idea what she'll say. If she wants me. If she likes women, or likes
anyone.

Because the last person I slept with, I put my blade through his head when I thought it would help Tori. And I'm not sure I've changed.

She licks her lips, a quick dart of a pink tongue.

I get to my feet, pulling my hands away.

"I have to go." Forcing the words out feels like vomiting broken glass.

Does she hesitate for a moment? As though she was waiting for me to say something else? "Good luck."

First a side trip to Sister Cadua's. She has what I need.

Then the market, which never really sleeps. A bottle of Jyashtani wine, costing far too much scrip.

Then to Zarun's tower.

One of his crew is on guard at the door, a boy who blanches at the sight of me. I'm wearing the same outfit I had on the night of the Council meeting, sleek, tight-fitting leather and crab-shell armor, the blue tracks across my skin standing out in the lamplight. I tell him I'm here to see Zarun, and he hurries inside with the message, then reappears to escort me. He takes me up a floor via an echoing metal staircase, then raps at a door.

"She's, uh, here," the boy says. "The Deepwalker."

"Very good," comes Zarun's voice from inside. "Get lost."

He swallows hard, nods to me, and hurries away. I push the door open.

Zarun's chambers aren't as gaudy as I expected. There's a front room with a large table and chairs, and a desk pushed into one corner. Through a rear doorway I can see a bedroom, with a huge bed in the Jyashtani style. Another room is curtained off. Zarun is standing in the bedroom doorway, wearing a black silk robe belted loosely at the waist. It hangs open enough to show off his smooth, well-muscled chest.

"Deepwalker. Not who I expected at this hour."

"I thought we could have a drink." I hold up the bottle.

"A drink?" He raises an eyebrow.

I keep my voice level. "A drink."

"Well. Let it never be said I wasn't accommodating to a guest."
He goes into the bedroom, comes back with a pair of sparkling crystal glasses and a corkscrew.

"Have a seat," I tell him.

He takes one of the chairs. I open the bottle and pour, as he smiles at me, bemused. It gives me the chance to let the little sachet of dried mushrooms fall into his glass. The wine is a deep red, and the mushrooms dissolve almost immediately, but my heart is still beating hard when I hand it to him. If he has suspicions, they don't show. He raises his glass, and I raise mine, and we both take a long swallow.

"So, if I may ask," he says, "to what do I owe the honor of this visit?"

"Frustration, if I'm being honest." I refill the glasses.

"Frustration?"

It's my turn to raise an eyebrow. His eyes widen slightly, and if I'm not wrong there's a hint of embarrassment in his grin.

"You have an odd way of flirting," he says, taking another long drink.

"I'm not used to flirting," I say, honestly. "Back home, when I wanted a boy, I'd usually say something along the lines of, 'Hey, let's go upstairs and rut.'"

"Subtle."

"At least it keeps things honest."

"To honesty." He raises his glass, and I follow suit. "Is that why you haven't come before this? Because I was beating around the bush?"

"You were clear enough. I was . . ." I pause, and sip the wine, which I've been too nervous to taste. It's good, actually. "Until now, I needed your help too badly."

"Until now? I *am* still master of this clade." His smile disarms the comment.

"Now I feel like we have a mutual understanding."

"We're using each other, in other words."

"Exactly. I needed to be sure you had a use for me other than in bed. In my experience, that doesn't lead to reliable partnerships."

"Reliable partnerships," he says, smile widening. "Oh, I *like* you, Isoka. You are a cold little reptile, aren't you?"

"It's kept me alive."

He leans closer. "You never let personal feelings get in the way?"

"Of staying alive?" I snort. "Do you want to know how many people I've had to kill because a personal feeling made them do something stupid?"

"I wonder if your total is higher than mine," he says. "Honestly, I haven't kept track. It feels like there's one in every batch of fresh meat." He frowns. "There was someone like that in yours, wasn't there? I made an example."

"An idiot. And then his sister."

He doesn't even remember. Why should he? He's a monster.

Like me.

"Ah, yes." He looks back down at the wine bottle, half-empty already. "Well, Deepwalker. Let me speak your language. Would you like to go into the other room and rut?"

"I thought you'd never ask." I make my voice a low growl.

In a few moments, we're kissing, his hands on me and mine on him, trying to stumble back toward the doorway without pulling apart. We lurch off course, and my back slams into the wall hard enough to sting. He presses his palms against my shoulders, pinning me there, and kisses my neck down to my collarbone. My fingers curl in his hair.

There's nothing wrong with what I'm doing. Not with the rutting, anyway. It's not like Meroe and I have said anything to each other, made any promises. I'm within my rights to dally with a pretty boy, to kiss him as thoroughly as I wish, to let his hands creep up under my leather top, feeling the tightness in my chest, the heat sinking down through my belly. To pull him through the doorway at last, back to the bed.

And, when my eyes are closed, if I'm thinking about darker skin, a softer body with a different shape, thick dark hair, and clever fingers . . .

There's nothing wrong with that, either, I suppose.

* * *

It would be poetic justice to say that, for all his handsome face and obvious self-regard, Zarun made for an indifferent lover. Truthfully, though, he was attentive and patient, and by the time we were finished I lay comfortably beside him on the silk sheets, sweaty and satisfied. He had his head against my shoulder, one arm thrown over my breasts, and I stared at the ceiling and waited while his breathing deepened into the steady rhythm of sleep.

Sister Cadua really does have a mushroom for everything. This one, she assured me, makes for a gentle potion when dissolved in wine. Just enough to make you drowsy, and ensure a good, uninterrupted night's sleep once you've dozed off.

That's all I need. When I'm sure Zarun is well and truly dreaming, I slip out from under him. A lantern is still burning in the other room, and by its dim light I wriggle into my clothes. I carry my boots in my hand, padding barefoot and silent through the carpeted suite, around the corner, and into the curtained-off room.

As I suspected, there's a desk covered in papers. Running a clade takes work, just like the street gangs of Kahnzoka. There are notes on outstanding scrip, bills from the other officers, all written on little slips of scraped-down, recycled paper still spotted with old ink.

In the center of this mess is a rough set of maps, an eye-twisting jumble that I just recognize as the Stern. Much of the area is blank, unknown except for a few tentative pencil marks, especially on the lower levels. Passages twist and turn in a complex three-dimensional maze, with rusted-out walls and floors adding extra opportunities for confusion. Someone has attempted to impose some order on this disaster, numbering the levels and assigning labels to a grid. Coordinating a search.

As I'd hoped, the information I need is obvious. The map on the top of the pile has a section clearly marked, annotated with reports from the scouting pack. Fresh holes in the deck and half-eaten crabs—sure signs that the dredwurm is nearby.

I pause long enough to make sure I can find the place, then replace the papers I'd disturbed, I hope close enough that no one would suspect I was there. Padding out again, I glance at the bedroom, reassured to find Zarun still sprawled and snoring. I put my boots on and slip out the door.

He won't be surprised to find me gone, I think. I certainly wouldn't, if our positions were reversed. We are, as he said, only using each other. He just doesn't fully understand how.

19

I have almost convinced myself Meroe isn't glaring at me while my back is turned.

We descend, level by level, into the depths of the Stern. This is where we came to fight the shaggies, a maze of corridors, stairways, and rusty holes, instead of the bridges and pillars of the Center. I know where we're going, but not exactly how to get there, so we search, argue, and occasionally backtrack. Eventually, though, we always manage to find a way to go down another level.

As Meroe predicted, both Berun and Aifin were willing to join us. Berun seems even more nervous than usual, clutching a round metal shield and with a sword at his belt. Aifin is surprisingly calm, having claimed a pair of short swords for his own. He has his slate and chalk, and we worked out a few simple gestures for emergencies.

Berun walks beside me as we descend yet another flight of stairs, holding up a lantern to light the way. It's getting darker the farther down we go, the weight of *Soliton*'s metal blocking the morning light filtering in. As the lantern bounces, our shadows spin wildly around us, flicking long and sinister along the walls.

"You're certain you know where to find the dredwurm?" Berun says, for the tenth time. I'm not sure whether he wants me to say yes or no.

"I have an idea, at least. It may have moved on."

"If we'd brought Thora and Jack—"

"You're almost as strong as Thora now," I tell him. It's not quite true, but I hope it's close enough. "We can handle this."

"But . . ." He subsides, slinking back to walk beside Meroe.

I find myself preferring Aifin's company. At least he's quiet.

In truth, the farther down we go, the more I wonder if I've made a mistake. Crabs are relatively scarce—plenty of packs have come this way in recent days—but the passageways are steadily more over-grown by mushrooms, thick shelf-like varieties on the walls and puffballs that crackle underfoot and hang from the ceiling. I can smell them, a dry, spicy scent, and when the lantern light hits them they reveal brilliantly colored flesh, blue and green and crimson. It's like walking into another world, an alien, lightless place.

Somewhere in here is the dredwurm. A nightmare. I've killed nightmares before, of course, but . . .

I catch Meroe's eye, and she nods to me, encouraging. I think of the Scholar's map, and Hagan's cryptic warning.

The Scholar might be wrong. But I can't take the chance. Tori's life depends on it.

I just wish Meroe didn't insist on putting herself in danger, too.

Aifin stops, holds up a hand. I halt, too, looking at him curiously. Berun and Meroe come up from behind.

"What—" Berun says.

"Shhh," I tell him.

"I thought he couldn't hear," he says, looking at Aifin.

"*I* can," I say, irritable. "And I'd like to try."

Aifin tugs at my sleeve, then points down at the deck. He crouches, putting his hand flat against the metal, and I do the same.

Then I feel it. A vibration, the deck shaking against my palm. It makes my teeth buzz in sympathy.

"It's here," I say. "We're close."

Berun swears, quietly. Aifin stands up, catches my eye, and points to the direction where the vibration felt strongest. I nod agreement.

We walk down the corridor, through the narrow clear space be-tween the encrustations of mushrooms. A little bit farther on, it ends in a T-junction. The mushroom puffballs on the wall are swaying visibly with the grinding vibration.

"Stay here," I tell Meroe. "I'll take this side, Aifin will take the

other, and we'll see if we can spot it." I gesture to Aifin, who quickly
gets the idea.

Berun clutches his shield a little closer. "What if it turns up here?"

"Try to slow it down, then run for it. We won't be far."

"We'll be fine, Berun." Meroe catches my eye and nods. I pad
around the corner, moving quietly, listening to the hum from the
walls.

Berun's devotion to Meroe would be touching, if he weren't so
craven otherwise. I shouldn't blame him, but I can't help a prickle
of irritation, especially when Meroe takes his hand.

She doesn't feel like *that*, though. Not about Berun.

And what if she did? I taunt myself, twisting the knife. *You didn't
tell her anything. She hasn't made any promises to you, any more than
you did to her, before you went off and slept with Zarun.*

Focus, *Isoka. This is—*

There's something moving in the wall. A thick stream of gray
motes, what the Scholar called Eddica energy. In the Deeps it was
everywhere, but here in the Stern it's less common. I hesitate for a
moment, then put my hand up against it.

I assure myself it's not personal. If Hagan is real—if he's really
Hagan—he might be able to help us. My eyes search the darkness
as I whisper, "Hagan, can you hear me?"

"Isoka." His voice is stronger than last time, with less of the
strange distortion. ". . . hear you."

"Blessed's *balls*," I swear. Because what am I supposed to say to
him? "Is that really you?"

". . . think so . . ." And there's just a twist of irony in his voice
that's so like the old Hagan it makes me wince.

"Are you . . ." I swallow hard. "Are you dead?"

". . . not sure."

I freeze, because what I want to ask next is, *Do you remember me
stabbing you? And are you angry about it?* Instead, I'm silent for a
moment.

"The anomaly," he says. ". . . coming *soon*. No one . . . survive."

"The Rot. Do you mean the Rot?"

"Rot? Maybe . . . *it* says anomaly . . . sense out of it . . ."

"*What* says?"

"No time. The rogue . . . you're . . . danger."

Rot. The flow in the wall is weakening, fading away as I watch, and his voice fades with it.

"Hagan, why is the Captain taking us into the Rot? Can you speak to him?"

"Don't . . ." His voice fades, then returns, thick with effort. "Find the Garden. Forward. The Bow. Safe there."

"The *Bow?* We don't know the way."

". . . help you. Like before. Find a strong enough . . ." His voices rises. "Rogue. Go, Isoka!"

There's a scream from behind me, and the vibration redoubles. A moment later, Meroe comes running around the corner, with Berun trailing her, hand in hand.

"It's coming!" Berun shouts.

Okay. Some mysteries will have to wait.

"Through the deck," Meroe pants. "Spikes. It's below us."

"Rot." I look down the narrow corridor. The floor is shaking violently, and bits of mushroom cascade from the walls. "We need more space. Come on."

We run. The corridor lets out into a larger room, which is more to my liking. Even better, I spot Aifin on the other side, hurrying toward the vibration. He pauses when he sees me, and I gesture for him to stay put.

Something punches up through the floor, near where we came in. It's a long black spike, needle thin, parting the metal of the deck as easily as cheese. It retreats just as rapidly, and another one comes up a few feet farther on, closing in on us. Berun and Meroe back away.

I raise my blades. "Berun, the next time it does that, try to hold it in place."

He swallows hard and nods. A moment later, a spike slams upward, only a foot in front of my face. It's close enough that I can see the serrated edges, gleaming with a dangerous sheen. Blue light materializes around it, Tartak bonds gripping the thing as tight as Berun can manage. It tries to retreat, tugging against the magic, but it can't move, at least for the moment. I swing both my blades inward, closing them like a scissor, biting into the base of the spike. It's tougher than I expected, and heat flares on my arms as my power struggles. With a blast of green light, the blades cut through, and the spike clatters to the deck.

The sheared-off surface is smooth and featureless. No blood, no internal structure, just tough, metallic carapace.

Underneath me, the deck shudders. I hear a wild *scree,* the slashing of talons against metal. I barely have time to leap aside before the deck plates buckle upward, opening outward like a flower in a shower of sparks. More black spikes tear at them, forcing the hole wider, and inch by inch the dredwurm pulls itself up.

It's roughly cylindrical, maybe twenty feet long, thickest at the head and tapering to a thin, whipping tail. The black spikes are set on multi-jointed limbs, which protrude from its segmented body in rings, a dozen at a time. It doesn't seem to have a sense of up and down—the spikes hold it off the floor and anchor it to the ceiling, both at once, scraping against the metal with hideous screeches.

At the front of it, there are three triangular mouths, ringed by rows of inward-pointing teeth. Each mouth is surrounded by another ring of limbs, smaller than the big leg-spikes but just as sharp. A final barbed spine tips the thing's tail. It's a dull black all over, carapace scraped and scratched from its passage through the metal. The only hint of color is in the center of its head, between the three mouths, where a faceted crystal pulses with a bloody red light.

It looks . . . familiar.

I am now *firmly* convinced this was a bad idea.

I glance at Aifin, give him the "okay" sign we agreed on. Back at home, we'd settled on a tentative plan. Aifin would work to draw the creature's attention, while Berun tried to slow it down, and I would see about actually hurting it. Simple enough, when you're not faced with tons of black armored monster.

Aifin, to his credit, doesn't hesitate. Golden light blooms around him, drawn from his Rhema Well, and his shape blurs. He skates forward, sliding across the deck so fast he leaves trails of sparks in his wake. The writhing spiked legs of the monster make it difficult to approach from the side, but he threads his way between them like they were standing still, and he puts all his weight and speed behind one of his swords, aimed right at the seam between two segments of the dredwurm's body. It sinks in, halfway to the hilt, and sticks there.

The screech comes not from the monster, but from the metal of the floor and ceiling as it grips hard, turning toward the source of the pain. Aifin darts backward, trailing golden sparks, as spiked limbs slash in his wake. He's good, but I wonder how long he can keep it up. I'd rather not have to find out.

"Berun!" I shout. "Try to clear me a path!"

He wipes sweat from his eyes and raises his hands, the blue glow of Tartak. The closest half-dozen legs to me are wrapped in blue light, locking their joints. I can tell it won't hold, the things are already trembling, but it gives me a second or two to sprint forward without having to dodge. I get to the thing's side and grab a leg, hoisting myself off the ground.

Aifin has retreated through a doorway. The dredwurm plunges after him, its limbs ripping the walls apart to make a space wide enough for it to pass. Mushrooms explode into fragments as it barrels down the corridors, legs digging into ceiling, walls, and floor, pulling it forward faster than a charging horse. I can see Aifin's golden light, only barely staying ahead of the monster. I keep my head down, bits of mushroom and scraps of metal glancing off my armor.

Time to do some damage. Locking one arm around the monster's leg, I swing my blade inward, driving it into the dredwurm's armor-plated side. Melos power flares and crackles, but the energy skitters along the surface, scoring a line into the dull black armor without punching through. The dredwurm, still focused on Aifin, doesn't even seem to notice.

I close my eyes for a moment, concentrating, and refine my power into the penetrating shape I used against the blueshell. It still doesn't come naturally, but I can force the energy into new channels, flooding into my right hand until my skin crackles, uncomfortably hot. The long Melos blade shifts into a short, pointed spike. I wind up, pushing away from the dredwurm's skin and swinging back down with all my weight behind the blow.

This time, the energy blade sinks in, until my knuckles scrape against the dredwurm's skin. I release the pent-up energy inside the creature, braced for a furious reaction. But the blast feels muted, contained, as though the monster didn't *have* any insides to shred, only more layers of armor. It barely reacts, shuddering slightly, legs still churning in its wild pursuit of Aifin.

Well. Rot. Now what?

Aifin is having trouble. He rounds a corner, and the dredwurm follows, slamming itself against the wall and scraping away a carpet of mushrooms. I hang on for dear life, armor flaring to protect me from countless minor impacts. Aifin's golden aura is flickering, sparks of bright energy exploding off it, and he's slowing down. He turns again, and I see we're headed back toward the room where we left the others. Meroe is visible in the doorway, waving Aifin frantically to one side.

"Now, Berun! Stop it!" Meroe screams.

"I—I can't. . . ." Berun hesitates, hands raised.

"You *can*!"

Berun's hands close into fists. Blue energy sparks around him, and Tartak bindings wrap themselves around the dredwurm's head, trying to lock it in place. I see them snap under the thing's enormous momentum, magic shattering in showers of sparks, and with every sundering Berun winces as if he'd been struck. But he keeps trying, lashing out again and again, and the dredwurm slows. Steam is rising from Berun's clothes as the heat plays over his body.

I push off from the creature's side again, bring the armor-penetrating spike around in another roundhouse swing. Once again, it sinks in, but the blast of energy that follows doesn't seem to have any effect. This isn't working, and I need to move. Taking a deep breath, I put my weight on the embedded blade and use it as a handhold to swing forward, grabbing for the next ring of legs. I get a grip and clamber through as they swing and strain, trying to drive the creature onward against the flaring pressure of Berun's magic.

The dredwurm has nearly halted, pulling itself forward only inch by inch, its head wrapped in a coruscating aura of brilliant blue. Berun's mouth is open in a soundless scream, enveloped in a matching nimbus of scintillating energy, but he's got it stopped. Aifin is still on his feet, golden sparks gathering around him, holding his remaining sword in both hands. I swing forward again, pushing through another ring of squirming, straining legs, only one segment back from the creature's head.

The eye. That red jewel. If the dredwurm has a weak spot, that has to be it.

Then it all goes wrong.

The dredwurm *twists,* folding itself nearly in half, with more agility than I thought possible. With its head locked in place, its tail comes around with lightning speed, striking Berun in the stomach with the force of a cavalryman's lance. The long spike goes all the way through him, emerging dripping crimson from his back. With a flick, the dredwurm throws him off, his limp body slamming into the mushroom-covered wall and flopping bonelessly to the deck in a pool of gore.

As his bindings vanish, the freed dredwurm rolls over, swinging me toward the deck. I have to leap free or be crushed, hitting the deck with a painfully hot flare from my armor. The thing's tail comes around again, sweeping back toward Aifin. He dodges the tip with preternatural speed, but there's nowhere he can go to avoid the length of the thing, and it catches him in the midriff. He folds up around it with an *oof,* and the monster slams him into the wall with a spray of broken pieces of mushroom.

Meanwhile, its head turns in my direction, and it advances on me as I struggle back to my feet. Free to move, its spiked legs screech horrifically against the metal of the floor and ceiling as it drags itself forward. Around its three mouths, the smaller limbs reach out for me, tight nests of interlocking blades. In the center of that horrible shape, the eye, glowing a deep, malevolent red.

Suddenly I know where I've seen that eye before. When I met Hagan, in the Deeps. The angel's eye glowed blue, but otherwise it looked the same.

The angel—

The dredwurm isn't a crab at all. However monstrous they look, the crabs are *animals*, with muscles, organs, and brains. This is something else, something animated by the same forgotten magic that powers *Soliton*.

Rogue, Hagan had said. A *rogue* angel. He'd tried to warn me. Which means . . .

Well, it means we're all in the Rot.

Meroe is shouting my name, though she's barely audible over the dredwurm's screeching.

"Get the others clear!" I shout back. Assuming they're still alive. Aifin's impact with the wall might have been cushioned by the mushrooms. Berun—I don't want to think about Berun.

Survive first.

The dredwurm comes forward, and I step up to meet it, blades slashing. I manage to sever two of its spikes as others slash across me, held away by shimmering Melos energy. The pressure has already made it hot enough to hurt, though, and I back away, breathing hard. Armor or not, I can't fight this thing head on.

Which means, since it doesn't show any signs of being distracted, that I can't fight it at all. Rot, rot, *rot*. If Jack were here to get its attention, or Thora to pry its limbs away—

If I'd told the Scholar to shove his offer up his arse—

Focus, Isoka. You're not dead yet. Neither is Meroe.

I feint to the left, and the dredwurm follows the move, coming on slowly but steadily. It has no eyes, but it's clearly able to see me. Or hear me, like the crabs.

It's an *angel*. No wonder my bursts of power didn't hurt it. The thing must be *solid*, no guts or muscles or skeleton, like a statue come to life. It doesn't even bleed.

Hagan had stopped the angel, back at the ruined village. So where in the Rot is Hagan now?

The thing lurches forward, backing me toward a corner. I parry a half-dozen slashing strikes, sever a spiked limb on the riposte, and feel another blade slam into my armor. Heat and pain shoot across my body. I see Berun behind my eyes, impaled and limp, blood spurting as he flies through the air. I'd been frustrated with his cowardice. For a moment, the image twists, and it's Meroe I'm looking at, her body shuddering, the life draining from her eyes.

Focus, *Isoka*.

The Scholar said this was a power I had, too. Even if he's mad, even if his notion about the spirits of the dead is insanity, maybe he was right about *that*.

Maybe I can use it.

I try reaching out to the dredwurm. I can feel my heart pounding, blood rushing in my ears, my armor crackling and spitting with power. The strange gray energy is there; I can feel it, even see it—tiny motes, coursing through the dredwurm like blood. But no matter how I strain, they don't move.

Hagan had spun ribbons of the gray light to wrap around the angel. I try to remember what it felt like, watching him.

The dredwurm lashes out, and I take another step away. My back comes up against the wall, my armor pressing into the mushrooms. Green lightning crackles across them, leaving scorched, blackened trails. The puffballs burst into phosphorescent shards.

Nowhere left to run.

I try to remember what it felt like in my dreams, the dead watching me, the hovering motes of gray.

Something shifts, a tiny break in the flow of gray light. The dredwurm halts for a moment, its movement stuttering, like a clockwork toy with a stripped gear. The light from the red gem flickers.

I reach out again, as though this *were* a dream, straining to hold on to that sense of unreality. It's a strange, transient feeling, a state of mind that will disappear if I look at it too closely. Like making two people overlap by crossing your eyes. I can see the flow of energy through the dredwurm, a ludicrously complex pattern of gray light that animates it, moves its limbs, drives it to kill. As I thought, it's not *alive*, not really. It's a machine made of magic and stone, and it has gone horribly wrong.

I don't think I could understand the structure of the thing in a thousand years of study. Fortunately, fixing something is never as hard as breaking it. I reach out, take hold of the delicate filigrees of light, and *pull*.

It doesn't give way as easily as I thought it would; size and strength are deceptive in this weird twilight world. But whatever I manage to do brings the dredwurm to a halt, its limbs stretched and stiff, vibrating with its need to tear me to shreds but unable to move. Its red eye pulses with light.

Carefully, like a performer walking with a spinning plate balanced on her nose, I step forward. I feel my mind wobble, my control over the strange energy slip. The spiked limbs of the dredwurm move fractionally toward me, then halt again. I take another step, right up against the thing's head.

Its jewel-like eye is level with my face. I raise my blades, Melos energy flickering. Still moving slowly, I pull my arms back.

Then I strike. One blade goes in above the eye, the other below it, driving as hard as I can into the rogue angel's tough flesh. The sudden movement topples me from my perch, makes me drop the plate, and whatever control I had over the gray energy vanishes. The dredwurm's limbs close in around me, points scraping against my armor, heat blooming across my back as though I were being roasted over a fire. I ignore it, forcing my blades around in a circle, carving away the flesh beneath the eye. The creature grows frantic, ripping at me, and I hear the sizzle of burning skin. I scream.

My blades meet with a fat spark of Melos power, and the eye comes free. It falls, hitting the deck with a metallic *clunk*. The dredwurm goes still at once, dozens of limbs freezing in place. I carve one out of the way as I pull myself back, gasping. As soon as I'm free I let my armor drop, the air cool as clean water against my abused skin. I can smell myself, burnt cloth and burnt flesh, and my back is a mass of agony.

I've had worse. I clench my teeth as I bend to retrieve the eye, feeling skin stretch and crack, and then look around for the others.

*   *   *

I find Berun first, by the splash of red he left when he hit the wall. He's lying facedown in a pool of blood. The dredwurm's tail has left a sizable hole in his stomach, and I can see right into the torn purple mess of his guts. The air stinks of blood and shit.

But he's not dead. Not yet. Bubbles of blood burst around his mouth as he breathes weakly.

He was only here because Meroe asked him. Because I *told* Meroe to ask him. I'd thought—

Rot, rot *rot*.

"Meroe! Where are you?"

I turn and find her hurrying across the room. Before I can stop her, she wraps me in a hug, the pressure painful on the skin of my back. I hug her anyway.

"Oh, gods, Isoka, I thought you were going to die. I thought we were all going to die. That thing just—It just *stopped*—"

"I'm fine," I say, which is a lie. "Meroe, Berun's alive. You have to help him."

"He's . . ." Meroe looks over my shoulder, down at the dying boy. She swallows hard. "I . . . I don't know. . . ."

"You can do it." I pull back, putting my hands on her shoulders, looking into her eyes. "You saved me. You can save him." She has to. It was a mistake to come here, *my* mistake. He shouldn't have to pay for it.

"You don't understand, Isoka." She pulls away from me, drops to her knees beside Berun. "It's not the same. This is . . . too much."

"Try." My voice is tight. "Please."

"It might not work."

"He's *dying*."

"It might . . ." She swallows again, and nods. "I'll try. Find Aifin."

I clap her on the shoulder. Aifin is on the other side of the room, lying in a heap of broken mushrooms. When I reach him, I'm glad to find he doesn't seem too badly injured, though he's not conscious. I check him for broken bones, and when I don't find any I pull him out into a more comfortable position and leave him for the moment.

The black bulk of the dredwurm is starting to *dissolve*, falling apart into loose black ash. I limp past it again, back to Meroe's side. Her hands are on Berun's body, and they're sticky to the wrists with blood.

"This is . . . not going to be easy," she says. "You just had broken bones. I need his body to rebuild. . . ." She shakes her head. "I don't know if I can."

"You can."

She looks up at me, smiles, and then turns to the dying boy with fierce concentration. Light gathers around her hands, a weird, glittering purple. Ghul light. The Forbidden Well. I suppress the in-ground urge to step away.

The light flows into long, looping strings, from Meroe's hands into Berun's wounds, like she's working on a loom. There's a hum in the air, and a sharp metallic scent stronger even than the smell of blood. Berun's hand twitches.

Then he lifts his head back, dripping blood from his nose and forehead, and gasps for breath. Meroe scrambles out of the way as he rolls over, trailing strings of gore. He takes another deep breath, and I can see the wound is *shrinking*, new pink flesh spreading from the ragged edges like frost closing over a lake.

"It worked!" I grab Meroe's shoulder. "It rotting *worked*!"

I see her face. Her eyes are very wide, with tiny pupils. She shakes her head minutely.

Berun sits up, in spite of his shredded stomach. His head is distended, *bulging* on one side, hair parting around a dome of expanding skull. Something shifts in his shoulder, the bones changing, a pointed growth stretching his skin like a tent. It splits, and whorled bone issues forth from underneath, wet and red with torn meat. One of his legs starts to shiver, and sprouts feathers.

Berun starts to scream.

The sound he makes is barely human, and it gets worse as the Ghul energy Meroe has unleashed churns inside his body. Parts of him start to grow, muscles bloating, skin coming apart like rotted lace. His fingers are melting where they touch the deck, becoming pseudopods that stretch outward like the blind roots of a plant. One of his eyes is wide and terrified, while the other is changing, pupil splitting over and over until there are a hundred black dots in a sea of white.

"No," Meroe is saying, over and over. "No, no no no *no no no*—"

She's screaming to match Berun. Maybe I am, too. I drag her away, back from this bloated, spreading monstrosity she'd created, a mound of bulbous flesh that gets bigger by the second, with Berun's terrified face still visible in the center of it. I see his ribs, grown into barbed spikes, tear their way out, then dissolve into white goo. There's nothing left but flesh, a spherical ball of flesh, growing outward fast enough that for a moment I'm afraid it will engulf us, engulf the whole *ship*, the world—

Then it explodes, painting the walls with blood.

20

"I'm afraid," Arin says, "that the master is occupied."

"This is important."

"He can't be disturbed."

"Tell me," I snarl. "Would it *disturb* him to have to clean bits of his bed warmer off his front step?"

It's a nasty thing to say to a girl who doesn't deserve it, but I'm not in a forgiving mood. Arin—she really is nearly identical to Erin, apart from the way she braids her hair—keeps a stoic expression, but she can't hide the flush in her cheeks. It must be hard, being an iceling and having your skin show the slightest blush.

I have to give her credit. The fear is obvious in her eyes, but she manages not to flinch. After a moment, she turns away, closing the door behind her. I start a mental count. I'll give it a hundred before I start tearing the place apart.

The door opens again before I get to fifty. The Scholar is waiting, cane in hand, adjusting his spectacles as though the sight of me is a surprise.

"Deepwalker," he says. "You've returned. Come in."

He steps aside, and I stalk past. I pull the dredwurm's eye out of my pocket. The surrounding flesh crumbled like the rest of the creature, but the jewel-like eye remained intact, still shimmering with a faint red glow. I slam the thing on the nearest table and turn to the Scholar.

"I got your rotting trinket."

"I see that." He raises an eyebrow. "You don't seem pleased. And you gave poor Arin a fright."

"Arin can go to the Rot. Which is where we're all going, if I believe you. You *knew* what the dredwurms really are, didn't you? That's why you wanted this thing, for your rotting experiments."

"I suspected, yes," he says, calmly. "I haven't had a specimen to study, for obvious reasons."

"We thought it was a *crab,* not a rotting *angel!*" I take a deep breath. "Berun, one of my pack, is dead. Some of the others are . . . hurt."

"I'm sorry to hear it." He shrugs. "But I hardly see how you can be angry with *me.* Crab or angel, you knew the dredwurm was dangerous, and you and your pack chose to take the risk."

"Because you wanted a trophy!"

"It's not just a trophy, as you know." He reaches out for the eye, and I pull it away. "It may be the salvation of everyone on this ship."

"You're going to take me to the Captain," I say.

"That was our agreement."

"And I'm going to get him to turn this ship around." Even if I have to put a blade to his throat. Anger flares inside me, as hot as powerburn.

"As to that, I make no guarantees. But it's possible you will have greater success than I have." He starts across the floor of the tower, cane *tap-tapp*ing. "Meet me at midnight, where we held the Council audience. I will guide you from there."

"Why not now?"

"Mundane reasons," he says. "I will have to adjust the rotation of the guards, to ensure you will not be found."

"Fine." I stuff the eye back into my pocket. "I hope the Captain stays up late."

The Upper Stations are still buzzing with packs trading information about the dredwurm. I wonder if Zarun has woken up yet, and if he's realized what happened. The mushroom I dosed him with should only have left him groggy, which would be easy enough to write off to wine and a busy night.

When I arrive, Jack and Thora are sitting in the common room of our quarters, roasting something in a pan. Thora is staring intently at the fire, but Jack bounces up, indecently cheerful.

"Fearless leader," she says. "I perceive that you have gotten an early start on the day!"

"More like she didn't actually finish the night," Thora said. "I hope you ended up somewhere good."

"I was with Zarun," I say.

Thora looks up at Jack with a grin. "Told you. That's two bottles you owe me."

Jack heaves an exaggerated sigh and puts a hand on my shoulder. "I believed in you, Deepwalker."

"Were you *betting* on who I would rut?"

Jack blinks, as though the thought that I might object had never occurred to her, then puts on a shifty look. "Possibly."

"And what did you put *your* bottle on?"

"That Princess Meroe would get her dainty fingers into your underthings before our illustrious clade master. I've seen the way she looks at you."

I suppress a powerful urge to punch her in the face. Instead, I turn away and head for my bedroom.

"Do you know what's going on with the others?" Thora says, her attention back to her cooking. "I haven't seen anyone else today."

"No idea." The words are a growl as I push through the curtained doorway.

Thora's not stupid. We won't be able to keep what happened from her for long. Berun is dead—my mind helpfully supplies an image of his screaming face, disappearing inside a mass of bulging, tumorous flesh—Aifin is hurt, and Meroe . . .

Meroe is curled up on her sleeping mat, facing the wall. I sit beside her.

"I talked to the Scholar," I say. "He's taking me to the Captain tonight."

She doesn't respond. Her breathing is quiet and snuffly.

"This is going to work. I will *make* it work. We will get off this rotting ship, and find Tori, and . . . and I don't know where we'll go after that, but you will come with us."

Meroe shifts slightly, pulling in her knees a little tighter.

"It wasn't your fault, Meroe."

When her voice finally emerges, it's a whisper. "Of course it's my fault."

"None of us would have been there if not for me," I say. "I thought . . . I thought I was strong enough that we'd be all right."

"Berun only came because *I* told him to," Meroe says. "He has—had—a crush on me."

I hadn't known she knew about that. She does a good job of seeming oblivious.

"And then," Meroe goes on, "I tried to help him, and he turned into that *thing*. And then he rotting exploded. So don't try to tell me it's *not my fault*."

"He was dying," I say. "I told you to help him, even though you didn't think you could. There was nothing—"

"Rotting gods, Isoka, will you *shut up*?!" Her voice is a croak. "I'm not your rotting puppet. *I* decided to help you, to try to save Berun, everything. I *decided*. And that means . . ."

She trails off, and there's a long silence. After a moment, I tentatively put a hand on her shoulder.

"Don't *rotting* touch me!"

I snatch the hand back, as though I'd touched a hot stove. Meroe curls herself tighter, her shoulders shaking with silent sobs.

"My father," she says after a while, "made the wrong choice, sending me to *Soliton*. He should have slit my throat when he had the chance."

"Meroe, please." There are tears in my eyes.

"Don't pretend you aren't thinking it," she says. "I know what I am. A rotting *ghulwitch*. Anyone who can do something like *that* can't be allowed to live."

I sit beside her, head bowed, and I can't find anything to say.

"Would you kill me? If I asked you to?" Meroe says.

I swallow. "No."

"It could have been you, you know. It's only dumb luck that I saved you, and it didn't end up like *that*."

"You knew you couldn't help Berun," I say quietly. "You *told* me."

"I'd do it myself, but I know I'm too much of a coward." She takes a deep breath. "Don't worry. I'm sure somebody on *Soliton* will be willing to kill me, if I tell them what I am." She snorts a laugh. "Maybe I'll ask the Butcher."

Another silence. I take a long breath.

"When I was eleven years old," I tell her, very quietly, "I decided I wanted to die. It had been . . . a bad year. My friends, the boys and girls I'd spent my childhood with on the streets, were dying. Two boys got the red fever and puked up their guts. The rest of us left them to rot under a bridge. My best friend, Seria, got taken by the kidcatchers." I close my eyes. "She must have put up too much of a fight. We found her naked in an alley with her throat slit. It seemed like Kahnzoka *wanted* us to die. That was just what was supposed to happen to street children. And I was cold and so hungry and tired of fighting it."

I knot my fingers together in my lap. Meroe says nothing.

"One night I was sitting there, with Tori leaning against me, half a blanket wrapped around both of us and still shivering. And I thought, Why not? I had a knife, a little thing barely more than a potato peeler, but I knew how to reach the heart." One of my hands goes to my own chest, the spot on the left side behind my breast, the gap in the ribs. Where I'd put my blade into Shiro. "It would hurt for a moment, and then it would be over.

"But there was Tori. She was seven years old. If I died, she wouldn't survive long, between the kidcatchers and the cold. So I put her in my lap, and I took out my knife. And I tried to work up my nerve.

"I thought she was asleep. But when she felt the knife against her skin, she opened her eyes. She didn't scream or cry. She just looked up at me, only half-awake, and she smiled and said, 'You'll come, too, right?'"

I had never told anyone about that night. Not Hagan, not any one of the boys who'd shared my bed. I don't even know if Tori remembers. Maybe she thinks it was a dream.

"I couldn't do it. Obviously. I couldn't hurt Tori, and I couldn't leave her behind. That meant the only thing to do was protect her."

I let out a breath. "It wasn't long after that that my Melos powers came, and I found out that hurting people was something I was very good at. But it was all right, because it was for her."

I open my eyes. Meroe has rolled over, watching me from behind a fringe of disheveled hair.

"Why are you telling me this?" she says. "Is it supposed to make me feel better? *My* sisters wouldn't stop to piss on my grave if I died. One less obstacle between them and the throne."

"They can go rot. I'm not going to kill you, Meroe, and I'm not going to leave you behind."

"You just get to decide that, without consulting me?"

"It's my choice to make."

She sits up. Her face is streaked with tears, and her hair has escaped from its knot to hang curly and loose across her face.

"I should never have let you help me," she says. "I should have left you to die in the Deeps. You stupid, arrogant—"

I kiss her.

It's a tentative kiss, a brush of my lips against hers. For a moment she sits frozen. Then she leans into me, her mouth opening under mine, desperate and hungry.

I close my eyes, and so her foot slamming into my gut catches me completely unaware. I double over, gasping, as she scrambles away, her back to the wall. Her eyes are very wide.

"Get out," she says.

"I'm sorry." My voice is a wheeze. "Meroe, I'm sorry. I shouldn't—"

"Get. Out."

I get to my feet, clutching my stomach, and stagger to the door. Meroe stares after me, her face a mask.

That night, I climb the long stairs up to the deck, trudging around the spiral until my legs burn. The dredwurm's eye is a weight in my pocket.

Why did I do that? For a moment I'd been so *certain*. I'd thought—

What? That Meroe would appreciate being suddenly slobbered on?

Blessed's balls, Isoka, how would you feel if some strange woman started kissing you without so much as asking?

And now I'd knocked the whole thing into the Rot.

I just hope—oh, Blessed, I hope so hard it makes my chest hurt—that she doesn't do anything stupid before I get back.

And the Captain had better hope, for his own sake, that he has some good answers.

Another three turns to the top.

I could have *hinted: So, Meroe, did you have crushes on any stable-boys back at the palace?* Or . . . Something like that, but not stupid.

Jack had said . . . but Jack is a little bit crazy.

Rot, rot, *rot*. Focus, *Isoka*.

I reach the top, and get my bearings. There's no one waiting to guide me, but the Captain's tower looms overhead, a black slice cut out of the starscape. The breeze of *Soliton's* passage ruffles my hair—longer, now, than I usually let it get—and flaps my shirt against the still-tender skin of my back.

A single light is burning in the empty space where the Council held its audience. The Scholar waits between the two silent angels, cane in one hand and lantern in the other. His spectacles are circles of darkness obscuring his face.

"You're late," he says.

"It's been a long day," I say. "If someone else is offering you a dredwurm's eye, you're welcome to deal with them instead."

He grins. "Zarun and the others have found no sign of the dred-wurm's passage today. They are . . . unhappy."

"Then let's get this over with."

He nods. I glance up at the angels, but they're dark, with no sign of a faceted gem, blue or red. For a moment I try to twist into the strange state of mind that let me pull at the gray energy, but I don't have the concentration for it, and it only makes my head hurt. I scowl, and hurry after the Scholar.

We take a roundabout approach to the tower, walking a circu-itous path across the deck of the ship and cutting through the shad-ows of several rusted-out structures. The Scholar's cane taps out a steady rhythm, so I don't bother trying to move quietly.

"Your . . . energy. What you call the Eddica Well."

He looks over his shoulder. "You still don't believe me, I take it?"

"I believe that it *exists*. I just don't think you've got the whole story." I hesitate. "If the spirits of the dead are powering the ship, can we speak to them?"

"No," he says. "Eddica taps the *energy* of the dead. Not their minds, not their essence. Those are gone."

I want to tell him he's wrong, just to wipe the smug look off his face. But something tells me I'm better off keeping a few cards to myself.

We'll see what the Captain has to say first.

Finally, we make our approach to the Captain's tower, from the side instead of straight on. It's longer than it is wide, and canted slightly backward, like an oval pipe plunged at an angle into *Soliton*'s stern. There's a small doorway here, covered by a scrap-metal door. A canvas shelter stands beside it.

"This is normally the guardpost," the Scholar says. "Fortunately, arranging the rotations is among my duties. I doubt anyone will notice the lapse."

"What about the angel?"

He nods, fishes in his pocket, and presents me with a small silver necklace, the kind of thing that you might buy for a sweetheart if you were moderately well-off and cloyingly sentimental. I frown at it.

"*That* is the key to the tower?"

He shrugs. "It's just a token of the Captain's permission. There's no magic to it." He holds it up by the chain, puts his cane under his arm, and extends his other hand.

I pull the eye out of my pocket and hand it over, taking the necklace in return. The chain slithers into a heap, cool against my skin.

"If you're lying . . . ," I begin.

"Then the angel will tear you to shreds?" He grins.

"Then you'd better hope you're right about the spirits of the dead," I say. "Because I'll come for you."

"Fair enough." He inclines his head, then offers me the lantern. "I hope you find what you're looking for."

*   *   *

The bottom floor of the Captain's tower is completely dark and very, very still.

I hold the lantern high, but it's a tiny light in a vast space. The ceiling is at least thirty feet overhead, meaning this chamber takes up a substantial portion of the tower. There are no other doors that I can see, just the blank metal deck, with rusted patches like anywhere else on the ship.

At the rear of the chamber, a set of steep stairs, nearly a ladder, goes straight up the slightly canted wall of the tower. In front of those stairs, its head nearly brushing the ceiling, stands the angel.

This one is more humanoid than most. It looks a bit like two men standing side by side, but merged at the shoulder, down one side of the torso, and along their central leg, giving it a grand total of three. The body is mannequin smooth, without definition, hands and feet just shapeless lumps, its two heads blank. But three human faces, rendered in great detail, stare out from its massive, merged chest. One laughs, one screams, and one weeps.

I don't know who designed these things, but they belong in a madhouse.

I take out the silver necklace and hold it by the chain as I approach. The angel doesn't stir, for all the world as though it were simply a statue. But it isn't. As I get closer, I can see motes of gray light running through it, just below its surface, and hear voices babbling at the edge of hearing.

Spirits, the Scholar said.

Rot. Dead is dead.

Either way, I give the thing a wide berth, edging around it to reach the stairs. Whatever the necklace is, it works, because the angel doesn't so much as twitch. I shove the charm back into my pocket and start to climb, awkwardly holding the lantern in one hand.

When I get to the second floor, it's disappointingly ordinary. Some kind of storeroom, half-full of crates and barrels, all of which are old enough that they're crumbling with rot. The lantern light illuminates patches of colorful mushrooms, but not much more. I continue onward.

The next level looks more like a barracks. A half-dozen Jyashtani-style beds line one wall, plain and utilitarian, while heavy trunks are pushed against the other. There's no sign of the occupants, though, and once again everything looks *old*. The sheets are frayed to translucence, with patches of mold growing across them. Bits of floating fungus and dust shimmer in the air when they catch the light, like drifting snow.

The ceilings in here are high. From the height of the tower, the next level must be the last. I grit my teeth, and keep climbing.

Unlike the rest of the tower, this level is divided in half by a wooden partition. The stairway ends in what looks like a nobleman's dining room, wedged awkwardly into the metallic semi-circle. There's a huge hardwood table, surrounded by chairs trimmed in crumbling velvet. A silver candelabra is nearly black with tarnish. More heavy wooden furniture sits against the walls, a sideboard and a chest of drawers, bronze fittings turned green and the wood itself starting to flake away. Fungus and mold are everywhere, waterfalls of the stuff dripping from the table and hanging in curtains on the walls. The floor, once covered with thick carpets, sends up bursts of swirling dust whenever I take a step, which hangs in the air as though trapped in liquid.

The wooden wall is falling apart, too, one section dangerously bowed. There's a door in the middle, which hangs open a few inches. I pause for a moment, listening, but there's no sound at all.

What in the *Rot* is going on here?

There's no point in trying to hide my presence, since my boots made enough racket climbing the stairs to wake the dead. But I find myself reluctant to shout, anyway. The silence has the same oppressive quality as a library, or a tomb. I manage to clear my throat and say, "Hello? Is anyone here?"

There's no answer. I step forward, raising a cloud of disintegrating carpet, and head for the door.

It swings open a few more inches at my touch, hinges groaning. I slide through, and find myself in a bedroom, as opulently furnished as the antechamber. There's a huge four-posted bed, with moldy sheets and ragged lace fringes. A wardrobe, its doors hanging open, revealing the tattered remnants of someone's finery. And another table, with a single wing-backed chair pulled up to it. There's a set of pens and a desiccated inkwell, along with some scraps that might once have been paper.

In the chair, reclining as though at ease, is a corpse.

It's still mostly intact. One arm has fallen away at the elbow, but the other rests in its lap, bones covered with withered scraps of skin. It wears a fine silk dressing gown, with a layer of hanging mold and dust. The skull stares at me, eye sockets gaping wide, tiny red-capped mushrooms pushing up from within. Here and there, gold gleams in the lantern light. A necklace, rings, a bracelet. The trappings of power and wealth.

Of a captain?

"Hello?" It's a stupid, stupid thing to do, but I can't *not* speak. Dead is dead, except that maybe it isn't. I don't *really* expect the skeleton to move, to stand up and speak, to lurch forward, grasping fingers extended—

—but I have my blades ready, just in case—

Nothing happens, of course. Dead *is* dead. And the corpse is just a corpse, left here for long, long years, undisturbed.

I cross the room, raising more dust. Behind the table, there's a set of shelves, and here the room shows signs of being recently visited. Another set of footprints is visible in the dust, and the ghostly imprints of objects that have been removed. Books, from the look of things.

"What in the rotting Blessed's name is *going on?*" The rage bubbles up in me, all at once. I lash out, kicking the old table, and it goes over in a shower of dust and floating spores. The skeleton glares at me, its frozen expression disapproving.

"Now, now," says the Scholar, from behind me. "That's not a very nice way to treat poor old Mahjir's furniture."

I spin, blades igniting with a *crackle-hiss*. Before he can take a single step backward, I'm on top of him, Melos energy spitting a half inch from his throat. I watch him swallow.

"Only me," he says. "Sorry to startle you."

"What is *this* supposed to be?" My voice is low and dangerous.

"The Captain's tower?"

"So where's the *rotting* Captain?" I snap. "This bastard has been dead for a century."

"His name was Mahjir Sepha," the Scholar says. "I found his journal. He was a nobleman from Jyashtan, who came into his power young. A little mad, I think, if we're being honest. He'd heard the legends of *Soliton* and determined to offer himself and some of his mage-blood retainers as a sacrifice." He gestures at the room. "You can see that he liked to travel in style."

"And?"

"He set up shop here in the tower. Seemed appropriate, since he wanted to be the ship's master."

"He became Captain?"

"He *called* himself Captain."

I press the blade closer to the Scholar's skin. Green lightning arcs to his collar, crackling down his robe. "Start explaining. Was this Mahjir Captain or not? What happened to him?"

"He died. I'm not sure exactly how. Obviously he didn't write that part down." The Scholar nods, carefully, to the corpse. "It doesn't look like it was violent, though. This is just the way he was when I first saw him."

"So the Captain is dead." My throat has gone thick, tasting of dust and mold. "That's what you're telling me?"

"No, Deepwalker." The Scholar sighs. "What I'm telling you is that there *is* no Captain. There never was."

"That," I tell the Scholar, "doesn't make any rotting sense."

"Karakoa never told me," he says, "but I think it was Jarli who came up with the idea. She was the first one to come in here and find old Mahjir. By the time they brought me onto the Council, it was already . . . tradition."

"The Council knows? About . . . this?"

"Of course."

"Then why—"

"Think about it like this," he says. "If there's a Captain, then the officers are merely representatives of a mysterious, all-powerful force. If there *isn't*, then they're just a bunch of high-and-mighty bastards who are unaccountably in charge."

"It's all a *lie*?" My hand is trembling, which makes him flinch. "Just for your *convenience*?" I shake my head. "That still doesn't make sense. Does the *Council* control the angels, then? Who sets the ship's course?"

"You still don't get it?" Beads of sweat stand out on the Scholar's forehead. "The ship *runs itself.* It goes where it wants. The angels do what *they* want. None of us, no *human*, has ever been able to command it or turn it or change one rotting thing."

"You mean it's *alive*?"

"Some of the others think so. Karakoa seems to regard it as a kind of god." He shrugs. "I've seen the Eddica energy that drives it. I told you, it's a *machine,* made out of steel and magic. It's not alive any more than a . . . a clock is alive, or a waterwheel. It's just a *thing*, doing whatever it was built to do."

For a moment, all I can do is stare. The Scholar coughs uncomfortably.

"If you're not going to kill me," he says eventually, "would you mind . . ."

"Why shouldn't I kill you?" I force a savage grin. "You lied to me. I took my pack to find the dredwurm because you said you could get me to the Captain, and now you tell me there's no such thing. Which means Berun died for nothing, so you could have some trinket." I press closer, and he flinches as crackling energy singes his skin. "Talk fast, Scholar."

"I have . . . a plan. To save us. To save everyone. I needed the eye—ah!"

I lower the blade a fraction. "Why not tell me from the start?"

"Would you have believed me?" He's breathing hard. "You needed to see *this*. Now you understand."

"A little, at any rate." With a sigh, I dismiss the blade and let my hand drop. The Scholar heaves a sigh of relief. "You said the Council knows. And the Council offered the bounty for the dredwurm's eye. So why did you need me to get it for you?"

"The rest of them don't understand what the eyes are. There are all sorts of legends about them, but the one the officers believe is that the dredwurm's eye will let you command an angel."

"Will it?"

"Possibly. The eye is a focus for Eddica power. If you or I used it, we might be able to take over an angel, but the possibilities go so much deeper than that. We could change the course of *Soliton* itself."

"You told the Council," I guess, "and they don't believe you."

"Of course they don't. Even if they did, they wouldn't risk it. The last two eyes that have fallen into their hands they've destroyed."

"Why?"

"The Council works because the clades are in balance," he says bitterly. "What do you think would happen if one of the officers had an *angel* on his side?"

"All right." My anger has faded a little. "So you needed someone to get to the eye who wouldn't just hand it over to the Council, and I'm the perfect idiot who volunteered."

"You're the Deepwalker," he says. "I hoped you would be strong enough. But it's more than that. If I'm going to make this work, I need your help." He steps closer, his fear apparently forgotten. "You can touch Eddica more deeply than I can. You have a better chance of being able to use the eye."

"To turn the ship away from the Rot."

He nods. "We're still sailing east. We don't have much time."

"And what is that going to take, apart from the eye?"

"The . . . mechanism that controls the ship is buried deep," he says. "We can't reach it from here. But there is a place where it can be accessed. I've tried to . . . map the currents, you might say, the flows of energy. Beyond the Center, close to the Bow, there's—"

"The Garden." My voice is a whisper.

"What?" The Scholar steps closer again. "How do you—"

"That's the place, isn't it?"

"I . . . think so." His speech is getting faster as he gets excited. "Some of the old books talk about it. Mahjir mentioned looking for it in his journal. It's supposed to be full of food, water, everything people need. But *sealed*, against the crabs and the Rot."

"Sealed? So it would protect us, even if we couldn't change course?"

He shrugs. "Legends scribbled by dead men. Who knows? But no one has ever been able to *find* it. Or at least if they have, they haven't written down how."

I think of Hagan, his urgent warning.

"I may be able to get us there," I say, slowly. "But I need to talk to someone first."

"Then we should go," the Scholar says. "Now! I will prepare a team for the journey, and you will do . . . whatever you need to do. The sooner we leave, the better chance we'll have."

"That won't be necessary," a deep voice says from the outer room. The Scholar turns, and swears in Jyashtani. Karakoa is standing in front of the stairs, arms crossed. Zarun lounges beside him, one eyebrow delicately arched. "You'll be coming with us, Deepwalker."

21

"Don't," the Scholar hisses to me, "do anything—"

He cuts off, but I get the drift. Stupid. Violent. Such as killing these two and making a run for it.

There was a time when I'd have considered it. But I've seen Zarun fight, and I doubt I could take him and Karakoa together. And, unlike back in Kahnzoka when I was cornered by the Immortals, I have something to lose. If I die here, Tori dies with me, and Meroe as well if the Scholar is right.

So this time, I let them take me. It turns out to be the right move. Zarun is no fool, and there are a dozen armed crew waiting nervously outside the entrance to the Captain's tower.

"I'll work this out," the Scholar says. "Don't worry."

We're not bound and gagged, but the circle of guards marks us clearly as prisoners. We descend via the cage, in carefully managed shifts so I'm never alone. I'm honestly impressed—the Ward Guard in Kahnzoka would have given me a dozen chances to slash someone's throat and make a run for it by now. Zarun catches my eye and smiles, as though it's all one big joke, but Karakoa's expression is grim.

"So what happens now?" I ask, when we're on the deck.

Karakoa shakes his head. "It has yet to be decided. For the moment, you will be detained." He glares at the Scholar. "And *you* will explain your actions to the Council."

"Gladly," the Scholar says. "Maybe this time you'll actually listen."

That doesn't make Karakoa any happier. They take us to the First Tower, at the corner where *Soliton*'s side and rear walls come

together. I'd expected to be shoved back down in the Drips, where
Pack Nine had originally been quartered, but instead there's a long
hallway fitted out as an actual cellblock. Guards open the door to
one of four small rooms and gesture me inside. I hear the clatter of
bolts and bar after they close it.

As cells go, it's not bad. Sleeping pallet, chamber pot, water ba-
sin. No rats. I've paid good money for worse rooms, frankly. I stretch
myself out on the pallet, suddenly feeling the exhaustion that's been
hovering somewhere behind me since last night. I haven't slept since
before we went after the dredwurm, and my eyeballs feel like they've
been wrapped in wool.

For a while, though, I can't rest.

There is no Captain. There *is* no Captain. But the Scholar thinks
he can control the ship.

Which means, presumably, I should go along with the Scholar,
at least until the time comes to stab him in the back.

So why are my instincts screaming at me that something's wrong?

Why do I feel like he *knows* more than he should, and he's
telling me what I want to hear?

Does Meroe hate me?

Focus, Isoka.

I open my eyes. There's a small candle on a shelf, but I haven't
bothered to light it, and no light is seeping through the cracks in
the door. But I can see, just barely. A tiny trickle of gray light runs
up through one of the walls, pulsing strong and fast. I edge over to
it and press my hand against the metal.

"Hagan, are you there?"

It's a moment before his voice comes. ". . . weak. Can't hold . . .
long."

Rot. I have so many questions, it's hard to stick to the most
important.

"If I get to the Garden," I say, "will I be able to turn the ship?
Avoid the Rot?"

Another pause. ". . . no. Not enough . . ." His voice fades, then
returns. ". . . Garden will *protect* you."

"Just me?"

"Whoever reaches it." His voice is strained. "Hurry. It's . . ."

He fades away again, the river of gray light dwindling to a trickle, like a dying spring.

"Hagan?"

No answer.

I don't remember falling asleep, only waking to a sharp rap on the door. I sit up, head full of fragments of dream.

"Who's there?" I call out, before I fully remember that I'm stuck in a cell.

"'Tis Clever Jack," says Jack. "Here to see the business done."

"Jack?" I shake my head, trying to rouse myself. "What are you doing here?"

"I am charged with escorting you, so you might bear witness and understand. But I must have your word that you will not attempt to escape."

"My word?" Back in Kahnzoka, I would have rolled my eyes at this, and happily made whatever promise she wanted. For some reason, here it brings me up short. "I . . . yes, I promise. I won't run for it."

"Well and good," Jack says. "I would hate to have to kill you, but such is the fearsome duty that has been laid on me if you violate your oath. Now, bide a moment."

There's a heavy *clunk* as the bar is removed, and a metal screech as Jack shoots the bolts. I blink against the light from the corridor, which outlines Jack in her hunting leathers. The guards are nowhere to be seen.

"So you're not breaking me out?"

"Only temporarily, I'm afraid. But I have every confidence you'll be all right in the end."

I stand up and stretch. At least the pain in my back has subsided a little.

"Have you heard what happened?" I said.

Jack catches my meaning. "I have. When Zarun made it clear to the Princess he knew the outlines, she confessed everything. I am sorry about Berun."

"Me too." I pause again. "And does Meroe . . . is she all right?"

Jack frowns. "I'm not certain, in truth. But she has emerged from isolation, which is something."

"Good." I swallow. "That's . . . good."

"Now come," she says. "You wouldn't want to miss the show."

"Where are we going?" I ask, following Jack out of the cell. To my surprise, she doesn't turn toward the entrance, but rather farther down the corridor.

"By secret ways, to secret ends," Jack says. "More precisely, through a gap in the wall to listen at keyholes. Here."

At the end of the corridor, a panel of scrap metal is bolted to the wall, with a rusted-out section visible behind it. Jack steps up and does something to one of the bolts, and the whole thing swings loose, leaving us looking into a dark space. It's not quite a corridor—a long, solid-looking beam occupies the top half, so we have to stay crouched after we duck to pass through the hole. Jack leads the way, confidently making a couple of turns, until she stops in a narrow alcove where we can stand up. There's a slitted grating just above my head, with light shining through.

"What's in there?" I ask.

Jack lays a finger to her lips and speaks in a whisper. "The Council's private chambers. They will begin their deliberations soon."

My eyes narrow. "Zarun sent you, didn't he?"

Jack shrugs, but she looks very pleased with herself.

"Why?" I ask. "What does he want me to hear?"

"Listen, and find out."

It's not long before voices filter back into the wall. It takes me a few moments to sort them out—Karakoa's deep bass, Zarun's pleasant tenor, the Butcher's drawl, and Shiara's crisp, unaccented Imperial. And, of course, the now-familiar voice of the Scholar. It was maddening not to be able to *see*, though. It felt like watching a stage play from behind the curtain.

BUTCHER: This isn't like you, Scholar. I knew you were mad, but this is rotting reckless, too.

SCHOLAR: When catastrophe is imminent, inaction is reckless. I have to act because you all refuse to do so.

KARAKOA: We've heard your reports. But there is still plenty of time for *Soliton* to turn south before it reaches the Rot.

SCHOLAR: You have *no idea* how much time there is, and neither do I. No one knows how far beyond the shores of the island the influence of the Rot extends.

SHIARA: If, in fact, it extends at all. The ship may sail past in perfect safety.

BUTCHER: We're not here to have this rotting argument again. We're here because you did something stupid.

KARAKOA: Indeed. Showing the Deepwalker the truth of the Captain's tower was . . . unwise.

SCHOLAR: I need her help to *save us all.* Apologies if that broke the rules.

KARAKOA: They exist for a reason. The myth of the Captain keeps order among the crew.

SCHOLAR: Why? So that everyone can die in an orderly fashion?

SHIARA: You've been awfully quiet, Zarun.

BUTCHER: For rotting once.

ZARUN: Apologies. I've been thinking.

BUTCHER: For rotting once.

KARAKOA: Enough. Have you come to any conclusions?

ZARUN: I must say I am inclined to think the Scholar, while he should have informed us, had the right idea.

BUTCHER: *What?*

KARAKOA: Explain.

ZARUN: The Deepwalker is a unique figure.

BUTCHER: My frozen arse. She's a rotten piece of gutter quim—

ZARUN: She killed a *dredwurm* with a pack of four. How many of you would have taken less than twenty to that fight?

SHIARA: That just proves she's a fool.

ZARUN: I think that, in the long run, we will have to admit her to the Council. So the Scholar's sharing the secret with her is . . . premature, but not a catastrophe.

SCHOLAR: There is no rotting *long run*. Have none of you been listening?

BUTCHER: And I'd freeze my tits off before I let that bitch on the Council. One is bad enough.

SHIARA: He has a point.

KARAKOA: Enough! You all know the penalty for transgressing the Captain's tower is death. I am in favor of applying that penalty. Rules must be respected. What do the rest of you say?

BUTCHER: I want the bitch's severed head to shove down my toilet and piss on.

SHIARA: I . . .

ZARUN: Rare to see you uncertain.

SHIARA: The Deepwalker's popularity is troublesome. I worry that executing her may lead to discontent.

ZARUN: My vote is to enlist her, not kill her.

KARAKOA: That means we are divided. What if she challenges?

There's a spate of rapid whispering, what sounds like Shiara and the Scholar, too low for me to hear. I turn to Jack.

"What does he mean, challenge? Like when I challenged Ahdron?"

Jack nods. "If the Council are divided on a punishment, you're entitled to challenge for your life. If no one is willing to face you, you go free."

Small chance of that.

ZARUN: I certainly won't face her.

SHIARA: Nor I.

KARAKOA: I admit I am . . . reluctant. Perhaps we should reconsider—

BUTCHER: To the Rot with that. I'll rotting fight her, if you're all such frozen cowards.

ZARUN: You're certain? We all know she's quite powerful.

Ship of Smoke and Steel 285

BUTCHER: Don't make me laugh, you miserable prick. I'll kill her with one hand jammed up my arse, and have enough left for you, too, if you want some.

SHIARA: Karakoa, we need to speak. In private.

More whispers, and the sound of people moving about. Jack beckons me away from the grate, and we hunch down once more and retrace our steps.

"So because Zarun won't agree to execute me," I say, "I get to fight the Butcher in the Ring?"

"Quick on the uptake, our fearless leader," Jack says. "That's the gist."

"He knew this was going to happen?" I shake my head. "Of course he did. He was practically baiting her."

"Zarun and the Butcher have been at daggers drawn since I came aboard," Jack says. "Only the pressure of the other two keeps them from open war. Which is, of course, the point of having rules. If the officers could fight each other we'd soon all be crab food."

I remember Zarun's smile, the day he'd taken me to look for dresses and we'd run into the Butcher.

"You wanted to know why I'm helping you? It's because she hates you. You made her look weak and foolish when you came aboard, and every inch you rise is a twist of the knife in her back. She never could get over a grudge."

"So you're helping me out of spite?"

"Don't be silly. I don't hold grudges. Hate makes people stupid. If this keeps up, sooner or later she'll make a mistake. And then . . ."

"He set her up," I say quietly. "He saw this coming, and now . . ."

He's using me, a knife he can afford to lose. If I kill the Butcher, all the better for him. If I die, then he hasn't lost much.

Rot.

"He didn't send you into the Captain's tower," Jack says, sounding a little offended. "If he hadn't argued on your behalf, you'd face simple execution, with no chance to fight your way out."

"I'm sure another occasion would have presented itself." If I hadn't given him the opportunity, he would have created one. "Is the Butcher as tough as she looks?"

"Tougher, if anything," Jack says, with obscene cheeriness.

"What are her Wells?"

"She has a touch of Rhema, for certain." Jack shrugs. "Scuttle-butt says she has Melos as well, but no one's seen her use it."

We reach the hole in the wall, leading back into the cellblock. Jack steps aside to let me go first, and I pause.

"This is where you would kill me, if you were so inclined," Jack says. "The guards are at the other end of the corridor. You might make it."

"I swore I'd go back, didn't I?"

"You did. But does that mean anything to you?" She cocks her head.

I climb through the hole, stretching once I reach the wider corridor.

Jack smiles, climbing through after me. "And what should Clever Jack tell Zarun?"

"Tell him . . . I'll think about it."

"Think quickly," Jack advises. She shuts the door behind me, and I hear the bar slide back into place.

There's no question of going back to sleep. I use the chamber pot, wash as best I can, sit back on the pallet, and wait for my next visitor. I have a feeling it won't be long.

Sure enough, the bar slides away again a few hours later. I compose myself, and when the door opens I barely twitch. I was expecting Zarun; instead, it's *Shiara* in an elegant black-and-red *kizen*. The Scholar is behind her, leaning heavily on his cane.

"Welcome," I say. "I'm sorry I can't offer any better hospitality."

Shiara gives a thin smile. She picks her way into the room as though the floor were covered in dung. The Scholar follows her and closes the door behind them.

"Deepwalker," Shiara says. Her Imperial has an upper-class accent, but it sounds studied to me, as though she's deliberately putting it on. "I regret we haven't had the chance to get better acquainted."

The Scholar just frowns, hands twisting around the head of his cane.

"The Council has deliberated as to your punishment," Shiara says, then glances at the Scholar. "And his. The penalty for trespassing in the Captain's domain is death."

I bark a laugh. "Oh yes. I'm sure he's very angry with me."

"Mythology has its uses," Shiara says tightly. "I wouldn't expect you to understand the fine points of leadership."

I refrain from pointing out that I was boss of the Sixteenth Ward, which had ten times as many people as live on *Soliton*. I just shrug, and she sets her shoulders, looking annoyed.

"*Therefore*," she goes on, "you are facing execution. But we hope to avoid that, if you are willing to . . . behave."

"You're worried I'm too popular," I translate.

"Quite." Shiara's expertly painted lips quirk. "The Scholar has, let's say, implored us to let you accompany him on an expedition to the so-called Garden. The Council has agreed that, if you wish to take the risk, we could commute your sentence. Assuming you were prepared to leave quietly."

"Isoka, please," the Scholar says. "This could be our only chance."

"It is certainly *your* only chance," Shiara says.

"Unless I fight the Butcher," I say brightly.

They both freeze, and the smile drains from Shiara's face. I mime astonishment.

"I'm sorry," I say. "Was I not supposed to know about that?"

"Zarun told her," the Scholar says. "Of course."

"Zarun is not thinking in the interests of everyone," Shiara says. "These are dangerous times. The last thing we need is a leadership struggle."

"But as long as he doesn't agree with the rest of you, I have the right to challenge," I say.

"You do." Shiara sighs. "But you should consider what would happen afterward, even if you win."

"Isoka—" the Scholar begins.

"Do you think," I say to Shiara, "that your colleague and I could speak alone? As the two who would be going on this . . . expedition."

She looks between us, suspiciously, and then sighs again. "I suppose. I will wait outside. Don't take long."

When she's gone, the Scholar lowers his voice. "I know you don't trust her, but this offer is genuine. Shiara may not be convinced that I'm right, but she's at least concerned."

"I don't have any particular reason to distrust her," I say. "It's not the offer I'm worried about."

"Then what?" His voice is a hiss. "If we don't turn the ship *soon,* everyone is going to die."

"I'm not convinced we can turn the ship, even if we find the Garden."

His eyes narrow. "Why?"

"I have . . . my own sources." I still don't trust him any further than absolutely necessary. "But I think the Garden will *protect* us from the Rot, if we can make it there."

"Then we might as well try," the Scholar says. "At least—"

"If that's the case," I cut him off, "then I'm not leaving without Meroe and the rest of my pack."

His eyes widen in understanding, and he taps his cane on the floor. "I see."

"So if you want my help," I continue, "find Meroe and tell her I need to see her. Tell her . . ." I hesitate. "Tell her I'm sorry."

"We're running out of time."

"Then hurry." I gesture around the cell. "I'll wait."

I hear the Scholar and Shiara talking in the hall as they leave. The Scholar sounds insistent, Shiara annoyed.

I don't know what I'm doing anymore. I had a plan to get to the Captain, and it blew up in my face. Now I'm playing it by ear. It seems like I have something everybody wants—the Scholar needs my power, Zarun wants me to kill the Butcher, and Shiara and the rest of the Council don't want me throwing a wrench into their carefully planned administration. And Hagan . . . I don't know if Hagan is helping me or taking some kind of elaborate revenge from beyond the grave.

All I know, at this point, is that it's been nearly a day since I've seen Meroe and I can't forget the feel of her lips, her body pressed against mine. If there's no turning back from this choice, I have to see her again before I step over the threshold.

22

An hour later, there's a knock at the door. Not the sharp rap of a jailer rousing a prisoner, but the quiet tap of a polite request to enter.

My princess. I sit up at one end of the pallet and clear my throat. "Come in."

The door opens. Meroe is flanked by two nervous-looking crew with hands on swords. She steps inside and they close and bar the door behind her.

I clear my throat again. "Hi."

"Hi." She's wearing a dress in the same style I first saw her, airy and colorful, with the same silver bands on her arms. "I heard . . . rumors. I didn't realize they'd actually locked you up."

"It hasn't been that bad."

"Isoka, you should know . . ." She looks at the floor. "Zarun came and asked me about the dredwurm. He already seemed to know most of it, so I didn't see any point in lying to him."

"It's all right," I say. "I heard from Jack. No one has tried to threaten you or Aifin?"

She shakes her head. "Zarun's people are watching us, I think. But that's all."

There's a pause, which stretches on uncomfortably. I shuffle sideways on the pallet.

"Would you like to sit?"

After a brief hesitation, Meroe gives a tight nod. She lowers herself carefully, keeping as much separation from me as the small space allows. Her shoulders are hunched, nervous. Rot, but I want to wrap my arms around her. Another pause.

"We need to talk," we both say, at almost the same moment. She looks up at me, and I can't help but smile. She breaks out in giggles.

"Sorry," I say. "Do you want to go first?"

"I . . . not really, but I suppose I should." She takes a deep breath. "If you ask me what I *want* I'd say it's to hide in my room for the rest of my life and never talk to anyone again. But that's probably not practical."

"Probably not."

"Okay." She squares her shoulders, as though she's marching to her execution. "You . . . kissed me."

"I'm sorry. I shouldn't have."

"It wasn't . . . ," she begins, then stops, swallows. "You shouldn't have. Not without asking. But I . . . afterward, I should have talked to you."

"You're under no obligation to me," I say, remembering my night with Zarun. *We've made no promises.*

"I'm under the obligation that I—you and I—" She stops again, collects herself. "Have you ever done that before?"

I raise an eyebrow. "Kissing?"

"With a . . . a woman."

"No." I take a deep breath. "I know you don't—"

"I have," Meroe blurts out. "It's . . ." She blinks, and there are tears in her eyes.

"We don't have to do this, Meroe." I put my hand, tentatively, on top of hers. "Just forget it, all right? Forget it happened."

"*No.*" She shakes her head violently. "I'm sorry. This is just . . . harder than I thought. But you told me about you and your sister."

"It's all right."

"Please just listen, Isoka?"

I nod.

"When I was . . . twelve, maybe, there was a girl. Sarama. A daughter of one of my mother's attendants, from a noble family, but wild. She liked to explore the castle, and one day she found her way into my garden.

"I didn't have many friends by that age. Everyone was so *careful* around me. My father wanted it that way. Princes and princesses didn't have the luxury of friends, he said. Sarama was different. She was a little younger than me, and she wasn't afraid of anything. And that made *me* feel different. Ever since I was old enough to understand"—she looks down at her hands—"what I am, I'd been careful, too. But not with her."

She pauses, pressing her knuckles into her eyes. I squeeze her hand, and she takes a deep breath.

"One of the servants caught us. I think my sister Boloi tipped her off. It was the kind of thing she would have done." Meroe swallows. "We were in the garden, back in one of the flower beds, and we were kissing. The servant told my father everything."

Her eyes are filling with tears again. "It wasn't Sarama's *fault*. The kissing was . . . I told her it was a game. I was the one who talked her into it. She just wanted to run around the garden and pretend we were fighting bandits.

"The next day, my father's guards picked me up from my room and marched me down to the basement. My father had Sarama and her parents there, and he accused her of defiling the Princess. Her mother screamed at her, and her father. I tried to scream, too, but the guards stopped me. I had to watch while Sarama's parents beat her bloody. All to please my father, of course. They were desperate to keep their station at court, and Sarama was only a younger daughter, and a troublesome one besides.

"Afterward, my father asked me if I knew why he'd made me watch. I called him awful things, said it was me who'd started everything. He said he was well aware, and that was why he wanted to teach me a lesson. He couldn't beat *me,* you see. Not without telling the whole court that I wasn't . . . what I was supposed to be."

"It's not allowed, in Nimar? For two women to be together?"

Meroe shakes her head. "It's all right for *boys* to run around and suck each other's pricks. That's all just in good fun until they're of age. But girls have to be pure, and princesses doubly so." She looks at me, hesitantly. "I heard it was different, in the Empire."

"I guess." I scratch my head, embarrassed. "It's not exactly . . . *usual,* but nobody gets beaten over it."

"In some parts of southern Jyashtan married women are expected to keep unwed girls as lovers," Meroe says absently. "It's supposed to keep them out of trouble."

"That . . ." I try to picture it, and shake my head. "What happened? Did you ever see Sarama again?"

"No. Her parents sent her back to their estate and kept her there." She rubs her eyes again. "So when you kissed me, I just . . ."

"I understand," I say, though I wonder if I really could. If I'd had a father, and he'd done that to me, I'd have killed him, king or not. "Like I said, we can forget it ever happened."

"I don't want to." Meroe turns to face me, and my heart double-thumps. Goose bumps race down my arm. "I *want* you to kiss me, Isoka. Gods, I've wanted that practically since we first met. I just need to . . . get used to the idea."

"You . . ." Rot, rot, *rot*. Something is wrong with my brain. "Honestly?"

"Honestly." She smiles cautiously. "Why are you looking at me like I just swallowed a live fish?"

"Sorry."

"And stop apologizing."

"Sorry," I say, automatically, and then start laughing. Meroe laughs with me, and our fingers intertwine.

"Thank you," she says, after a while. "For telling me what you did."

"I felt like an idiot," I say. "It's not exactly an uplifting story."

"It was your story," she says. "That's good enough."

We stare at each other for a long moment. The tension has drained away, replaced by a warm feeling I can't put a name to.

"Okay," Meroe says. "Now that the important stuff is out of the way, do you want to explain why exactly you're sitting in a cell waiting for execution?"

I start laughing, and when I'm finished laughing I tell Meroe everything.

Somewhat to my surprise, I tell her *everything*. It comes spilling out of me, like pus from an infected wound, a river of ugly, stinking truth. Meroe takes it all and doesn't flinch. I tell her about Shiro's death, and Hagan's. About Tori, with her perfect house and her perfect life, and what I've done to keep her safe. And about Kuon Naga, how he wants *Soliton* for his war, and how he ruined everything. Her hand tightens on mine.

Then it's just a matter of explaining what went on between me and the Scholar, the deal we made, and what had happened between me and the Council after I'd been captured. And Hagan, of course.

"He's a *ghost*?" Meroe says, her voice a squeak.

"I'm . . . not sure."

"Okay." Meroe takes a deep breath. I can't help but think she's dealing with this remarkably well. "And this ghost-friend of yours agrees with the Scholar that the ship is going to sail to the Vile Rot and kill us all."

"Yes."

"And the Scholar thinks if he can get to this Garden he can change course."

"That's his theory. Hagan said it wouldn't work. But he said the Garden would *protect* us if we got there."

"Right," Meroe says. "And the Council is offering you the chance to go with him and find out. In the meantime, Zarun wants you to fight the Butcher."

I nod. "That would get me out of the execution. But it doesn't help us if Hagan's to be believed." I shake my head. "I think I have to go with the Scholar, Meroe."

Meroe looks at me, carefully. "Then what happens to everyone else?"

"I told them I wasn't leaving you behind." I squeeze her hand. "I said my pack, actually, so Aifin, Jack, and Thora are welcome if they want to come."

"But what about the others?"

"What do you mean? The rest of the Council?"

"All the *people*," she says, patiently. "The crew. The ones who stay behind."

"Maybe the Scholar can turn the ship around," I say. "If not . . . I don't know. But probably nothing good."

"Then we can't do that, can we?"

I stare at her. "Why not?"

"We can't run off, save ourselves, and leave a thousand people behind to die!"

"What choice do we have?"

"There has to be a way," Meroe says. "We just have to find it."

"We're not in *charge* of everyone." I wave a hand vaguely. "That's the Council's job."

"Are they doing it?"

"I—"

She crosses her arms, as though that were a conclusive argument. I sigh and run my fingers through my hair.

"Look," I say. "I know you were raised in a palace. But things are *different* in the real world. You're not responsible for everyone."

"It's not about being responsible," Meroe says. I expect her to be angry, but she's not, which honestly makes *me* irritated. "It's about helping people when you have the ability to help them."

"But—" I grit my teeth. "We *don't* have the ability to help them. If Hagan is right and the Scholar can't turn the ship, then people are going to die no matter what we do."

"How many people would fit in the Garden?"

"How many . . ." I stop. "You're not serious."

"How many?" Her tone is gentle, but firm.

"I have no idea!" I'm shouting now. "Hagan said it would protect everyone who gets there, but I don't know if he meant *everyone*."

"Still. It's the best chance they have."

"Except that there's no way we'll be able to convince them to go. The Scholar barely got the Council to agree to send *me*. They're not going to pack all this up and haul it across the ship."

"Forget the Council," Meroe says. "Just talk to the crew. Tell them the truth. If they choose to follow you, the Council won't be able to stop them."

"How exactly am I supposed to do that when I'm stuck in a cell?"

"At a public event where nearly everyone will be watching," Meroe says.

The penny drops. "Like if I were to fight the Butcher, you mean."

"Like that, for example." She grins.

"Rot." I stare at her. "You really mean it. You want to help *everyone*."

"Someone has to."

I want to—I don't know. Yell at her until she realizes how insane this plan is. Lie to her, tell her I'll do it, then tie her up and drag her off with me and the Scholar and leave everyone else to burn.

Kiss her. Because she's a better person than I could ever hope to be.

Then she looks at the floor, and all the certainty drains out of her face.

"What's wrong?" I ask.

"I . . ." She swallows. "Be honest with me. Can you beat her?"

"The Butcher?"

She nods. "I realized I just assumed you could do it. I think I'd believe you can do anything. But . . ." Meroe shakes her head. "Please, Isoka. Don't just tell me everything will be all right. If you—if something happens to you, then it's all for nothing. Can you?"

This is my way out, I realize. If I want it. If I say I think the fight is hopeless, then I'll be able to talk Meroe down, get her to come with us. We'll be safe. Maybe.

Or else I roll the dice. Save everyone, or die trying.

Rot.

I don't care about everyone. Maybe that makes me a monster, but I've always known that. To save Tori, to save Meroe, to save my own skin, I'd kill every crew on the ship if I had to. But—

There's more to saving Meroe than just keeping her alive. If I take her with me, and we live when everyone else dies, then she'd never forgive herself. The goodness in her, the part that makes her care, might be snuffed out forever.

Then she'd be a monster, too. And I can't accept that.

"I can beat her. I beat the hammerhead and the blueshell, and they were both bigger than she is."

"Right," Meroe says. "Sorry. I didn't mean to doubt you. It's just if you went in there, because I asked you to, and . . . got hurt, or anything—"

"I'll be fine," I tell her. And I will be. For her sake, if not for mine.

"I'll start laying the groundwork," she says. "There's a few people I know who can probably help."

I raise an eyebrow. "Have you been starting a revolution without me?"

"Not . . . exactly," she says. "But you kept talking about getting close to the Captain. I thought we might need some support eventually."

"Be careful."

"You too."

She looks up at me, hesitates, then leans forward impulsively. Her lips brush mine, as light a touch as a butterfly's wing, less a kiss than a promise of things to come. She backs away, eyes wide as though amazed at her own daring, grinning like a fool. I think there's a matching smile on my own face.

Without taking her eyes off me, she gets up and bangs on the door to the cell. I stand up as the guards pull the bar and let her out, drinking in the sight of her as long as I can.

"Wait," I say, once she's gone but before they can shut the door again. Both guards tense, as though they expect me to try something.

"I need you to find Zarun," I say.

"Zarun doesn't have time for you anymore," he says.

"He will. Tell him . . ." I pause, then shrug. "Tell him I'm ready to kill the Butcher for him."

"Not bad, for a cell," Zarun says, looking around. "I didn't realize we kept prisoners in such luxury."

"It's feeling less like a cell and more like an audience chamber," I say. "I've had half the Council in here so far."

"I'd expect nothing less of the mighty Deepwalker." He looks down at his nails, flicks away a bit of grit. Today he's dressed soberly, in shimmering black velvet and crimson ribbons. "I ought to be very angry with you."

"For stealing the dredwurm's eye, or for seducing you first?"

"My memory of that night is a little fuzzy, but I don't believe I took much seducing." He grins, then lets it fade. "I'm sorry about your man. You shouldn't have gone after it with a pack of four."

"They were the only four I could trust."

"Jack would be hurt, if she heard that."

"We both know Jack and Thora work for you first and me second."

"True." Zarun sighs. "Ah, well. I can't find it in me to hold it against you. The hunt for the eye was always a distraction, and truthfully I'm glad to have it over with. Things are difficult enough as it is."

"Do you believe the Scholar?"

"*Soliton*'s never gone close to the Rot before. I still have a hard time believing it would do something so dangerous. Why collect us all, only to kill us?"

"The Scholar says it isn't alive. Just a kind of a machine. It may not understand."

"There's still a few hundred miles to go. And even if we stay on course, nothing says we'll get close enough to the Rot to be in danger." He pauses. "Do *you* believe him?"

"Let's say that I think he has a point."

"And yet you sent the message that you'd be willing to kill the Butcher." Zarun looks at me curiously. "You didn't like the offer the others made you?"

"I can always go *after* I've won the challenge," I say. "If the Scholar is wrong, it'd be nice to have somewhere to come back to."

Zarun laughs. "Poor Shiara worked so hard to convince everyone it would be better to get rid of you quietly. It's a shame to waste all her effort."

"Not from your point of view. This is what you wanted me for from the beginning, isn't it?"

He runs his eyes up and down me, with a faint smile. "Not the *only* thing."

"Well. Now you've gotten everything you wanted."

"And yet I find myself unsatisfied," he says.

He steps across the room, closer to me. I'm standing by the sleeping pallet, my back to the wall, and I look up at him without giving ground. His smile widens.

"Have you given any thought," he says quietly, "to what happens after you win the challenge?"

"Do I get to be on the Council?"

"It's not quite that simple. To be on the Council, you need a clade, a power base of your own. There will be a . . . realignment. One that is potentially very favorable to me." He leans a bit closer. "And to my partners."

"Partners. There's a slippery word."

"Would you prefer something more . . . solid?"

"Are you making me an offer?"

"You are a remarkable woman, Isoka Deepwalker. I find that I want you for more than a pawn or a quick rut." His voice drops. "You'll have a place by my side in the Council. Authority in the clade. Safety for you and your pack."

"And all I have to do is warm your bed?"

"I consider that a benefit, not a drawback," he says. "But if you kill the Butcher for me, I will owe you a considerable debt. And I hate owing debts."

"An attractive proposition," I deadpan.

"I thought so."

"How about this? I kill the Butcher for my own reasons. As for the rest, we'll see." I shoot him a challenging stare. "Maybe I'll just keep you in my debt."

"You never give an inch, do you?" He sounds genuinely impressed.

"Not if I can help it."

Zarun grins like a wolf.

23

And so I find myself in the Ring. Again.

I had thought the crowd was impressive the last time I was here. This time, it rises up around me like a bowl. They stand on boxes, and tables, and barrels, and bookcases. Now and then there's a splintering crash and a wave of laughter as some priceless, overburdened object gives way.

On the dais sit the officers. Zarun is taut, expectant, eyes gleaming. Karakoa looks on with interest, while Shiara affects boredom. The Scholar is sullen, arms crossed, tapping his cane nervously. The Butcher's chair is empty.

Meroe is on the other side of the arena, pressed against the jury-rigged rail. I'm glad to see Aifin by her side, along with Jack and Thora. There's a chance that things could go very badly today. Worse comes to worst, I hope they can keep her safe.

As for me, I've been given the opportunity to bathe, though not to change clothes. So I'm still in my hunting leathers, stained with sweat and blood, which is perhaps appropriate. My hair is tied back and pinned up. As I wait, I stretch, feeling the tug of half-healed burns on my back. In spite of its scars, my body feels light, energized. I bounce on the balls of my feet, and smile at the roar of the crowd.

Then the Butcher arrives.

Rot, she's big. Not just big for a woman, but bigger than a human has any right to be, with barrel-thick arms, fists like knots of sausage, legs like tree trunks. She's made all the larger by her armor, the same elaborate kit I saw her in the first night I arrived. Her blond hair is concealed under a narrow-visored helmet, and overlapping plates of crab shell cover her torso, her shoulders, her knees. Her hands are swathed in long leather gauntlets, with the white flash of the razor-sharp tooth on the back of each palm. Her sword is a rectangular thing like a cleaver, with no point but a gleaming, freshly honed edge.

Enough. It's not like I haven't fought big bruisers before. Never so elaborately equipped, to be sure, but how much difference will that make against Melos armor and blades? Jack said that the Butcher has a touch of Rhema, which means she'll be faster than she looks. And maybe Melos as well, though she can't be very strong, or why rely on that monster sword?

My eyes find Meroe in the crowd again, and I take a deep breath. I can do this. I *have* to do this.

The deck doesn't actually shake as the Butcher makes her way across the Ring. That has to be my imagination.

"Hello, Butcher."

Her lip curls. "I knew I should have killed you for talking back."

"I knew I would have to kill you eventually."

"Better girls than you have tried." She leans closer. "When I'm finished taking you apart, I'm going to take your princess and cut her into tiny pieces. Just remember that when you're bleeding out."

I let out a breath, feeling strangely calm. "You won't."

"You think Zarun will protect her? That two-faced prick? He'll sell her to me for half a bucket of crab juice once you've failed him."

"Meroe can protect herself."

"Her? The girl who stood there and whined about her father while I beat her bloody?" Her lips part in a nasty grin. "That's the funniest thing I've heard all day."

"Isoka Deepwalker." Karakoa's voice booms across the Ring, and the spectators quiet. "You stand accused of trespass in the Captain's domain. Since the Council is divided as to your punishment, your challenge has been accepted. Do you still assert your innocence?"

"I do," I say, as loud as I can. If everything goes according to plan, I'll be asserting more than that.

"Then we will see if the Ring proves your case." He sits back in his chair. "Begin."

I ignite my blades with a *crack-hiss*, familiar energy coursing down my arms. The Butcher is raising her sword, but it's too heavy and she's too slow. I'm already dodging around her left side, one blade swinging, the other on guard against a sudden lunge.

I'm expecting a trick, waiting for one. But the blade connects, slashing across her crab shell armor in a spray of green energy, leaving a scorched, smoking path. Where two plates join, I feel it slip through and bite into flesh, and as I dance away I can see blood blooming on her flank.

"Ooh," the Butcher says, turning to face me. She has her huge sword held in front of her now, as though its weight were nothing. "That stings."

She's still smiling, and I can see why. This could be a problem. Her vulnerable spots are well protected, and she's so big that I'll have a hard time doing lethal damage unless I can get to her face or throat. Meanwhile, on the one hand, if I get tagged by that sword, it's going to hurt, armor or no armor.

On the other hand, staying out of the way of the huge blade shouldn't be difficult. And she's still *human*. If she's bleeding, she'll go down eventually.

Golden light shimmers around her, as though she were briefly outlined by an invisible sun. Rhema, the Well of Speed. When she moves, she's faster, though not as blurringly fast as Aifin. Touched, like Jack warned me, rather than a full adept. I give ground for a few steps, getting a feel for her speed and reach. She swings the cleaver blade back and forth, a steady, rhythmic attack that cuts the air with a *thrum*. It's easy to predict, and I dart forward as she goes into the backswing, aiming my blade at her leg.

She can't get the sword around in time, but she slashes at my chest with her off hand, using the tooth like a punch dagger. My blades slam into her armor, and crab shell breaks with a *crack*. The Butcher grunts as Melos power leaves a long, bleeding line on her thigh. At the same time, her tooth skitters across my body, repelled by shimmering armor. I feel the impact as a line of heat, warm but tolerable.

I come to a halt a few yards away from her, and she turns to face me, big sword whirling in front of her. She's wearing a thoughtful expression.

"You're as good as everyone says." She nods, as though acknowledging me. "A full Melos adept."

"You're welcome to give up, assuming that's allowed," I tell her. "I'm not really clear on the rules."

"Oh no." She chuckles. "You're going to be begging me to kill you quick. I'm just going to have to show off a little, that's all."

She comes forward, cleaver-sword flashing in a dangerous figure eight. Again, I go for her unguarded side, moving around her before she can turn. This time I aim for her shoulder, hoping to slip my blades under the plate there. Her off hand comes up again, and I have a moment to register that there's a shimmering aura around it, a halo of magical energy that matches the crackling green of my armor. Suspicious, I abandon my attack, darting back, and get far enough out of range that her fingers barely brush against my stomach.

There's a brilliant flash, and *crack* like the world's largest branch breaking. Heat rolls over me. For a moment I can't see, my vision full of flaring afterimages. Green lightning crawls across my body, earthing itself in long arcs to the deck.

The kick comes out of nowhere, slamming into my stomach. Even with the Melos armor, it would be enough to knock me off my feet, with all the Butcher's weight behind it. I go limp, letting it carry me, ready to hit the deck and roll—

—but the Melos armor doesn't flare. There's no crackle of green fire or spray of lightning. Just a *thump* of bone-cracking impact, and an abrupt spike of pain.

I don't even notice when I hit the deck, skidding across it to sprawl on my back. The world spins around me, the sound of the crowd an oceanic roar in my ears. Every breath is an agony, not the familiar pain of powerburn but something sharp and nauseating.

Rot, rot, *rot*. *Get up, Isoka.*

I raise my head, expecting to find the Butcher bearing down on me, but she's still several yards away, propped on the hilt of her oversized sword. I force myself to roll onto one shoulder, gathering my legs under me. Blood gushes from my midsection, splashing across the deck. I put my hand to my stomach and find a neat hole in my leathers and the flesh beneath, torn skin hot against my fingers. The Butcher has one of those sharp, triangular teeth on her boot, too, and it's now dyed red.

She makes no move to attack as I shakily regain my feet, one hand still pressed against the wound. Once I'm up, she straightens, stretching her shoulders and heaving that monster sword into the air again.

"Bit of a shock, isn't it?" she says, conversationally. "Not used to having holes punched in you."

I close my eyes, concentrate. My blades shimmer to life with a crackle, but the warmth that my armor should conjure doesn't follow. When I open my eyes again, the Butcher is holding up a closed fist, wreathed in sparking green energy.

"Won't work," she says. "Not until I let go. I never had enough control in Melos to protect myself, but I learned *this* trick from a Jyashtani boy. Interference, I think he called it." Her grin turns vicious. "How do you like being mortal, you rotting bitch?"

Then she comes forward, sword swinging, trailing the golden light of Rhema as she moves with preternatural speed. I back up, dodging, not daring to parry a blade that heavy. Every move tears at the hole in my stomach, the leather around it now sodden with blood. I can barely think through the pain.

When we reach the edge of the Ring, I have to do *something* or get backed into the barrier. The Butcher is coming at me with big sideways swings, all power and no finesse. I slip in behind one, feinting low and then jabbing one blade right at her face. She takes the feint strike on her thigh, Melos energy crackling over armor, and blocks the high strike with her off hand. As I spin away, she pulls back, and the tooth on her gauntlet leaves a long cut along the length of my arm. Fresh pain blooms, and blood spatters the deck.

"Getting a little weary?" she says, watching me sway. She slaps the spot on her thigh where I cut her and grins. "I can keep this up all day."

She's rotting right. Even if I *could* trade cut for cut with her, I'll drop long before she does. Sooner or later I'll be slow enough that she'll catch me with that sword, and without armor one hit would cut me in half.

I'm backing up again, staying out of range. Something roils in my gut, around the pain, that's so unfamiliar it takes me a moment to identify.

It's fear. It's been a long time since I was afraid in a fight. I'm suddenly *aware* of my body, not just as an instrument for delivering death, but in all its horrible fragility, its soft skin that parts so easily beneath a blade, its bones that break under pressure. There had been a moment, when the hammerhead had me pinned, but then it had been do-or-die. Now I'm faced with this grinning monster, and I'm practically running away, feeling thick, hot blood squirt between my fingers.

I feel like I'm twelve years old again, before my powers came to me, when all I had to defend me and Tori from the next slaver or rapist was a two-inch knife and whatever strength an underfed kid could muster. We were always, always running. In my dreams, we were cornered by laughing shadows.

I try to force myself to move. To *fight*, rot it. But the Butcher's blade whirrs, and the razor teeth on her armor gleam, and I fall back.

Blessed's rotting balls. Is this how Meroe feels all the time? Is this how *Berun* felt, when we guilt-tripped him into coming with us, fighting monsters without the benefit of magical armor? I feel like I would go and hide in a dark corner and never, ever come out.

The Butcher is right. I'm only brave because I'm *strong*. Take that away and I'm falling to pieces.

To the Rot with *that*.

I dive sideways as we reach the barrier again, the Butcher's sword whirring over my head. She kicks out, the tooth nicking my leg, but I'm already rolling away. I get back up, breathing hard, my vision starting to swim. Not long left, now.

But if she thinks I'm going to give up, she's wrong. I might have been scared, before I gained my power, but I kept going. The scars that mar my skin are a record of beatings, knife fights, frantic scuffles in the dark. Every time, I got back up, standing between my sister and the world that wanted her dead.

She's still behind me, somewhere. So is Meroe.

This rotting monster has to have a weakness. She's too confident, for one thing. She could have cut me down while I was surprised by her trick, ended this in one strike. But she had to lecture me first, make me understand how badly I'd lost. What else?

She's practiced this style of fighting, the slow, brutal cuts, wearing an opponent down until one connects. She's comfortable with it. When I get in close, she relies on her armor to keep me from doing serious damage.

—relies on her armor—

A slow smile spreads across my face.

The Butcher isn't the only one who can make the Melos Well do tricks.

I concentrate as I back away, letting one blade vanish, shortening the other into a vicious spike. Melos energy builds up in my arm, bringing it to an uncomfortable pitch of heat. I hadn't considered this before—against most human opponents, it would be too dangerous, reducing my reach and leaving me no way to parry. But now—

—I launch myself forward, before I can think about the consequences.

The Butcher swings her sword, and it forces me to the side. Her off hand comes up at the same moment, a short jab sparkling with golden Rhema light. I accept the blow, the long tooth punching into my chest under my breast, its edge grating against a rib. I grab the Butcher's wrist to hold myself in place and swing the spike, aiming for the join between two armor plates on her side. Melos energy screeches against crab shell as I drive it in, punching deep.

"Ow," the Butcher says, sounding more annoyed than angry. "You—"

I release the energy built up in my fist, and she screams.

Her skin is lit from within for a moment by a flickering green light, bleeding forth through the gaps in her armor. Her wide-open mouth throws an emerald beam, and two more burst out of her eyes. Her muscles lock rigid for a second, keeping her upright, and I stagger back and away. Then, with a clatter of plate, she collapses to the deck.

The crowd has gone silent. I step forward again, carefully. Under her helmet, the Butcher's exposed skin has blackened and cracked. Wisps of smoke rise from the gaps in her armor, and the air stinks of burnt meat.

I blink and look up at the crowd.

Now what?

There was something I was supposed to do, something I was supposed to say to all these people. Meroe had coached me, but all the words have fled my mind, draining away with the blood flowing freely from the two holes in my torso. I try to fill my lungs, but all that does is make me cough, and the pain from *that* drives me to my knees.

Someone is running across the floor of the Ring. I look up to see Meroe kneeling beside me, halfway to tears already.

I try to apologize, to tell her that the plan isn't going to work, but all of a sudden I can't hear anything because everyone is screaming.

Something big is moving through the crowd. At first I think there's a fight going on and people are trying to get away from it. Then the crab rises on blue, spindly limbs, towering above the assembled crew. A blueshell. All around the ring, knots of panic and rising screams indicate it isn't the only intruder.

After a stunned moment, the air suddenly fills with the flash and bang of flying magic. Bolts of Myrkai fire erupt, washing over the blueshell, blooming in balls of flame on its carapace or missing entirely to burst among the crowd. More screams, the shouting of pack leaders trying to organize a defense, the panicked rush of people determined to get out of the way.

The blueshell stalks forward, clawed arms rising and falling, already tinged with blood. The mass of sword-tipped tentacles at its mouth stretches out, slashing and skewering, lifting bits of torn flesh to be consumed. I see a boy rolling on the ground, clutching at the stump of his arm, moments before the tentacles descend and silence him for good. One big claw grabs a younger girl, lifting her screaming into the air. She lashes out desperately with her Xenos Well, twisting waves of shadow battering the monster, but its grip tightens inexorably. She shudders and goes limp, spine bent at an unnatural angle, and her sorcery fades away as the crab feeds her into its whirling razor-sharp tendrils.

I look up at Meroe, who is staring around with wide eyes. "Help—" I cough, which sends me into a whimpering ball of pain. Teeth clenched so hard they're about to crack, I force myself to grab her hand. "Help me up."

"Isoka?" Meroe looks down at me. "Gods, stay still! You're bleeding—"

"Help." I swallow. "We have to help."

She shakes her head, and reaches down to put my arm over her shoulder. "We have to get you *out* of here."

I'm too tired to argue. Too tired, in fact, to get very far. We manage to stumble a few steps past the Butcher's steaming corpse, and then my legs give out, and I slump back to the deck. The blood that patters to the metal is a deep, rich red. I stare at it, fascinated, as the puddle starts to spread.

"Isoka!" Meroe's voice is a shriek, but it rings hollowly in my ear. "Get up. You have to get up." I feel her arms around me, trying to lift me, but she's not strong enough. It hurts, when she tries to move me. I want to tell her to stop, to just let me rest awhile, but I can't force the words out.

The blueshell enters the Ring, moving with quiet, eerie grace. Most of the crowd is gone, now, leaving a few hastily organized defenders. They surround the thing with swords and spears, splashes of Myrkai fire and Rhema speed. Blood leaks from it in a few places, but as I watch it lunges forward, claws clacking. A big iceling man is picked up and hurled through the air like a rag doll, crashing to the deck a hundred yards away. An Imperial woman with a long spear stands her ground, stabbing at the crab's mouth, but its tendrils wrap around the weapon and yank her closer. One long blade-tentacle slashes her open from crotch to breastbone, spilling her guts in a gory mass. The crab steps gently over her still-twitching body, coming in our direction.

"Meroe." My voice is a croak. "Run."

"No." She bends closer, to whisper in my ear. "Hold on, Isoka. I'm going to heal you."

I remember Berun, screaming. I feel Meroe's hands grow warm on my arm, the energy coiled inside her, ready to burst forth. I can feel her hesitate, trying to force the power out and hold it back, pushing and pulling on the door at the same time.

It won't work. She can see that as well as I can, and no words are necessary. She leans forward, wrapping herself around me, putting her body between me and the crab.

"It's all right." I'm not sure if I mean it. I'm not sure if she can hear me.

There's a flash of green.

Zarun stands only a few feet away. His elaborate, immaculate outfit is splashed with blood in several colors, and his hair is sopping with the stuff. But none of it seems to be his, and he's ringed in a crackling, writhing aura of Melos power. The crab swings its claw down, a strike with the weight of a falling boulder behind it. Zarun meets it head on, throwing up his arm, a circular shield of Melos energy flickering into being and holding the crab at bay with spitting arcs of lightning. Irritated, the blueshell brings its other claw up, and Zarun throws out his other hand. Bands of pale blue Tartak force wrap around the huge limb, holding it in place.

"Any minute now, you muscle-bound idiot!" Zarun shouts, above the *snap-hiss* of magic and the shouting all around.

Karakoa comes up behind him, at a run. He's at the center of a storm of Melos power, too, his hands held together to grip a long, curved energy blade, like a two-handed sword but impossibly thin. He skids to a halt under the blueshell's claw, weapon humming. After a moment's pause, the crab rears back, but its claw stays in place, severed at the joint. Zarun lets it drop, spinning wildly on the deck and spewing dark blood. Karakoa pivots, lunges, and slashes the long blade through the blueshell's second claw, which falls away as easily as an autumn leaf. Zarun lets his shield disappear, and his arms sprout blades like mine. Together, the two of them move in.

But my eyes are closing. I have time to think that I'm going to have to get him to teach me to do that, and then darkness engulfs me, sucking me under like thick, black oil.

24

"You're luckier than you have any right to be," Sister Cadua says. "This one bled like a bastard, but it only tore the muscle. I've put some fellspike powder in with the bandage, so it shouldn't fester." She draws a needle through my flesh, purses her lips in satisfaction, and bites the end of the thread before tying it off. "The other one got caught in the rib and missed your lung, or we wouldn't be having this conversation."

"I'll try—ow!" She gives me an uncharitable grin as she finishes the knot with a tug. "I'll try to get stabbed a little less next time."

"Good. We're a little swamped at the moment."

Meroe, sitting at my side with my hand held tight in her lap, says, "Thank you, Sister Cadua."

"You're welcome, dear." The Jyashtani woman smiles at her. "Remind this stubborn girl that if she tries fighting anytime soon, those are going to open right up again."

"I'll do my best," Meroe says, with a dark glance at me.

Sister Cadua leaves and there's a knock at the door. We're in the First Tower again, a significantly nicer part of it than my old cell. It looks like someone's bedroom, hastily repurposed as a hospital. Several sets of sheets have been sacrificed to make bandages and towels.

"Come in," I manage. Meroe pulls the bedsheet up to cover my bare torso, swathed in bandages, before the the door opens.

The Scholar looks none the worse for wear, his cane tapping, but his features are drawn. When you go around prophesying doom, I suppose it's something of a mixed blessing to be proved right. He looks over his shoulder and closes the door behind him.

"It's good to see you so . . ." He waves a hand vaguely. "Alive."

"Doesn't mince words, does he?" Meroe says.

"Not that I've noticed." I shift, wincing at the pain. "What's happening?"

"The packs have retaken the walls," the Scholar says. "Crabs are still coming, but a little slower now."

"How did they get over the walls in the first place?" I say.

The Scholar shrugs. "Nobody expected every crab in the Stern to come at us at once. I've never seen anything like it."

Blessed's balls. Hagan had warned me there was no time left.

"It's the Rot," I tell the Scholar. "It's . . . doing something to the crabs. Egging them on."

He frowns at me. "It's a theory. But we're still hundreds of miles off."

"Which means it's going to get worse. You wanted to know what happens to everyone? This is it."

He swallows, and straightens up. "If that's true, then it's already too late."

"Maybe not." I glance at Meroe. "We have to get to the Garden."

"That's what I came to ask you. You and I can set out at once—"

"Not you and me," I say. "All of us. The whole crew. I don't know if it's possible to turn the ship, but even if it is, it's obviously too late for that. The Garden will *protect* us."

"How can you possibly know that?" he snaps.

"You have your sources, and I have mine," I say.

He snorts. "Even if I believed you, what then? Move *everyone* the length of the ship? It can't be done."

"I think it can," Meroe says. "I've been . . . planning."

"Regardless," I say, "it's not your decision. Tell the Council I need to talk to them."

"They're not going to want to listen," the Scholar says.

I exchange another glance with Meroe. "They're not going to have a choice."

* * *

The Council's meeting room is more impressive from the other side of the grate. A big, ornately carved wooden table practically fills it. We arrive well before the others, so Meroe has time to help me to a seat, hovering protectively beside me. The Scholar takes his position with bad grace, hands tight on the head of his cane.

The others come in, one by one. Shiara is in yet another silk *kizen*, this one green and black, with a pattern that puts me in mind of a poisonous spider. Her lips and nails are colored to match. Zarun has managed to change, but there are still traces of crab blood in his curls and on his skin. Karakoa wears a full suit of wooden armor, a weird, insectile helmet held under one arm.

"Deepwalker," he says. "Congratulations on your victory."

Some victory. I'm full of holes. I shrug.

"Ordinarily, this would be when we would come to some kind of . . . accommodation. But," he goes on, "I'm afraid we don't have time for negotiations at the moment. People are dying on the walls as we speak."

"A hammerhead brought down a whole section near the Fourth Tower," Zarun says. His bravado is dulled by exhaustion. "I've never seen them attack the barricades like that."

"We're still hunting down all the little ones that got through," Shiara says.

"I appreciate all of that," I say. "But I need you to listen to me. This isn't going to get better. It's the Vile Rot that's driving the crabs crazy, and the closer we get the madder they're going to be."

The three of them exchange looks. Karakoa turns to the Scholar. "Is this true?"

"It's . . . possible," the Scholar says. He looks sour. "Isoka isn't willing to share the source of her information, so I can't say for certain. But I have always guessed that approaching the Rot would be dangerous."

"They surprised us," Shiara says. "But we've beaten them back. If they keep coming, we'll keep killing them." She shrugs. "Eventually they'll run out of crabs."

Zarun shakes his head, wearily. "There's no *end* to them. *Soliton* is huge, and for all we know it's packed with crabs from bow to stern. My packs are already getting tired."

"I agree," Karakoa says. "This can't go on forever. I suggest we retreat to the Drips. The tunnels are more defensible."

"We won't be able to hide behind barricades," I say. "You just told me a hammerhead broke through. If we're packed tight in a tunnel, that would be a disaster!"

"Besides," Zarun says, "what happens when the *dredwurms* come after us?"

"So, what?" Shiara turns to me. "We give up? Cut our own throats?"

There's something different about them, all three of them. They've always been fractious, proud, quick to snap at one another. Now they're afraid. They can all see what's happening, even if they don't want to admit it.

"We take the crew forward," I say. "To the Garden."

Shiara snorts. "The Garden's as much a myth as the Captain."

"She is correct," Karakoa says. "Jarli went looking for the Garden. If anyone could have found it, it was her."

"She didn't know the way. I do." I hope.

Zarun glances at the Scholar. "You believe this?"

"Again, I have no proof," he says. "But I think it's worth investigating."

"Which is why I offered to let you two try," Shiara says. "Instead, she chose to kick the table over, at what turns out to be the worst possible time. Some of the Butcher's packs are already fighting each other."

"There isn't time to investigate," I say. "There isn't time for *anything*. We have to go *now*."

They're all staring at me now, even the Scholar. I take a deep breath, feel a sharp pain as it pulls at my stitches.

"Isoka," Zarun says. "You have to know we can't."

"That's too much risk for a single throw of the dice," Karakoa says.

"I'm not asking you," I say. "You're right; this isn't a negotiation."

"Excuse me?" Shiara says. "You may have escaped execution, but you're not—"

"Meroe?" I interrupt.

"There are two options here." She stands up, with a smooth smile on her face. "First, the Council can agree with us, and we'll present a united front. Or, second, once we're done here Isoka and I go outside and start telling everyone the truth. The Captain is a lie, the ship is headed for the Rot, and the only way to safety is reaching the Garden."

"What makes you think they'll believe you?" Shiara says.

"They'll believe the *Deepwalker*," Meroe says. "Who was caught in the Captain's tower. Who killed a dredwurm. Who fought the Butcher and won."

There's a long moment of silence. I can see the three of them working it out, and coming to the same conclusion. They look at one another.

"Or," Zarun says slowly, "we can make sure you don't walk out of here."

"Don't be stupid," the Scholar says.

"It's not stupid," Shiara says. "She's *threatening* the Council."

"I have made a few friends," Meroe says. "They're expecting me. If I don't show up, there's a letter they're supposed to open."

"Let me guess," Shiara says. "It says that the evil Council has imprisoned or murdered you."

"Something like that," Meroe says. "When news gets around that the Council has turned on the Deepwalker, after she won her freedom by challenge . . ."

"Enough," Karakoa says. "We will not be murdering a wounded young woman with no justification but our fears. I am not so lost to honor as that."

"Then what?" Shiara says.

"If telling the rest of the crew the truth frightens us so," Karakoa says, "then we should face the possibility that she is in the right."

"You're taking *her* side?" Shiara says.

"Meaning what?" Zarun says. "Go along with this plan? Pack up *everyone* and hope this Garden is real?"

"We can barely defend the walls," Shiara says. "How are we supposed to make it past the Center?"

"Actually, I've thought a bit about that," Meroe says. She takes out a sheaf of *Soliton*'s speckled, scraped-down paper, covered in pencil sketches. "Let me show you something. . . ."

The arguments go on far longer than I would have liked. Far longer than I have stamina for, in truth. I excuse myself and limp back to my bed while Meroe is still debating with the Council, though it's clear she has the upper hand. The Scholar accompanies me, leaning heavily on his cane.

"I hope you know what you're doing," he says. "For all our sakes."

"So do I," I mutter.

When I wake up, Meroe is in charge.

It seems like a few moments between the time I close my eyes and the time I open them, but by the sunlight streaming in through gaps in the deck it's been at least ten hours. One of Sister Cadua's young assistants arrives to help me clean up and change my bandages, but my efforts to get any news out of her are thwarted by the fact that she's clearly in awe, bobbing her head and averting her eyes like I was the Blessed Emperor. Once she's done, I put on a robe and walk outside—carefully—to find out for myself.

I have to interrogate a half-dozen hurrying crew until one of them will tell me where Meroe is. People are running back and forth on all kinds of errands, carrying bundles outside or bringing back information. It doesn't look like we've been entirely overrun by crabs, which is a cheering thought. Those who recognize me step out of my way as I limp past, murmuring, "Deepwalker," with a reverence I find seriously uncomfortable.

Outside the First Tower, the market has been cleared away, replaced with a bustling camp. At the center is a pile of waterskins, bottles, small kegs, anything that will hold a significant amount of liquid, which is growing by the minute as crew run to arrive with more. There's cloth, too, in a bewildering variety of colors and shapes, curtains and carpets and clothing of all kinds. Well-armed crew are standing around in groups, and a few small dead crabs are in evidence.

I find Meroe simply by following the crowd. She's standing at a table in front of the piles, with the Scholar on one side and Shiara on the other. Spread in front of them is a mess of paper, covered in hasty lists and sketches. A dense ring of people, most of whom I recognize as pack leaders, surrounds the table. I grimace, not relishing the prospect of forcing my way through, but as soon as one of them notices me they step out of the way.

"Deepwalker," says a huge iceling, wearing crab-shell armor and a sword nearly as big as the Butcher's.

"Deepwalker," an older woman echoes, her blue-tinted hair flopping over as she inclines her head.

I blink. What in the Rot am I supposed to say?

Fortunately, Meroe sees me. She says something to the Scholar, then hurries over, taking my arm in hers and helping me away from the crowd. Behind us, the chaos of shuffling paper and shouted orders goes on.

"Isoka!" Meroe says. "How do you feel?"

"In quite a lot of pain, to be honest." I put one hand to where the bandages bulk under my robe. "But I can walk without bleeding, at least. What's going on?"

"Well, you talked the Council into trying for the Garden." Meroe waves her hand vaguely. "We've just been working out the details."

"It looks like you're tearing the town apart."

"There were some fights over that at first. Karakoa threatened to cut one of the scavengers in half if he didn't get out of the way, and that clarified things." Meroe looks at the piles. "My biggest concern is water. Everyone's going to have to carry some. At least food shouldn't be an issue. There's going to be plenty of crab."

I half-smile, thinking this is a joke, then decide it isn't. "They're still coming?"

She nods. "Zarun and Karakoa are out at the defenses now. We've had to pull people off the walls to give them some rest, so we're stretched pretty thin."

I shake my head. "Is all of *this* part of a princess' training, too?"

Meroe looks surprised. "Of course. A princess of Nimar must be prepared to lead an army in the field, if necessary." She looks a little embarrassed. "I admit it's mostly reading and theory on my part. But while I was talking to the Council, it turns out I'm the only one who's read Anjustius or Gero's *Campaigns,* so the others agreed that I should . . . organize things."

They agreed, just like that. I find myself grinning at Meroe. "You're . . ."

"What?" She looks at me, then down at the deck. "I'm sorry I couldn't consult you, but there wasn't *time*—"

"Please." I grip her hand. "It's fine. What in the Rot do I know about putting together an . . . an *army*? You're better off without me."

"We're not, believe me." Meroe squeezes my hand back. "In fact, now that you're awake, do you feel up to a short walk?"

"Where to?"

"Crossroads. That's where people are resting. I think it would be good for morale if they could see you."

"Good for *morale*? Why?"

"You're the *Deepwalker,* Isoka." Meroe lowers her voice. "Most of these people have never left the Stern. Even the hunting packs and scavengers don't go into the Deeps, or beyond the Center. You're living proof that it can be done. And you went against the Council because you knew this was coming, and fought the Butcher to convince them—"

"That's not true! I didn't know anything, except what the Scholar had already told them. And I fought the Butcher—"

"*I* know that," Meroe says quietly. "So does the Council. But the rumors have gotten . . . overheated. At this point, it's probably best to just let them believe what they need to."

Rot. Bad enough that I had to get perforated fighting that monster. Now they're trying to make me into some kind of saint for it? I shake my head.

"This isn't going to work, Meroe. I'm not . . . what they want me to be. *You* know. I'm a girl who likes to hurt people, and I'm pretty good at it. That's all. Not a . . . a leader, or a savior."

Meroe leans closer, putting her head beside mine, her lips to my ear. My skin pebbles to goose bumps at her touch.

"How do you think I feel?" she says. I can hear the panic in her voice, deeply buried but still there, like lava bubbling underground. "Because I read a few books, they're treating me like some great general! I am making this up as I go along, and every *second* I expect someone to stand up and say, 'Hey, Meroe, you don't have any rotting idea what you're doing, do you?' And then I realize that the reason no one does is because *none of them know any better*, and I can't decide which is more terrifying. They ask me to decide things and I do the best I can and people are *dying* on the walls."

I slip my arm around her shoulders, pulling her closer. I can feel her shaking.

"I'm not what they think, either," Meroe says, pressed against my chest. "I'm a *ghulwitch*. If they knew that, they'd have torn me apart by now. But I'm going to keep faking it because I haven't got any choice, and I need your help." She looks up, her face close to mine, and my breath catches in my throat. "Please?"

"Of course." I put on a shaky smile. "We'll fool them all together; don't worry."

Crossroads had also been cleared, its tables and chairs pushed to the edges to leave a broad space. Sleeping pallets and blankets occupy about half of it, covered with exhausted-looking pack members, still in their armor with weapons nearby. The other half is a hospital, with the casualties laid out in neat rows, while Sister Cadua and her people move from one to the next and kneel beside them. Most of the injuries are relatively minor. A few who are worse off groan in pain, or lie ominously still.

Meroe takes my hand again as we approach, squeezing painfully tight.

"Some of them are going to have to be left behind," she whispers. "We'll carry a few, but the ones Sister Cadua thinks are dying . . ."

"Blessed's balls."

"It's not that many," Meroe says, desperately. "And some of them may recover before we're ready to leave."

I lower my voice even further. "You could help them."

"I tried," Meroe says, miserably. "Of course I tried. But the power just . . . wouldn't come. I'd try to focus, and all I could see was Berun's face, hear him screaming. I . . ."

She trails off, and all I can do is keep squeezing her hand.

We're recognized before long, and crew start flocking around. None of them want to get too close, so we end up in a sort of bubble of clear deck, surrounded by a dense, quiet crowd. Looking around at the faces, I feel close to panic. It's like—

Every so often, back in Kahnzoka, someone would come to me as ward boss and just . . . beg. I'm used to people asking for favors, for business arrangements, or peddling a sob story. But every so often, a petitioner looks at me and I can feel the raw desperation coming off them. No attempt at bargaining or plea for sympathy, just *need*. The feeling that this is the end of the line, the last chance.

I grant those petitions, as often as I can. Most of the time, they don't ask for very much. It's good for my reputation, and honestly I just get uncomfortable with the way they look at me. Now, as I stand in what used to be Crossroads, every face has that look. Men and women, Imperials and Jyashtani and icelings and Akemi and southerners. Kids—so many kids, boys and girls of twelve or thirteen, more than I imagined. Most of the people I've dealt with were part of the hunting packs, who tended to be at least my age, but the officers' clades and scavengers are full of soft young faces, working behind the scenes. Now they're here, the children who mop the floors, cook the food, clean the clothes, stained with sweat and blood, staring at me like I'm the Blessed One come again.

"Isoka," Meroe whispers. "Say something."

"What?" I try a smile, and it ends up as a corpse's demented rictus. "What am I supposed to say?"

"Something hopeful."

Hopeful. Right. I swallow.

"Um. Hi."

Not a great start. Did my voice always sound like that?

"I know things aren't . . . great. But we're working on it. Meroe is helping; the officers are helping—"

I'm babbling. I'm almost glad when a voice from the crowd cuts me off, a young man.

"Where are we supposed to go?" he says.

"The Garden," I say. "We'll be safe there."

"How do you know?" says a stick-thin girl, her arm in a bloody sling.

"It's hard to explain," I say. *A ghost told me* lacks a certain something as an explanation, I have to admit. "But trust me, we can get there."

"Why is the Captain doing this?" a younger girl says. "Why would he steer us into the Rot?"

I meet her eyes, and immediately regret it. She's Tori's age, and she has the same intensity as my sister, the same wholehearted belief.

What am I supposed to say? That the leaders they've all put their faith in have been lying to them for years? That there's nothing in the Captain's tower but the skeleton of some mad nobleman? That none of us have any clue what controls the ship, and for all we know it could be taking us to the ends of the world?

"I don't know." The lie burns my throat. If you'd asked me, a month ago, what I would do in a situation like this, I would have told you I'd give them the hard truth. Now, staring at those faces, I can't do it. It's one thing to kill someone. It's another to destroy them. "But the Garden is the only chance we have."

"The Garden's a rotting myth!" someone at the back shouts.

Mutters rise, on both sides. I hold up my hands and get quiet, for a moment.

"Look," I say. "You don't have to believe me. But at least you should know that *I* believe it. What would be the *point* of a lie? It's not like Meroe and I, or the other officers, are going to send everyone off while we stay behind. Right or wrong, we're all going to the same place. Either everyone will be safe"—I risk a sideways glance at Meroe—"or we're all going to die, together. That much I can promise."

* * *

We take things slower on the way back. My wounds are hurting badly from even this modest exertion, burning pain stabbing with every breath and every step. Meroe stays by my side, keeping to my pathetic pace. I grit my teeth to keep from screaming.

"Some good I did as inspiration," I say, after a while. "I basically told them we were all probably going to die."

"I don't think you said 'probably,'" Meroe says, with a slight smile. "And you were honest with them. I think it's what they needed."

"I wasn't, though."

"About the Captain?" She gives a shrug, though I can see it troubles her, too. "Sometimes there's value in a myth."

"A lie, you mean."

"It's not the same thing, exactly."

I don't quite get it, but I don't want to argue. The streets are empty of vendors and hawkers, the stalls crushed or ransacked in the aftermath. Dead crabs lie here and there, scorched by Myrkai fire or cut to pieces.

"What happened to Aifin and the others?" I ask, ashamed I hadn't thought of it before now. Some pack leader I am.

"They're all right," Meroe says. "Aifin has been helping with my scavenging work. Thora and Jack are with Zarun at the walls."

"Oh. That's . . . good." In truth, I feel numb, distant. "When are we leaving?"

"Tomorrow morning," Meroe says. There's a slight tremble in her voice. "I wish we could do more to prepare, but if the crabs keeping coming . . ." She trails off.

"You've done everything you can," I say, quietly. "I don't think anyone could have done better."

"It's not enough," she says.

It will never be enough. Not for her. That's what makes me want to wrap myself around her and keep her safe from the world. But Meroe is not like Tori, to be kept in blissful ignorance of the blood at the foundation of her fake, beautiful life. She *understands*.

She doesn't want me to keep her safe. She just wants me to help, to try to be as good as she is.

Rotting Blessed, I want to kiss her.

25

By morning, there's still not enough water, not enough food, not enough medicines or boots. But we're leaving anyway, because there's no time left.

The beginning is the trickiest part, a classic disengagement in the face of the enemy in a manner (Meroe tells me) straight out of Gero's *Campaigns*. Everyone gathers together in the shadow of the First Tower, except for the bare minimum of fighting crew needed to hold the walls. Seven or eight hundred people, battered and dirty already, some of them injured. They pick up improvised packs, filled with a little bit of food, a little spare clothing, and as much water as they can carry and still stagger.

Zarun and Karakoa are still leading the defense, so Shiara and the Scholar assist Meroe in getting the column moving. Pack leaders fan out, taking to the edges of the crowd, making sure no one shirks their burden or gets left behind. Carts would make this easier, even without horses to pull them, but carts would never manage the spiral steps. So everything has to go on someone's back, or not at all.

The youngest scavengers act as runners, darting off into the abandoned city to get messages to the walls. As the column moves off, heading away from the First Tower toward the Center, the fighting packs have to fall back to join it, but not so quickly that we all drown in a horde of crabs. It's a delicate piece of timing, and I feel completely useless, walking next to Meroe and trying to ignore the pain of my wounds. She listens to returning messengers and gives them answers, telling pack leaders to move in ten minutes, or twenty, or to hold out for more instructions.

She manages it, somehow. The hunting packs come hurrying back to join the column, exhausted and bloodstained. I catch sight of Jack, still somehow with a spring in her step, and she gives me a jaunty wave as she bounces beside Thora. Meroe assembles them into a rear guard, protecting the column as it winds its way through the Upper Stations.

The crabs are coming. We've blocked off the stairs down to the Middle Deck and the Drips, but once the packs retreat from the walls there's nothing to stop the monsters from wandering into the city. A few of them charge the rear guard, where Myrkai fire and Tartak force take them apart. I can see blueshells clinging to the First Tower, brightly colored in a shaft of sunlight, and a swarm of scuttlers working its way over Crossroads.

I don't have to look at Meroe to know what she's thinking. Not everyone joined the column. A handful were too hurt to walk; Sister Cadua had left each of them with a knife, for the crabs or for themselves. More had simply refused to leave, including several of the Butcher's old packs. They'd holed up in the towers, or down in the Drips, determined to fight. Watching the crabs swarm across the city, I don't think anyone has any illusions that we'll be seeing them again.

Eventually, the head of the column reaches the barricaded door that marks the boundary between the Stern and the Center. Here the crew contracts to a dense huddle, reorganizing. I see Zarun and Karakoa for the first time since the Ring, particolored with the gore of a dozen types of monster. The two of them and the strongest of the hunting packs wait while we dismantle the barricade. I stand with Meroe, Shiara, and the Scholar by the door, listening to the sound of fighting behind us. The crabs are silent, as always. It's the humans who blast them with fire, throw them against the deck with a clatter, or scream in agony.

Two Tartak adepts from Karakoa's clade pull scrap metal out of the way, straining visibly as they wrap the barrier in blue light. As soon as there's a clear space, crabs start to squirm through. Scuttlers, at first, and other small monsters that the hunters spear or fry. Then, once the gates open, larger beasts. A hammerhead, a pair of blueshells, even a shaggy. Others I don't recognize.

I'd never seen a real hunting pack take on a crab. It makes me realize how makeshift Pack Nine's efforts had always been, how much I'd relied on my own powers to handle things. Even tired, the packs operate with efficient teamwork, Tartak bindings holding their targets in place long enough for Myrkai fire to blast through their armor.

In places there's a flare of green, a Melos blade, but not often. I'd always known Melos is one of the less common Wells, but I'd never really appreciated the difference it made, how it set me apart. Zarun and Karakoa are the only full-fledged Melos adepts apart from myself. They stride through the fight like glowing green gods, rending and breaking.

Eventually, the mass of crabs on the other side of the door thins out. The packs advance, pushing onto the long bridge that arcs into the great void of the Center, fighting their way toward the first of the big support towers. We follow in their wake, through a horrible landscape of twisted flesh and scorched chitin.

Most of the mangled pieces lying around us belong to crabs, but not all. A young man lies impaled on a blueshell's claw, which in turn has been severed at one of its armored joints. The top half of a pretty young woman lies faceup, wearing an expression of blank surprise, her body below the hips trailing off into a red smear. I recognize Attoka, one of Zarun's pack leaders, only by her white-blond hair; the rest of her is so tangled with the corpse of a many-limbed crab that I can't tell where one ends and the other begins.

Somewhere behind me, there are retching sounds. One of the youngest starts to cry.

Thankfully, we leave the mess of bodies behind as we make it onto the bridge. Only a few dead crabs line the way, and we push those over the side. The rear guard contracts as the last of the column pushes through the door. The entire population of *Soliton*, minus those we left behind and the bodies that line the way, is now trudging across the long, narrow bridge, hanging in the darkness above the Deeps.

"I'm telling you," Zarun says, "I can't ask my people to push any further. They're barely on their feet as it is."

"We're all tired," says Karakoa. "But—"

"We can't stop here," Meroe says.

We're on the broad ring around the first support pylon. The entire crew doesn't fit, of course, so they spread a little way back along the bridge. Packs watch the rear, and other bridges that lead from this circular platform off into the darkness. The officers, along with me and Meroe, are meeting on the far side of the pylon, out of easy earshot.

I can see the tiny flecks of gray light moving up and down, just under the metal skin of the pillar. Part of what the Scholar describes as a great machine, like a pipe for magic instead of hot water. When I put my hand against the metal, I imagine that I can feel the prickle of the energy on my skin. But it's weak, here, not enough to try to contact Hagan.

"This is a fine spot," Zarun says. "I may not be as well-read as our 'military expert' here, but I can see this place will be easy to defend."

"It's not about defense," Meroe says. "It's about water."

They all look at her.

"We have maybe three days' worth of water," she says. "Here in the Center, there's no way to get more."

She'd explained the problem to me, before we left. *Soliton*'s crew collected water from where it gathered on the decks after rains, then strained and boiled it to make it safe to drink. Here in the Center, where there are no decks, only bridges and platforms, there's nowhere for water to collect. Far below in the Deeps, we'd found a pool, but I knew better than to suggest we try to repeat *that* journey.

"So we have to reach the Garden before we run out," Meroe goes on. "That means we have to push on as far as we can before we rest. There will be other platforms we can defend."

"That's easy for you to say." Zarun scowls. "We're the ones going up against the monsters."

"Zarun." Karakoa puts a hand on his shoulder. "She is right. We can press on a few more hours. It will be easier, on the bridges."

Zarun looks up at the big Akemi and sighs. The two of them turn away, and Shiara follows. The Scholar taps his cane on the deck, looking at me.

"At some point, of course," he says, "you'll have to direct us to the Garden."

"When we need direction, I will." I match his questioning stare. "For now, all we need to know is that we keep going forward."

"As you say." He rubs his bad leg and grimaces. "Don't push *too* hard, Princess."

When he's gone, I lean back against the pillar. Meroe settles herself beside me, our shoulders touching.

"How are you doing?" she says.

"Keeping up, so far." I put my hand against my bandages. "It's not enough. I should be helping."

"You know what Sister Cadua said," Meroe chides. "This much walking is bad enough."

"I *know*. Rot. I just feel . . . useless."

"You're not. You're—"

"The Deepwalker." I growl. "What good is that doing anyone?"

"They're watching you."

"They're watching me limp along like an old woman."

She turns to face me. "Isoka—"

"I know. I *know*." I keep looking off into the darkness. In the distance, colored lights shift, ever so slightly, and flicker.

Meroe is going over some kind of plan with Shiara and the Scholar. I sit with my back to a support pylon, my breath ragged. I should eat something, but the thought is nauseating.

We don't have a "camp" in any real sense of the word. No tents, no fires, just a mass of people stretched out on a hard metal deck.

Myrkai adepts conjure a few lights. Some people chew on dried meat or mushrooms, but most are too tired to eat.

The rest of my pack have drifted in nearby. Jack, her dapper suit torn and bloodied, lies with her long limbs curled into a tight ball, her head in Thora's lap. The iceling woman has a hand on her partner's shoulder, stroking her with gentleness surprising for her size. Aifin sits down beside me, sweat running freely down his face. He takes a long swig from his canteen, then looks over at me.

I gesture, *You okay?*

He blinks, reaches for the slate that hangs at his belt, then thinks better of it and just gives an exhausted shrug.

I'm drifting into a doze when someone else sits down opposite. It's Zarun, looking more haggard than I've ever seen him, dark bags under his eyes as though he's taken a beating in a bar brawl. I watch him through hooded eyes, and wait for some banter, a superior grin, or a not-terribly-subtle double entendre. But he just stares at me, until I stir slightly.

"What?" I say.

"Your princess," he says. "She doesn't stop, does she?"

"Not that I've seen."

"Freeze and rot." He lets out a long sigh. "I don't think I've ever been so tired."

A week ago, he would have added *except after our lovely evening together, of course,* or something similar. I hesitate, then say, "Your packs have been doing well."

He nods, bleakly. "Did you know Ghelty? About your age, five foot tall and skinny as a twig, but rot, what a fighter. She was right in front of me, fighting a scuttler, and a blueshell came up behind her. I shouted something, but she just . . . missed it. Too tired. Rotting thing cut her to bits. I killed it afterward, but what good does that do?"

"I'm sorry," I say, and somewhat to my own surprise I mean it.

"Meroe was right," he says. "She made the right decision, and people are dying anyway."

"Believe me." My chest feels tight. "She knows."

"Ghelty used to dance," he says. "She was such a proper little thing, most of the time, but if you got a couple of drinks into her she'd dance, and it was—"

"Can I ask you something?" I say, hoping to change the subject.

"What?"

"That . . . shield you make, with your Melos power. How do you do that?"

"It's not hard," he says. "Just try to picture the armor opening out, like a flower. It takes a lot of energy, though."

"Did someone teach it to you?"

"Jarli." He shakes his head. "God, I wish she was here."

"Did she teach Karakoa the sword he uses?" I raise my hand. "Half the time my blades just scratch the surface of crab shell, but he cuts right through it."

"Good trick, isn't it?" Zarun grins, and looks like his old self for a moment. "He's a Myrkai talent, you see. Never uses it to throw fire around, but he spreads that energy through his Melos blade. The heat helps it cut clean."

I'd never heard of two Wells being *combined* like that, even in people who could use more than one. Though it wasn't much help to me, since I didn't have even a touch of Myrkai.

"Glad he's on our side."

"Me too." He cocks his head. "Are you angry with me? For using you against the Butcher?"

"I probably should be, but I'm too tired. Are you angry with me for stealing your dredwurm's eye?"

"Let's call it even."

"I *did* seduce you."

"Is that how it went?" He gives a crooked grin. "Well. I didn't mind. If we live through all of this . . ."

He makes a vague but nonetheless obscene gesture. I can't help but laugh.

I wake up in the morning—if it is morning—to find Meroe huddled beside me, her head resting on my shoulder. She looks so carefree, sleeping, that for a while I don't move.

The second day's march goes much like the first. At the head of the column, the hunting packs flush out the crabs and cut them down, a never-ending fight that leaves more and more crew stumbling away injured. Sister Cadua and her assistants can provide only bandages and crab juice, then a pat on the back as the pack members return to the fight. In the rear, the attacks are less intense, but we still have to stay on guard.

Fortunately, the center of the column is relatively safe. The youngest crew gather there, and the injured, and those whose Wells are too weak to be any use in a fight. It's where I'm walking, too, when a long, red leg slips up from underneath the bridge and plunges into the crowd.

The farther we've come, the less familiar the crabs have been. The scavengers have names for some of them, but we've come far enough that there are creatures even they have never encountered. This one is certainly beyond my own experience, a towering, spindly giant of a thing with eight legs, each only as thick as my wrist but several times longer than I am tall. Far above us, they support an oval body, shaggy with brown fur. A central mouth bristles with fangs.

The air fills with screams as the thing swings itself up. It must have been nestled against the underside of the bridge, somehow patient enough to wait until the front line had passed it before attacking. Smart, for a crab, or maybe just lucky. Either way, it's waded into the most vulnerable part of our line, with anyone who can fight several hundred yards away behind a mass of panicking people.

The bridges aren't the safest place to panic, either. Some sections of a rickety metal railing remain, but most are long since rusted away, leaving nothing between us and a sheer drop. As the young and the injured flee from the red-armored crab, they pack together, pushing the crowd dangerously close to the edges.

Near me, I can see a girl Tori's age fall to her knees. Her shouts are inaudible under the general panic, and before she can get up someone kicks her in the side, sending her sprawling toward the drop. The crab takes another step forward, and the crowd surges, shoving the girl over the edge.

Once again, I'm moving before I'm conscious of making a decision, sliding toward her as she overbalances and begins to fall. Her hands claw at the unyielding metal, desperately, and I go down on my stomach and grab her wrist before she disappears forever into the dark. The weight of her nearly jerks my shoulder out of its socket, and her nails dig into the back of my hand, drawing blood. She swings sideways, scraping my arm against the edge of the bridge. I get her in my other hand out just before my grip gives way, and start to heave her back up. Muscles clench and strain in my chest and back, and on my stomach I feel the *pop* of a stitch giving way. A hot gush of fluid dampens my shirt.

I manage to get the girl back on the bridge. She clings to my hand even after her feet are back on solid metal, and I have to pry myself away. More screams draw my attention back to the crab, which is chasing the mass of people pressing toward the rear of the column. Its furry body dips down, like a bird taking fish from the water, and snatches a boy out of the crowd. He shrieks as it lifts him high into the air, hanging from its underside, long, flexible mandibles slowly closing around him.

The only accessible parts of the thing are its legs. I ignite my blades and charge, but a swing against the armored limb only produces a long scorch mark on the red plate. Even driving a spike into that armor isn't going to help, not from here, which means there's nothing for it. I jump, gripping the leg in both hands, and start to climb.

The crab takes notice when I pull myself up past its second joint. It pauses in its slow ingestion of the screaming boy to shake its leg, like a dog with a burr. I do my best burr impression and hang on. The crab raises a second leg and tries to scrape me off. I grit my teeth, letting its taloned foot press against my armor, the familiar crackle of Melos power raising heat on my back.

At least my armor *works* again.

Another body length and I'm close to the screaming boy. I grip the crab's leg between my thighs, freeing my hands, and reignite my blades. I don't dare simply cut him free—we're high enough above the bridge now that the fall would be dangerous—so I go for the crab's body, punching my glowing green weapons into the furry mass. The core of the thing is surprisingly small, and much softer than its legs. It twitches with each strike, and the blood that bubbles out is disturbingly close to human red. I focus on where its legs meet its body, and before long the creature is leaning sideways, wobbling closer to the abyss.

The boy's leg is close enough to grab. I dismiss one blade, take hold of him, and deliver a final strike to the crab's core with the other weapon. It staggers, its jaws spasming, and lets the boy drop. I let go at the same time, pulling him close to me as we fall, wrapping my body and my Melos armor around him as I once wrapped Meroe for a much longer plummet.

This fall is thankfully brief. We hit the bridge hard enough to knock the wind out of me, a spray of green sparks earthing themselves in the metal all around us. Above me, the red crab weaves drunkenly, then collapses, its body tumbling over the side of the bridge, followed by a tangle of legs.

The boy on top of me is still screaming, which means he can't be too badly hurt. Unfortunately, I can't say the same about myself. There's a lot of blood around us, and I think it's mostly mine.

I don't quite pass out, but the rest of the day goes by in a blur, a shifting mass of visions that change whenever I blink.

Someone carries me. Or several people. I think it's Thora, at first, but later it seems like Zarun. I can hear the roar of Myrkai fire in the distance, and shouted commands, as though my ears were stuffed with cotton.

Meroe walks beside me. That's the one constant. When we stop for a while, she pulls up my shirt to change my bandages, which are soaked alarmingly red. I try to say something to her, but it comes out as a croak, and she shushes me.

Sometime in the afternoon, I fall asleep. When I wake up, we're on another support platform, with a spiral stair wrapped around the central pylon. Everyone is sprawled on the deck again, so the day's march must be over.

My head is clearer than it's been since the fight, though I still feel as weak as a kitten. I look around for Meroe, and find her nearby, carefully pouring water from a skin into a larger clay jug.

"Could I . . ." My throat is dry, and I swallow. "Could I have a drink?"

"Isoka?" Meroe looks up, and her face is like a punch in the gut. Her eyes are red from crying, and every line of her speaks of exhaustion. Nevertheless, she hurries over, the half-full waterskin glugging in her hand. "Here. Be careful."

I drink, wincing with every swallow. I can feel the pressure of bandages, and the wet squelching when I move tells me I'm still bleeding. That seems . . . bad.

"You were supposed to stay out of it," Meroe says, while I drink. "Sister Cadua warned you."

"Nobody told the crabs." I finish the skin. "No one else was close enough."

"Isoka, *please*." She closes her eyes. "I know you want to help. But if you do this again, you could die. And if you die, I . . ." She swallows, and continues in a more level voice. "If you die *we* won't have any way to find the Garden."

"I can't just hide when a crab is eating people." I pull myself up a little, grimacing at the pain. "They're only here because *I* told them it would be safe."

That's the difference, I realize, even as I say the words. Back in Kahnzoka, if monsters had been tearing the Sixteenth Ward apart, I would have gotten as far away from it as possible. The ward boss didn't have a responsibility to *defend* the ward, only to enforce the rules. The only promise I'd made was the promise of pain for those who'd stepped out of line. But here—

"I know," Meroe says.

"You were the one who wanted to save everyone." My throat feels thick.

"I *know*."

There's a long silence. Meroe's hands are clenched tight in her lap, skin stretched across her knuckles.

I let my voice drop. "You have to heal me."

She blinks. "I can't."

"You *need* me up and fighting. I've seen how much Zarun and Karakoa can do, but it's not enough. Another Melos adept—"

"I *can't.*" Meroe looks down at her clenched fists. "I tried healing people before we left, and I couldn't do it. The power wasn't there."

"What happened to Berun wasn't your fault," I say. "You told me you couldn't do it, and I pushed you into it. That's why it went wrong."

"You don't know that," Meroe says.

"You healed me once." I touch the line of blue marks across my face.

"Maybe I just got lucky."

"I'll bet on that luck again."

Meroe shakes her head. "If it . . . goes badly, then we won't have any way to find the Garden."

"At the rate we're losing fighters we're not going to *make* it to the Garden." I'd seen the wounded stumbling back from the head of the column, and the bodies pushed to the sides of the bridge.

"I . . ." Meroe looks up at me. "You'd trust me to try? After . . . after everything?"

I nod, wordlessly.

She unclenches her fingers, one by one, and I can hear the joints pop.

Finding privacy in the midst of the tight-packed column isn't easy, but fortunately *Soliton*'s twisted architecture provides. The camp sprawls out around a support pylon and its ring-shaped platform, and a spiral staircase wraps around it, leading to more ledges above and below. Meroe helps me negotiate the staircase down an agonizing couple of turns until we reach another, smaller platform, thickly overgrown with mushrooms and mold. Meroe tells Thora to wait at the top and not let anyone bother us.

"There could be crabs down here, you realize," Meroe says, as we take the steps one at a time.

"I'll handle them," I manage, between gasps. It's a joke, because I can barely support my own weight.

Finally, we reach the ledge. There are no crabs visible, just a thick carpet of spongy gray-green mushrooms broken by towering spires of larger growths. Meroe helps me sit, and the fungus makes for a surprisingly comfortable surface. The noise of the camp above us is a distant buzz, and a little bit of lantern light outlines the platform and the bridges leading off from it. In every other direction, there are only the distant motes of the Center's colored lights.

"Okay." I'm sitting across from Meroe, suddenly uncertain. The last time she did this, I was unconscious. "What should I do?"

"Lie down, I guess." Meroe tugs nervously at her hair. "You might pass out."

I lie down. "Do I need to undo these bandages?"

She shakes her head. "I don't need to see the injury. I can . . . feel it, I guess? It's hard to explain." She takes a deep breath. "Are you *sure* you're okay with this?"

I nod, quickly and decisively, trying not to betray the roil in my gut. Sitting by my side, ready to lay her hands on my skin, is a *ghul-witch*. Foul, unclean, the incarnation of filth.

And if she gets it wrong, I'll end up like Berun, bloating and bursting and screaming the whole time.

But she won't get it wrong.

"Meroe?"

She's staring at her fingers, stretching them. "Hmm?"

"Can I kiss you?"

Silence. My heart stops.

"You said you needed some warning," I say, desperately. "But I thought"—*no, don't say* just in case, *rot rot rot; think of something else*—"if you're not ready, that's fine, I just wanted to check it's—"

"Isoka."

"Yes?"

"Please be quiet."

She leans over me, supporting herself with one hand. Our lips meet, a dry brush at first, and then more, her mouth opening against mine, hot breath tickling my skin. I push against her, desperately, craning my neck when she starts to pull away. The wound in my chest gives a stab of pain, and I fall back to the deck.

Ow. Rot.

"You can do this," I tell her.

In spite of her hollow eyes and gaunt cheeks, Meroe is smiling. "I can do this."

She puts her hands on me, and does it.

If you ever have the chance to be awake while a ghulwitch heals you, I do not recommend you take it. A gentle heat throughout my body contracts to burning fever where I'm torn and bleeding. I feel something *move* inside me, as though there were rats under my skin, burrowing around and looking for an escape. The heat changes, becoming something else, raw energy that stimulates every nerve at once, simultaneously orgasm and agony, sensation too strong to touch, like staring directly at the sun. It lasts for roughly ten million years, and then stops. I slowly become aware that I am still breathing.

"Isoka?" Meroe's voice is distant and timid.

"Am I . . ." My own voice sounds like a stranger's. Blood roars like the ocean in my ears. "Am I about to explode?"

"I don't think so," Meroe says. "I think it worked."

I open my eyes. Meroe is leaning over me, looking worried. I put one hand on my stomach, worm it down under the bandage, to where I would expect to find the ragged edge of the wound. There is only smooth skin, slicked with leftover blood.

"How do you feel?" Meroe says.

The answer is, as though I'd been struck by lightning, full to the brim with a strange, crackling energy. I sit up—too fast, my head spins—wrap my arms around her, and kiss her again. The energy seems to flow into her, too, lighting her up from the inside. She kisses me back with the same desperation I felt, moments or millennia before. My hands are sliding down her flanks, and hers are fumbling under my shirt, undoing first the bandages and then my chest wrap.

"Meroe." I speak in fragments, between gasps. "I don't. Exactly. Know what I'm doing."

"I have. Mmm. An idea." When I pull back for a moment and

raise an eyebrow, she gives me an innocent look. "I had . . . instructional books."

"Of course you did." I grin, and kiss her again, and pull her close. "You're a very strange princess."

26

"Hagan?" I keep my voice soft. Meroe is lying beside me, snoring gently, one brown shoulder protruding from where my shirt serves as makeshift blanket. "Are you there?"

Eddica energy flows in a thick stream through the pillar behind us, stronger down here near the Deeps than it was back in the Upper Stations. I'm hoping that means it'll be easier for Hagan to talk to me, but I'm still surprised when he actually appears, gray motes drifting out to form the approximate shape of a human and then slowly sharpening into detailed features. It apparently surprises him, too, because he looks down at his hands with exactly the goofy smile he used to wear. Something inside my chest clenches.

"Hi," he says. His voice is clearer now, with only a touch of the strange distortion. "I'm glad you're okay."

"So far." I sit up a little, tugging the blanket. "I should have listened to you earlier."

He gives an awkward shrug. "I'm not sure I would have listened to me, in your position."

My heart is beating fast. This is the most coherent he's been, by far, and I have to ask. "Hagan, how did you *get* here?" I hesitate. "Do you know that you're . . ."

"Dead?" He nods. "Honestly I wish I could tell you. I don't remember anything from before you came aboard, and even then not much until you found that node in the Deeps. How did *you* get here?"

"Kuon Naga," I say, and he winces. "And after I found that . . . place?"

"It felt like . . . waking up." He frowns, groping for words. "Or going from being *nearly* awake to wide-awake, maybe. Ever since you came aboard, I was *aware*, but it felt like I didn't have enough strength to do anything, not even think much. Then when you got near the node, suddenly I could . . . feel that there was a . . . a larger space nearby, and I moved into it." He shook his head, frustrated. "It's hard to explain."

"You stopped an *angel*. And you showed me the way out. How?"

"I could feel *it* trying to touch your mind. It found out what you wanted, and then decided you weren't . . . allowed here, I guess. I tried to stop it, and . . ." He looked down at his hands. "I'm sorry. I know *what* I did, but I don't have the words for it."

"It's all right," I say. "When you say *it*, you mean the *Soliton* itself? The ship?"

"I . . . think so. It's everywhere, anywhere the energy touches."

"Is it really alive?"

"I don't know. It can . . . make decisions, I think, but it doesn't *feel* like a person."

Blessed. There's a hundred more questions I want to ask, but the stream of power is visibly thinning. I clear my throat.

"We're almost there, I think. To the Garden. But I need you to show me the rest of the way."

"I've been getting it ready." Hagan raises one hand, and a ball of twisting gray motes materializes. Once again, he tosses it at me, and it sinks into my chest, leaving only a single twitching thread of gray on the outside. "You're right; it's not far now. But you have to hurry, and there are so many of them. . . ."

"We'll make it." He's growing dimmer. "Hagan, why are you helping me?"

He raises one eyebrow, in a well-remembered, infuriating expression. "Why shouldn't I?"

"You know, don't you? That I . . ."

"That you killed me?" He nods, translucent now. "I remember."

"Then . . ."

"And I understand why." He flicks his eyes up at the platform above us. "You're bringing them all to the Garden. You didn't have to."

I look down at Meroe's peaceful features. "I know."

"I always thought you were . . . better than the life we lived, in Kahnzoka." When I looked up, Hagan has vanished, but his voice is still a whisper in my ear. "I'm glad you got the chance to prove me right."

My throat is thick, and I blink away tears. The flow of Eddica energy dwindles to a trickle, and then vanishes. For a long time, I sit in silence, until Meroe stirs and opens her eyes.

"Were you talking to him?" she says. "The ghost?"

I nod. "He says the Garden isn't far, but there are a lot of crabs in the way."

"It'll help to have you on the front line."

She yawns and sits up. My shirt falls away, leaving her uncovered, not that it covered very much to begin with. I drink in the glorious sight of her, the soft curves. I can feel her staring back.

"What are we going to tell them?" I ask. It's been preying on my mind.

"About what?"

"About what happened here." I gesture to myself. "We come down together, and now I'm healed. Someone is going to guess what you are."

Meroe shrugs, smiling. "You were already mostly healed. Whatever you took down in the Deeps must have had a lasting effect. You were just worn-out, and then I dragged you down here to rut."

I snort a laugh, then hesitate. "You don't mind? Telling everyone about . . . this."

Meroe looks at her hands. "I'm not going to shout from the rafters about it. But . . . gods, Isoka, this is what I want. My father can go to the Rot."

I lean in and kiss her. For a moment, I think we're going to start all over again, but with an effort Meroe pulls herself away.

"They're waiting for us," she says.

"Rot." I sigh. "If we survive—"

"Indeed," Meroe says. "Let's survive."

* * *

Meroe had stuffed the outfit I'd worn to the officers' audience into the bottom of her bag. I change into it now, leaving my half-shredded, bloodstained things behind. Tightening the straps, I take deep breaths, reveling in the sensation of stretching without pain. This time, there aren't even marks on my skin to show where the wounds had been.

Of course, as Meroe said, it's possible we've just gotten lucky. Just because her powers have saved me twice doesn't mean they won't turn me into a bloated monstrosity the next time. I can't get careless.

Still, I feel good. Great, even, the mad charge of the healing blending into postcoital satisfaction and a night's rest, leaving me with a bouncy energy. Once I'm dressed, I ignite my blades, listening to them part the air with a soft hiss, and feel the heat from my armor. I dismiss one blade, and try envisioning an opening flower on that arm, as Zarun recommended. To my surprise, it works. The armor dims around the rest of my body, leaving me with a round shield of green light. I practice shifting back and forth several times, but it already feels natural.

I wonder if, had the Immortals caught me young, they'd have taught me these tricks in the Legions. In the Sixteenth Ward, the raw power of being a Melos adept had always been enough. Only on *Soliton* had I realized how much there could be to learn about a power that had always felt instinctive. If we survive, I have practicing to do.

If we survive. Like Meroe said, let's survive.

The officers are surprised to see me at the morning council. Zarun and Karakoa both sport bandages, and I recognize the smell of Sister Cadua's powerburn poultices. The Scholar looks gaunt, his cheeks hollowing out, his cane tapping nervously. Shiara seems untouched, her lip paints and makeup still perfect, but underneath even she is showing the strain.

"We're almost there," I say, as I join their circle. "But there's a lot of crabs in the way."

The Scholar's eyes widen. He can see the thread of intangible gray energy that spools out from my chest, leading into the darkness of the Center. He stares at me for a moment, and I raise an eyebrow.

"That's certainly good to hear," Shiara says. "Morale has . . . not been good."

"I know," I tell her. "I'll be joining the vanguard today."

"You seemed pretty badly hurt yesterday," Zarun says. "Though I hear your actions were quite heroic."

I tap my face, the blue lines. "I heal fast, it seems."

"Indeed." Zarun's eyes are unreadable.

"In that case," Karakoa says, "I recommend that I take rear guard. We are spread very thin."

I glance at Meroe, who has come up behind me. She nods.

"If there's anyone not in the hunting packs who can touch Sahzim," she says, "I'd like to gather them just behind the vanguard. They should be able to tell us if any more crabs are hiding under the bridges."

Everyone nods in approval. Wielders of Sahzim, the Well of Perception, were usually scavengers rather than hunters, but this was a good way to use their talents.

"We should move as soon as we can," Meroe says. "We're not sure how much ground there is left to cover."

"I'll get my people started," Zarun says.

The others disperse to their various tasks. I give Meroe a grin as she goes back among the column, then turn to Zarun, who is watching me with what looks like concern.

"What?" I ask him.

"You're certain you're all right?" he says. "It's not going to do morale any good to have the Deepwalker collapse from blood loss in the middle of a fight."

"I'm fine," I say.

"If you say so." He stretches, wincing. "I wish I was. It's been a long time since I had to push this hard."

For a moment, I feel guilty. Meroe can't help everyone. Even if she could, half of them would probably go into hysterics at the thought of being touched by a ghulwitch, and she'd end up getting lynched.

If he's feeling a little pain, though, Zarun seems hale enough, running through a series of exercises to loosen sore muscles. By the time he's done, other fighters of the vanguard are gathering. Thora and Jack are there, and other pack leaders and hunters I recognize from Crossroads. For the most part, I don't know their names, but every one of them knows me, and I hear a low buzz of conversation as they realize I'm going to fight with them.

I don't need Meroe to tell me that now is the time to say a few words. But I still don't have much to say.

"We're nearly there," I tell them. "We should reach the Garden today, if we can push through the crabs. Let's get this finished."

Not much, but it seems to serve. "Deepwalker!" someone shouts from the back. The others take it up, one by one. "Deepwalker! Deepwalker!"

Zarun gives me a sardonic glance. I grin at him, raise one hand, and ignite my blade with a *crackle-hiss* and a flash of green.

At first we cut through the crabs like a hot knife through butter.

For the first hour, I barely have to work at all. Tartak bonds lock the crabs in place, keeping us safe from their sudden leaps, while a rolling wave of Myrkai fire blasts them to cinders. Zarun and I walk in front of the advancing line, cutting down the occasional larger crab that emerges from the firestorm maddened and burning. Behind us, the column advances, step by step, and behind them the rear guard fights its own battle.

After falling into such an easy rhythm, the arrival of the first blueshell is a rude shock. The huge crab bulls through the bolts of flame like so much hot air. Light blue Tartak bonds snatch at its legs, slow it down, but they stretch and snap in the face of its prodigious strength. Its two huge claws strain toward us, mouth full of sword-tentacles writhing.

"You can break its armor, can't you?" Zarun says, as the thing strains closer.

I nod. "But last time, I had to hit it in the brain to bring it down."

"We don't need to be quite so ambituous. Left claw first. Come on!"

He jogs forward, looking almost cheerful. I follow, warily. The monster shifts, bearing down on him, and with a wave of his hand he generates a Tartak binding holding its right claw in place. The other claw swings toward him, and Zarun parries with his Melos shield, the impact driving him back a pace in a maelstrom of green sparks. He leans into the shield, pushing against the crab with all his weight.

"Now, Isoka!"

I summon the Melos spike, gathering power in my right hand, and dodge around him. Before the crab can pull its claw back for another swing, I jam the spike home, punching through its armor. Melos energy ripples into the limb, cracking chitin, and bursts of blue blood spray from the joints. The claw goes limp, dragging on the deck. The crab rears up, ripping its second claw free of the restraints and bringing it down; again, Zarun blocks it, and we repeat the process. With the beast effectively disarmed, a squad of Myrkai adepts steps up to close range to punch through its hide with firebolts.

"Very neat," Zarun says, approvingly.

"Much less painful than last time," I agree.

They keep coming, though, and gradually the battle takes on the aspect of a nightmare. I work with Zarun to cut down another of the long-legged red variety, let Jack distract a bulbous, pseudopod-covered juggernaut while I slice my way to its heart, and stand between Thora and a thing like an enormous dandelion puff as she rips it to pieces with Tartak force. A rain of Myrkai fire from behind us blasts the things off the bridge or cooks them in their own juices.

And it's not enough. Zarun and I can only be in one place at once, fighting one enemy at a time. There are other adepts among the hunters, but we're the strongest, and when we're distracted it's left to the others to engage the cart-sized monsters with fire, force, and spears. I hear screams from behind me, and the grisly crunch of breaking bodies, but I can't spare the time to turn away. I'm breathing hard now, sweating freely, my hair matted and my skin tender with premonitions of powerburn. I kill, and kill, and kill, and it's not enough.

When we come to a platform or a stairway, I follow the gray thread in my chest, and the others follow me. Zarun doesn't question, not now. The path leads us forward, but also down, taking spiral stairways and long ramps that lead steadily toward the base of *Soliton*. We're going back to the Deeps.

The rear guard is fighting hard, too. Once I hear shouts and blasts of flames halfway along the column, something that got through. There's no time to investigate, and I can only hope that Meroe and the others have it handled. Once again, I find myself praying, as I haven't since the first night they hauled me aboard.

Blessed, if you're listening, keep her safe. I can't bear to lose her. Not now.

We're getting close. Foot by foot, yard by bloody yard, we push down the bridges and stairs, until I'm certain we must be near the plain of white sand where Meroe and I landed. Instead, the last staircase leads to a broad expanse of deck, stretching into the darkness in every direction. There are no more of the star-like lights ahead of us, only behind. I can see something else, though, a softly glowing pillar, extending up and out of sight toward the deck so far above.

"Now what?" Zarun says, when we pause for a moment. There are fewer crabs here, as though they don't like the solid ground.

"I think that's it," I say, pointing to the tower. He just blinks, confused, and I realize he can't see it. The glow must be Eddica energy. Ordinarily, it's only visible close up. Whatever's out there must be absolutely thick with the stuff.

"It's going to be hard to hold the line here," Zarun says, looking around. Unlike the narrow bridges, this flat deck leaves us open to attack from any direction. "But they seem to be thinning out—"

"Deepwalker!" A boy runs up to us, gasping for breath. "They're attacking the rear guard. There must be hundreds of them!"

Blessed's rotting balls. I grit my teeth, trying to think, but Zarun answers first.

"I'll go and help," he says, then turns to me. "You say we're close?" I nod.

"Take half the vanguard and push forward. I'll get the column running. The rest of us will bring up the rear."

No time to make a better plan. I nod again, and he hurries off, shouting instructions. Then he's gone, pushing backward along the column with a group of hunters, as the remainder gather around me. He's left me Jack and Thora, I'm glad to see.

"We're going to run for it," I tell them. "Kill anything that gets in your way, but *don't stop*. They're coming in from behind, and Karakoa and Zarun won't be able to keep them back for long."

Grim nods. I ignite my blades, *crackle-hiss*, and gesture. We form ourselves into a loose wedge, and charge into the darkness.

Crabs loom out of the shadows with startling suddenness. Scuttlers launch themselves from the sides—I intercept one on the edge of my blade, block another with my new Melos shield, and cast it aside. Myrkai fire and Tartak force rip them out of our way. Jack runs beside me, her hair spiky with sweat, her jaw set, no silly quips to be heard. Her shadow runs beside her, fluid black slipping over the deck without any source of light. She eludes the crabs, her body turning shadowy and shadow turning solid, gets behind them for a quick stab with a long blade, then runs on.

The first big crab, a hammerhead, charges out of nowhere, bulling into the left flank of our formation. A big iceling boy gets caught in its jaws, his scream cut off abruptly. Without prompting, Thora and a dozen hunters peel off, surrounding the thing. Her Tartak bonds fix it in place, while the others close in with spears. The rest of us keep moving.

This whole time, the tower has been growing, getting closer. It's bigger than I thought, which means it's farther away. In the soft ghost light of the Eddica current, I can see that it's a cylindrical structure, much larger than the towers of the Upper Stations, rising out of the deck and stretching as far overhead as I can see. The line in my chest leads right to it.

The Garden. This must be it.

We're close enough now that the others can see it, too. Real light glows from big square doors at the base of the thing, not firelight but something closer to sunshine. It looks warm and inviting, and the hunters fight harder the nearer we get, slashing and tearing through the crabs that throw themselves at us in a frenzy. A blueshell rears up and is cut down by a dozen blades, hunters taking wounds from its sword-tentacles and ignoring them in their hurry to kill it and move on. I barely have time to reach it and finish it with my armor-piercing spike. Then we're past, and the glowing doors are just ahead. I pull up short, blinking in the sudden radiance, and the rest of the vanguard slowly comes to a halt around me.

The tower is dark metal, like the rest of the ship. But through the doors, we can see another world.

The light *is* sunlight, golden and warm. A shallow slope rises up from the doorway, a gentle hillside, made of rich brown earth, not steel. Tufts of grass at the edge give way to a solid carpet of green, tall stalks waving in a wind we can't feel, dotted by clusters of trees and bushes. It's a perfect park, in high summer, somehow dropped here in the depths of this steel leviathan.

The Garden.

I'm only a few feet short of the door, but it's a moment before I can bring myself to cross the threshold. I walk forward, expecting a trick—invisible glass, a field of magical energy, something to keep me out. But I step past, and my boot sinks a little in the soil. New smells fill my nose, wind and grass and the aftertaste of rain. I look up, and the sun blazes in a cloudless blue sky.

No. Not quite. The sky is there, and the sun, but I can see *past* them, to a ceiling only a couple of dozen yards overhead. It's a fake, but a convincing fake. And the plants are real, the soil. I reach down, touch the grass, and shiver.

Then I turn, and find pandemonium coming after me.

The column has lost all semblance of order in this last, desperate sprint. The first wave of civilians is following directly behind the vanguard. They reach the doorway, halting briefly in confusion, but they're pushed forward by those still coming from behind. A crowd develops, and I can see the situation threatening to spiral out of control.

"Keep running!" I give it my best shout, cutting through the babel. *"Into the Garden! Clear the way for the people behind you!"* At the rear of the mass of humanity, I can see the glow and flash of magic. "Vanguard, *stay here,* with me! We're going to have to hold them back!"

People pour past me, running flat out, not even pausing now on the edge of the sanctuary. I see Shiara, in a small bubble of calm maintained by a few of her own hunters. The Scholar hurries past, supported by his servants Erin and Arin. Scavengers and street vendors, servants, cooks, and porters, everyone who'd scraped a living in *Soliton*'s harsh streets. Children, in smart uniforms, silks, or tattered rags. The better part of a thousand people, rushing into the Garden.

The rear guard comes into view as the press subsides. There's been no sign of Meroe, and for a moment panic rises in my chest, but then I catch sight of her at the tail end of the column, just behind the fighters. Of course she would wait, let the others rush past. Aifin stands beside her, a blade in either hand, edged by a slight aura of golden Rhema light.

Beyond her, hunters fling fire into the darkness. I see the green glow of a Melos blade moments before Karakoa appears, dragging a stumbling Zarun with one hand and brandishing his long, curved weapon with the other. There are too few in the rear guard, far too few considering how many Zarun took with him. I ignite my blades and hurry to Meroe's side.

"Isoka!" The relief on her face makes my heart stutter. "Is it safe inside?"

"I think so." I look past the hunters, into the dark. "What happened?"

"A whole wave of them came at us at once." Meroe's face is ashen. "They broke right through the line. It was . . ." She swallows. "Zarun's people stopped them, when they arrived."

"Are they still coming?"

Meroe nods. "But we'll be safe in the Garden. Won't we?"

The rear guard, falling back, has reached the doors. Now I can see the crabs advancing behind them, shadowy monsters with no eyes and too many limbs blending into a single, amorphous mass.

A blueshell pushes ahead of the rest. It lunges forward, through the door, and its spindly feet dig into the soil of the Garden. I hold my breath, waiting for a bolt of energy to strike it down or drive it back, but nothing comes. One claw snaps out, grabbing for a young woman pouring a stream of Myrkai fire at another crab. Before it can reach her, Karakoa is there, leaving the panting Zarun on his knees. He swings his long blade with both hands, cutting through armor like it was cloth, and the blueshell rears back.

"Isoka," Meroe says. *"Now what?"*

"I don't know." I look around frantically. "He said we'd be safe here."

"Well, rotting ask him!" Meroe says. "They're going to get into the Garden!"

"Hagan!" Over the chaos of battle, I doubt anyone but Meroe can hear. "Hagan, how do we stop them?"

Eddica energy is all around me, here. The whole Garden is thick with it. He has to be able to hear me.

Meroe grabs my arm. "The doors," she says. "Look. See where they fold?"

I follow her pointing finger. On the Garden wall, steel is folded up like a paper fan on either side of the huge doors. I imagine that metal flexing, straightening, blocking the entrance. She's right; she *has* to be right. There has to be a way to close them. But there are no pulleys and cranks, nothing to grab on to, and the steel sections must weigh tons.

Everything on this ship operates by Eddica power. I try reaching out for the doors, as I reached out for the dredwurm, but there's nothing there to twist, no flow of energy.

"There has to be *something*. Hagan!" I turn around, wildly. "Close the rotting doors!"

There's a tug at my chest, as though someone had yanked on the thread anchored there. For a moment, I hear Hagan's voice in my ear, thick with pain and distortion.

"Isoka, he's here. You have to help; I'm trying, but I can't get *out*—"

It vanishes, abruptly.

Oh, rot. Oh, rot rot *rot.*

"Meroe, I have to find the Scholar."

"What?" She turns to me. "Why?"

"No time. Just trust me."

"I—" She shakes her head. "Of course I trust you. Go!"

I run, back toward the line. Karakoa is standing just inside the doorway, but the rest of the hunters are beginning to edge away. A few have already run into the Garden. I told them they'd be safe here, didn't I? I can't blame them for believing it.

"Hold here!" I try to shout over the sound of battle, and I can barely hear myself. "You have to hold here!"

I skid to a halt beside Karakoa. Thora, Jack, and the rest of the vanguard are gathered around, looking uncertain. The big Akemi looks down at me, blade purring softly in his hands.

"This is the Garden?" he says. I can hear the doubt in his voice.

"This is the Garden," I say. "I'm going to get this door closed, and then the crabs will be locked out. But you have to *hold here* until I can. If they get in, it's not going to matter!"

For a moment, I think he's going to argue. His jaw moves from side to side, as though trying to crack a nut in his teeth. I notice for the first time that he's wounded, bloody cuts in several places on his arms and legs and the telltale scorch marks of powerburn on his shoulders. None of it seems to slow him down. Zarun, a few paces away, tries to get up off his knees and fails. He's bleeding, too.

Karakoa nods.

"Go," he says. "We will hold here, as long as we can."

"Thank you—" I start to say, but he's already raised his voice into a bellow that cuts through the shouts and blasts like a trumpet.

"Stay at the door! Do not let them pass!"

The hunters who'd drifted away jerk to a halt, as though someone had tugged on their leashes. The vanguard who'd accompanied me throw themselves into the fight as well. With a narrower area to defend, they have a chance, even with thinned numbers. Karakoa wades forward, blade slashing, and Zarun finally clambers to his feet. His shirt hangs open, and there's a bloody slash across his chest, washing his light brown skin with gore.

"I'll be back," I tell him.

He nods, too. I can't tell if its belief or resignation on his face. I turn and run.

My first thought is to find someone who'd seen the Scholar, but the thread of gray energy in my chest is still tugging. It's changed direction, leading not toward the center of the Garden, as before, but off to the side. Playing a hunch, I follow it, the springy grass unfamiliar under my feet after so much time walking on steel and mushrooms.

Along the edge of the big circular chamber, there's a staircase, hard to see from a distance. It ascends in a curve, following the wall, and passes through the fake sky. The thread leads me to the bottom, and I pound up it, boots clanging on grated metal steps.

Above the sky, there's a metal ceiling. The stairs cut through it, and onto another level. Instead of grassland, there's forest, overgrown tree trunks stretching away as far as I can see. Something chitters from the canopy overhead. A fat raindrop lands on my arm.

The thread stretches, the pull getting stronger. I sprint up the steps, gasping for breath, my thighs on fire. Another fake sky, another metal ceiling. And then—

The pull of the thread shifts abruptly. The stairs continue, winding around and around the endless tower, but the thin line of gray light now points inward. This level has no soil, only ordinary metal deck. There's a corridor, like the corridors all over *Soliton*. Here, though, no rust mars the metal. Brushed steel gleams as though it were polished yesterday, and pale, sourceless light washes out all shadows.

I slow, leaning against the wall, straining to breathe. I force myself to walk, down the corridor and in the direction of the increasingly frantic tugs on the Eddica thread. The hallway continues, monotonous and featureless, until the exit has dwindled to a dot behind me. Then, ahead, another dot appears, expanding to a set of double doors, which stand open. There's brighter light beyond. I start jogging again, gritting my teeth at the pain in my knees.

Beyond the doors is a huge circular chamber. The walls are a metal filigree, interwoven beams, pillars, and girders in a complex web. Between the larger pieces are smaller ones, metal rods the size of my arm, crisscrossing like threads in a loom, and then others smaller still. All of them glow bright with gray Eddica power, pulsing through the room in regular waves, like a heartbeat.

In the center of the room is a circular pillar, about my height, with a flat top like an altar. Energy flows toward it, from the walls into the floor, and up from the floor into this single place. A beam of soft gray light rises from it, shining upward until it disappears into a matching pedestal extending down from the ceiling.

Behind the pillar, there's an enormous gray stone, like an egg the size of a small house. I ignore it for the moment, because in front of the altar-like structure stands the Scholar, one hand on his cane, the other holding the dredwurm's eye over his head. The crystal glows a deep, sullen red, like a hot coal, and Eddica energy swirls around it.

Erin and Arin, looking as tired as I feel, are on their knees on either side of their master. Hagan hangs over the altar, suspended in empty space with his dangling feet a yard above the metal. He's spread-eagled, bands of gray energy wrapped around his wrists and ankles. As I enter, he screams. It's not a human sound, half keening bird and half watchman's whistle, sliding across the octaves and into weird modulations that scrape across my mind like fingernails on glass.

"Stubborn," says the Scholar. He looks over his shoulder and smiles at me. "Hello, Isoka. We've been expecting you."

27

I step into the chamber. "What in the *Rot* are you doing?"

"Taking control of *Soliton*, as I told you I would," the Scholar says. "This is a friend of yours, I take it? A dead one."

"Let him go."

"'Him'?" The Scholar turns to me, spectacles slipping low on his nose, the eyes behind them full of fire. "There's no *him*, Deepwalker. This *thing* isn't human. It isn't even alive. It's a mistake, a broken cog, a stripped gear. A stray batch of memories you installed by accident." He grins maliciously. "It's been getting in my way, but I'll have it removed in a moment, never fear."

"I don't care what you think he is. I need him to close the door to the Garden. The crabs are breaking through!"

"Don't worry. We're perfectly safe here."

"*Safe?* Everyone is going to die!"

"Everyone down there, yes." His smile widens. "Regrettable, but necessary."

"You have got to be rotting joking." I take a step forward, and Erin and Arin tense. "Let Hagan go *now*."

"Or what? You'll kill me?" He pushes his spectacles up his nose. "Then you'll never be able to bring *Soliton* home to your beloved Blessed Empire. That's what you want, isn't it?"

There is a moment's pause, a silence filled with the crackle of my blade.

"Which sort are you? I wonder," he says. "You seem too smart to be a patriot, doing it all for Emperor and Empire. A mercenary? What kind of fortune did they promise you? Or was it the other kind of promise?" He cocks his head. "Yes, that seems more like the Kuon Naga we all know and love. Who does he have? Your lover? Your parents?"

"My sister." The words force their way out before I can bite them off. I grit my teeth. "How . . ."

"How do I know?" He pushes his spectacles up with one finger. "Poor Isoka. Do you really think you're the first young fool the Emperor's spider has sent to try and take *Soliton*? Do you think you're the *tenth*?"

He laughs, and my head whirls.

"I killed the first few," the Scholar says. "Seemed logical. Eliminate the competition. It took me some time to realize I'd *over*estimated Kuon Naga. His attempts were shots in the dark, wild guesses. His agents weren't dangerous. Most of them got themselves killed anyway. Some gave up as soon as they got here. I think Shiara was one of those, actually."

"You . . ." I shake my head. *Focus, Isoka.* "You're here for the same reason, aren't you? To try and steal *Soliton*."

"I was. His Royal Majesty the King of Jyashtan, Master of the Six Thrones and rightful ruler of the world, bade me capture the great ship to add to his navy for our next attempt to crush the unrighteous. He promised to make me a prince if I succeeded." He shrugs. "I may still take him up on the offer. On the other hand, even the King doesn't really understand *Soliton's* power. Maybe I'll just take the throne for myself."

He leans forward. "The difference between us, Isoka Deepwalker, is that *I* was prepared. In Jyashtan we're not so obsessed with burning old books as you Imperials. His Royal Majesty knew that Eddica, the power of the ancients, was the key to *Soliton*, and so he sent me here. Your Kuon Naga just got lucky when he chose you. Tenth time's the charm, I suppose.

"The Well of Spirits. We thought that meant the ship would be haunted, but it's not like that at all. The spirits are stripped of everything that made them human, all but a few leftover memories, like a fading stain. They're changed into raw energy and channeled into the mechanism. The greatest source of power you can imagine. And this *thing*, this incomparable machine, has just been wandering around the oceans of the world because it's slipped a gear and no one can figure out how to catch it." He laughs again. "Have you ever heard of anything so absurd?"

I've heard enough. "Close the *rotting* doors. *Now.*"

"I'm afraid not. *Soliton's* basic controls are too powerful for you or me to take command of, under ordinary circumstances." He pats the dreadwurm's eye. "But this focuses and amplifies Eddica power. That is, the power of spirits. The power of death. For which our little massacre downstairs is a convenient source." He taps the deck with his cane. "When it builds high enough, I'll rewrite the machine to recognize me as its master."

"You rotting bastard." I'm within a few paces of him, now. "They're fighting and dying downstairs."

His lip curls. "That's what they're for."

I thrust for his throat.

A pair of Melos blades cross in front of mine, catching my weapon. Fat green sparks jump between them, energy crackling and popping. Erin stands on one side, Arin on the other, each with a green energy blade emerging from her forearm.

"Isoka's usefulness is at an end, apparently," the Scholar says, with a sigh. "Kill her."

Instinct takes over. I dismiss my blade, escaping the bind, and hastily backpedal a few steps. When they don't follow at once, I settle into fighting stance, ignite my blades, take a breath, watch.

The twin sisters look perfectly calm. They fight with opposite hands, Erin's left and Arin's right, each half-turning toward me to lead with a single Melos blade. I don't see the telltale crackle of Melos armor around them, though. So they're not full adepts, which means I should have the advantage.

If they don't have any other tricks. The Scholar is too confident. He's seen me fight, so he knows—

"You don't have to do this," I tell the two girls. "I don't know what he's promised you—"

"He's going to take us home," Erin says. Arin nods, silently. Rot. Worth a try.

Arin comes at me first, footwork smooth as fine silk, feinting high and then cutting at my waist. I parry the blow with my left-hand blade, and she spins past. It leaves her open, and I lash out. The blow would cut deep into her side, but she's not there, fading away like a shadow with a liquid spray of dark energy.

I'm already turning back, knowing what comes next. But Erin surges forward, much faster than I anticipated, her limbs outlined in golden sparks. She twists her blade neatly around my parry, and I'm just able to turn in time to take a long slash across my belly instead of a hard impact. Melos energy spits and wars as blade and armor meet, and violent heat stabs at my skin. As I stagger away, I can feel blisters forming along the line drawn by her blade.

Xenos and Rhema. Shadows and Speed. Rotting wonderful.

The sisters look at each other, and something passes between them. Some plan, no doubt. They've clearly trained together, and I need to break up that coordination. So I charge at Erin, blades swinging horizontally, before they can set up their next attack. She dances backward, spinning out of reach of one of my blades and parrying the other with a fat green spark. I whirl, just in time to catch Arin coming at me from behind. She fades into shadow at my thrust, materializing to one side, blade swinging at my face. I bring my left hand up, dismissing the blade and unfolding my armor like a flower, summoning a shield of Melos energy that intercepts her weapon with a screech. She hops backward, pausing, and we square off again.

"Nice trick," says the Scholar. "Zarun taught you, did he? He's a tenacious little cockroach, that one."

Erin and Arin come at me together, a coordinated flurry of swinging blades. I give ground, parrying furiously, staying ahead of them only by blocking strike after strike with the shield on my left hand. Their style is elegant, studied, nothing like the street brawlers I'm used to facing. Erin is *fast*, so fast she nearly gets around me more than once, and Arin switches positions with her shadow, trying to trip me up.

Rot. I don't have *time* for this.

Elegant forms have their advantages, but so do street brawlers.

I surge to the side, switching my shield back to a blade and driving Erin away with a furious combination. She backs up for a moment, and I turn on Arin. This time, I'm watching her shadow. She's expecting the first strike, which she evades by shifting postion; expecting the second, which she blocks, her blade held vertically. She's *not* expecting me to bull forward afterward, my knee coming up hard into her stomach. She doubles over, gasping, and I spin around her, driving my blade into the small of her back. I rip it free with a twist and a spray of blood, and she collapses onto her knees, then falls forward.

"Arin!" Erin's scream is high and piercing. Golden light flares around her, speeding her up until she's a blur. She comes at me at a run, subtlety forgotten, trying to push through my defenses with brute force. I fade sideways, and it's barely any effort at all to leave one blade hanging in front of her. It punches into her chest, my clenched fist pressed against her sternum as the spike of Melos energy emerges from between her shoulders. She coughs blood on my arm, where it sizzles against my armor, and then I step back, dismissing my blade. Erin staggers drunkenly for a moment, and then falls shuddering across the body of her sister.

I step around them, toward the Scholar. He's watching me through his spectacles, unconcerned at the demise of his servants. Still too confident. Which means he still has a trick—

There's a *crack*, like a tree branch breaking. The red glow from the dredwurm's eye in the Scholar's hand is matched, suddenly, by another. The great gray egg, behind the pillar, has sprouted a crystal like the one the Scholar holds, pulsing with crimson light in perfect time.

With another *crack*, part of the egg separates from the whole. It shudders, changing shape, becoming a leg, long and multi-jointed. Another *crack*, and another, as the thing comes apart.

Slowly, the angel rises to its feet.

* * *

Too late, I lunge for the Scholar.

A slender leg of hard gray stone comes down between us before my blade reaches him. Melos energy slashes against the angel's flesh and rebounds, leaving little more than a burn scar. I dodge around it, but another leg intercepts, and then another comes straight at me, tipped with a vicious claw. I jump backward, and look up.

The angel is a sphere, held off the ground just a bit higher than my head. The glowing red eye pulses in the center, while around it the stony flesh is shaped into a sea of twisted, screaming human faces, one melting into the next, covering its entire surface. The faces *shift* as I watch, mouths widening, eyes darting, one swallowing the next and being swallowed in its turn. From the churning mass extend long, stick-thin legs with five or six joints, spread evenly over the surface like a halo of pins sticking in a pincushion. Underneath the angel, the legs fold in on themselves to support its weight, while those protruding from the sides and top hinge down to jab at me with horrible agility.

"I hope you didn't think I was relying only on those two to protect me," the Scholar says. He steps sideways as the angel advances, its legs passing neatly around him in a complex ballet. "I may not have control of the whole ship, but it's simple enough to use the dredwurm's eye for this."

I keep retreating, drawing it forward. A leg swipes at me, then another, and I block them with my Melos shield.

The dredwurm was a rogue angel. I killed it, so I should be able to deal with this one the same way. I don't have Aifin to attract its attention, but—

Focus, Isoka. I reach out to the thing, feeling for the currents of Eddica power that animate it. Last time, I gave those a twist, and it froze the creature in place. Just a little twist—

When I take hold of the energy churning inside it, it feels like being slapped in the face, a jolt that leaves every muscle twitching. I stumble, and the angel swats me, a claw scraping across my armor. Heat ripples through my chest, and I feel myself tumbling through the air, landing hard against one wall.

The Scholar is laughing.

"I imagine that's how you killed the dredwurm," he says. "I should have known. A good try. But a dredwurm has nothing driving it, no force behind it, just a leftover loop of energy cut off from its natural state. *This* is an angel, and the will behind it is mine." He grins nastily. "You will not be able to subvert it so easily."

Rot. So much for that plan.

I get up, my back to the wall. Eddica energy pulses through the metal behind me, and I can hear tiny almost voices, like whining gnats. The angel, moving ponderously on its folded legs, swings a dozen limbs in my direction, closing them around me like the jaws of a trap. I duck, dodge, and swing both blades against one leg, right into the joint. My arms get hot as I pour in power, and with a mighty *crack* the joint gives way, the last third of the leg sheared off and crashing to the floor. The angel twists, swinging the damaged leg away and bringing a dozen fresh ones to bear.

One down. At least twenty to go, and the skin on my arms is already burning. This is not going to work.

The eye. If I'm going to kill it, it has to be the eye. I push away from the wall, dodging claws or letting them scrape my armor. I grab a leg and lift myself up, swinging closer to the angel like a monkey pulling itself through the jungle canopy. More legs close in, the forest getting tighter and tighter around me, until I'm facing a solid grid of gray stone. Through the gaps, a foot away, the angel's eye gleams mockingly. For a moment I'm poised there, straining, the angel with all its legs folded inward like a dying insect. Then it uncoils, hurling me across the room.

I do my best to brace, wincing at the impact and the blast of heat it sends through my armor. Eddica power pulses in the wall where I hit, rising briefly before returning to its regular rhythm. I stagger back to my feet and start to run, straight for the Scholar, ignoring the angel.

"You tried that already, Deepwalker," he says. Legs snake out, blocking my path like reaching vines. "Getting desperate?"

He has no idea. I shove my arm through a gap in the wall of limbs, one blade reaching toward the Scholar's head. Letting the other blade vanish, I pour power into the outstretched weapon, lengthening it into something closer to Karakoa's two-handed sword. The blade grows, stretches, and the Scholar jerks backward as the crackling tip swings wildly in front of him.

But it's not enough. I can't make the blade any longer, and the angel has ahold of me now, throwing me backward again. This time, when I hit the wall, I'm not so quick to get up. My limbs feel like lead, and the skin of my back and shoulders is already charred from powerburn. I just manage to get to my feet as claws arc down toward me, blocking the strikes with my Melos shield. Each impact rings me like a gong.

Hagan is hanging limp in the luminous gray bonds. His body is flickering, blurred, as though on the other side of lumpy glass. But I hear his voice, just for a moment.

". . . Isoka . . . follow . . ."

There's a familiar tug in my chest. For a moment, I think a claw has taken hold of me, but I see the thread of gray light that led me to the Garden has gone taut again. It wraps around me, leading into the wall.

The wall—

Not *just* into the wall. It leads to a large, cylindrical strut, which pulses with gray light, heavily loaded with flowing Eddica power. I risk turning my head, and see the thread join the flow, right where the big strut meets two smaller ones. They merge in a complex knot of power.

Time to place the big bet.

The angel rears back, raising four legs at once to batter my shield. I spin sideways, letting the shield fade away, summoning both my blades. Instead of slashing at the enfolding legs, I swing both blades against the wall, right where the thread from my chest joins it. Melos energy *cracks,* and there's a rush of heat along my arms as my blades cut into the metal. The knot sags for a moment, and then gives way.

Like water spilling from a broken pipe, a torrent of Eddica energy blasts from the shredded metal, spraying into the air in a million tiny gray motes. I reach out and take hold of the flow, bend-ing it with all my strength. It twists, fighting like a raging python, but just for a moment I manage to direct it where I want it to go.

Right against the eye of the angel, looming over me.

I can feel the organized, looping structure of the thing, the magical machine the Scholar is so fond of, come apart under the blasting pressure of the wild, chaotic energy. The angel spasms, then freezes in place, its legs shuddering to a halt.

I can't hold the flow for long, and I have no idea if the angel will recover, so I move fast. I grab a leg, swinging myself up and over, traversing the creature like an obstacle course, heading for the Scholar. He takes a half step back, not quite realizing what's happened, and then I see panic breaking across his face. He throws up one arm, as though that would protect him from my blades—

And then I'm past him, the dredwurm's eye in my hands, red light draining out of it like blood from a wound.

"No!" He turns on me, eyes wide. "Give it back! Quickly! The ship will—"

Hagan's scream returns, sliding from high and terrified down toward a bass roar, a thundering growl that sets the room around us to shaking. The bands of gray light that had wrapped him dissolve, and he drops into a crouch on the pedestal.

"Give it to me!" the Scholar shrieks. *"Please!"*

I stand stock-still, waiting.

With a *shriek* of twisting metal, conduits and pipes all over the room tear themselves away from the walls, animated by the wild pressure of the Eddica flow inside them. They converge on the Scholar, jagged ends lancing toward him like spears. His scream rises as he's pierced a hundred times over, disappearing in a matter of moments inside a compacting sphere of broken, twisting metal. After a few seconds, the bottom of the sphere begins to leak blood, thick and red.

Hagan tries to rise, stumbles, and falls to his knees. His body still flickers with distortion, growing fainter by the moment.

"Hagan!" I rush to the pedestal. "The doors. You have to close the doors!"

He looks up at me and nods, face clear for an instant before the distortion sweeps over it again. I feel a rumble through the floor, the sound of metal shifting far below.

"Thank you." I reach out a hand to him. "Are . . . are you . . ."

And then he's gone, fading into a spray of gray light that dissolves like mist. A quiet settles over the room. The angel is still, the bent and torn pipes fixed in place. The Scholar's blood drips metronomically into a spreading puddle.

I pick my way out, past the splayed metal, past the still bodies of Erin and Arin. In the corridor, in spite of the pain all through me, I start to run.

They're waiting for me. The ones who are left.

Meroe meets me at the bottom of the stairs, wrapping me in a hug tight enough to send spikes of pain through the burnt skin of my back. I ignore it and hug her back, just as tightly. Her braids are crusty with blood.

"You did it," she says. "Gods, Isoka. You did it."

I blink tears out of my eyes, and look past her.

The long curve of the door is closed, the unfolded steel sheets sealing off the entryway. I can hear crabs banging on it, distantly, but the metal doesn't even shiver. They're locked out. And we're locked in.

Inside the door, bodies are piled in heaps. Crab bodies, blown apart or fried or cut to pieces, and human bodies, torn or slashed or mangled. Blood in every color imaginable has soaked into the soil, churned now into thick mud. There are dead hunters, the men and women I fought alongside on the way here, but so many others, too. Scavengers and servants, porters and children, lying in drifts like windblown sand.

"They came back to help," Meroe says in my ear, as I walk forward. "Not just the fighters. Everyone who could hold a blade or a spear."

"You wanted to save everyone," I say, my eyes locked on the corpses.

Meroe squeezes my hand. "We saved everyone we could."

The living are gathered just upslope of the carnage, sitting in stunned knots on the grass. A few are at work on bandages, helping the injured, but most just sit and stare at the closed doors, unable to believe that the nightmare is finally over. I see a few of the hunters, pitifully few. Aifin, Thora, and Jack are sitting together. Thora's asleep, head resting on her lover's shoulder, but Jack is awake enough to give me a little wave. I see Zarun, protesting feebly as Sister Cadua goes at him with her needle and thread.

Karakoa lies on the hillside, on his back, eyes closed. At first I think he's asleep, too, but then I see the deep cuts in his coat, the crimson stains that surround them. The cuffs of his sleeves are scorched from powerburn, and I shudder to think what the flesh underneath must look like. His lover, the young man I'd seen at the officers' council, kneels beside him, prostrated in an attitude like prayer.

"He fought to the last," Meroe says quietly. "Sister Cadua told him to fall back, to get help, and he refused. You could smell his skin burning. When the doors finally closed, he walked back here and just . . . lay down."

"Oh." I put my arm around her shoulders, pulling her tight against me.

"Deepwalker."

I turn, reluctantly. Shiara is standing between two tired-looking hunters, her *kizen* frayed at the edges, her makeup slightly smudged. By her standards, she might as well be naked.

"What?" I ask her.

"Where is the Scholar?" she demands. "He was seen going up the stairs."

"Dead." No need to elaborate on how.

"Oh." She seems to deflate a little, then squares her shoulders. "What happens now?"

"What do you mean? We're safe."

"For the moment." She waves a hand. "Will the ship keep going, past the Rot? Where does it stop? Will the doors open again, or are we trapped in here?"

I feel eyes on me, from all directions. Stares. Even Meroe is watching me.

What makes them think *I* have the answers?

"Deepwalker?" Shiara says.

Epilogue

Soliton continues on.

There's food in the Garden, and freshwater. We're short of clothes, furniture, the sort of thing the scavengers used to retrieve, but we survive. The old clades are dissolved, and even the Butcher's crew is joined into our single community, united by the trauma of our flight and final, desperate battle.

The crew looks to Shiara and Zarun for leadership. They look to Meroe, who organized the march and saved them. And, for reasons I don't understand, they look to me. They call me Deepwalker, like it means something, and nod quietly when I pass by.

Rot. I will never understand people.

We bury the dead, a novelty on *Soliton*. When we recover our strength, we explore the rest of the Garden. There are several more levels, different environments, different plants and animals. Meroe and I agree that we need to be careful with it. We take fruit from the trees; a few unfamiliar animals for meat; berries and vegetables. But not too much. This place is a refuge, and we don't know how long we'll need it. Or when we'll need it again.

Eventually—there's no way to judge the passage of time in the Garden, where the fake sun always shines—the door opens. We venture out, cautiously, but the killing frenzy that drove the crabs has passed. They are back to their old selves, wandering and only occasionally dangerous, and the hunters quickly go back to hunting. Scavengers venture forth, into fresh, rich territory near the bow of the ship where no one has gone before, and return with rich booty.

A new town starts to take shape, around the base of the Garden, with barricades and crude shacks that grow by the day.

Meroe, Jack, Thora, and I go on an expedition, climbing the staircases from platform to platform until we make our way, exhausted, onto the deck. It's night, and a blaze of glorious stars stretches from horizon to horizon. There's no sign of land, no city lights, just the endless stretch of dark ocean.

Meroe says that she can get a rough idea of where we are from the stars, which surprises none of us. We wait, staring upward, while she sketches and calculates, tongue sticking out of the corner of her mouth. Finally, she announces that we have left the Vile Rot far behind. We have passed beyond it, beyond the Central Ocean, where no ship has ventured for a thousand years. And *Soliton* is still heading east, cutting smoothly through the water, taking us farther and farther from everything we've ever known.

There will be questions, when we get back. People will ask me when we'll reach land, whether there'll be more sacrifices, what happens next.

Hagan hasn't appeared to me since the Scholar died. I've pressed my hand to the Eddica streams that still flow through the ship and called his name, but he never responds. It's possible what the Scholar did destroyed him. Sometimes, though, when I let my thoughts run along with the strange gray energy, I can feel . . . something. I don't know. I don't know *anything*.

I hope wherever Hagan is, it's somewhere he wants to be.

Thora and Jack wander off, to find a private corner. Meroe and I lie on the deck, side by side.

"I have to get back to Kahnzoka," I say. "Tori is waiting for me."

"I know," Meroe says. She levers herself up on one elbow, then leans over and kisses me. "We'll get there."

In that moment, in spite of the fact that we're going in the wrong direction, in spite of the fact that there are crabs and the Vile Rot and Blessed knows what else in the way, in spite of *everything*, I believe her.

Hold on, Tori. I'm coming.

We are coming.

ACKNOWLEDGMENTS

This book represents my first venture into the world of YA. Doing something new always carries with it the fear of screwing it up royally, and so I've been enormously grateful to have a great crew of people much more knowledgeable than me helping me along the way. (Any royal screwups that *do* result are, of course, my own responsibility!)

When I first started thinking about this project, I consulted my resident YA expert, Casey Blair, who provided me with an extensive, annotated reading list and endless input along the way. Liz Bourke provided another great swathe of recommended reading. Later, she and Iori Kusano were generous enough to look over a draft as sensitivity readers, in which capacity they were enormously helpful.

My agent, Seth Fishman, performed wonders as usual, finding the perfect home for my odd little project. I'd also like to thank the rest of the team at the Gernert Company: Jack Gernert, Will Roberts, Rebecca Gardner, and Ellen Goodson.

Special thanks to my amazing editor, Ali Fisher, who was perfectly in sync with me from day one. It's always wonderful working with someone great! I've loved Richard Anderson's art for a while now, and having him do a cover for me was amazing; thanks to him for his wonderful work. At Tor Teen, I'm grateful to everyone from the legendary Tom Doherty on down: Kathleen Doherty, Seth Lerner, Elizabeth Curione, and Karl Gold. And my thanks to everyone on the Macmillan and Tor/Forge marketing and sales teams who work hard to make this book a success.